ISLANDS

OF MICE

Lucy Jacobs

First edition.
Copyright © 2024 Lucy Jacobs
ISBN: 978-1-0687647-1-4

Cover Design: Stephanie Hoffmann
Find out more at: www.lucyjacobs.co.uk
Follow me on Instagram: @lucyjacobsauthor

All rights reserved. This book or any portion thereof may not be reproduced or used in any manner whatsoever without the express written permission of the author.

The excerpt on page 123 is from "The Well of Loneliness" by Radclyffe Hall.

This is a work of fiction. All characters and events in this publication are fictitious and any resemblances to persons (living or dead) is purely coincidental.

Prologue

"Damn teacher's late," Gunnar says, peering down off the edge of the quay. "It's too cold to be standing around like this."

He's right, of course. It is cold, even wrapped tight against the weather. The wind is lazy and thin off the winter sea, cutting through the material of her coat without any effort at all. The ruined dockside walls do little to stop the wind's path, sending it whipping instead around corners with ferocious speed. There's a smell in the air that still feels burnt, charred, despite the usual sea-salt tang.

It catches at her throat, making her cough and wheeze, and she pulls the collar of her coat across her face, filtering her breaths through the serge. Nose and mouth at least mostly covered, Solveig presses her hands further into her pockets, curling them into fists around the lining. The slushing snow is seeping through a crack in her boot where the sole meets the upper, and the toes inside are stiff and frozen.

"You're alright," she says, "with that blanket of a beard."

He shifts his gaze to her from the sea, watching from the corner of his eyes. For a moment, his lips stay pressed in a thin line, and then he smiles and opens his arms. Solveig rolls her eyes - she's not falling for the sharing body heat suggestion. Gunnar drops his arms, steps forward, and instead rubs his gloved hands up and down her arms, the friction more painful than warming.

"Get off," Solveig protests weakly, pushing at his chest. "You'll shake my brain out of my ears like that."

"Well anyway," he says, stepping back, "we'll lose the light soon, and I don't want to make the crossing in the dark."

The harbour master says the coastal waters have been swept and are clear of mines. The fisheries mean too much to their occupiers to risk one of their own unexploded bombs rising unexpectedly to the surface. There's no danger, they're told, to the fishing fleet, or to private vessels, or to the Navy.

No danger at all, if you're obeying the rules.

There's been no incidents, either, but two weeks ago the crew of the Swan out of Veiholmen said they saw a dark shape pass close under the boat that might have been a mine. It's not worth taking the risk, chancing their necks for some outsider with a teaching qualification and a *Nasjonal Samling* membership card. They stand there close together for a few minutes more before a woman comes swinging into view around the corner.

She's smartly dressed - too smartly, perhaps, for a trip in Gunnar's open boat. The hat pinned to her hair just covers the crown of her head, but the small half-veil drops over her eyes. Her ulster is an unblemished shade of beige, matching high-heeled shoes that elegantly pick their way along the wharf's snow-shovelled path. The outfit looks new, and as though it should cost more than an entire year's clothing rations. You can get anything, Solveig supposes, if you're friendly enough with the Germans.

"I'm sorry to have kept you waiting. It's just, with the place like this..." She gestures carelessly behind her, to the wreck of Kristiansund, and shrugs apologetically. Her voice is light, cheery. It's as though she thinks the locals have left the city in disarray, like children with toys they never tidy up.

The thought rankles, and Solveig shifts on the spot. She is about to step forward, say something, when six or seven young soldiers come struggling round the corner, their arms piled high with trunks and suitcases. Two, those carrying the largest between them, slide on the icy path, and their grips on the handles slip.

"*Vorsicht!*" the stranger calls out, hand held out in warning. She crosses to them with fast, precise steps, arms held stiffly by her sides. When she reaches them, she breaks into a stream of guttural German too quick for Solveig to follow.

The soldiers look cowed under the onslaught, and Gunnar and Solveig share a look, her eyes coming across to meet his. He pulls a face, and she has to hold back a snort of laughter. Her press-ganged porters brought once more to heel, the teacher turns, hand again outstretched, this time in greeting. Solveig stands up straight, away from Gunnar, straightening the coat across her shoulders and smiles.

"Liv Sunde. You must be Solveig, like my letter says?"

Her voice is pure Oslo, a city girl. She waves a piece of paper in their direction - the letter, presumably, or German mandated identification - before taking Solveig's hand between both her own.

"That's me. And this is Gunnar Josøy."

Liv Sunde's eyes slide across Gunnar's face, barely stopping long enough to take him in; they linger on Solveig, on her trousers and battered boots, the dark patches of crusted sea spray. Solveig had been out on the islands, watching the sheep, and hadn't bothered to change. Perhaps I should have, she thinks, feeling the wear in her clothes, the unfashionable cut of her hair. She itches under the teacher's observation, aware suddenly of her appearance and all its defects. Her hand is still trapped, and the frank stare and closeness are overbearing, and she steps away.

The teacher's easy smile returns.

"Miss Eik, Mr Josøy. Pleased to make your acquaintance."

Gunnar nods a hello, tilting his chin back in recognition.

"Need to hurry up and load your things," he says, moving off towards the boat. "I don't want to have to do this in the dark."

He could, of course. Gunnar and his family have been on these waters right back as far as anyone can remember, making their living from the sea. Far enough back that they'd likely made their living from lands they found across the sea: from trade and plunder and nighttime raids. You could guess at it from the look of him - wide shoulders, tall and bearded. But despite the current ferocious set to his face, Gunnar is the product of generations of niceness, viking anger and rage slowly leaching away down the generations. But the teacher doesn't know this, and follows him, peering down at the boat, a frown creasing her face under the veil.

She takes a last drag on her cigarette, letting the smoke linger in her mouth, grinding the butt into the outside of a silver cigarette case, pocked and marked with use. She blows the smoke up, over her shoulder, away from Solveig and Gunnar.

"I thought there'd be a ferry."

"Not at this time of day. Especially not given the circumstances."

She just nods, stiffly, and motions for her Germans to carry on. Trunks and bags are lashed to the deck, covered roughly with a tarpaulin. The women, too, climb aboard, and the engine kicks over once, twice, before pulling away.

The sea surges between the side of the boat and the dock, the space widened by the press of Gunnar's boot. He points them out to sea, heading for the islands. The sea is slate grey as always, the failing light rapidly leaching the colour from the world. The wind has picked up, just as Gunnar said, and the waves are coming in tall and fast.

"It'll be a bit bumpy," calls Gunnar from his place by the engine, "but I'll get you there."

Huddled together in the bow, they hunker down against the wood to save their faces from the spray. The water is cold, and stings where it catches uncovered cheeks, the bite of the salt irritating their eyes. Solveig, of course, is used to it. On the islands, you virtually grow up in boats like this, and she crouches easily, rocking on her heels in time with the plunging swell.

The teacher looks miserable. One hand clutches at her seat, the other pressing her hat tightly to her head. Her face, as Solveig squints through the gloaming, is slowly turning green.

"Are you alright?" She has to shout to be heard, voice rising above the steady chug of the engine.

"I thought -" A particularly fierce swell sends them falling down the side of the water, trunks straining under their ropes with an ominous creaking. She stops, throat constricting, hand flying from her hat to her mouth. She swallows convulsively and takes a breath. "I thought there'd be a ferry. I'm not much good with small boats."

Solveig can only wonder why she's come to Smøla, where there are no roads or cars, just boats, and almost all of them small.

Whatever the truth, by the time the boat reaches the edge of the islands, she's bent over the edge of the boat, head hanging down over the wooden railing. Her face is just inches from the sea's choppy surface, hat and veil dripping with salt droplets. Solveig crosses to her, presses her hand to the small of her back in comfort. She waves the help away, turning her face away from Solveig's concerned gaze.

"I'll be fine, Miss Eik," she says, a hint of anger in her voice.

Then another wave of nausea seems to hit her, sending her face back down into the sea. As they move between the rocky outcroppings, the waves drop slightly, and her head comes up. The sun has virtually disappeared over the horizon already, but the outlines of houses and boats are just about visible against the skyline.

"Tie us off, Solveig," Gunnar says as he brings them alongside.

Solveig jumps from the boat, sure-footed even as it lurches against the wooden dock. The teacher stands more carefully, bending to hold on to the sides of the boat, working her way towards the safety of solid ground inch by inch. She stops, one high heel resting on the side.

"It's alright. I'll pull you up."

Her hand grips Solveig's with surprising strength, the fine leather of her gloves creasing across the knuckles. As she lands on the decking, her ankle twists slightly on the wet wood, falling off the point of her heel before righting herself. Gunnar joins them on the planking, ties the boat to metal rings, and then starts up towards the darkened house.

"Excuse me," she calls after him, "but what about my things?"

Gunnar doesn't stop, his back retreating into the darkness. Beside her, Solveig stretches her hand out, resting it lightly on her arm. In the dark, the teacher doesn't see her move, and jumps.

"He can't move all that on his own," Solveig explains, gently. She feels sorry for the woman, her striking face dripping with sea water, still pale and blotchy from the seasickness. "My brother-in-law will come down now that they know we're here."

Gunnar must reach the house, for the path down to the water is suddenly illuminated by light from the kitchen. Silhouetted in the doorway, Solveig's sister - the previous schoolteacher - waves.

Threading the teacher's arm through her own to stop her falling, Solveig guides them up the path. Just before the door, outside the square of yellowing light, the pressure of Miss Sunde's arm stops them. She fidgets with her hat and veil, tucking wisps of hair behind her ears.

"Do I look alright?" Her voice is low, urgent. Nervous. "After, you know, the boat..."

Solveig reaches up with her free hand and straightens the hat slightly. Her hair is stiff under the veil, forced chemically into place and barely moves. As she draws away, her fingers brush against her cheek. The skin is soft, warm in the chill night air.

Pulling away, Solveig nods and the teacher fixes a brittle smile across her face.

"Good."

Liv Sunde shakes herself, squares her shoulders as if for battle, and marches on ahead.

One

It has been snowing all day, all week, and even the salted soil of the islands is covered in thick drifts, crunching underfoot and turning to sheet ice on the wooden jetties. The old dog refuses to leave the house, stretched in front of the wood burner, nose between his paws.

Outside, the thin, yellow afternoon light is fading quickly, surrendering to the dark nights, as the sow screams for her dinner. In the near-darkness, her piglets can't be seen, huddled in the shelter, lying under the straw and each other. Solveig can smell their warmth as she pours the bucket of meagre slops over the wall.

"There we are," she says, reaching to scratch the sow behind her ears. "Dinner time."

The piglets, drawn by their mother's grunt, are inching their way forward, sniffing at the fish skins and tomato pulp. They shiver in the cooling air, climb into the trough where with no motherly compunction the sow swings her head to knock them, squealing, out again.

The dying sun is trying to break through the clouds, warming the patches it touches. Solveig shuffles down into the thick serge of her coat, leans on the wall and watches the pigs, in no rush to head back inside, despite the cold. The piglets are growing fast. Their mother will keep them for now, milking their meals off her own back, but weaning won't be long and then Solveig will have to find them their own dinner.

Still, out here her family are better off than those in the towns, at least, if she's to believe the papers. Thank God, her father says, that the Germans haven't found a way to ration the fish in the sea, yet.

Gunnar doesn't have to shout: Solveig hears him arrive, his boat changing the pattern of the waves against the rocks, the slap of water against the jetty. She turns her head to watch him, the practiced drawing in of his oars, the turn of the boat, its sideways slip into its mooring. He holds up a hand, beckons her down to the water.

Solveig nods in silence, pushing off the sty wall. She casts a look back at the house, windows blacked out, her mother nowhere to be seen.

She jumps down into the boat just as the sea lifts the boat above the dock, landing as the swell retreats. Gunnar points them out into the sound, heading for the schoolhouse.

"What d'you think, then?" he says after a while.

He doesn't need to explain.

Solveig sniffs, puffs air through her coat to warm her cheeks. The teacher had been nothing but polite friendliness, even as she'd click-click-clicked her way across the quay towards them, her high heels spotless and deliberate.

"Good looking, I suppose, well dressed. Clever, definitely. Tried to be charming and sophisticated and all that, but, you know. One of them."

Solveig shakes her head in irritation. With all her poise and education, Liv Sunde should be a leader of the underground: editing an illegal paper, hiding enemies of the Führer. If nothing else, she could be charming secrets from the Occupiers, laughing and flirting her way into their confidences, then passing her newfound knowledge on. She's the type: cool, calm, the kind to inspire loyalty and devotion from her followers, of which Solveig could be one. Instead, so disappointingly, she's the opposite of all that.

He gives her a look that says a bland description wasn't what he was after.

"Anyway," Solveig carries on before he can ask again, hunching her shoulders against the wind. "You concentrate on not sinking us into this freezing sea."

He won't, of course. They grew up out on these waves together, could make this trip in gales. But it's not the islands that she's concerned about, not jagged coastline and half-submerged rocks.

Solveig looks up, checks their progress. The sun has virtually disappeared over the horizon already; her home, the lighthouse, is a black column against the skyline, light extinguished.

The islands all used to wink at you on approach, small windows of friendly light shining from homes and barns. But tonight, it's as dark as it can be, the pinpricks of starlight Gunnar's only guide. Blinds and curtains across the islands are pulled, shutters firmly closed. The penalties for breaking the blackout are harsh - but nothing compared to the bombs, the planes guided by the homing beacons so helpfully provided up and down the coast.

Gunnar's oars cut silently and easily through the water, the shoreline sliding past. The schoolhouse jetty floats out from the platform that runs the perimeter of the buildings, supported on wooden poles set deep into the shore. In the spring, when the ice water melts on the mainland and the moon's pull is at its strongest, the tide comes almost to the door and students step straight from boat to desk. The waves now are small and gentle, a far cry from this morning's trip - then Gunnar's motorboat had been full of the new arrival's possessions, low in the water and slow. In the brittle winter sunshine, the schoolhouse had seemed doubled in size, its reflection shining white in the water below, the red-tiled roof blending with the swell of land behind it, rusty heather and winter sea-grass only just disappearing under their winter blanket of snow.

They've done this fifty times, at least, but now the house at the top is occupied. Solveig sticks to the shadows in the lee of the rocks. Tonight feels different, tense, more fraught with danger. Not just a little mouse biting an elephant, but a real risk, an actual act of war. The new teacher eats, sleeps, or sits reading, just a few feet from Solveig and her co-conspirators.

Solveig can picture it: Liv Sunde, pride of Norwegian fascists, will be sitting there, head lolling back against her chair, drink cooling on the side, while Mein Kampf dangles limply from her fingers. But too loud a noise, and she'll startle into wakefulness. They'll be found, and then everyone knows what will happen next.

A firing squad, somewhere public, somewhere obvious. Here, perhaps. The Germans would line them up against the school wall, friends and neighbours kept back behind the chicken-wire fence. She'd be brave, of course, no tears. She'd meet their eyes and their bullets with her chin held high. At the execution, Solveig's mother would cry, and Gunnar's family would blame the Eiks for years.

It would be worth it, Solveig thinks, as she slips the rope around the mooring bollard. A noble death would spur reprisals all along the coastline. Ships and guns and barracks sabotaged in the night, her name inked across the ruins. Solveig Eik, people would say, shaking their heads sadly. A true Norwegian. Defying the oppressors right to her last breath.

"Solveig!" Arne's hiss brings her back to the present, and the sting of patriotic tears is just the sting of the night air. Her brother-in-law is watching her, waiting for her and Gunnar to join him in the schoolhouse doorway. The door swings open, and they slide inside. Their footsteps sound loud on the wooden floor, but they've been at this long enough to avoid walking into the desks and chairs.

There are boxes of books everywhere, still left where Solveig had unloaded them that morning. There's just so many, box after box, layers of paper and stories packed carefully together. Undset, Lie, Garborg's translations of the Odyssey. All names she should know, a list of the great and good. There are others too, less familiar, modern works in translation. It's too dark to read the titles, and no doubt Miss Sunde will notice if anything's out of place.

Solveig makes her way across the room behind the men. In the back corner, Arne reaches up and pushes a board from the ceiling, hands slipping into the hole. He pulls himself up, disappearing into the roof space.

That feeling at the bottom of her back won't go away, sitting ominously heavy at the base of her spine. Solveig checks out of the window for movement as Gunnar too climbs up, before leaning through the gap, hand held out for hers. There's nothing moving that she can see, so she turns to him, allows herself to be hauled through the roof. The jump used to be hard, when they first moved the radio here a year ago, but she's practiced at it now, and slides through the opening easily.

They fit the board back in place, plunging themselves into darkness.

"We need to find a new hiding place now that *she's* up there in the schoolhouse," Solveig says as Arne fiddles blindly at the radio. "It's not safe here anymore."

"It's not safe to move it, either," Arne says. "Getting it down and out while that woman's here, just to start."

"We can be careful," Gunnar says.

Solveig isn't convinced. The teacher strikes her as a clever type, calculating. Not the kind to miss a stream of people traipsing in and out of her territory.

"We'll bloody have to be."

Finally, sound crackles from the wireless' speakers, distorted and fuzzy.

"Dette er London."

The same words, every night at seven, from across miles and miles of dark sea. Flying above the waves, they skim the battleships and the mines, the barbed wire defences and patrolling guardsmen. Right over their heads and down into the radio and out. Solveig can picture it, the air shimmering with radio signals as though with heat.

The reports are busy, full. There's so much action in them, Solveig thinks. Bombs and fires and heroic ARP wardens and firemen. Oh, terrible to live through, of course, but still. Her own war is bland, banal. She still looks after her sheep, Gunnar still fishes. They've food enough and the soldiers are, for the most part, irritatingly pleasant.

Every Sunday at seven, or as close to it as they can manage, the three of them crowd round, waiting to hear the news. Arne comes in the week as well, passing the news on when well out at sea, away from listening ears. Tonight, there's extra programming. Øksnevad's voice goes on for longer, summarising the week's news from across the continent and abroad.

It's hardly more encouraging than the papers they're allowed to read. The news is still full of German victories: the sinking of this ship or other, their names unfamiliar and strange, the desolation of cities many times larger than Kristiansund, increasing reports of shortages in Oslo and Trondheim, food and clothes and fuel running low, allocated elsewhere. But at least, they console themselves, this news comes from a friend's mouth, and not the enemy's.

Tonight, the news seems tailored to their location. Reports are beginning to filter through from Oslo and the other towns of teachers who refused to join the NS. The Nasjonal Samling, the Norwegian Nazi Party, was still small, a cancer in the population, but powerful.

Solveig stamps down a shiver of fear as she thinks of her sister, what those camps would do to her. She can feel, though she can't see, Arne thinking the same. The space between them is hard, and the silence carries the sound of grinding teeth. She puts a hand on his arm, gently.

"Arne, let's go. We've heard enough." He shakes his head, ears still bent towards the radio, concentrating. "Arne, please. I've got a bad feeling. That teacher..."

She can't explain it, not properly. A feeling that crept over her this morning on Kristiansund quay, that Miss Sunde represented a sudden change in their lives together. Not physically, not immediately, but that somehow her presence on the islands had changed things irrevocably.

"What about her?"

"I don't trust her, of course. She's NS, and remember what Asbjørn said, about her soldier friends in Molde. If she finds us..."

The radio clicks off, the inhuman jollity of the voice fading into silence.

"OK. Come on then."

They slip down through the ceiling, pulling the board back into place and cross hurriedly to the door. Arne leans against it as always, listening.

"All quiet out there - go."

Two

Solveig is two steps beyond the door when the ground is swathed in light. She pulls Gunnar with her, presses them back flat against the schoolhouse wall, the lines of the planking pressing through Solveig's coat, digging into her shoulder blades. She motions to Arne, and the door pulls shut, the turned handle muffling the lock's close.

"Who's there?" The teacher is silhouetted against the light, a torch in her hand. She's not holding it so much as a light source, but a weapon. In its light, Gunnar's boat is clearly visible, bobbing lightly against the dock, rocked by night-time tides. "I know you're here."

She doesn't sound frightened, the hard edge to her voice searching for a fight.

There's no time to run, no route to the water without being

seen. They should have moved the radio while they still had time. Think, Solveig urges herself. Given how little you know about the new teacher, what is your best choice?

And then she remembers the piles of books, their faded, thumbed covers, love story after love story spilling from their pages.

Solveig pulls Gunnar around the corner of the school building by his coat, out of the teacher's immediate gaze. The movement will draw the teacher's eye, she knows, but it gives them the few seconds and space they need. They cannot be seen next to the schoolhouse door. It would suggest they'd been inside, and Liv Sunde would check, and Arne would be caught, and the firing squad would be called.

"Kiss me," Solveig whispers. Despite the darkness, she can see his look of surprise. It's not like that between them, never has been, although her parents have always assumed that it was only a matter of time. He doesn't move, just stays there, careful not to touch. She tugs closer, shakes him by the edges of his coat, leans his weight against her own, runs her hands down his arms. "Gunnar," she says, making her voice insistent, "kiss me."

He suddenly understands that she's serious, and leans forward, cradling her head between his hands. His mouth is cool, shy, the press of his lips against hers uncertain. It sparks nothing for Solveig, all her attention focused beyond him, behind him, on the teacher's approach in the darkness. She brings her arms up around his shoulders, keeping him in place. From the corner of her eyes, she can see the edge of the torch' beam come ever closer.

Gunnar's hand slips from her head to her shoulder, then

further down. His palm rests on her coat and, through layers of material, her breast. He's forgotten, it seems, the teacher's approach. His kiss is no longer shy, but firm, demanding. His beard rubs and scratches at her face, his hands pinching and pulling at her clothing.

"What are you doing?" As they start away from each other, away from the wall, Solveig takes care to keep their hands linked. She hides behind Gunnar, pressing her head into his shoulder, trying not to wipe her lips clean. "Well?"

Liv Sunde is barely three years older than Solveig, but her voice carries all a teacher's authority.

"I'm sorry," Solveig says, and the torch beam comes up, shining straight onto her face. Closing her eyes in a wince, she holds up a hand as a shield against the brightness. "It's just that, well, Gunnar and I... we want to be married, but we can't. Not until he has his own fishing boat."

Solveig turns her head out of the beam, her reflection in the schoolhouse window moving with her. Solveig sees herself suddenly, sees herself as a stranger must, as this Liv Sunde must.

Tall for a woman, almost as tall as Gunnar, and broad shouldered, square-jawed. Her arms and legs are solid, her stomach flat, built out from rowing and wrestling sheep. When she squeezed her own arms, proud of the muscle lying underneath the pale skin, she felt like an unripe plum, unyielding but with a hint of softness. If it weren't for her dark hair, tied back out of her face, she'd be the spitting image of a German propaganda poster. Staring into the distance, sleeves rolled up and forearms corded as she churned butter or pushed a hand-plough, wandered arm in arm through fields of wheat; strong and capable, ready to breed for the glory of the Reich.

She's not dressed like a propaganda poster, no swishing skirts or sensible pinafores. She's in trousers, not wide enough to be movie star fashionable, and an old fisherman's jumper, the heavy-knit pattern turning lumpy and frayed with wear. Her coat is thick serge, the blue stained and faded from salt-spray, collar turned up against the wind. It's not the usual outfit you'd expect a girl of twenty-two to go courting in.

Twenty-two - not a child anymore, but not a real woman either, not married, not a mother. Not even close to being either, and just as far from being her own idea of a Resistance hero. She turns away from the smooth glass, ignores the pull of her reflection, elbows Gunnar in the side.

"My own boat," he repeats flatly. He's not much of an actor, Solveig knows, but at least he has the sense to play along.

"Miss Eik," the teacher says, a note of resigned recognition in her voice. "Somehow, I knew you'd be trouble. That doesn't explain why you've chosen *my* house to conduct your torrid romance against."

"My parents wouldn't approve, and..." Solveig trails off, trying to sound contrite, in love. Anything other than treasonably guilty.

There's a long pause. Solveig's mouth fills with coppery fear, her hand tightening around Gunnar's.

"And nor do I," Miss Sunde says. "This is a school, not a brothel."

She lowers the torch, its light now pooling at their feet. She sighs, wraps her dressing gown tighter around her, a poor defence against the chilly night air and the sea breeze. In the moon's half-light, Solveig can see her hands are shaking, ungloved and stiff. Her legs, too, are exposed, shoes covering bare feet.

"Go home and find somewhere else to meet next time." She turns, heading back to the house, taking the light with her.

For a moment, Solveig and Gunnar lean against the wall, the cladding pressing lines into their backs. Solveig hears the door shut behind the teacher and allows herself to sigh. Gunnar takes her hand in his and pulls her in for another kiss. At the last moment she turns her head, and his lips land against the frozen skin of her cheek. Her coat bunches beneath his fingers, the material gaping between the buttons, and she shakes her arms until the material lies smooth again.

"Come on," she says. "We need to go."

Gunnar takes the oars, as always, and Solveig sits in the rear, facing out towards the sea. After a moment, she turns back.

Arne will still be in the school, pressed against the walls, waiting for the light to go out. She wonders if he'll climb back up to the radio, in case the teacher checks for more uninvited guests. It's what she'd do, but the thought of a night in the school roof is less than appealing. At the end of the attic there are loose boards where snow slants through gaps in the old wooden cladding, and icicles form on the beams.

In the darkness, there's a small square of light leaking from the schoolhouse. Clearly visible, Liv Sunde stands in the window, watching them row away. Her outline stays still, unmoving, for long moments, although she surely cannot see them at this distance now the moon is hidden behind clouds.

"We want to get married, do we?" Gunnar's voice is soft, uncertain, unexpected in the darkness. The image of Liv is cut off by a falling blind and Solveig turns back around, laughs nervously, unprepared for the fallout. She'd half-known it was coming. Perhaps that was why she'd looked back, why she'd focused so intently on the back-lit figure.

"It was just something to say, a cover, an excuse for us being there."

He should know to drop it, know to leave it there. Solveig's never been very good at keeping her heart from her sleeve: if she wanted him, he'd know by now. He stops rowing, and the boat smooths to a stop, bobbing gently with the waves.

"I know," he says. "But Solveig, I'm game for it, if you are."

Somehow, his proposal is not what she expected, not what stories and songs and her mother's reminiscing had led her to imagine. It should be, she thinks. It's just the situation the heroine of one of Liv Sunde's books would find herself in: barely escaping from a dangerous enemy, a handsome conspirator, love against the odds.

It's the moment for declarations, for grand passion. And yet his gentle offer has left her empty, hollow in the place her feelings should be.

"Well, you don't captain your own boat yet." It's a joke, but in a shaft of moonlight the disappointment on Gunnar's face is clear to see.

"Well," he says, "the offer's there if you want it."

As he sits back, hands once again on the oars, he looks out over the water and the corners of his mouth pinch down into a frown.

Three

Christmas Eve, for Solveig, holds none of its usual delights. The other post-Invasion years hadn't seemed so bad, somehow, remnants of the festive spirit clinging to life. But this year there's no lavish feasts of lutefisk and sausage and ham, no church, no royal broadcast. The flagpole - usually so proudly adorned with the red and white and blue of the Norwegian flag - remains bare.

The family have already arrived, cramped together in the lighthouse's kitchen and large sitting room, and no-one else seems to notice the missing Christmas spirit. At the piano, her mother leads them in the traditional carols, defiantly playing those the Germans have banned the loudest. Her father and uncle drink too much, their singing off key and slurred.

After the meal, weeks of rations but still meagre enough, Solveig escapes the press of motherly attention, the intense debates on old disputes, the constant rattle of dice against the sides of her cousin's new board-game, and sets off for the sheep. The waters are empty and cold, splashing around the bow, breaking against the skerries and sea stacks. She takes her time shaking out the hay, the few beets, counting each sheep.

There's something wrong with her, she knows, to be upset at how little the war has changed things. She should be happy that her family are safe, that Gunnar is safe. She should be happy with Gunnar, with his steady kindness. But what other suited people, made her friends sigh with satisfaction, what filled their dreams, had never appealed to her.

She wanted adventure, excitement. She wanted to see more of the world than the islands, than her sheep. She wanted someone to see it with. Before the war, when there were more options, she'd left the islands, taken a job in Molde. Rented a room in a boarding house, had time and money of her own. She'd had friends, had someone who...

Solveig shakes herself, stamps her feet as a distraction.

No. No thinking of ifs and buts and what could have been. Here she was, back again, and there was no use daydreaming.

Eventually, it's too cold to stay out any longer, the biting at her ears through the rough wool of her hat, threatening an earache. When she returns to the lighthouse, Solveig and her cousins make their way upstairs early, while they can still feel the warmth of their dinner. The topmost room is already cold, even through the jumper and long, thick socks she had layered over her pyjamas. At least she's been allowed to keep her own eiderdown, if not the room it belongs in.

She'd also been made to give up the bed to the boys, and take an old camping mat up with her. The floor underneath was hard and cold, a draught blowing from somewhere, but if she curled up tight and stayed still, she'd be warm enough.

Johan, her youngest cousin, falls asleep almost instantly. As his breaths lengthen out, his brother Karl turns over, swings his hand down the side of the bed, brushing Solveig's leg.

"Hey - you still awake?" He doesn't wait for an answer, carrying on in a hushed whisper. "I've got something for you that I didn't want to give you downstairs."

"Why? What is it?"

"Nothing bad," he says. "Just don't want my Mor to worry about me, you know? She's bad enough as it is."

He twists, reaching under his pillow. His brother stirs, his feet disturbed. There's a crackling rustle and then the darker shadow of a hand hovers over her face.

"Here," he says. "Have this, pass it around."

She reaches up, feeling her way up his wrist. It's paper, several pages folded and bound together, and she can feel the raised type in thick columns along the surface.

She knows what it is.

"I'll read it," she says, slipping it under her own pillow. "And I know who to give it to next."

"Be careful," he says. "Don't tell them where you got it."

It'll be pretty obvious if she passes it to Arne or Gunnar where it's come from, and Karl must know that. Her cousin visits, and suddenly she has resistance newsletters and gossip? Even the pigs aren't that stupid, but she promises anyway: "I won't."

She turns over, burrowing down into the thin mattress, cold despite her layers of clothes. She tucks her hands between her legs, presses her nose into her shoulder and tries to warm her face with her breaths. Winter was so long this year, and she was so tired of being cold.

A yawn overtakes her, bringing tears to her eyes.

"Night Karl."

This won't happen to her when she's a proper hero of the resistance - bumped out of her own bedroom by her aunt, left to freeze to death in a room of snoring boys. If she's going to freeze, it'll be hunkered down behind a snowdrift, binoculars trained on the enemy.

The Hun will be massed down on the fjord banks, and in the crisp snow-fall air their harsh shouts will carry clearly, up to where she lies beyond the tree line, her platoon waiting on her orders.

"You'll think this is cold?" she'll ask them, kicking derisively at the snow. "Try lambing at three in the morning, on a rock that barely breaks the surface of the sea. That's cold. This? It's just a bit chilly."

Eventually, long after other commanders would have failed, she'll give the go ahead. Silently, they'll ski down, each man in the tracks of the one before. Solveig will go first, carving the line down the slope. The Germans won't be watching, looking in the wrong direction to see the white-suited blurs hurtling down the mountainside behind them.

At her signal, they'll stop right behind the waiting railway cars in that smart flurry of snow she's never yet been able to master. The men will do their jobs, whatever it is - maybe stealing supplies, food rations to distribute perhaps, or something more dangerous: fixing explosives to train carriages' undersides, setting the timer for miles down the track, the bridge over the mountain pass.

Solveig herself will keep watch, pressed against the edge of the truck, rifle unslung from her shoulder, safety off and ready to fire. There will be a fight, of course, shots fired and a sprint chase across the snow, German patrols skiing hard behind them. But Norwegians are born with skis on, and Solveig and her team will weave easily between the trees, take hidden jumps at full pace, climb up into their mountain hideouts with ease.

There, in some abandoned summer farm or other, they'll light the fire, drink akevitt and Scottish whiskey dropped by plane the week before, stretch out in the warmth, socks steaming in front of the fire. And the resistance leader, the mastermind behind it all - another woman, most likely, tall and reserved and blonde and put together - will lean over and refill her glass, chinking against her own.

"I'm so glad we found you," this woman will say, "that I found you. I'm so glad that you, above all others, saw through my disguise - we'd be lost without you, Solveig Eik."

At least, that's how the dream goes, and Solveig smiles in her sleep, no longer disturbed by her cousins' gentle snoring.

A crick in her neck pulls her awake. It's too early to be up on her only day off apart from her birthday: the room is dark still, the winter sun not yet high enough to do any real good. It's Christmas still, she reminds herself, and her present is that her father will check the sheep, his city-living younger brother uselessly in tow. She tries to go back to sleep, wriggling into the thin mattress, but it's no use.

She's awake.

In the end, she lights the lamp, angling its glow down on the floor. She'll take the chance to read Karl's secret missive in private, before the others are up and likely to walk in on her.

The pages say nothing much, similar plain reports of unofficial news. There are a few updates on the war outside Norway, but mostly the news is provincial, barely straying beyond the borders of Kristiansund. They sit uncomfortably next to more impassioned speeches that continue to urge all decent Norwegians, all freedom-loving, King and God-revering Norwegians, to stay true to the cause.

KONGEN LIV

23 DESEMBER 1942

PHOTOGRAPHY NOT APPROVED HOBBY

A few days ago in Tustna, a German soldier arrested an amateur photographer for taking pictures of the Trondheim sound, saying they captured German fleet movements. However, no fleet movements were reported at that time and it is strongly suspected that the arrest was motivated by a cowardly NS informer's report. The photographer's house and possessions have already been requisitioned by the invaders. It is believed the man himself has been transferred to Grini prison.

"BRAVE VOLUNTEER" RETURNS HOME

Yesterday the police raided the house of well-known NS members in Oslo. It is believed that their son, reported by neighbours to be an eager volunteer for German military service in both Finland and Russia, has deserted his commission with the Wehrmacht. The "courage" of volunteers is again proved inferior to the bravery shown by our boys, who continue to resist our oppressors. We salute both those who escaped to England and those continuing the fight on the home front. Other family members are believed to be in the Kristiansund municipality, where he may be attempting to shelter. We want to advise residents in the suburbs of Kristiansund of the danger - as a coward and a traitor, he is likely to be dangerous.

FIGHT THE GOOD FIGHT, MY FRIENDS

My fellow citizens, the war grinds on and you may feel that there is no end in sight. Even the most resolute amongst us may feel our natural patriotism and revulsion for the enemy weakening, our resolve threatens to shatter. After all, as Christians, does not the Bible urge us to obey those in charge, who now happen to be the German Reich and its puppets?

"Let every person be subject to the governing authorities. For there is no authority except from God, and those that exist have been instituted by God."

(Romans 13:7)

When St Paul wrote these words, the world was no less cruel and savage than our own. The Roman Empire still flourished, with its slaves and gladiatorial games and crucifixions. Should we not also submit to the rule of the authorities, lay our efforts at the feet of slow, incremental reform rather than bloody and outright resistance?

No, I tell you - look to the Old Testament. Look at the kings laid low in Daniel, look at Sodom and Gomorrah. Turn to the midwives who kill innocent babes (Exodus 1:15-17), to Daniel ignoring Persian law (Daniel 6:10), and to Daniel's friends refusing to bow to the king's image (Daniel 3:14-18).

These jack-booted invaders are no God-given authority. They stole what they have, by threats and force. It is the duty of every God-fearing one amongst us to resist the evil of tyranny and oppression, to ignore man's law when obeying would force us to disobey God's.

Rise up, my brothers, and do God's work.

Solveig strongly suspects the last piece to be written by a striking minister with too much time on his hands. The news sheet is hand-typed, and by the pastor's article the ribbon has begun to wear out, leaving an irregular pattern of ink across the sheet. She looks at the last line again, and it makes her eye twitch in frustration. Would it have killed him to type two extra words: Rise up, my brothers and sisters?

You'd think, reading the rest of the paper, that Norway had become a country populated entirely by men.

The dim light and irritating reading makes Solveig's eyes dry and itchy. She sniffs and turns out the light, folding the news sheet back under her pillow. The mattress is still uncomfortable, and the room still cold. Eventually she drifts off, enjoying her rare late morning, only to be woken again far too soon by Johan's foot colliding solidly with her shoulder.

"Hey!" Solveig moans, rolling onto her side to protect from any further attacks. "Careful, Johan!"

"Sorry Solveig! I forgot you were there!"

Before her eyes are fully open, or she's had a chance to wipe the drool from the corner of her mouth, he throws himself down next to her, face smothered in her shoulder, his arm flung out across her chest.

"Merry Christmas! Come on," he says, shaking her with excitement, "get up! I want to play my game again!"

He leaves at a run, his heel connecting this time with the inside of her elbow, bashing it against the wooden floor in his hurry.

"I'm coming," she says, "I'm coming. Two seconds, alright?"

Karl is more careful where he puts his feet, offering his hand to pull her up from the mattress.

"Sleep alright?"

"Well enough," she says, stretching her arms behind her head. "Eventually. You don't half snore, Karl."

They move together, smoothing the covers of the boys' bed, leaning her camp mattress up against the wall. Karl throws the curtains and shutters open, blinking against the sudden light.

"I'd forgotten," he says, leaning on the windowsill, head

craning to see the mainland, "how quiet it is out here. Listen - there's nothing." A burst of laughter from the kitchen ruins his moment, and he rolls his eyes. "Apart from them."

He pauses again, looking out at the empty sea, the humps of islands and skerries in the distance.

"A man could hide out here and never found, get lost, fall off the map." He looks as though he's thinking, considering something. "A little mouse's bolthole to rest and recover. I bet you feel pretty cut off out here, like the war's a completely different world."

"Sometimes. We're not exactly first in line for news, unless it's about the movement of cod." Solveig pulls her hair into a rough bun, throws on her slippers. "But you know, don't you? What's going on out there?" She picks up the piece of folded paper he'd given her last night, holds it up for him to see. "That's what this is about, right? You hear the news better than we do."

Karl shrugs, shaking out the blanket across the bed.

"There's not much news, not really. The Germans are good at propaganda, at making sure only their version gets through. But we hear things, about Stalingrad, about the war in Africa and so on."

"About Stalingrad?"

Solveig had heard a little about it on the radio, the spare details the BBC's Norwegian programme had cared to provide. She hadn't known, at first, where Stalingrad even was when the reports started filtering in. She'd had to look it up, flicking through the pages of her parents' encyclopaedia, convinced she'd just missed the entry. The books had been a wedding gift and took up an entire shelf in the big living room; there was no way a city the size of Stalingrad had been ignored by the compilers.

In the end, she'd asked her father, and he'd turned to the next section, away from S and into T, his finger underlining a completely different place.

"Changed its name," he said. "Back in twenty-five or so."

What a strange thing, Solveig thought. It had been known as something else - Tsaritsyn - for hundreds of years and then, just like that, Stalingrad. How long did it take for people to adjust to the new name, their new identity? They can't have woken up the day after, pulled on their trousers and Cossack hats and said to their wife, I'm off to Stalingrad now.

It would have been halting, hard work, full of cut off sentences and only half-uttered words. And now that was the name everyone in the world knew the place by - news reports and locals and official war documents and Norwegians in lighthouses two thousand miles away - the old name erased as completely as if it had never been.

There must still be old people who refused to accept the change, who clung adamantly to the old ways, to the name their grandfathers used, the name that had a meaning based in history, in geography, not just the actions of some dictatorial upstart.

She understands, can sympathise.

"They say it's terrible - much worse than here. That the rats have left the city, that people are eating their pets. I spoke to a man who'd seen it with his own eyes and he told me that the river burnt."

"What?" His words make no sense. "How can water burn?"

Solveig tries to imagine it, the seas around Smøla on fire, bright flicks of flame washing up along the shores. Out of the window, she can see the white walls of the schoolhouse reflected in the water below. They'd burn too, if the water was alight, the dust of the schoolroom and the paper in the books catching quickly, white hot with heat.

"I don't know," Karl says. "Oil got in the water, perhaps. He said thousands are dead."

They're both quiet for a moment. The scale of it, of the war on the Eastern Front, far eclipses their ration lines and curfews, the petty disappearance of women from the news sheets.

"Makes the war out here look great, eh?"

"Not great," Karl says, "but not as bad as it could be." He's serious again, his eyes fixed on Solveig, on her face. "They need to be stopped, Solveig, sent packing. If they're not, Stalingrad's just the start."

"And you're the one to do it, are you?" She means it as a joke - Karl is just turned seventeen, too weedy and short-sighted to make any kind of soldier. She can't imagine him outrunning pursuers, climbing or swimming his way out of danger. He doesn't know boats, how to read the wind and bird signals, like she does - he couldn't hold a wriggling ewe still if his life depended on it. Taller than her, but thin, lanky. Not enough weight, not enough grip.

"I'm trying."

He's entirely serious behind his glasses, his eyes wide and magnified.

"No. Come on, not really."

"Yes really! Some other local chaps and I are in contact with

London. We've got orders: get to Scotland if we can, come back trained."

Honestly. That's taking it too far, surely. There's wanting to be involved, and then there's just plain fantasy.

"I don't believe you," Solveig says flatly, shaking the sheets smooth with more force than necessary. "You're not a soldier."

"Not a soldier, exactly, but..."

"But you can barely fire a gun at a deer, let alone at an actual person."

"You couldn't either!"

"I could," she insists. "Do you not remember how you cried over that doe when we were, what, fifteen?"

He cuts her off.

"This is a war, Solveig, and we all have to do what we wouldn't normally do. Even if that means killing."

Perhaps it wasn't a striking minister - perhaps it was Karl himself, hopped up on self-righteousness.

"I bet you couldn't do it, though. Couldn't actually pull the trigger."

"I could, if I had to."

Her aunt calls up to them, banging something against the bare wood of the stairs.

"Karl! Solveig! Are you ever coming down?"

Karl turns from the bed, shrugs.

"Sorry Solveig," he says, "got to follow orders."

At the door, Solveig catches his sleeve. He might be making things up, but if he's not...

"If you need me to do anything, you know, to help - I'll do it."

He smiles, nods. She's gripped with a sudden feeling he doesn't believe her, won't really come to her for help. "Karl, I mean it. Anything you need. *Anything*. Just ask."

Four

The new ewes cannot be put off any longer. Solveig spends long days out on the water, island hopping to check their shelters, break the ice on their water troughs. At each stop, she shakes out a few beets and waits for the ewes to come running over. While they gobble down her new year offering, she checks them over, making sure they have no injuries, no chesty coughs. She squeezes their backs, right over the bones of their hips, feeling the depth of their fat. They need worming and feeding, conditioning before the real winter sets in. They've lost weight everywhere but their stomachs, their bones creeping through their skin even as their bellies swell. There's still a fair few months of winter left, and they'll need the energy stored in the covering flesh to get them and their unborn lambs through.

When she makes it to the main island, a new poster is nailed to the red wall of the boathouse. Against a white background, heroically outlined, is a German soldier. The posters are appearing everywhere, a call to action, to arms, to the willing defence of their new fatherland. *Alt for Norge*, they shout, as their grim-faced portraits stare into the middle distance.

There's a rumour going around, a joke, about posters in Oslo, warning the citizens to behave. You will be shot if you do this; you will be shot if you do that. And someone, brave, foolish, has written: you will be shot if you have not been shot.

That's alright in Oslo, where there are enough suspects for the culprit never to be caught. But here, with just a few hundred families clinging to rocks in the middle of the sea, it would be easy enough for the soldiers to match the handwriting. And then - bang! - you will be shot.

There's no-one in sight, no approaching chug of motors. Solveig reaches up and pulls the paper from the wall, the corners left in place, scraps of colour under the nails. She grinds it into the dirt with her heel, then scratches a 'v' into the wood with her penknife. V for victory. She half thinks about continuing, adding the rest of the King's symbol, but there's always the chance of discovery, so she settles for throwing the poster into the sea, and watching as the colours bleed and fade.

In the sea between islands, the noise of an approaching motor is obvious. Too small for one of the fishing fleet, too well-oiled to be another farmer. The shout, then, is unsurprising.

"Halt!"

She stops rowing, lets the boat drift sideways in the motorboat's wake. The old dog wakes from his place in the bow, bares his teeth at them, barks once.

"Hey, it's alright," she tells him. "Just another day."

Just another spot inspection. They would be boring if they weren't so regular and unwelcome. As they pull alongside, the Germans anchor their boat to hers with a long pole, one hooked at the end, ensuring she won't just row away.

"What are you doing? Boats must stay close to the shore." His Norwegian is good, marked only lightly by traces of a Danish accent.

"I'm going out to my sheep on the small islands, and this is the quickest route." She rummages around for the cartons of wormer, the movements drawing the muzzle of their guns in her direction, and holds one up to show them. "I always row this way."

"Your papers, please."

She hands them over, the identity card hard to read, blurred by salt spray and creased from living in her pocket. The soldier squints at the photo, making a show of comparing her to her picture. Then he nods, brusquely, and waves her on.

"This time only, Fräulein," he says, emphasising the German word. "For your own safety. There may be enemy mines in the water."

It's nothing Solveig hasn't heard before - they really ought to come up with a new spiel - and so she says nothing. Sure thing, she thinks, enemy mines. They should be his enemy, not his friends, his employers. But then that was volunteers, she thinks - they'd rolled over at the first sign of trouble, went belly up and tails tucked between their legs. Yes Herr Hitler, they'd said, no Herr Hitler, anything you like Mein Führer.

The hook detaches from the gunwale carelessly, scratching a deep line through the paint and into the wood beneath.

"*Leck mich am Arsch,*" Solveig mutters once they're out of earshot, her school-girl German more insulting than useful or correct. At least Norway hadn't given up so easily. Solveig consoles herself with that, even if it's to be expected - Norwegians have always prided themselves as having the same solid backbone as their country.

As Solveig rows, her mind churning with disgust at these volunteers, these traitors, her thoughts return to Liv Sunde. School will have started back after the holidays, Miss Sunde's pupils once again trapped with their German lessons, their incessant brainwashing. Their parents can't be happy about it: no-one else with half a brain on Smøla thinks the Germans are a good thing, apart from Magnus Løvik, three islands over. He runs a good business, always makes a canny deal for his wool. It doesn't make sense to deal with the devil, with those monsters, when he could stand with his kin and countrymen.

Except, of course, if he's decided - if Miss Sunde has decided - that this German domination was the new permanent state of the world. Then it would be sensible to be in cahoots with the overlords, cozied up against their hot, steaming flank like a winter piglet with the sow.

God, she thinks, as her bladder suddenly announces itself. I should have gone at home first. She turns around, leg bouncing distractedly, throwing off the rhythm of her oars, and looks over her shoulder at the approaching shoreline. How far is that? Forty strokes? Fifty?

She counts down in pairs. Fifty, forty-eight. A quarter of the way, half. The boat slithers over the water, oars cutting cleanly. Her muscles bunch and pull together, used to this, conditioned for it, and it feels good to be strong and coordinated.

Eighteen, fourteen. Up through the surf, the breaking crests pushing her closer.

The problem with sheep, more than any animal, is that they know they're going to die. It must be passed down, ewe to lamb, the inevitability of their mutton-y destiny. They skitter and skip away from her, apparently terrified for their lives, legs flailing in all directions. Then, as she squats awkwardly, they return, nosing at her coat sleeves, cautious, wary, but curious.

"Get off," she shoos them, waving a hand so they tense and jump sideways. "Give a lady some privacy."

When she's done, it's down to worming.

Clearing the holding pen of its accumulated moss and dirt is only marginally easier than steering the sheep into the funnel. The old dog these days is slow, hobbling to keep up. She should train a new one, find someone with a pup for sale. But that's another mouth to feed, another portion of meat or fish to find every day. Besides, she likes the old dog, the slow thump of his tail, the way he knows what she wants to do before she does. Often, she feels that he's the farmer and she the assistant, following his suggestions before she's had a chance to come up with her own.

By the time she's drenched all the ewes with wormer, hair plastered to her forehead, mud and other dirt caked to her trousers, the sun is making a rapid descent into the sea.

"One, two, three, five, ten, thirteen." She counts the ewes, one by one, finger tracing the air outline of each woolly back. One missing. She counts again: one, five, still thirteen. No mistake, and no rustling in the scrub. Lost then, or at least as lost as something can get on an island barely big enough to earn a name.

"Stay here," she says to the dog, "I'll be back."

Solveig sets off inland, boots crunching against the stiff matgrass. The grass tops are dry, but the undergrowth is soggy, water running in rivulets along sheep tracks, cold enough to freeze except for the salt.

"*Sau!*" she calls. "*Sau!* Where are you, bloody thing?"

The sheep doesn't answer. It was foolish to expect a helpful bleating, or for the sheep to come trotting towards her, but she's disappointed, anyway. People in offices don't have this problem. She never did when she was working as a bookkeeper in Molde, warm in her office on her high chair, the scribble of pen nibs around her and the promise of a canteen lunch after. Even nurses, teachers don't have this problem.

Well, she supposes, teachers might, their charges less controllable than sheep, if her sister Bjørghild is to be believed.

There are caves here that her grandparents forbade them to enter as children. They'd explored anyway. The old holes were dark and dank, unappealing even to children fuelled by myth and legend, but large enough for a sheep to hide from the biting wind.

At the cave entrance a scrap of wool, caught in lichens against the rocks, flutters in the wind, a speck of dirty white against the grey. It could have been there for ages, but something about the waxy feel of the wool says it's recent. Inside, something - a mouse, maybe - skitters in the darkness.

Solveig stands at the cave entrance, hand against the exposed stone wall, aware of the day dwindling at her back. The snow built up around the cave mouth provides a makeshift barrier against the wind, like the ice houses of the Sámi up in Finnmark or Tromsø. But unlike those, the air from the cave feels damp, colder than the air outside.

"*Sau?*" she calls into the cave, hearing her voice come bouncing back at her from all angles. "Where the hell are you?"

A vague rustling comes from the darkness, but no answering bleat.

"If I have to come in there, I will," she threatens uselessly. The ewe can't understand her, isn't going to listen to reason.

In the dark, something moves just out of the edge of her vision. She takes a few steps into the cave, feeling her way, fingers trailing the rough rock wall.

"*Sau?* You in here?"

There's nothing this far south that could really do her any damage, but the trolls of her childhood are not easily shaken. She can feel eyes creeping up her back, but when she turns round, she sees only the entrance of the cave.

"*Sau?*"

It's not a sheep moving through the cave. In the darkness, she can just about make out a face. Eyes glint above a beard, not trimmed like her father's or Gunnar's, but wild, ragged at the edges, curling over the sheepskin of a leather flight jacket.

"Stop there." The voice is low, quiet, but the press of cold metal against her neck gives it power. "Who are you?"

She doesn't answer him, she can't. It's a simple question, but her mind is blank.

"Tell me who you are," the man repeats slowly. "Speak before I fucking kill you."

Solveig nods, the sharp knife edge cutting into her skin with every movement.

"I'm... I'm Solveig," she says. It becomes clear, as her eyes adjust to the dim light, that the cave's lived in: the thin pallet against the rock, the fire remnants, the dried meat hanging from the ceiling. No-one would brave the islands' winter nights unless they had to. Anyone official would stay nearby and only come out to the small islands in the short daylight. Which means the man isn't official, isn't supposed to be out here among her sheep. He's hiding from someone, and these days that can only mean...

She takes a breath, a chance.

"I'm a friend," she says. "Long Live the King."

The knife shivers against her neck, and she waits for the sharp, sudden pain of being stabbed, the furious rush of blood. Defiant to the end, she reminds herself. Except that this is hardly the noble death she'd imagined. No patriotic campaigns are run in honour of girls lying rotting in caves, surrounded and nosed at by inquisitive sheep.

She won't need one this time.

The press of the knife eases.

"Get in here," the man says, "let me have a look at you."

She takes a few nervous steps, and the body belonging to the bearded face moves behind her, blocking her exit. She turns around, hands on her hat and lapel. The man must recognise the meaning of the paperclip, for the face in darkness nods, stiffly. He lights a match, letting it flare, flickering in the damp, before setting it to the wick of a lantern. The cave lights up, darkness receding into the corners.

"What's your name?"

"I'm Solveig," she repeats. "Solveig Eik."

His eyes flicker up at that, a moment of sharp interest.

"Eik? From the lighthouse?"

"Yes, that's me."

"You're the local do-gooder, I hear."

He's not exactly how she'd imagined a resistance fighter: there's not much of the classically heroic about him. A hero's jaw should be strong, square, his arms capable of carrying the wounded with ease, his hair fair and windswept.

She checks herself. That's unfair: the man can't help not being handsome. Not everyone can be blessed with Liv Sunde's complexion, with her easy poise and confidence.

He's not in uniform, either, and somehow she's always pictured the resistance in uniform. Tatters of pre-war Norwegian kit, long worn thin, or in new brown serge and British sigils. Saboteurs in British uniform, Karl had said, are less likely to bring down reprisals on the local population. Enemy agents at work, rather than local resistance that should be taught - or frightened - into knowing better.

"I'd like to think so."

"Alright then," he says. "What good are you going to do me?"

He's a disappointing resistance fighter all round. Not

handsome, not in uniform, not even polite. But he is in need of some good deeds: his hiding place is pretty awful. Cold and damp and uncomfortable, poor shelter for sheep on the worst nights - hardly suited for human habitation. If Solveig were hiding, she thinks, she'd head into the city, where she could slip unnoticed in the crowds, where her unexceptional face would blend in with all the other tallish, dark-haired girls. Or maybe, if that wasn't possible, she'd head out into the mountains, lose her pursuers in the vastness of the countryside. She wouldn't come out to Smøla, where people have to have known your grandfather to trust you and any stranger sticks out like a sore thumb. Unless, of course, she knew where to find people willing to help her, if she'd been told who to ask for when she got across the sound.

"Karl sent you here, right?"

The man doesn't reply, simply tucks the knife back into the waistband of his trousers, covering the handle with the back of his jacket.

"He sent you here, but the light's not on in the lighthouse and you just overshot."

There's a long pause, the man watching her steadily, unspeaking.

"Of course," Solveig says into the silence. "You probably can't tell me. I'm safer if I know nothing and all that. But you're on the run, you're lying low, and you've come out here to do it." It's a brave plan. Especially without warning her of his arrival. "They can't get you to Sweden?"

That is what Resistance people do, after all, when the going gets too much and the Gestapo get too close. They're hidden, given fake papers, and smuggled across the border to live out the rest of the Occupation with unrationed food and peace.

"Sweden?" He seems incredulous. "Why would I go to Sweden?"

Of course - that was stupid. Sweden's a last resort, something that only happens when all other options are exhausted. He will just be hiding out, waiting for the search to move onto someone else, before he can go back to his resistance circles. But for now, he's been sent to her.

"So tell me," she says. "How can I help? I'll carry messages for you, I'll sabotage their boats, I'll do anything."

It's hard to tell, turned as he is into the semi-darkness along the cave walls, but Solveig thinks she sees him smile. Then, finally, he nods.

"I need food and blankets. Will you do that?"

Her voice seems to have dried in her throat, sticking to the roof of her mouth. Your country needs you, Solveig. To fetch and carry, to cook and probably clean. To be a good little woman.

Some hero, confined to the kitchen.

Her silence is obviously not welcome.

"Look, sweetheart-"

"Sweetheart!" He might be a resistance fighter, and he might have a gun. He certainly has a knife. But no-one has called her that in years, not since some patronising old man in Molde when she was fifteen. No-one's dared since. The islanders know her, have seen her castrate piglets and throw bags of sheep feed over her shoulder like they were nothing, have been on the wrong end of her temper. "Don't call me that - not if you want my help."

"Fine," he says. "Look, Solveig, if you want to help us, this is what you have to do."

She swallows her disappointment. She needs to earn his trust first, convince him of her loyalty. And afterwards, she'd work on persuading him to include her in the top secret stuff, in disguises, codes and plotting, in the things that would change the course of the war.

"How do you think I'm going to do that? You know food is rationed. At this time of the year, there's nothing growing. The soldiers took our spare blankets, our quilts."

They'd tried to take everything, but the lighthouse is old, its floorboards loose.

The man moves closer, right up against her, until she can smell the rankness of him, the warm gush of his breath. His hand closes around her shoulders, strong fingers crushing into her flesh.

"I need food and blankets. Are you a friend or not?"

She nods, mutely, and he lets her go.

"Alright. Food and blankets. Anything else?"

"Just that." The man, crouched by the embers, makes a show of fiddling with his knife. His eyes shine in the flickering, the light casting shadows across his face, hiding his expression. "And your silence, of course."

There's a moment of silence while she thinks of what to do, what to say. Even as it's leaving her mouth, she can feel how stupid it is, considering the meat hanging above them, the heap of dirty wool piled next to the mattress, the stink of blood by the fire.

"So, have you seen my sheep?"

At least now, without the ewe to treat and catch, Solveig can make a quick escape from the island. In the fading light, she's glad of it - though the cave is out of sight, she can feel the man's eyes on her, the weight of his expectation, the strength of his fingers. Her left arm is tender, sore; she can feel the bruise spreading, developing under her clothes. But a bruise is nothing compared to the punishment the Germans will hand out if she is discovered hiding the enemy.

Out on the water, she watches for any trace of him, any sign the island houses more than sheep. So this time, the shout is a surprise.

"Fräulein!"

The oars jolt in Solveig's hands, rough wood catching in the waves and pulling forward, sending a splinter into the skin of her palm. She swears, and the old dog stands up, paws on the seat, barking at the approaching patrol boat.

Perhaps the man in the cave was a trap, a ploy to test Norwegian loyalty. There are other rumours, printed in the underground presses, of Norwegians acting as decoy refugees, bringing down trouble on any who help them. Although, that being so, it would be a specific trap: other than her, who visited that tiny island? Her father and, in better weather, the odd courting couple eager to escape their parents' watchful gaze. Hardly a hub of resistance activity.

It's a fresh set of soldiers than from the way out, and their faces are stern.

"*Was?*" Even with her limited German, she keeps her tone

deliberately belligerent, scowling up the gun-grey side of their boat.

"Your business?"

The rifles pointing over the gunwales are intended to reinforce the seriousness of the question, but there's only so many death threats that frighten in one day.

"What business brings you out on the water?"

"Returning home from my sheep on the island."

They confer in low, hushed voices, and then hands are extended in place of guns, hauling her roughly from one craft to the next. The old dog is grabbed too and hoisted into the boat beside her. She puts a hand down, strokes the rough hackles on his neck, curls her fingers into his fur. It's as much for her as it is for him.

"We will tow you and your boat to the shore. It is not safe for you on open water."

In the twilight, the officer stands beside her, hands folded behind his back in some kind of parade rest. It's probably meant to be neat and efficient, but Solveig thinks it just makes him look older than he is. And more pompous.

"My brother and father are farmers," he says after a while. "Dairy cows, in Wesermarch." He drops his hands, bends down to her, conspiratorial. "I never liked the mornings." He winks at her, and Solveig forces a tight smile. "Must be different farming here, though. All stones and salt water!"

He's trying to be friendly, as though he's completely unaware of the islanders' policy of ignoring the Germans and their collaborators, freezing them out. Perhaps he is. Solveig stands mute, teeth pressed together, jaw muscle flexing in a way she hopes is visible. He says nothing if he sees it, but keeps talking on. They've got used to it, the Germans, the way every decent Norwegian ignores them as fully as they can.

"My Norwegian is improving, don't you think? Especially now we have the new teacher helping us."

That, at least, draws a reaction from Solveig, a quick head-snap in his direction.

"Liv Sunde is teaching you?"

"Yes," he says, pleased to have found a topic of conversation she'll engage in. "I think we are harder to teach than her usual students. Far more trouble."

Solveig reassesses her opinion of the teacher. She's not just NS for survival, then. It's not's just self-serving cooperation, but active collaboration. All that potential, wasted. Worse than wasted: squandered, frittered away, on these men and their halting command of language.

Well, it won't do her any good in the long run, Solveig thinks savagely. She'll be stuck with them for all her company. Even her pupils will turn against her. Maybe that's what happened in Molde, that's why she left.

"Well, here you are, Fräulein. Don't let me see you in open water after dark again." He salutes, face hard and serious, but then lets himself break into a smile, hand dropping down into a static wave.

Solveig waits on the shoreline, boat bobbing in the surf, until they're out of sight. Damn Liv Sunde, and damn the Germans. On the wall of the boathouse the poster has been replaced, and although she spits at it, sticky gob sliding down the printed face, she now has bigger tasks at hand.

Five

"So what's she like, the new teacher?"

Solveig has to squint at her friend, the low winter sun in their eyes. They're smoking a crumpled cigarette as they walk, paper thin and burning fast, passing it across between drags. The Germans have better quality, if you're willing to sink that low.

"As German-loving as we heard." Her answer is restrained, held back, despite the fact that she is itching to discuss Liv Sunde: her clothes, clearly bought with loose morals, the tap-tap-tapping of her unbalanced walk on those ridiculous heels, that smug superiority across her chiselled profile, her torchlight in their eyes. "I don't really know; I didn't speak to her much. Just drove the boat, unloaded her endless boxes of books. That's it."

Overhead, gulls circle, their black backs brief glimpses as they wheel through their aerial manoeuvres, screeching. Solveig and

Aase walk on, still passing the cigarette, Solveig rehearsing winning arguments in her head. *If you only met her, Aase, you'd understand then. You can't talk to her without feeling she's hearing everything you're not saying. Without her watching you, judging you, like she's weighing up whether to turn you in or not. You just watch, she'll be trouble. I know it.*

Gunnar jogs up from the water line, the thin smattering of snow crunching underfoot, interrupting Solveig's silent monologue. The girls pull apart.

"Not disturbing any secrets am I, ladies?" He smiles an easy, lazy hello at Aase. "Do you mind if I steal Solveig for a moment?"

Aase steps away, giving them a moment of privacy, a knowing smile on her face. Gunnar takes Solveig's arm, pulls her in close, whispers in her ear. She knows what it must look like, what people will think.

"See you later. Usual place. Don't be late this time."

When he's gone, broad back disappearing down to the shore, Aase returns, fiddling with the fingers of her gloves.

"So that's why you've been distracted," she says. "You are seeing him, after all. Though you swore blind that there was nothing like that between you."

Solveig blushes, grinds her heel into the harbour wall.

"There isn't," she mutters. "I told you."

She can picture it, their lives together. It'll happen like this: there's long periods where he's at sea, and Solveig lives her life much as it is now. Sheep and boats. When he's home they sit quietly, in chairs opposite each other, Gunnar reads and she, well, Solveig supposes she'll read too, or knit, darning his socks, carding wool from the lambs. Over her task, whatever it is, she watches the room around her change, fade, the old walls getting older, Gunnar's hair and beard speckling slowly, as though he's caught the snow around his ears and mouth. It's a good enough life, she thinks, happy enough - steady and predictable - it would suit some girl one day.

But Aase ignores her.

"I'm so glad you've found someone then, Solveig, finally, because, well..." She stumbles over the words. "We are twenty two, you know, and I won't be young forever..."

"So Per asked you, then."

Solveig's voice comes out flatter than she intended. If they'd been boys, things would have been different. They could have gone to sea as they'd dreamed about as children, their boats chalk outlines on the hard beside the lighthouse. Properly, not like Gunnar and Arne in the coastal fishing boats, but in great ships that carried akkevit and other, more exciting, goods across the equator and back. They'd have got drunk in foreign ports, fought and fucked their way through exotic towns and returned home with their pockets full, with tales to keep the old men up at night.

Instead they're girls, and so they'll be good and get married, like Bjørghild and Maret and Gerd, all the girls they knew at school. With Aase marrying too, Solveig knows the pressure on her will only get heavier.

Solveig smiles, bright but brittle, and pulls her friend in, closing her arms around her.

"Congratulations, Aase."

The ring, Solveig can't help but think, is ugly. A thick, heavy band of gold with a small diamond set flush with the metal. Per's grandmother's, apparently. Full of emotional resonance and romantic symbolism, of course, but still ugly.

"It'll be you next, Solveig, you'll see."

Solveig tries not to look as horrified at the thought as she feels.

Along the street, the shop windows have a hollow look. In the butcher's, stringy mutton chops crowd together in the centre, some dried fish, a stale cake no longer fit for eating but still pretty enough. From the counter a queue of people snakes out of the door and down the street. Soldiers with dogs patrol a few paces away, waiting for rebellion, resistance, conversation.

Solveig and Aase join the queue, eyes focused safely on the floor, on the shoes of people ahead. Like children, Solveig thinks, outside the classroom. Waiting for someone in authority to give permission, half expecting them to say no. Mothers speak to their children in fierce whispers, telling them *wipe your face, don't scuff those shoes, stay close by me*.

Solveig's glad the children have been dragged on their mothers' shopping trip - they're a distraction for the soldiers, movement to follow, noise to decipher. Today she wants as little attention as possible on the meat queue. She needs something to feed the man in the cave, and she's decided the butcher will help her. She's not tried it before, not needed to, but Olav has a reputation - he can be trusted, he can be relied upon.

Eight pairs of sensible boots, old but serviceable, shift and stamp in the cold between her and the counter, the line broken in the middle by blue heels and stockinged legs. Everyone else stands quietly, shoulders hunched against the cold and pugilistic, occupying stares. But not Liv Sunde - Liv Sunde bends down to pat the dogs, smiles winsomely at the soldiers, waves at her pupils as they pass. She even smiles, calls out to Solveig, who flushes with embarrassment. With her face burning and her plans crowding her thoughts, time crawls.

Eventually, there's conversation at the meat counter.

"I'm sorry, Miss Sunde," Olav says. "We don't have any mince left."

Liv Sunde puts her hand to her forehead, rubbing as though at a headache.

"None at all? That was the very last?"

"The very last, Fräulein," he says. Snide titters run shivering through the waiting ladies. "We're all sold out."

Liv nods, fidgeting with her ration book and purse.

"Well then, just the fish, please."

He wraps it for her, motions quick with practice. She leaves the money and ration stubs on the counter, snatching up the fish to her chest. This time, Solveig tries to catch her eye, to smile. It doesn't hurt, after all, to be kind. Liv just trains her gaze on the floor and hurries out.

As she reaches the exit, the woman in the queue behind her places her order loudly.

"Mutton, please, Olav, and mince."

Each person between then and Solveig is handed their share of mince, carefully weighed against the ration stubs. Solveig looks down at the ration cards in her hands, counting how much she can afford. At the counter, she squares her shoulders, standing straight on to the butcher.

"My mother's usual, please. Except..." She takes a breath, and lets the next part out in a rush. "Except this week she needs double the mince."

Behind her, Aase's fingers dig into Solveig's back.

"Double mince?"

Solveig nods resolutely.

It's not for Liv Sunde.

That would be daft, wasting money and risk on one of Quisling's followers, no matter how meekly she'd swallowed the obvious lie.

It's for the man, she reminds herself, a decent proportion of the food she's promised him. The resistance fighter getting the traitor's rations. It seems like a fair deal, in wartime, a kind of poetic justice.

Even so, she can't help but feel bad for the teacher - that's only human, only decent manners - but she can't help her.

"That's what she told me."

"What for?"

Solveig can see his suspicion, can feel it.

"I don't know, I just eat it." Her laugh feels forced, her face tight with the smile, while he looks at her, hands resting lightly on the counter top. Finally, he sighs, closing his eyes as he decides.

"I can't, Solveig. Not even for you."

Oh well. It was stupid to try, to risk exposing herself and her new friend in the cave, to risk being associated with an NS member. Olav wraps her normal portions tightly and hands them over.

"Will you do me a favour though?" he asks. "I borrowed a book from your father - take it back for me?"

He gestures round the side of the shop, to the back door. She nods and pushes her way out of the door, squeezing past women in aging winter coats and shiny, worn out skirts. The soldiers watch her go, apparently unconcerned. The back of the shop stands open, long chains hanging over the doorway to keep flies out. Olav doesn't appear immediately, and Solveig can hear him serving customers out front.

She leans against the doorway, sending the chains swinging against her hand.

Erik the butcher's boy looks at her sideways but says nothing, turning back to the scales and the pile of mince at his side. She watches him work, parceling out meagre portions into thin paper, sealing and marking each one carefully. At one time, before, men like Gunnar would have eaten that much in one meal, let alone in a week. They'd been lucky, she realises now, their rural lives overflowing with fish and meat. In the early days, when the shortages started in the cities, they heard rumours of fist-fights in the street, occupation soldiers left battered and bloody while their assailants vanished into the night. It didn't feed anyone, but there was satisfaction, of a sort.

The pile of mince is quickly whittled away. It's no wonder there's none to spare, even as a favour to the daughter of a friend. Erik wipes his hands on his overalls, and looks her over.

"Solveig," he says, tilting his chin upwards in greeting. "What d'you want?"

"Olav has something for me. A book, for my father."

"Is that right?" He leans back, mutters to Olav through the connecting door. Olav waves from across the shop, his line of customers undiminished. Erik disappears for a moment and then comes back, a book in his hands.

"Olav says to make sure this goes straight back to your father," he says, handing over the book and, hidden underneath, another packet of mince. "And to no-one else. Understand?"

It's not one she recognises, the cover worn and fading at the end of the spine. She opens the cover looking for a title and a loose sheet of paper, densely printed, flaps in the wind.

FRIHETEN

2 FEBRUAR 1943

It has come to the attention of the editors that pilots from the Kampfschwader KG-26, responsible for the terror-bombing of Kristiansund, have been honoured as heroes by Luftwaffe command with the German Cross in Gold and the Knight's Cross, variously. It is only right that the most conspicuous bravery, coolness and determination during severe operations of a prolonged nature is rewarded and so we too add our congratulations. Hurrah for the Kampfschwader KG-26!

Unfortunately, the war has a habit of distorting time, of making two years feel like ten, and so the editors would like to take the opportunity to remind Nordmore of their heroic actions. As the assault was on a defenceless civilian target, rather than any military installation, it was felt too dangerous to use novice pilots during their actions against Kristiansund - all crews had previously trained against other civilians in Spain and Poland. This allowed the planes to fly without fighter escort, avoiding detection by legitimate and resistance forces, and to drop the bombs in a carefully rehearsed pattern: first they dropped explosive bombs, then firebombs with a seven minute delay fuse. Machine-made confusion complete with death and destruction.

This tested bombing strategy ensures that there is sufficient rubble and debris for the firebombs to ignite - the very model of the famous German ingenuity and efficiency. Having dropped the first bomb load, the pilots turned back to Vaernes where dinner was waiting. While the pilot heroes took their meals, so generously provided by as yet unbombed local residents, their aircraft were reloaded with fuel and ammunition and bomb charges. After all, their job was not quite completed yet - they had another four days of hard work ahead of them.

So, congratulations to the bomber heroes of "Løwengschwader" KG-26, as brave and noble as the lions painted on their aircraft.

"Don't read it here, idiot," Erik hisses. "You'll get me shot."

Solveig grins at him, her most practiced fake smile, all teeth and nose and no feeling.

"Thank you, for returning my father's book."

She turns to go, but he stops her.

"Ration stubs."

She hands over next week's allocation, enough for the mince, and steps outside. The queue is dwindling, Smøla's housewives returning to their kitchens. The teacher, delayed by another queue at the greengrocer's, is already some distance down the road, retreating fast. She'll have to go hungry this week without her meat ration - Solveig doesn't think she's the kind to fish for herself, to have enough friends to barter and trade.

Aase's waiting, chatting to some relative or other next to the shop doorway, out of the wind. At Solveig's reappearance, she makes her goodbyes and steps out into the street. They take a couple of steps, Aase waiting until they're out of earshot before she speaks.

"Double mince? What for?"

"Ask Mor, not me. It was her who wanted it. Didn't get it anyway. I suppose they can't, not with the queue like that and bloody soldiers everywhere."

There's a long pause while Aase scratches her face. She doesn't believe it.

"So what took you so long out back, then?"

Solveig shrugs, holding the book up for Aase to see.

"Something of my father's that Olav wanted me to return."

Aase pulls up short, looking through her bag.

"Blast," she says, scrunching her face in frustration. "Forgot the greens. You coming back with me, or heading on?"

Down the road, Liv Sunde is still in sight.

"No," Solveig says. "I think I'd best be getting on. Take this lot back to Mor, tell her about the mince."

Aase looks up from her bag, then she deliberately turns her head, stares in the direction the teacher had walked.

"Right," she says, slowly. Solveig remembers how well Aase knows her, how well she's always been able to read her. "Of course. See you later, then."

"See you later."

"Solveig!" Aase calls after her, her voice clear in the cold air. "Don't be stupid."

Solveig doesn't look back, covering as much ground as possible without running.

"Miss Sunde!"

The teacher either doesn't hear or ignores the call, hunching her shoulders down, leaning into the wind. She must hear the panting up behind her, but she doesn't look round or turn, doesn't slow down. Solveig has to run to catch up to her, bag bumping against her legs.

This is stupid.

This is crazy.

This only makes things more complicated.

"Miss Sunde!"

Solveig is closer now, her voice too loud to ignore. The teacher turns, waiting. It's clear she's trying to look fierce, shoulders held tight, her shopping clenched in her fist like a weapon. The reflected light from the snow and the winter sea is blue and cold - a harsh light - and in it Liv Sunde looks brittle.

Solveig holds the mince out between them, almost as protection.

"The butcher sent me with this. There was more, out the back, that he'd missed."

Liv's gaze is flat and knowing. Eventually she nods, and forces a twitch of a smile onto her face.

"Thank you, Miss Eik." She holds out her ration coupons. "Take what the butcher needs. And tell him - tell him I said danke."

Solveig's burst of laughter catches them both by surprise. Liv smiles with the side of her mouth, pleased at the success of her own joke. She takes her cigarette case out of the pocket of her coat, fits one between her lips, and fumbles for her matches.

"Here," she says, holding the case with one hand, the other trembling the lit match close to her face. "Want one?"

"Thanks."

Solveig takes one from the edge, taps it like her cousins do when they want to look suave and sophisticated, before leaning forward for Liv to light it with the last of her match. Liv's face, her sharp profile, her sculpted jawline, are close enough for Solveig to see every detail, every line and freckle, every imperfection. Solvieg swallows, wrestles her mind under control, steps back.

Liv shakes the flame out, dropping the spent match on the ground.

"Have you got yourself a boat yet?" Solveig asks, trying to steer the conversation and her thoughts back to safer ground. Liv smiles around her cigarette, squints against the winter sun.

"Yes, though I'm afraid it still doesn't agree with me."

Solveig puffs smoke over her shoulder, away from Liv.

"Must have been difficult for you then, coming out to the islands."

For someone so seasick, it's a strange decision.

Liv shrugs, changes the subject.

"How's your sister these days?"

"Fine," Solveig says. "Grumpy, at getting so big."

"I spoke to her on the telephone once before I took the position," Liv says, her tone confiding, us versus them. "About the class, the school, things I should expect and so on. She didn't half make things hard work; she hasn't stopped now I'm actually in post."

"Oh, she does that." The words are out of Solveig's mouth before she can stop them. That was disloyal, she chides herself, running down Bjørghild - her own flesh and blood, a good Norwegian patriot - in front of this stranger, this mini-Quisling. "But I always say that sisters can say anything they like about each other, you know. But for someone else, someone outside the family, almost a stranger..."

"It's rude." The teacher's so quick to correct her mistake that Solveig feels almost petty for making a fuss. "You're right, of course it is. I'm sorry - didn't mean to offend."

"You didn't, I suppose."

There's a long moment of silence as they both smoke awkwardly, Solveig prising a rock from the edge of the path with her toe.

"Do you have siblings, Miss Sunde?"

Liv holds her cigarette between her lips, digs through her purse, searching for something. After a moment, she pulls out a picture and hands it over.

"A brother."

The man in the photo is tall, clean shaven, in a pre-war army uniform, hair slicked back from his forehead. He's laughing, one arm slung carelessly around his sister. The resemblance between them is striking. They're far closer in looks than Solveig and Bjørghild. They've the same jaw, same eyebrows, same arrogant tilt to the chin. Cut off the teacher's hair and put her in a uniform and they could be twins.

"He's handsome," Solveig says. "A soldier?"

"Yes, signed up when he was seventeen. The men in my family have always been military, generations of us."

It's just light chit-chat, a breezy charm that seems to come with money and a university education - even Bjørghild can grudgingly muster it when needed, though never directed at Solveig. It must be drilled into them alongside their Greek and economics. Philosophy and politeness, Socrates and social awareness.

It's meant to mean nothing, but this time it might be revealing. A career soldier, Solveig thinks, a peacetime recruit. That means there's pretty much only two options for him: in London with King Harold, or fighting in the woods with the remains of his regiment, a ragtag band of resistance. He might be dead, of course, but wouldn't Liv have said that?

I had a brother. Killed in action in 1940. Something like that.

A brother wanted by the Nazis might be reason enough to become a card-carrying member yourself. Hiding in plain sight, showing them you're no threat, all of that, and meanwhile passing messages to her brother. It's entirely likely, entirely possible.

One of the patrolling soldiers has caught up to them.

"Move on," he says, pointing down the street. "*Keine anhalt hier.*"

Liv Sunde nods at him, flicking the cigarette after the match, and picking her bag up from between her feet. With a smile and a press of her free hand against Solveig's arm, she sets off down the road. Solveig turns on her heel, smoke burning to a stub between her fingers, the ghost of Liv's fingers against her skin, watching the teacher pick her way home.

One cigarette, one conversation, and her opinion of the teacher has changed again.

She's almost forgotten the soldier stood at her side, and his voice makes her jump.

"You too, Fräulein."

Six

Solveig and her parents shiver together in the lighthouse, the world through the window white with snow and sea foam. The bite of the weather is worse for the new ewes, still unused to sea storms and the way the salt and wind drop the temperature over the exposed brackens, with only their three-sided shelters for relief. They need fresh straw and extra feed in case the weather really rolls in and they have to be alone for a while.

That's at least one good thing about working for your father, Solveig thinks - there's always time for a decent lunch, especially when the weather outside is awful. You're not constrained by proscribed break hours, perched on a tall stool, forbidden to talk or yawn, counting the minutes left till home time. And not, like Bjørghild and now Liv Sunde, having your meal interrupted by the petty complaints of the schoolyard - grazed knees and squabbles and sandwiches dropped into the dirt.

Instead, she can sit at the kitchen table, feet stretched out, idly eating eggs and reading the previous day's paper from Kristiansund, the paper thin and the ink already smudged from her father's fingers.

"Nazi trash," he'd muttered as he'd passed it over, "but what else are we to read?"

Most of the front page is dedicated to the tenth anniversary of the election of the National Socialists in Germany and the first anniversary of Quisling's tenure as prime minister. There's a big picture of the man himself, right in the centre, staring out at the reader in his most statesman-like manner, the text bunched up round him.

SMØLA DAGBLADET

12 MARS 1943

A GREAT ANNIVERSARY FOR US ALL

How well our efforts to progress our food, labour and cultural life are continuing under Herr Quisling's leadership, along with the help of our Germanic brothers in Denmark, Austria, Czechoslovakia and elsewhere in the world. Almost a year on from that unforgettable day in our nation's history, we also celebrate the decade that has passed since the election of the

National Socialist party as the government of Germany. As we look to the next ten years, we are sure that, as our Führer says, the force of the National Socialist ideals will propel the war to unequivocal victory. On the home front we must fight as well - to gather and present a single united people, as Harald Hårfrager did. The New Norway Lives!

German arrogance knew no bounds, as usual. The newspaper carries other news as well - bank reopenings, marriages, weather forecasts - in smaller type, the language less extravagant. Underneath the bluster and propaganda is a small advert, requesting the use of a decent sized motorboat for a weekend's fishing. More like a weekend trip to England, she thinks, for someone equally fed up with German Norway.

"You'll never believe it," Solveig's mother says, bursting through the door. She stops to untie her headscarf, checking the edges of her hair are still neat beneath it. "It's all over the news. Everyone's talking about it."

Solveig and her father wait for her to explain.

"Talking about what?"

"The Krauts have surrendered at Stalingrad. Given up, completely."

It's news enough to stop Solveig's fork on the way to her mouth.

"What? Really?"

"Except they say it's a tactical retreat, or some such."

"Well," her father says emphatically, "its good news for us. I knew they'd overreached themselves going into Russia. Look at Finland - those Bolsheviks are ruthless, just ruthless."

"Oh, quiet Far. Let Mor tell us the details."

"I don't know that much, just what Fru Nygård was saying in the queue - I think her boys listen to London on the wireless, you know. She always seems to have news to pass on." The groceries shift on the counter, threatening to fall completely onto the floor, forcing a pause. "Anyway, the ones left are half starved, they say, and more than half frozen."

"Well," her father says, "Napoleon could have told them that. Him and his Grande Armée. They outnumbered the Russian troops, were better equipped, better trained. Were winning battles all over the place. That wasn't the problem. The thing that really did for them was that the Cossacks burnt their own villages and crops and so on. I can't remember how many French they said starved - something like half a million went in, and barely any came out."

Her mother stops unpacking the groceries, leans for a moment on the counter, hands either side of the meat, bloody and warming in its paper. Solveig rolls her eyes, trying to cut off a long and involved history lesson.

"Forget Napoleon - I could have told them that. The damn Nazis can't even go two winters here without requisitioning blankets - how did they expect to manage out on the steppe?"

Her father isn't listening, still caught up in Napoleon's losses.

"It'll be in the encyclopaedia somewhere. I'll get it." He heaves himself to his feet, hands on his knees, and heads for the living room in a haze of academic curiosity. Solveig sighs, scraping the last of her eggs from her plate onto her fork.

"You've set him off now, Mor. He'll be talking Napoleon for days."

Her mother shrugs, pouring herself a thin cup of ersatz coffee and settling down at the table.

"Oh also," she says, as this were a side thought, unimportant, "I ran into Fru Josøy on the way home. She tells me Gunnar's proposed."

"Really?"

For a moment, Solveig has to fight down an unexpected, irrational flash of jealousy. How dare he go and offer himself to some other woman, when he was hers by right, when she hadn't even given him an answer?

It better not be Liv Sunde, she thinks. Swanning in here with those legs and books and smart cut city clothes, smelling of perfume rather than sheep, with hair and makeup straight out of Hollywood.

"Who to?"

"Honestly, Solveig. As if you don't know." Behind her mug, her mother rolls her eyes. "To you."

"Oh, that."

She knows her voice is flat, trapped. There's a curious empty feeling in her chest, where her heartbeat ought to be. Where the excitement of a proposal, a wedding, a husband should be. The tin in her mother's hand hits the kitchen table with a solid thunk, heavier than it ought to be.

"Yes that, Miss. Were you ever going to tell us? Or were we expected to divine it somehow - at the sight of you in a bridal gown, perhaps?"

"Of course I'd have told you, if I'd really been proposed to. But he wasn't serious," Solveig says around her last mouthful of eggs. "Not really marriage serious, anyway. It was just something he said, a joke, you know?"

"That's not what his mother made it sound like."

"Well, that's what it was."

She really doesn't want this conversation, can't stand to hear her mother bang on again about how she ought to be married already - I was, when I was your age. You don't want to leave it too late now. All the good men will be gone, and who will give me grandchildren then?

"Right," she says, wiping her mouth on her sleeve, brushing any egg or toast onto the floor, "I'm off out to the ewes. Promised Far I'd feed them for him today."

Her mother sighs, knows the evasion for what it is.

"Be back early," she says, with a glance at the ominously bleak sky. "That weather's coming in."

Solveig presses a kiss to her cheek, squeezes her arm in reassurance.

"I know, Mor. I won't be long."

The wind stays fierce as she rows, sending Solveig's ears stinging red at the edges of her hat as she tends to the sheep. The waves, too, are high, splashing at the rocks, sending freezing spray up the edges of the islands. On the smaller islands the snowbanks shrink and shrivel, grow fragile, the wind opening up glassy patches of ice through the centre of fields. The ice in the lakes and ponds and puddles cracks like gunshots through the nights as warmer seawater surges up through channels and gullys, refreezes harder and stronger before people wake in the mornings.

She's not been back to the caves since that first meeting, has half decided she won't, the memory of the man's eyes in the darkness frightful. But now, three days later, she must go to the sheep, and her pride insists on helping the man as well. After all, Solveig Eik, hero of the resistance, can't be a hero if she's afraid.

Neither food nor blankets are easy to find. Smøla doesn't have it as bad as the cities, but food is tightly rationed, and there are quotas on what you can grow and catch. From the sow's previous litter, three are destined for the mess hall on Edøya, requisitioned at three days old, and two are promised to neighbours and friends in return for milk, salt, ersatz coffee. The remaining meat will have to last the winter, supplementing shop-bought rations until the spring comes and last year's lambs are ready. There'll be blood sausage too, to be stored and eked out, and fat. The offal, the viscera - ears and eyes and feet - are destined for the dogs. And now, perhaps, her own personal resistance fighter.

Solveig takes what she can, a few salt fish from the barrels in the cellar, some beet, a few potatoes from the store, and hides them in the box under the seat of her rowboat. Enough not to be noticed, hopefully enough to keep the man alive a little longer. Her great-grandfather - a mainlander by birth - had never quite got used to the islands, where his mother and then his wife belonged.

Not enough snow, he said, not enough land. And all of it too wet by half.

He'd kept ponies here, shivering flank to flank with the cows, and rode around the islands like an old Jarl. Her grandfather remembers, if Solveig does not, and delights in retelling the same few stories over and over again, while her father and aunt laugh indulgently along. Horses in boats, horses in the sea, the time Olav Jenssen fell and broke his arm.

The ponies are, of course, long gone, and the six cows have been whittled down over the years to just two. One of the low beams still supports a saddle, leather cracked and mottled with age and the damp cold of the barn. Somewhere are trunks, boxes, filled with other equestrian paraphernalia: bridles and stiff-bristled brushes.

As children, the horse remnants were better than horses. Solveig was always a Viking, fighting up and down the Scottish coast, while her sister rode off into the sunset with the hero of the month - perhaps Harald Halfdan or Thor, or the heroes of the Icelandic sagas. Since then, she supposes, they've been packed away, waiting for more horses or more children to arrive.

The box had opened reluctantly, lid sticking to the sides, hinges groaning at the unexpected movement. Accumulated dust and dirt were sticky under her fingers, sliding thickly under the pressure. The contents smelled old and damp, once carefully placed piles of leather bridles and stirrups now tangled and messed, carding combs and hoof picks snared and hiding in the dark, waiting for unwary hands. And there in the bottom, packed in paper so yellowed and stiff that it crumbled at her touch: her ultimate prize. Folded neatly, free of mould and mostly faded, two thick horse blankets, straps and buckles still attached.

There are a few patches, threadbare and mouse-nibbled, where the fabric has worn away, and the air moves through. Still, they're better than the blankets some families have left, better than the Germans' cast offs and left behinds. These will do for the man in the cave, for a start.

Across the barn, one cow was watching her vacantly, chewing easily.

"Mind your own business, or you'll go the way of the horses."

The cow shivered, sending a cloud of heat-seeking flies buzzing briefly along her back, before turning back to the hay.

The man, this time, has seen her coming and stands waiting at the mouth of the cave. As she climbs the shallow slope towards them, the clouds make good on their promise and it starts to rain.

"You came back then," the man says. "Didn't think you would. People say anything when they're afraid for their own skin."

"I promised, didn't I?" Solveig says, holding up the blanket and the bag of food.

He laughs.

"Not such a mouse, after all," he says and Solveig bristles.

Mice could do surprising amounts of damage if they went undetected long enough, could chew through thick mooring ropes, setting boats adrift. Could riddle a house with secret tunnels and hiding spots. Could spoil a winter's rations and leave a family thin and hungry.

"Come in," the man says, dismissing her outrage with a wave, "too cold away from the fire."

He turns back into the cave, squatting near the flames, watching. Solveig pulls her coat shut, forcing the lapels together with her scarf.

"I've brought you some things," she says needlessly, holding up the blankets and bag.

She hands them over, nervously, and smiles awkwardly at him, before he pulls her by the elbow towards the fire. She shies away from his touch, gently removing her arm from his. He reaches forward, pulls a ladle from a pan hanging above the fire.

He's older than she first thought, the white in his hair catching the firelight. At least thirty, eight, ten years older than Karl. But then, Solveig supposes, the resistance can't just be formed of groups of classmates, rigorously divided by age. It'll take all sorts to make up an effective group. And now that's a group she's part of.

"Here, sit down," he says, "you're making me nervous. Have a drink."

Solveig can see how little he's brought with him. There's a pile of dried grass and heathers banked up against the cave wall. It's the kind of bed she makes up for her sheep when the stocks of wheat straw are running low. He has a good coat, aged but solid boots, and very little else.

She feels embarrassed, suddenly, by the scraggy modesty of her offering. Two loaves and a few fish might once have fed five thousand, but this will sustain him for only a few days.

"The bread's terrible, I'm sorry." She holds up the loaf, lumpen and dark. "It's been getting worse for weeks. The bastards take the best for themselves, of course."

He doesn't look up from the fire. He must be used to girls swearing around him - there's no time for unnecessary politeness when you're fighting for your country.

"Well, it's yours anyway."

"Takk," he says. But once her hard come by provisions are handed over, he seems less impressed, picking over the food with his finger, flipping her carefully wrapped parcels out of the bucket with one long nail.

"What is this?" He holds up one blanket, puts his nose to it, and rears away in disgust. You're not so fragrant yourself, she thinks. Certainly dirty enough to drop the attitude.

"A horse blanket - all I could find."

"It stinks of piss - and God knows what else. Not fit even for a dog, let alone a horse!"

He might be a great man of the resistance - he might just be their errand boy - but it's no excuse for ungratefulness.

"You can give it back, if it's that's bad."

He doesn't, just drops the blanket and food back into the bucket. Outside, the rain is easing.

"I've got to go," Solveig says. "The weather's coming in. I'm sorry I couldn't bring you more."

"No," he says, gritting the words out between clenched teeth. "You've been kind. Thank you."

He gestures towards the cave entrance, glancing over his shoulder, motioning for her to lead the way. He follows her closely, hand at the small of her back. As she's almost out into the light, she pauses.

"The weather will be bad for some days," she warns him. "Stay inside."

Seven

If only she could take her own advice. The boat pitches and yaws over tall waves, threatening to rip the oars from her hands.

Closer to shore, there's another boat. Not a German patrol this time, but another islander. Solveig holds up a hand in greeting, although, at this distance, she can't quite tell who it is. She doesn't recognise the boat, either - just a standard wooden dinghy much like her own.

After a few more strokes, perhaps ten, twelve minutes, she realises that the other boat's not moving under its own power, just drifting with the waves. Are they fishing? In this weather? With the wind and rain a roiling black bank over the mainland?

Then the figure spots her, standing and waving as the boat turns sideways onto the waves, sending its occupant staggering.

"Hei! Hello! Help!"

Of course - the absolute cherry on the cake. Liv Sunde, in trouble on the water. What was the point of being NS if the Germans left you when you needed them? Always there, questioning, requisitioning, and then nowhere to be found.

Three powerful pulls to the left, and Solveig sets herself on a course to intercept.

"Miss Sunde, what are you doing out here?"

Rain is starting to arrive, fat and intermittent drops falling almost soundlessly into the surrounding sea. The water is cold, and stings where it catches uncovered cheeks, the bite of the salt irritating their eyes.

Liv flinches and jumps at each drop on her skin, screwing up her eyes against the rush of wind.

"It's the bloody motor - I can't get it to work!"

Solveig ties their boats together and climbs across. "You've flooded it - just wait a minute."

"I thought I'd be home in time, before the storm."

The teacher's boat is too heavy to pull behind Solveig's own, with just the power of her arms, but they cannot wait much longer. The weather is closer now - slinging rain and sleet, sending the waves higher and higher against the sides of the boats.

Miss Sunde looks terrible, ghastly white, teeth chattering, turning at intervals to the sea to retch. She's more bedraggled than intimidating at the moment: her makeup is near gone and her hair's ruined. Her eyes are wide and dark against the paleness of her face, like a puppy pulled out of the river.

Finally, when Solveig thinks they can't wait anymore, she turns to the engine, hands fumbling for the ignition. The motor kicks, turns over, and coughs into silence. For long, empty seconds, Solveig's heart is similarly silent.

She tries again.

At the third try, the motor growls reluctantly into life. They have been turned and twisted about by the waves, and Solveig scans the horizon, no longer sure of her direction, searching for distinguishing features on the skyline.

The lighthouse should have been a steady beacon, a fixed point above the tossing sea.

The light should be on, she thinks.

She points the boat in the direction that feels most right, and hopes. The going is slow, the tied-together boats graceless and hard to steer. Down low on the seat, Liv Sunde is limp with sickness. Each roll and pitch of the boats has her groaning. Her time on the islands must have helped her at least a little, for her head stays inside the boat, well out of the reach of the sea.

"You all right, Miss Sunde?" Her voice is lost in the wind, caught and dragged over her shoulder before the words are fully formed. She tries again: "Are you all right?"

The teacher waves a hand in Solveig's direction.

"Fine," she calls, "just keep going." After a moment, she lifts her head and attempts a weak smile. "*Erwache mir wieder, kühne Gewalt*, and all that."

They seem to be staying just ahead of the worst of the weather, for it breaks around them almost as soon as Solveig guides Miss Sunde's boat into the school boathouse, and pulls her own up the slip onto the shore. Together, they run headlong to the schoolhouse, and stand frozen and shivering while the teacher struggles to put her key in the lock.

Inside, Liv pauses for a moment with the door open, watching the sea.

"You'll have to stay here tonight," she mutters, closing the door. "There's no way you're getting back to the lighthouse in this."

"Thank you, Miss Sunde," Solveig says, standing stiffly on the welcome mat just inside the door.

"You sound like one of my children," she says easily, shrugging out of her coat. Underneath, her clothes are soaked through, as are Solveig's own, and cling coldly to her figure. "Get out of those wet things - I'm sure I have something to fit you."

Solveig is taller, by more than a head, and the thought of her in the teacher's smart city outfits is ludicrous. Solveig almost resigns herself to an evening spent in damply clinging clothes, to the rub of wet seams against her thighs, the squelch of her thick socks over the floor, but Liv gestures to a pile of men's clothes with a shrug.

"Some things of my brother's," she says. "Everything got musty, dirty, in the move so they're freshly washed. They should cover you, at least."

"Thanks." Solveig takes the clothes awkwardly. "Is there... Is there somewhere I can change?"

"Yes, of course. Use my bedroom," Liv says. "Just pull the curtains, and you'll be perfectly private."

Liv's bedroom is plain, spare, gives nothing away. The bed is crisply made, the sheets neat and starched. There's a wardrobe, a vanity with a brush and some makeup carefully laid out in front of a mirror. It could be a guest room, for all it says about its occupant.

It still feels intimate to be in here, exposing, and Solveig rushes to change. She sets the fresh clothes on the bed, strips out of her own wet things, and inspects the outfit Liv has provided.

The trousers are brown, a soft blend, lighter and less hard-wearing than her father's. Trousers themselves are nothing new - far more practical for boats and sheep - but it's the fit that's different. The way they curve and hang, narrower than any movie starlet's, masculine enough to give her aunt an aneurysm if she were here.

At least they're warm, and long enough in the leg, once she's turned the hems over two or three times, even if they'd fall apart after a single day's decent work. The shirt is baggy over her figure, hanging loosely over chest, bunching about the braces. There's even a tie, red and coarse woven, and Solveig adds that too, adjusting the knot to sit in the neck of the jumper.

The effect, if she says so herself, is rather good; if you ignore the hair and the lack of a beard, from a distance she could be a boy.

She turns, posing, watching her new reflection pose in the mirror. She's sure it will be useful, this affinity for disguises, when the Resistance calls her properly, when she has to disappear into the mountains, hiding from pursuing armies. Something behind her moves, reflected in the mirror, and draws her eye.

"Christ," Liv says from the doorway.

Solveig turns with a start, sudden guilt rising at being caught. Then she remembers - she's in disguise. She leans back, one hand in her pocket.

"Got a cigarette?" she says in her best, deepest voice.

Liv laughs.

"You look ridiculous. Come on, come have a drink."

On the Kristiansund quay, that first meeting, Solveig had found her stiff, forced. But like the command to come inside, the invitation is easy, practised, calculatedly attractive. A society hostess at work.

Still playing her role, Solveig holds out her arm for Liv to take.

"Oh why thank you, sir," Liv says and takes it, her hand settling in the crook of Solveig's elbow, leading them in to the main room. The divan is low, old, the cushions solid and hard.

"I hope it's not too cold for you, Miss Eik. I've lit the fire, but it takes forever to heat the place. The house is rather damp, I'm afraid, rather cold."

"It's not that bad," Solveig says. "The top room at home is much worse this time of year. They're just old - well, the lighthouse isn't that old, but you know - and exposed."

"Draughty too," Liv says, rubbing her hands along her arms.

As if to prove her point, the chimney rumbles with the wind, stirring up the flames, making them shiver and dance. The curtains, too, swing towards the windows, pressing flat circles against the glass.

"Yes." Solveig rubs her hands on her trousers, willing some feeling back into her fingers. "There are some panels loose up in the schoolhouse's attic. Fixing those would help, I suppose."

Too late, Solveig realises she shouldn't know about loose boards, about attics. There's no reason for her to know that.

Liv hums, distracted. She's still in her wet clothes, hair frizzing in the warmth. She's hardly dressed for the weather - and the coat that's dripping onto her welcome mat is woollen, tailored, without a lick of waterproofing.

"If you don't mind me asking, Miss Sunde - Liv - why were you out on the water?"

Liv's eyes come up to meet Solveig's, a sharp question in them, before she shrugs.

"Seeing a pupil," she says. "I needed to speak to his parents, but they won't come to the schoolhouse." She shakes her head, and Solveig knows she's rolling her eyes. "Won't be seen seeking me out. So, needs must, Mohamed went to the mountain."

"You need a better coat," Solveig says. "An oilskin, something to keep you dry. And you need to be more careful when you go out on the water. I can't always be there to save you."

"You're the lighthouse, aren't you? I thought that's what you did."

The tie feels tight, restrictive, around Solveig's throat, and she loosens it.

"I'm sorry I don't have anything better for you to wear," Liv says, sitting down beside her, glasses and bottle in hand.

"Really, these are fine. Dashing even."

Liv laughs again, leaning against the opposite arm of the sofa.

"Oh yes. Very dashing. Akevitt all right?" She pours generous doubles, several fingers deep. Liv knocks back hers in one and pours another. "Right," she says. "You drink that while I change out of these things."

Solveig sips obediently at the drink, letting it burn its way down her throat. The half empty bottle looks good quality, its *linje* pedigree clearly marked.

It's too easy to like Liv, Solveig thinks, too easy to be swayed by good looks and gracious manners and the warming flush of alcohol. It's too easy to fall into a teasing back-and-forth, to ignore the outside world and just let them be two women, alone together.

While Liv is out of the room, Solveig is in charge of her own thoughts. Remember, she tells herself, whose house this is. Don't get carried away. You can't make a mistake with her, mustn't put a foot wrong. Any hint that you're up to no good, and she'll have you in front of the local garrison faster than you can say bang.

"I'll fix us something to eat." Liv is already at the stove, feeding the burner with wood. "Nothing fancy, I'm afraid, just soup or something."

She smiles at Solveig, who feels the warmth of that look pool in her gut. There's something there, beyond the obvious. Like calls to like, and she and the teacher are alike, Solveig knows. The only trouble is: working out which secrets they share is a dangerous game.

"Lovely," Solveig says. She's like Daniel in the lions' den, or Thor in the halls of the ice giants, treading carefully, looking for the exits.

She drifts around the room, not quite stopping at any one thing. Unlike Solveig's bedroom at home, the room seems quite devoid of personal trinkets - no accumulated childhood treasures, no picture postcards tacked to the wall, no shelves of ornaments or china decorations, just one creased and faded photo in an old-fashioned frame - a family on a beach. In the centre, between two boys that must be her brother and some kind of cousin, stands a girl with blonde hair, smiling crookedly at the camera.

Then there are the books, in shelves that could have been installed just for them. They draw Solveig in, the inevitable end to her schoolhouse tour. She closes her eyes, trailing her fingers across the neatly arranged spines. There's one Solveig recognises at once: the wound slash of red the only colour against the black and white, the darkly brooding face glaring out at her.

Mein Kampf.

She had almost forgotten, in their easy camaraderie, who - what - Liv Sunde is.

Her foot crashes against the bottom of the shelf in surprise, and the teacher turns round, pauses her cooking to check on her guest. It's my face, Solveig thinks, that gives me away. That, and the way she jumped at the realisation, holding the book out, between the tips of her fingers.

The line of Miss Sunde's jaw sets, muscles pulling teeth together. Solveig hands the book back and Liv takes it, hands smoothing the cover down, cradling it like a frightened cat, like something precious.

"Have you actually read it?" she asks, her voice taking on a harsh, accusing note.

The answer is, of course, no. Solveig has no intention of reading it either, something that she's sure shows.

"Of course not." That's too final, too hardline. Liv Sunde might be a book lover, but she's still NS, still dangerous, a fact Solveig had been too close to forgetting. If Solveig's wrong about the brother, about the NS membership being a smoke screen, then it's dangerous, talking like this. "I don't speak German, you see. Certainly not well enough to translate politics."

"Hmm. You're probably one of those who thinks we should have fought harder in 1940, should still be fighting today."

"Well, I can't..." Solveig keeps her voice light, polite. "I can't deny that it feels like we could have made a difference, right at the start, if only we'd done more."

Liv Sunde sighs as though this is an argument she's had a thousand times before, as though she's tired of explaining the simplicity of her point of view.

"Oh really, Miss Eik. It's basic mathematics, the kind I teach to ten-year-olds. There are three million people in Norway, give or take a few thousand." Her voice has taken on a teaching tone, one that itches for chalk and board to record her calculations. Solveig smarts under the hectoring tone, the assumption she couldn't work this out for herself. "And if we discount the infirm, the elderly, children, then that's a million gone. Then if you discount the women too..."

"Why discount the women? I'd fight."

"Could you? Can you fire and clean a weapon? Can you use a radio?"

"Yes." Solveig squares her shoulders, lifts her chin. "Yes, I can."

"Can you run or ski for weeks on end, living rough in the woods?"

"I could, if I had to."

"And can you take orders? Do what your officer says immediately, without an opinion of your own?" Solveig is silent, while Liv Sunde smirks victoriously. "No. So, discounting the women, what are we left with? A million fighting men, maybe? That's not counting the cowards who fled to England at the first sniff of trouble. And the Germans? They say one for every eight of us. By my reckoning that's, what, four hundred thousand?"

"Not even half the number."

"Yes, half the number. But do you really think that the Wehrmacht, professional soldiers with planes and tanks and discipline and training, do you really think they couldn't kill two boys with sporting rifles each?"

Solveig sighs into her drink, takes another large mouthful. This is a practiced argument, something Liv has clearly said before.

There's a long pause between them as Solveig stares at a corner of the room.

Liv places the book on the kitchen counter, carefully distant from her chopping board, from the sink. She straightens her shoulders, forces her face into a society smile.

"Do you like to read?"

It's as though the previous conversation has simply been turned off, the tap firmly closed at the source. For a second, Solveig thinks about pressing the point, about passion over orders, patriotism over obedience.

The mathematics might be simple, laid out bare like that, but surely the truth can't be that simple. But she's deep in the woods now, and Solveig remembers the old folk stories, remembers what happens to young girls lost, far from the paths.

"I do, actually," she says, only slightly too late to be natural.

"Not that I've ever had this many books."

"It's a bit of an obsession for me," Liv says, "a compulsion. My mother used to despair – we could never pass a bookshop without coming away with at least one. I think the tipping point for her was when I bought an eight volume collected works of some philosopher or other. I was only ten and I think they weighed more than I did."

"You were reading philosophy at ten?" The idea sends an unexpected wave of fondness through Solveig.

"No, I just liked the leather covers." The teacher rolls her neck, her shoulders, stretches her legs out in front of her. "And what kind of stories do you like? Romances, is it? All fluttering hearts and secret smiles?"

It's said lightly, teasingly, as though she already knows the answer.

"God no. Though I've suffered through enough – that's all Bjørghild and my mother ever read, so there was always one lying around the house somewhere and sometimes, when the weather was bad or something, I just got so desperate I gave in."

Solveig stops shelving the pile in front of her, book still in hand, idly flicking the page edges, feeling them riffle under her thumb.

"I like stories that move, you know, adventures. I loved the sagas as a kid – all those kings and gods and maidens."

"How terribly Norwegian of you. I can see it exactly – little Solveig, out on an island somewhere, her head full of stories, fighting off invisible giants and trolls -"

Solveig rolls her eyes. Somehow, she knows, just knows, that the teacher and her brother played the same games.

"You can mock all you like. But I'll have you know they were very dangerous adventures, and I was very heroic."

Liv smiles at her over the stove.

"I'm sure you were," she says, and winks.

To hide her blush, Solveig stops caressing the shelves and picks a book at random, pulls it from its home. She's disappointed with her choice. The plain brown cover, stripped of its dust jacket, is hardly inspiring. She turns the book over, bringing the front to face her. Black text scribbles across the middle, the author's name perhaps, their signature.

Idly, she turns to the first page and stark columns of words she cannot immediately read stare back implacably. It's English, she realises after a second.

"What's this?" Solveig holds it up for Liv to see, waving it in her direction. She doesn't look up.

"Read me the first bit," she says, "and I'll tell you."

So Solveig starts reading, slowly, the shape of the words unfamiliar and strange.

Not very far from Upton-on-Severn - between it, in fact, and the Malvern Hills - stands the country seat of the Gordons of Bramley; well-timbered, well-cottaged, well-fenced and well- watered, having, in this latter respect, a stream that forks in exactly the right position to feed two large lakes in the grounds.

She glances up at the outline of Liv's back against the window. The set of her shoulders is tense, hunched awkwardly over the saucepan, as though she were expecting a blow. Slowly, she turns, resting her hips against the counter, hands fidgeting at her sides.

"Oh," she says, lightly, "that one." Her tone seems forced, and Solveig can understand why. It's not so much the content of the book, which seems as dry and dull as reports of wool prices, but the language it's written in. An NS party member has no business owning books in English. "Long, and tedious. I don't know why I kept it."

Liv frowns at the book, holds out her hand for it, and Solveig passes it over silently. Liv's mouth opens, as though to speak, and then closes again.

"Before the war," Liv finally says, "I studied in Germany and Paris. Books in Norwegian were impossible to find, and English ones were cheap."

She slides the book back into place, spine flush with its neighbours. For a moment she stays at the shelves, pushing the books against the back of the shelf. The pan's lid rattles on the hob, and Liv turns away, back to the cooking food.

Solveig sits back on the sofa, curling her feet up under her legs. As she moves, she dislodges the books piled four high on the arms, slim paperbacks, their corners creased and dogeared.

"Poetry," Liv says, rushing from the stove to clear the books. "I'm trying to read more of it." She pushes them back into their shelves, unerringly finding small spaces Solveig would have missed. "One should read poetry, don't you think? Good for the soul and all that."

She says the words too brightly, too easily, like she's covering for something, like Solveig's discovered more of a secret than she expected.

"So I'm told." Solveig keeps her voice neutral, non-committal.

"Rather flat in translation, though, of course." Liv crosses back to the stove, reaching in low cupboards for bowls and cutlery. "Do you have a favourite poet, Solveig?"

Liv is still speaking in that too bright, too fake tone. An airy socialite passing the time. She doesn't expect Solveig to have a ready answer.

"I do, actually. A local man, born in Kristiansund." Solveig shifts further into the seat, settling her shoulders. She takes another drink of akevitt, and this time it doesn't burn enough. "Øverland. Perhaps you've heard of him?"

At first, Liv says nothing. She doesn't turn around, wipes her hands on her skirts.

"I can't say I have, no."

Without catching Solveig's eye, she picks up their glasses, refilling generously, the bottle now half-empty. As she moves back across the room, Solveig follows, leaning her hip on the edge of the kitchen counter.

"Don't dare to sleep, you know?" Liv's face is still studiously blank. Solveig tries to think of the words, remembering the times they've been spread - blazoned - across the pages of the resistance papers, read out on the airwaves. Prophetic, they'd been called, inspirational. Treasonous. *"Defend yourself, while your hands are still yearning, protect your offspring - Europe is burning."*

"Ah, that Øverland." The pot on the stove rattles, the stew boiling under the lid. "A criminal, no?"

"So was the Führer, once."

Liv smiles, and although it reaches her cheeks, her eyes stay blank. Solveig takes the two bowls and crosses to the settee, Liv following with bread. Liv pauses, pushing a stray loop of hair behind her ear. "My father always said: with guests, don't talk money, religion or politics. Then there can be no arguments."

An uninvited guest, Solveig is gracious enough to let her host off the hook.

"That seems...sensible."

For the rest of the evening, they stick to Liv's father's advice. Slowly, the light chatter and akevitt do their job: the tension in the room dissolves. The storm outside continues to batter the windows, but inside the schoolhouse is warm and quiet.

Maybe, Solveig thinks, in different circumstances, she and the teacher could have been friends.

Eight

They talk for hours, the conversation easy. Solveig doesn't push Liv on politics, doesn't pick at the exposed nerve of her English books. Next to her, Liv is relaxed, leaning back on the divan, her stockinged feet propped on the edge of the coffee table. Her face is flushed with akevitt, and Solveig knows her own is too.

In the soft firelight, Liv seems gentler too. Solveig can almost believe that they meant for this evening to end like this. The two of them curled up together in Liv's house, pleasantly buzzing from the alcohol, unarmed and open. Solveig wants to imagine they could do this again, that it could be a regular thing.

Drinking in her own living room, Liv could just be any pretty woman, her damp hair swept back to expose the long lines of her neck, the hollows of her throat. Solveig forces herself to think about something other than how soft Liv's skin looks, the line of her muscles, the warmth of her leg against Solveig's own.

When Solveig looks up, Liv is trying and failing to suppress a smile, the corners of her mouth twitching uncontrollably.

"What? What did I say?"

Liv won't meet Solveig's eye, picking at the fabric of the blanket she has thrown across her knees.

"Oh no, nothing." But the smile doesn't leave her face.

"Come on," Solveig insists, a nervous laugh trembling her voice, "what?"

"It's nothing. You just sounded very... rural, just then."

"Oh." Like a bumpkin, she means. Uneducated, unsophisticated. "Sorry."

Solveig can't keep the sting from her voice, and Liv notices.

"No, no," she says. She leans across, places a tentative hand on Solveig's leg, resting just above the knee, as though it's been there for hours, as though it has a right to be there. "It's charming, really. My grandmother's dialect is, well, hideous, but yours is just charming, I promise."

She might mean it. She sounds certain enough. But it could just be flattery, empty words to hide the scorn.

"Why did you come here?" Solveig's question is sudden, breaking their unspoken agreement. She hadn't intended to say it out loud, but the akevitt must be affecting her more than she thought. "Why did you come to Smøla, when you hate boats and think we're all so rural?"

Liv's father, no doubt, would disapprove. His daughter, however, seems to take it in her stride. She sits back against the arm of the divan, looking at the fire as her hand withdraws. On its retreat it brushes Solveig's, just lightly, edge of edge. For the briefest of seconds, it feels to Solveig as though Liv's finger curls around her own, a passing squeeze. The touch is electric, and Solveig pulls her hand away, cradles her glass protectively. There's a lump in her throat, like the build-up of tears, and she swallows thickly, bringing up the drink to cover her face. After all, there are things you know about people - like Liv Sunde is a traitor, a snob and a woman - and things you feel.

Solveig knows that Liv is someone to be avoided, to be shunned, that she is beneath contempt. But she cannot feel it. Not with Liv sprawled an arm's length away, legs thrown casually over her side of the chair, all slim angles and light up smile.

"Have you never wanted to live somewhere else?" Liv asks. "To leave where, and who, you are behind, and start afresh?"

"No." As Solveig says it, she knows it's a lie. All those games out on the hard, the years in Molde, the fascination with her grandfather's fairy stories. Even now, what else are her daydreams, her wild imaginings? The dreams that promise something exciting just around the corner. "Where else would I go? The Eiks belong here, always have."

"Of course," says Liv. "Of course. *Blut und Bonden.*"

The German, and the ease with which it's spoken, is jarring. Solveig looks away, down into her drink. She asked the question: she should be prepared for the answer.

"I forget, sometimes," Liv continues. "I am a product of city life, of this 'asphalt culture'. I've never really belonged anywhere."

They sit there in silence for a moment longer, both drinking too much, too fast. It must be the akevitt, burning warmth in her stomach, for Liv looks different. Her make up has faded and the hard set of her mouth relaxed a little. There's a strand of hair falling across her forehead, blonde and curling with the damp, and Solveig has to clench her hand into a fist to stop herself from brushing it back into place.

"It's not that I don't believe in Norway, not that I..." For a reader of poetry, Liv's ineloquence is surprising. Solveig would have thought she'd have a speech prepared, that she'd have to justify herself all the time, to any decent Norwegian she knew. "At university, everyone thought like you. You know, *ja vi elsker*, do and die."

"Not you, clearly."

"Oh, it's alright for you," Liv says, pouring another drink, "out here where nothing's changed. You should see Oslo, or Bergen."

The amber liquid sloshes too fast into the glass, splashing her hand, and Solveig watches hungrily as she licks the mess from her fingers. She blinks unwanted thoughts away, forces herself to look elsewhere. This was important to say, to get right.

"Everything's the same? Nothing's the same. How can it be? Kristiansund burnt for four days. Nothing will ever be the same - the whole place is wrecked, thanks to you and your pals."

The drink has loosened both their tongues, and Solveig's words come out harsher than intended. Liv snorts into her drink, and has to wipe the side of her mouth.

"Oh," she says dismissively, "thanks to me? Thanks to the British, more like. They're not a country of saints, you know, despite what people think. You should hear what they're doing in Germany, what the radios say."

Solveig's face closes, jaw tensing with the effort of staying silent. She had heard what the radio says, and the reports don't support Liv. She looks away, at the wallpaper, tracing the flowers' geometric patterns, looking for the joins between the sheets, where the briar stems fracture and slip. Her face feels tight, flushed with the heat of the fire and the drink. It must be bright red.

"I don't know why I expect you to understand," Solveig spits. "After all, what could you possibly know about what it's like to be me?"

Liv's face is warm too, and her breathing's heavy, her chest heaving.

"Oh I understand you very well, Solveig Eik," Liv says, before she leans across, closes the gap between them, and kisses her.

It's hard, angry, but Solveig kisses her back.

Her hands tangle unrelentingly in Solveig's hair, at the nape of her neck where the hairs are shortest, pulling her away from the back of the divan. Their legs crash together against the coffee table in front of them, pushing it out of its neatly ordered line.

The surprise knocks the air from Solveig's chest, and for a moment she's unsure what to do, how to continue. She doesn't have long to decide, for Liv is kissing her again, deft, experienced hands working at the buttons of her blouse.

Liv moves forward, her skirt sliding up around her thighs, swings one leg across Solveig's own so she is straddling her, grinding down into her lap, hands still focused on her shirt.

Solveig runs her hands up the back of her legs, against the smooth material of her stockings. It's ridiculous that she's wearing them now, in her own house, at night, when there's no-one to impress. It's not like silk grows on trees on the islands, and most women would kill for even one pair. Solveig wants to scratch, to tear, to rip the stockings from her and leave her bare and wanting.

Liv has her shirt open now, moves her mouth to suck and bite at Solveig's chest, at the tops of her breasts, along her collarbones and in the hollow of her neck. This isn't love, isn't anything Solveig's had before. No tentative fumble, unsure and searching. There's no affection in the movements, just pure want and need. Solveig pulls Liv to her, kisses her roughly, licking teasingly inside her mouth, feeling her gasp and moan.

"Fuck, Liv," Solveig says, wincing at too hard a bite, but Liv reaches up a hand to clamp over her mouth. Liv might look slender, but her grip is iron, as strong as Solveig's own on her hips.

"Don't speak," Liv says around Solveig's nipple, her tongue tracing circles around the stiffening peak. "Don't ruin it."

Solveig pushes her hand inside the stockings, rolling them down Liv's thighs, and inside her underwear. The space is tight, restricted by the press of clothes, but her fingertips slide effortlessly between soaked folds.

Liv hisses, and her hips pick up their rhythm to a frantic pace.

Liv's worked the buttons on Solveig's trousers too, has wedged her hand inside, roughly pushing past to Solveig's own aching need.

Solveig moans against the hand still clamped against her mouth, bites on the palm as Liv slides inside and starts pumping, matching the pace of her own hips. The motion has Solveig losing her place, slipping off centre, and she pushes upwards with the side of her hand, applying pressure to where she thinks Liv needs it most. With the other hand she reaches up, under Liv's shirt, to the soft skin of her back, and scratches her blunt nails hard.

It will leave marks, she knows, long angry red welts. She wants to mark Liv, leave evidence of her presence. Disrupt that perfect facade, ruin her for her precious Germans. She pretends she's better than Solveig, than the others, but here she is, desperate for the touch of Solveig's hand, the press of her leg against her core.

Solveig scratches again, and Liv's eyes slam closed, her head drops to Solveig's shoulder, her breaths loud and shaky in Solveig's ear.

Liv is marking her too, leaving bite marks across her chest. She slides out of Solveig, and her face twists into a satisfied smirk at Solveig's protesting moan. She shifts, giving herself more traction, and slams back in. It feels like two fingers, maybe three, the pad of her thumb hitting Solveig's clit with every thrust, her fingers curling and beckoning inside.

Solveig can feel herself clenching, the muscles in her stomach trembling, tightening with each thrust of Liv's hips and hand, with each lick and bite of her teeth and tongue. She knows Liv is close too, erratic, breathing hard, moaning as she grinds against Solveig's hand, arching her back into her scratching nails.

Liv comes quietly, suddenly, her teeth on Solveig's throat, biting harder than is comfortable, and the feeling tips Solveig over the edge too. They pant for long moments, not moving, not talking, both still shaking from the unexpected encounter.

"Well," Liv says, her voice strained with the effort of not sounding breathless, "you've done that before."

Solveig lets out an unspeaking hum, eyes closed.

"So have you, I'd say."

Liv shifts above her, as though she's about to speak. If her mouth is occupied, she can't say anything to break the spell of the moment, so Solveig follows, leaning in for another kiss.

As before, Liv's hand comes up to her shoulder.

This time, it most definitely pushes her away.

"Nothing happened, you understand?" She climbs off Solveig's lap, adjusts her skirt, smoothing it back down, tucking her shirt inside the waistband again. "You saved me from the storm. We had dinner. Nothing else."

Solveig sits back, closes her eyes against the sting of tears. Her chest is still exposed, shirt open and bra pushed down, breasts bare to the night air. She can feel the sting of the bite marks, feel the phantom press of Liv's teeth against her throat. She feels undone, still coming down from the orgasm. Her heart hasn't slowed enough to allow her to keep her cool, and she doesn't need Liv to see her cry.

"What else would happen?" she says. "We're both women, after all, and we don't even like each other."

"Exactly." Liv has regained control of her breathing. Sounds unflappable, controlled. "I'm glad you agree."

Solveig wakes by degrees - the chill air against her face, the blankets rucked up under her knee, the fuzzy furriness of her head and her mouth, the warmth of the body next to her. It's still early, the room pitch black even with her eyes open. In the darkness, she could be anywhere.

But it's not her room.

The sounds are wrong, the walls feel too far away, and in her room she sleeps alone.

Next to her, legs and knees flush with the edge of the sofa, Liv stirs, drapes an arm lazily over Solveig's middle.

Oh. Last night: the storm, the rescue, the akevitt. She cannot finish the list.

The drinking explains the rest, the pounding in her head, the way her stomach seems entirely too small, the very obvious realness of crawling under the covers with her enemy. Solveig slides backwards, sitting up, careful not to disturb the woman next to her, listens to their combined breathing.

She should get up. Put up her hair, put on her clothes, her coats and boots. Make her way home as fast as she can.

Forget that this morning ever happened.

Liv rolls her shoulders, one leg straightening to hang in midair, and her head moves closer, rests on the edge of Solveig's shoulder. Her breath is hot compared to the unheated air of the room, and her nose is cold against Solveig's neck.

She should get up, before there's any awkwardness with Liv, before her parents can worry too much, before the sun rises and someone sees her leave the quisling teacher's house. But the sofa is comfortable, wide and warm, and Liv's arm seems too heavy to move. She's trapped, like Thor under Hrungnir's leg, and too weak to free herself. She's almost asleep again, her eyes heavy and closing, when, from somewhere nearby, she can hear Bjørghild's disappointment: In bed with a traitor, Solveig. And a female traitor at that.

Solveig lifts Liv's arm gently, slides sideways out from under the blankets, and lays Liv's hand down into the hollow she's left. The storm is over; it's past time to go home.

The room isn't dark, the badly drawn curtains letting through the thin pre-dawn light. It smells sweetly, sickeningly, of the alcohol they'd drunk the night before. Their glasses are still on the side table, dregs of liquor still clinging to the bottom. The cushions of the divan are scattered, pushed out of their normal order, banked up against the arms.

Something about the disarray makes Solveig blush.

Her clothes, stretched in front of the cold fire, are dry now, stiff with salt. She looks at the clock on the mantelpiece. It is early, even by her standards, not yet time for breakfast. She can change into her own outfit before Liv wakes, make it back to the lighthouse before anyone sees her, before anyone sees anything.

Solveig stands, changes quietly, quickly, forcing her arms and legs into her cold clothes. She folds the clothes Liv lent her, hangs them back on the clothes rail in front of the fire.

They look wrong there, too obvious, too conspicuous, as though their very presence is damning. She moves them around - onto the back of a chair, onto the kitchen counter.

Back in her own clothes, Solveig feels more normal. More like herself. Her hair is a mess, flopping down across her face. Her hairpins have disappeared, mixed up somewhere amongst Liv's, their owner indeterminable. Never mind - she'll take the brush to it as soon as she's home, make herself presentable for now, and then steal some pins off Bjørghild later.

She thinks about leaving a note: thanks for the drink, see you soon. Thanks for the food, for the argument. Thanks for making me see stars, see you never.

Something, however, holds her back. Some remnant of pre-war politeness, perhaps, that prevents her from sneaking off with just a note as goodbye.

If she's going to be the better person, take the moral high ground and all that, she could tidy up a little at least, clear and rinse the glasses, sort the cushions, that kind of thing. So that's what she does, as quickly as she can. Every second she's in the house is a second that Liv could wake up, could hold her to some drunken night-time promise of friendship that the war and Liv's ridiculous politics make impossible to keep.

What is it about some people - otherwise clever, decent people - that drives them to cross that creeping line between good Norwegian and traitor while others stick firm to their morals, their conscience. The war should be between each Norwegian and each German. As the radio says, you have to fight for freedom - fight to keep it. After all, she remembered someone saying, the Norway they'd had before was like a glass bowl, very easy to break.

Easy to lose.

Just the washing up left now, rinsing the two bowls and their empty glasses. She wipes perfunctorily round the lip of the bowls, setting them on the side to drain. Liv's glass still has the imprint of her lipstick on it, fine pink lines spreading out from the rim.

Solveig stares at it for a moment, but her hands are wet and the glass slips back into the water, splashing her shirt.

Solveig reaches for the glass, feeling for it beneath the layer of soap. This time she grips it hard, curling her fingers around the rim. It won't slip from her this time.

Damn Liv Sunde.

She shouldn't have been out on the water if she can't control her bloody boat. Then Solveig wouldn't have had to rescue her, and then she wouldn't have been talked and tricked into staying the night, into casual conversation and everything that followed.

She'll just have to be more careful from now on, avoid the temptation of the teacher's company. It should be easy. She doesn't even like her that much - stuck up, over read Nazi - and they've the entire island chain in which to keep away from each other.

Solveig slams the glass down on the side with all the force of her decision. It shatters under her palm, glass shards scattering across the floor.

"Shit." The flesh of her thumb stings sharply, and when she lifts her hand to look at it, her palm is red with blood. "Shit."

The noise draws Liv upright, pulling the cord of her robe around her middle, blinking the sleep from her eyes.

"Solveig? Are you all right?"

"Fine," she says around the wound, mouth forming a seal to stop the blood splashing her clothes, Liv's floor. "Don't come any... I've broken some glass."

Liv steps forward anyway, her hand held out imperiously.

"Let me see." Solveig leans back, further into the safety of the ring of broken glass. "Seriously, I'm fine. I just... I was just washing up, smashed a glass."

Liv crosses the room, giving the smashed glass a wide berth, changes from her slippers to thicker-soled heels. Once in them, she strides back towards Solveig, and this time won't take no for an answer. She takes Solveig's hand, bending her head to peer more closely at the cut. She turns it this way and that, pulling gently at the edges of the wound to check for shining slivers embedded in the blood.

It's really not fair. Liv drank as much as she did last night - if not more - she shouldn't be this put together so early in the morning. There's barely a hair out of place and her face, scrubbed of makeup, is the very propaganda poster picture of good health. In front of such early morning perfection, Solveig's all too aware of her reflection in the mirror above the mantelpiece; hair flat and trailing from its style, creased clothes, blood oozing from her hand.

"It looks pretty deep," Liv says. She reaches round behind Solveig, feeling for something on the counter. It brings her close again, the soft heaviness of her breasts pressing against Solveig's arm. Her closeness is overwhelming again, bringing Solveig's urge to run back with a vengeance. From the counter top Liv picks up clean, dry rag and uses it to bind the bleeding hand. "There. That should help."

"Thanks."

"But you ought to see someone, get the doctor to make sure it closes properly."

"It'll be fine." Solveig laughs, trying to pull her hand away.

"I've had worse."

Liv won't let go, still peering at Solveig's hand, twisting it under the light. She seems to want something more, some kind of promise to look after herself.

"Honestly, I'll get my mother to look at it. She's always patching me and Far up."

Reluctantly, Liv lets her go.

"Well," she says. "If you're sure you're all right."

"I am."

"Well then," Liv says, "mind out of the way, let me clear this glass up."

Solveig steps carefully across the glass, back out towards the divan, towards the door. While Liv's back is turned, she forces her feet into her boots, readying herself to leave as soon as possible. They're still wet, sodden inside. She won't be able to wear them properly for days, not in this cold - they'll need to be replaced, though God knows how, given the rationing. Her mother's decent Sunday shoes have had to become her everyday pair and a new pair of fish skin shoes, badly tanned and poorly cobbled, reserved for special occasions. It's not like they've got Liv's under-the-counter fashion contacts, a German boyfriend to buy her mink coats and nylon stockings. The chink of broken glass sounds behind her, the shards sliding into the bin.

"There," Liv says. "All done. So - coffee?"

"No, thank you." Solveig wriggles her heel further into her boot, trying not to grimace as water wells up beneath her heel. "I've got to go."

"It's still dark." Liv wipes her eyes, stifles a yawn, motions to the newly clean kitchen. "Are you sure you don't want breakfast before you go?"

How is she so calm about this? How can she act like they just passed out on the sofa, like nothing happened between them? Solveig is in knots, spiralling closer and closer to panic with every second she stays.

"Thank you, but I..." Just the thought of breakfast has her throat tightening against a wave of nausea. "I really ought to go; my parents will be frantic by now."

"Of course."

The disappointment in Liv's voice seems barely concealed, but must be a figment of Solveig's imagination. The wrap on her hand, now spotted with blood, makes her clumsy, her fingers slow to respond to her commands, and Solveig fumbles with her laces. "Are you sure you're all right?"

"I'm fine."

The oars are rough against the wound on her hand. The salt spray stings through the rag. It's a reminder, Solveig tells herself, that no good can come from anything involving Liv Sunde, traitor.

Nine

Solveig is in the sty when the soldier arrives, sorting the younger sow's latest litter. The older piglets were moved next door to fatten weeks ago, making way for the newcomers. These piglets are just days old and still cling to that thin newness, heads too big for their bodies, legs still delicate and frail. They need their teeth clipping, before they start to bite and ruin the bacon. The piglets cry and squeal as soon as Solveig comes near, as though sensing her ill intent. If feeding the pigs is her favourite job, this is her least.

She's done one - small and unresisting, thankfully - when the sound of a motor makes her pause. Peering over the wall, she can see the prow of a boat coming alongside the jetty. The well-oiled thud of the engine is not one she recognises, not her father's, not Gunnar.

A grey trousered leg appears, then another, and, finally, the full uniform. She clips another mouth determinedly before looking up again, the soldier clearer now.

It's him, she thinks, the dairy farm German. Apparently alone, he looks up from tying a rope to the waiting bitts and waves. He actually waves, as though she should be happy to see him. He calls out something indistinguishably German, then drops his hand, and turns back to the boat.

A social call, then, she thinks, purposely turning her back to him.

"Good morning, Fräulein," he calls on his way up the path. He looks younger than before, boyish, no longer surrounded by rifles and unsmiling uniforms. She says nothing in reply, doesn't even acknowledge his presence. Eventually, one hopes, the message will have to get through. "Do you need any help?"

"No, I don't." He continues to stand, leaning against the wall of the sty, just watching her. The pig between her knees wriggles desperately, even with the clippers in its mouth. The young German smiles at her as she readjusts her grip on its head. Taking advantage of her lapsed attention, the piglet gives a final heave, sliding from her grasp too fast to catch.

"Shit." The edge of the clippers catches her hand, opening the scab along the palm. "Shit."

"Here." There is no question in his voice, none in his outstretched hand.

Gone is the farm boy: this is the voice of an officer, the actions of a man used to being obeyed. She passes the clippers over wordlessly. He climbs over the fence, the military shine fast disappearing from his boots. The piglets squeal among themselves, climbing over each other in an attempt to crawl deeper into the banked corner straw.

Solveig leans against the brickwork, face half turned into the sun, and watches him. He works competently, the sleeves of his uniform shirt rolled past his elbows, stiff collar unbuttoned. A lock of hair falls limp across his forehead, like a boy's, and from time to time he pushes it back in place with the edge of his hand. In the sun, fair skin bronzed and glistening, he could be the embodiment of Aryan values - straight and strong and beautiful.

On his fifth piglet, two more to go, Solveig finally speaks.

"You got a name, pig boy?"

"Heinrich," he says, clipping off a tooth and letting the pig drop. "Oberleutnant Heinrich Meyer."

He tries to click his heels together, but the muck underfoot makes his heel slip, turning his salute into a frantic scramble for balance.

"Perhaps just Heinrich."

Despite herself, Solveig laughs, and her mirth is answered by Heinrich's wide lipped smile.

"Heinrich," she says. "Alright then."

He finishes the last two piglets quickly, and climbs back over the wall, scraping the muck from his shoes. The drying mud on his trouser cuffs is spattered all the way up to his thighs and will not easily brush off. He pulls his jacket on, straightening his uniform.

"So...," he says, letting the end of the word trail off into silence. She can see him casting around for words, trying to force his new Norwegian into pleasing forms. His eyes drift from her to the lighthouse.

He wants to come in, she thinks, wants me to offer him coffee. He wants to be taken into the flock, adopted, wrapped in a blanket and put into the oven to warm like a motherless lamb in the springtime.

"So, thank you," she says firmly, decisively, "and goodbye."

She heads towards the house, clippers and bucket in hand. Perhaps if she disappears for long enough into the basement, he'll take the hint and leave. She loiters in the musty dark, kicking idly at old nails and counting off the time in her head.

She's been down there for ten minutes, maybe longer if her seconds were slow, and she can't see any boots through the small ground-level window. There's no whistling, no foot stamping, or shivery coughs. I'm safe, she thinks, he's gone.

Solveig opens the door, climbs towards the light, and there he is, waiting awkwardly at the top of the basement stairs. His back is to her, but she can see his arms working, wringing his hands together nervously. She has to pause while he steps back, making room for her.

"Fräulein," he says, breathless. Oh herregud, she thinks. "I was wondering if, maybe, you would..."

She knows what's coming. There'll be some forced laughter, maybe even a joke. Come dancing, he'll say, down at the mess. We have records, a gramophone. Technically, it's forbidden, but we bend the rules from time to time.

They're all the same, these fumbling approaches. And after all, quick rejection is a kind rejection.

"I don't step out with Germans," she says. The lighthouse

door shuts behind her, blocking him from sight.

It takes ten minutes, maybe twelve, standing alone in the entranceway, surrounded by shoes and damp coats, her back pressed trembling against the solid wood, before she hears the first sound of Oberleutant Heinrich Meyer's engine.

Ten

The weather stays bad, bitingly cold, well into March. It feels like all Solveig has heard in days is the incessant, hollow rush of wind past her ears and the crash of the waves against the rocks, like static on the wireless. Even quick trips out on the water make her face sting, numbing into red blotches that spread unevenly up her neck and jaw.

The nights are the worst, the cold seeping through the lighthouse walls. In some places patches of water cling to the wallpaper, making the pattern darken and distort, the flowers wilting. From the top room window, after scraping off the layer of ice frosted across the bottom and sides of the glass panes, Solveig can just about see the resistance fighter's island, if not the cave itself. She can see her breath in the room, misting the glass in small irregular patterns.

Overhead comes the rumble of plane engines, big petrol engines cutting through the night. They sound low enough to clip the top of the light, but even though Solveig cranes her neck, presses her face to the cold glass, she can't pick out their shapes against the blackness. There aren't any stars, either, just the moon and one wispy cloud in front of it.

It's been a week since she took him anything, and unless he has a rota of island girls ferrying him food, the man – Lars - will be hungry by now. No-one else is moving yet, her parents still asleep downstairs. The sea from the windows is quiet too, no patrols or passing warships in the sound, no fishing boat lights winking in and out. If she's going, it ought to be now, while the world is dark and quiet.

Silently, quickly, she collects the food she's stored for the man - more meat from Olav's back door, things her mother will not immediately notice, essentials - and stows them under the plank seat in her boat. It won't fool a search: the wicker edge of the basket is visible, sticking up from underneath the seat, pressing into her tailbone with every stroke. Perhaps, she thinks, in this weather the Germans will start their patrols later, when the sun at least takes the edge off the cold.

There'd been no boats the night after the storm - maybe she'll get lucky again. It's too early to set off really - only just light enough, the sea disappearing into darkness feet from the edge of the boat. Her hands are cold and stiff around the oars, and going is slow. The waves are higher than she thought, the tide against her, pushing her towards land. In normal years, normal winter mornings, the lighthouse would be a help, spotlighting rocky promontories and the edges of islands.

But not now.

"Hello again!"

The call is friendly and Solveig's hand is up, returning the wave, before she realises it. It's the Germans, the blond head of Oberleutnant Heinrich Meyer, distinguishable from a distance. There's no use trying to out-row them, to head for the island and stash the food under a bush somewhere. The grey boat pulls up alongside, forcing her to pull her oar into the boat, splashing cold water down her slacks.

"Papers, please."

"Really?"

Meyer - she can't call him Heinrich, not even in her head, not when he's about to arrest her, have her flogged for treason - has the good grace to look apologetic.

"It's protocol. So, your papers, please."

She digs in her pocket, stretches up to hand them over the side of the larger boat.

"You're out early," he says conversationally as he makes a show of checking her details, matching her face to her photo. "Off to see your sheep again?"

"Yes."

"All in order there, Miss Eik. But - and I'm sorry about this - we have to search your boat."

She thinks about resisting, about insisting on written orders. But that'll make her look suspicious, and that's the last thing she needs.

"If you must." She stands, throws the painter over the patrol boat's side, giving them no excuse to damage her wooden hull this time. They tie her to them, and Meyer holds a gloveless hand down to help her up.

"Any reason in particular?"

He shrugs.

"New orders. We also have to search empty houses and small islands. Following the..." He pauses, searching for the word. "...difficulties in Telemark, the High Command is concerned about the presence of *die Saboteure* - you understand? *Die Saboteure?*"

It wasn't a word covered at school - the extent of Solveig's classroom German extending to her name, days of the week, a few colours and numbers - but underneath his accent the word Meyer is saying doesn't seem that different from the Norwegian, and she can work it out.

"Saboteurs - I understand." Her voice is breathier, shakier than usual. "Well, that's not me! *Ich nicht!*" she says, trying to cover the lump in her throat with a joke.

"No," he says. "Not just here, but across Norway, across the Reich. We don't expect trouble here."

It sounds rehearsed, which it probably is. A stock line formulated by the ever generous Miss Sunde, carefully taught to patrolling officers for use when encountering friendly locals.

The man in her boat is going through the locker in the bow, pulling out lengths of rope and old, soggy cartons of sheep dip and feed. Solveig shifts her weight from foot to the other, grips the edge of the patrol boat with both hands. He seems to be quite thorough, for someone not expecting trouble.

"The gulls are very loud here," Meyer says, watching their white shapes trail lazily overhead. "Wesermarsch has different birds."

"I'm sure. Inland, isn't it?"

It's said to distract, without any real thought, Solveig's mind still focused on her own boat, rather than the man at her side. Meyer visibly brightens, takes her reply as an expression of interest.

"Our farm is, yes. Quite near to Bremen. But the coast is not far away." The man in her boat is done with the locker, it seems, and is now kicking through the hay bale set carefully behind her seat.

"Hey," she says. "Tell him to be careful with that - I can't have it going in the sea."

A little defiance is expected, surely, even if trouble isn't. Meyer's met her before, and over- compliance will look as odd as venomous resistance.

"You know, I wrote to my father about you."

That gains her attention.

"You did?" He's not going to be the persistent type, is he? The kind that won't take no for an answer. "That was a bit forward, don't you think? Considering that I..."

He laughs.

"Not like that. About your farm, about your island sheep." His Norwegian is coming on fast. Liv Sunde must be a decent teacher, to drill a foreign language into these helmeted heads. "He was impressed. Said it must be hard, raising animals where there should be fish, he said."

It's not all like that, she wants to say. There are lakes and good soil in places and the sea is as kind a friend as it is an enemy. And besides, the Germans are the ones who want Smøla, who have decided to take it by force.

Oh, she can understand why they'd want to, quite aside from any military purpose. Norway is wilder and more beautiful than anything they have at home in Germany, a land she imagines to be entirely full of sausages and beer halls and ruddy-faced men and buxom women. And compared to the cities - Kristiansund, Trondheim - the islands are wider, cleaner, the houses whitewashed and picturesque, and the view - on one side stretching out into the distance and on the other framed by the clean lines of the mountains as they meet the sea - is the very picture of Hitler's rural idyll.

A shout goes up from the man in her boat; he's found the box under her seat. Oh god, she thinks, pulled back to the moment.

Here it comes.

She takes a steadying breath, her pulse jumping hard in her throat. There's nothing to do but brazen it out. Meyer leaves her side, leans on the gunwale. There's a moment where all Solveig hears is shuffling, the knock of the boats as they bump in the swell, the call of the gulls overhead. She watches him lean over the side, reach down to lift the basket of food back into his patrol boat.

"What's this?"

She holds his gaze, shrugs as though it means nothing.

"My lunch."

Meyer looks at her, eyebrows vanishing into his fair hair. He looks back at the basket, at the loaf of bread, sausages and hunks of dried meat, at the blood pudding and sack of withering vegetables. All uncooked, all inedible. At least there are matches, somewhere down at the bottom beneath the food. No pan or plate, but the matches must go some way to corroborating her story.

"Your lunch?"

It's a week's food, and even a German officer - with his commandeered mess and meals, with orderlies to serve them - must be aware of the way food is rationed, eked out.

"That's right."

The soldier that found the food climbs back into the patrol boat expectantly, hand on the butt of his pistol.

"Oberleutnant?"

Meyer looks between the soldier and Solveig, weighing the box in his hands.

"And why was it hidden?"

"It wasn't. I was just keeping it dry, out of the spray."

Meyer stands impassive, and under the weight of his stare, Solveig can feel her face cracking, her eye twitching. She can feel the confession building, coiling into a knot in her stomach, threatening to leak up her throat and out into the air at any second. Lars is not worth being locked up for, losing her freedom, maybe her life. Besides, if they interrogated her, she'd spill, anyway.

It occurs to her, now she's been caught, that she's not cut out for secrets. She's not cut out for pain. She can control it, if she confesses now, absolve her family of any wrongdoing. And then, well, she'll deal with the rest - torture, imprisonment, Lars, the guilt of betraying Karl's trust - when it happens.

Meyer calls something over his shoulder in German, too light and cheerful to be an order to open fire. He laughs loudly, and his men cautiously join in.

Oh thank Christ, she thinks, a rare burst of relieved belief in divine intervention making her eyes well and prick with tears. That's the point of military power, she supposes, all that training and brainwashing. The officer laughs, and so you do too, without an opinion of your own.

Meyer motions sharply, and the weak laughter dies abruptly, their faces falling back into hard masks of suspicion.

"Get back to your sheep," he says roughly, thrusting the basket back at Solveig.

She climbs over the side, dropping heavily into the boat below. The boat rocks unsteadily, slopping cold salt water onto Solveig's boots. Their engine starts up again, right in line with her ears.

Meyer leans over the side as they begin to pull away.

"Oh, Miss Eik? I'd advise you to eat your lunch soon."

Solveig checks the sheep carefully, taking her time with each inspection. It's important for them - making sure those carrying twins or triplets have enough to eat, that those with only one lamb are not getting too fat - as well as for her.

She watches the horizon, listens for the chug of approaching engines. It wouldn't do to be followed.

When she finally heads up to Lars, he is pacing the cave,

pulling on his beard.

"Where have you been?"

His voice is thick and rasping with disuse and cold, and the shadows under his eyes have grown more pronounced. He'd looked wild before, unpredictable, but now, crouched by the fire, he seems ready at any moment to turn, to jump at her, pound her into the floor with a fist, with the butt of a pistol.

She ought to have brought a knife, her father's hunting rifle, some kind of defence. Lars stops pacing, drops his hands to his sides.

"I thought you'd fucking sold me out."

This might be the time to leave. Just drop the food and run, come back with Oberleutant Meyer and his friends and the safety of their well-oiled guns. They'd have to be lenient to an informer, a resister that lost her nerve before she'd begun.

In the old stories, men in caves never turn out to be the hero's friend. Especially not if the hero's actually a heroine, a younger daughter.

"I haven't." She steps forward into the dark, food held out in front of her. "I wouldn't do that."

She doesn't tell him about the incident with the soldiers.

He takes the basket from her, picking through her offerings with one long fingernail. This time, at least, it seems, meets with his approval - there are no angry outbursts, no dramatic refusal to placate. Solveig fishes in her pocket, fumbling for her pack of cigarettes. She lights two, hands one over.

"Thanks." She lets him smoke in silence, cooks him the streaky bacon, more fat than meat, and pebble potatoes, fried up together. It's not much, barely anything, but Lars attacks it as though he hasn't eaten in weeks.

"It's good," he says. "Delicious."

Solveig grinds a used cigarette butt into the dirt with the toe of her boot, watching the paper rip and shred.

"Look, I don't think you ought to stay here much longer."

"What?" He's on alert again, cigarette burning forgotten in his fingers.

"Nothing, nothing like that." She takes a few steps back, involuntarily. "I just meant that, there's got to be somewhere safer," she kicks at the floor, sending a pebble skittering into the cave wall, "somewhere warmer, more comfortable."

"What do you mean?"

"I've heard that, well, people are saying that..."

"Saying what?"

"That the Germans are searching the islands: empty houses, old boathouses, that kind of thing."

"Caves."

"Yes, exactly."

"So where then? I guess you've got a plan."

"I might. But I will need a few days."

Lars smiles, and it changes his face. He looks younger, happier, and for a second she sees a flash of a man who might have been handsome before the war. Washed and shaved his hair would almost the blond as Liv Sunde's, his eyes a startling blue. She can imagine he'd have been charming, once.

"I'll survive that long, I'm sure, what with this feast you've brought me."

Eleven

If she's going to move Lars, it needs to be done well. Professionally, as befits a true patriot and Resistance operative. That means there's to be no brushes with disaster, no relying on the kindness of Oberleutnant Heinrich Meyer.

The early morning won't be any safer than broad daylight, the Germans twitchy after their failures at Telemark and in Tunisia. The blaring headlines of her father's state-censored newspaper focus on other challenges, aim to distract their readership from thinking too hard about the war abroad.

SMØLA DAGBLAD

15 MARSJ 1942

FISHING TRAWLER KARIN SUNK; CREW FORCED TO SWIM

ASHORE

The fishing trawler Karin sank in the early hours of the 12th of March. She is thought to have struck a mine in rough seas five miles east of Kristiansund. The main cargo of Atlantic cod is lost. The crew attempted to deploy the lifeboats, but large swells and the rapid sinking of the ship prevented them. All crew members were able swimmers and managed to swim ashore, despite the strong currents and unseasonably cold weather. The value of the ship and her cargo is estimated at 18,000 kr.-. Captain S.E. Hegg, who had refused to be interviewed until yesterday, said: "I don't know how the accident came about, and I can't speak about the matter now. This is all very bad luck, as I have held a master's ticket for 35 years and intended to retire from the sea at the end of this trip. I have always taken every precaution for the crew's safety and am glad that no loss of life occurred."

The Harbour Master's office ensures all mariners that coastal waters and regular routes are regularly swept for mines by the Reichsmarine and are generally considered safe. If the Karin did strike a mine as alleged, it is likely a single remnant of the British actions in Norwegian sovereign waters in the early part of 1940.

HIS "NINTH LIFE"

Erik Gunnarsson Bygland, of Egeland, Stavanger, crewman in the Karin has been shipwrecked eight times before.

"I've had it," he said. "I'm done with boats. I'm going to find myself a nice quiet job ashore. Even cats only have nine lives, and I've used my quota."

A second crewman, Hjalmar Rutedal, of Bergen, has been

shipwrecked twice before.

NEW GERMAN-FINNISH PACT PROMISES BRIGHT FUTURE

In the traditional spirit of German-Finnish friendship and cooperation, a new trade agreement has been signed between Helsinki and Berlin. The outcome of the trade negotiations has been most satisfactory, and the agreement provides ample scope for further discourse and collaboration between the two countries, providing a solid base from which to continue fighting on both Eastern and Western fronts. The German Minister for Economics, Herr W. Funk, pointed to the many benefits the wider Reich and her allies will stand to gain.

"It removes barriers to Finnish exports across a range of products, including raw metals such as nickel, copper and cobalt, wood products, as well as their expertise in winter warfare," he said. But as ministers from both countries promoted the benefits for industry and the war effort, pressure is being placed by US and British ambassadors on neutral Sweden to reduce trade with Finland, aiming to starve the proud nation into submission and capitulation. President Rysti has taken to the radio to reiterate his belief that Germany and her allies will win the fight against the Soviet Union and the menace of Bolshevism. He will not bow to the bullying of the Americans or the British, those who have turned, in their desperation, against all sense, to Mother Russia and the empty promises of Josef Stalin. We, the Norwegian people, must not be swayed by such false rhetoric. If we, like our Finnish cousins, now put all effort into the battle of life and death that leads Europe against our combined enemy, we can protect our land, our homes, and our children.

We must work together, united, undivided. Then, and only then, we will be free of this Eastern threat.

It's accompanied not by a picture of fat diplomats shaking each other's sweaty hands, but by war reportage - German soldiers removing food and medicine from a landmine-blasted truck in North Africa.

The local people are smiling, grinning, all dressed in white tunics and fez hats set at jaunty angles, hands held out for the Germans' munificence. 'See?' the caption might as well read, 'look how kind the Aryan is to those beneath him'.

Her father pushes the paper away in disgust. Her mother, at the other end of the table, pulls it towards her, her face creasing into a frown at the headlines.

"What are your plans for today?" he asks, rubbing tiredly at his hairline.

Solveig ought to tell her father, ought to warn him about her plan to move Lars. It's his barn, after all, his name on the title deeds. Who would believe he didn't know about the man living so close to his house, in the barn he visits every day?

It would share the burden of Lars' upkeep. Her father could add to the rations she scrapes together, could fish and hunt, could run double trips to Olav. The thought is tempting, if only for half an instant.

Then she decides: Lars is her secret. She has enough to keep, anyway. This is just another to go unsaid.

She can protect her father if she's caught, interrogated. Wild horses and all the Gestapo's inventiveness won't drag Lars's secret out of her. She'll be stoic, noble, offer unbending silence in the face of even the harshest threats. She smiles, presses a kiss to his whiskered cheeks.

"Not much. Just checking, feeding the sheep."

"So," she starts, shivering in the chill cave air, "I have a plan. In fact, I have two. The first is easier, but..."

Lars pauses his exercises for a moment, sweat forming dark patches on his undershirt despite the cold. He hadn't stopped at her arrival, hadn't acknowledged her until enough press ups had passed.

"Fine. What's the first then?"

This is the tricky part: explaining her plans to him in a way he'll understand, a way that will show him the tactical brilliance of them. The trouble is the first one is risky, and the second more so.

"As I said, it's easy. We just get in the boat and go. Anyone sees us, we say we're stepping out together, you know, seeing each other."

"And that's going to work, is it?"

No, if she's being honest, it's not. Any local knows that Solveig Eik doesn't date, doesn't go about in boats with unkempt men. It's been hard enough for Gunnar - God bless his soul -, they'd say, and he's known her since they were tiny. It'd be all over the islands in an hour. But it's not the locals she has to fool.

"What I was thinking, you see, was that hiding works best

when you're not actually hiding, right?"

Lars pushes himself upright, rifles through his abandoned shirt pocket for a last cigarette. He leans back against the cave wall, one foot propped up behind him.

"And if a German patrol stops us?"

"I was hoping that... Well, do you have identity papers? Ones that won't cause the Germans to shoot as soon as they read them?"

He looks at her like she's daft.

"If I had clean identity papers," he says, "would I be living in a fucking cave?"

"*Ja.*" She says it on a sucked in breath, avoiding any real response. "Right. Of course. I had to ask, you know?"

"So you've asked." He shrugs, inhales a first lungful of smoke. "Now what?"

"Now we have to do it the harder way."

"This is ridiculous," Lars calls from the bow of the boat, his voice muffled by the steady chug of the motor. Even Solveig, who knows he's there, can't make him out beneath the crumpled tarpaulin and the remnants of hay bale piled up around his sides. "How long do you expect me to stay cooped up like this?"

"Not that long."

As short a time as she can manage, the engine's throttle pulled right out. It is ridiculous, really. The time she has something to hide, the ever-efficient Wehrmacht and Kriegsmarine are nowhere to be found.

She feels like standing up, shouting for them.

This is probably the most dangerous thing she will ever do, and there's no one around to witness it. The hardest part is getting Lars from the jetty into the barn without noticing. Solveig docks the boat and watches the kitchen window.

Her mother's outline moves back and forth, a dark smudge against the glare of the windows. The tarpaulin moves as Lars shifts, unfolds his legs so his boots poke out from under the cover.

"What are you doing?" his voice demands.

"We're just waiting for my mother to move away from the kitchen window," Solveig says.

"That could be forever." The tarpaulin lifts where he kicks it, sliding down the hay bales, pooling at Solveig's feet. "Bloody cold down here, and wet."

It will have been cold, hunkered down in the bow, straight onto the metal. Solveig can feel the bite of the wind, even through the layers of her dry clothes, and she shivers inside her woollen vest.

It was necessary, though.

They avoided the Germans easily, but had Lars sat up in the boat, they would not have done.

"You need to get your shitty boat fixed - it's leaking."

"It doesn't leak," she says, more sympathetic than she might be, given his tone. But she's nervous, anxious, too, her heart beating unsteadily. "It's just the spray, as we go over the waves."

Her mother disappears from view.

"Come on then," she says. "Up you get."

She's barely stopped speaking before Lars is stood up, making a mess of climbing onto the jetty. He wasn't lying about being wet:

his trousers are dark with water, dripping as he moves, and the leather of his jacket is stained in a tide where he's lain in the bottom of the boat. Hay clings to its sheepskin collar, to his hair, tucked into the laces of his boots.

"So show me where I'm to stay, then," he says.

"This way." She takes him quickly, not stopping to pick up his things, to check her mother's position or the sea horizon for approaching gunboats, not pausing to quiet the sows' noisy demand for food.

"Come on." She pushes him ahead of her into the barn, pulls the doors mostly closed behind her. "This is it. You'll sleep up there, with the hay and straw."

Lars moves forward, takes a few steps up the loft ladder, peering into his new quarters.

"It'll be warm enough and quiet. I'll bring your things up in a minute - the blankets and food and stuff."

"Thank you. This is..." He laughs, rubbing his arms with a mock chill. "This is already warmer."

"It's all right," she says. "We all have to do our bit, right? Bed and breakfast appear to be mine."

"Are there any rules to this hotel?"

"This is a working barn. Stay away from the animals. Stay away from the house. And if my father comes in..."

"Ja ja, I know. Stay away from him too, right?"

Solveig recognises that tone of voice, understands what Lars' childish petulance means. Despite the jokes, he hates being cooped up, hidden away, hates being useless while out there, somewhere, a war is being won and lost and he's not part of it. She knows the feeling all too well. But sympathy doesn't change the facts.

Even with the opportunity he represents, the chance to latch onto the links to the Resistance he's only ever hinted at, Lars is an unwelcome guest. He's rude and Solveig's war should be about fighting and spying, not cooking and cleaning for someone who is never thankful and she isn't sure she likes.

"Right."

She almost wants to take him back to the cave, to leave him there to fend for himself. He's not her responsibility, even if Karl intended him to be.

"Do you know what a risk I'm taking here?"

He huffs a laugh, as though the risk is negligible, as though she should be grateful to him.

"I mean it," she says. "Get yourself in trouble, get yourself found, and it won't be the bloody Germans you have to worry about."

She turns on her heel with satisfying co-ordination, sure she leaves Lars flapping gutless in her wake.

Twelve

Easter is late, and spring is too. The end of March drones by, wet and cold.

"Spring's not coming this year," her mother says. "I can feel it - we'll go straight from winter to summer, you watch. The Krauts have so upset things round here, they've driven the weather to extremes."

When she's not out with the sheep, Solveig stays in, barricaded against the unblunted island weather, the wind rattling the windows and sending the fire twitching. From her window, she can see the schoolhouse, watch the children come and go, note every evening a smart German motor-launch bobs in the shallows, tied up outside the teacher's door.

Arne and Gunnar are out at sea fishing, her parents tied up with Bjørghild's ever expanding belly. Even Aase is too busy to see her - wedding planning all consuming despite the wartime restrictions. It's a surprise, then, when the telephone rings late into the month.

"Solveig," her mother says. "It's for you."

"Look." Aase's voice crackles down the line, the connection disrupted by the wind. "You're turning into a hermit out there. It's been positively ages since I saw you. Come and see me, let's go out. Catch up. Have a coffee."

"Well, it won't be coffee," Solveig says. "That's for sure. Not out here, not unless you want to ask the Germans for some."

"You know what I mean. Something hot and sweetened. It'll do, right?"

"I suppose."

"Oh, come on." It's clear, even through the tinny connection, that Aase had imagined a warmer reception. "It's a good idea; you know it is."

"All right then," Solveig says. "I'll meet you by the boats, and we'll walk down together."

"You look different."

"Do I?" Aase pats the hat with a maternal fondness, setting the feathers in its brim vibrating. "It's new. Per bought it for me. Don't know where from. Gorgeous, isn't it?"

Solveig laughs, lets Aase thread her arm through the crook of her elbow and pull them along.

"But you haven't changed, all those months out alone with your sheep. You're just the same." She squints, pushing Solveig back to stand at arm's length as they walk along. She scrutinises the mud-spattered trousers and the woollen pullover in traditional red and white, sleeves rolled up to the elbows. "I think that's the same jumper as when I saw you last."

"It might be."

Aase laughs, unsurprised.

"It's nice to know you made an effort. You look good, either way. You look well."

As the road turns inland, a group of German soldiers pass them, swinging steps perfectly in time. One man, a thick-necked giant at the back, turns his head as he passes and lets out a low whistle.

"Good hat," he calls, "*und bessere Beine!*"

His squad mates laugh as one, a single block of mirth. Solveig doesn't know what they've said, but she can easily guess. Something lewd, sure enough. Something Aase would skin Per for saying to her, engagement or not.

"So," Solveig says, "how's Per?"

"Oh, he's fine, fine. He's well enough."

"Itching to be married, is he?" Solveig pulls Aase against her, jabbing an elbow into her side. "Lucky boy, eh?"

Aase gives Solveig a strange kind of smile, pulling her hand free.

"Something like that," she says. Despite the hat, despite the cheery greeting, there's something wrong, Solveig thinks. Something Aase's not sharing.

They make their way idly through the streets, Aase stopping to chat with almost everyone they pass. The day itself at least is dry, Solveig thinks as Aase reiterates her rapidly approaching wedding plans for what feels like the hundredth time, the sun trying but weak and useless under the wind. Perhaps the weather has drawn people out: the cafe is surprisingly busy, people glad of the temporary distraction that awful coffee and decent cake can give.

They order, take a seat by the window and end up, like everyone else, talking about the news, the new labour law that insists all men and women of working age enlist.

"I don't think they'll actually assign you... If you were still in Molde, then maybe. But you work in agriculture, for God's sake. It's not exactly unnecessary, is it?"

Solveig shrugs, not bothering to uncross her arms or lift them from the tabletop.

"Well, I'm not going. I'm not doing it."

They fall silent as the waitress brings them their coffee, steam rising from the mugs.

"I'd be more worried about me than you, to be honest," Aase says, "if it weren't..."

Solveig is struck, suddenly, by a memory of them as girls, up in the lighthouse. They'd sneak food right up to the top, and hide there together, leant up against the walls, talking. They'd known, with a certainty that Solveig struggles to recall, that if only they could be themselves, truly themselves, then there was nothing they couldn't do: leave the islands, travel, change the world. It was, Solveig remembers Aase saying, the rotating beam of the lighthouse illuminating her face with rhythmic regularity, absolutely the only way to live.

And that's the difference, Solveig decides, between Aase then and Aase now. Not just the fur collars and stupid hats, but that she has stopped dreaming, got very small. Somewhere along the way they'd forgotten that certainty, settled into adult respectability - jobs, husbands, families.

"Do you remember," Solveig says, interrupting Aase's worried reasoning, "those nights up in the lighthouse? When we'd talk about everything - God and morality and, I don't know, the importance of great works of love. You remember - all that stuff on poetic existence and all that."

Aase sighs, shakes her head. "Solveig..."

"You remember, right? How clever we were, how interesting." That, at least, gets a smile, before Aase looks down at her hands again, fiddling with her ring. "I don't talk to anyone like that anymore."

"That's because that's how children talk, Solveig, girls. And I'm not a girl anymore. In fact," Aase says, "I've got some news."

She puts her cup down, placing it precisely in front of her, twisting the handle till it lays flush with the edge of the table.

"Good news."

"You don't seem very convinced of that."

"It is good news. Very good news." Aase checks for listening ears, leans across the table on her elbows. "I'm going to have a baby."

"You're what?" Solveig isn't as quiet as she ought to be - people are looking at them. Two tables over, a group of her mother's friends have stopped talking, heads bent into their coffee, ears trained like the American's new radar in their direction. She cuts herself off, squashing the last remnants of cake under the prongs of her fork. "Does Per know?"

Aase gives her a strange look.

"Of course he does. Why do you think we're getting married so soon?"

"Oh. Right." Solveig tries not to be shocked. More precisely, she tries not to let it show. This time, she tries to keep her voice down, ask questions without exposing them. "How... how far along are you?"

"A few weeks," Aase says. "Six or seven. Something like that."

Solveig reaches out, grabs Aase's hand. "You don't know?"

"What do you want me to say?" Aase shrugs. "It's not me that's the hermit."

Solveig stirs her coffee with the handle of her spoon, watching the milk swirl.

It's harsh of Aase to keep going on like that, she thinks, like she's some kind of saintly spinster, alone through unattractiveness rather than design. After all, it's not that she couldn't be off in some bushes somewhere, pushed up against the back of a divan, or with her legs spread in the bottom of a boat, the burden boards uncomfortable under her back, if she wanted to. And she wouldn't be so stupid as to get up the duff either.

She resolutely does not think of the stupid decisions she might be making.

She picks a bobbled piece of wool off the cuff of her jumper, flicks it to the floor.

"I don't envy you and Bjørghild," she says, "that's for sure. Popping out babies in the middle of the war?"

"It'll be over soon enough."

"You don't know that."

Aase shrugs.

"It's what the papers are saying."

"But what if doesn't? What if it goes on for five years, ten, fifteen? Are you happy to have your child goose-stepping to school? Growing up, all: yes, Frau Mutter and no, mein Vater Führer?"

"The war doesn't stop time, Solveig," Aase says, more quietly, "and I don't want to wake up one day and find I've wasted my life and that I'm too old and I can't have children anymore. That's the deal, you see, between me and Per. He'd get a wife who would cook and clean and not get het up waiting for him to come home from the sea, and I'd get that house, him, and enough children to fill that house." She trails off, watching the waitress, the other patrons, people out on the street. "It's what we both want."

"But you couldn't have waited?" Solveig drains the last dregs of her coffee. "Or at least, you know. Been more careful."

"No," Aase says, sharply. "We couldn't. And anyway, don't you judge, after all that with... I haven't forgotten, you know."

Solveig only hopes her mother's friends have stopped listening.

"Come on then," she says. "Let's get going."

Just outside the shop, Solveig stops walking, uses their linked arms to steer them towards a nearby threadbare window display. For there, coming out of the bakers, is Liv Sunde in full NS uniform. Black skirt, black jacket. Solveig huffs at the window, misting the glass in two round patches.

Why must the woman insist on going about like that?

So obvious, so distinct from everybody else on the street. She must see how off-putting it is, how it's as good at attracting attention as a flare at night. She could wear normal clothes, try to blend in a little. Instead, she wears the black, buttons shining, face a mask of aloof indifference, and ends up surrounded by a bubble of space. She's not looking at anyone, which is just as well: the *isfronten* is as tight-knit as ever. Even the shopkeepers avoid eye contact, gritting out the prices owed in bitter, clipped voices.

"What are you doing?"

"Nothing - just looking in the window."

"Solveig," Aase says, disbelieving. "No-one's going to believe that you're interested in anything in there."

Aase's right - the window display truly is awful. The shop is - or at least used to be - a milliner's. The scarcity of decent material and thread has left the shelf almost empty, large cobwebs spanning the gaps between a pair of crimping scissors and a faded cross-stitch sampler. In the background, a half-dressed tailor's dummy is sitting at an angle, appearing to lurch drunkenly towards the glass.

"I was just thinking, maybe, about taking up sewing," Solveig says, tucking her head to her chin. Liv hasn't seen them yet, busy checking her shopping, turning each package over in the basket one by one.

With luck, she'll pass them by completely and Solveig won't have to make the choice to ignore her. They might not be lucky - Aase's new hat is eye-catching, to say the least, a capercaillie feather waving madly with every minute motion of her head. Liv knows this jumper too, has hung it out to dry in the warmth of her own fire.

"For fun, you know, a hobby. Mor sews, so does Bjørghild, but I... and I could always do with something indoors, for the winter."

Aase doesn't look convinced.

"Right," she says. "Solveig-"

At that moment, distracted by her own purchases, Liv walks straight into a woman coming the other direction. Solveig knows her, in the island way she knows everyone who grew up alongside her. Beate's not a close friend, barely an acquaintance, but Solveig can put the face to an identity, a few dances and pre-war parties, can just about summon up the names of the shared teenage crushes they discussed as they twirled round the floor.

The other woman's bag breaks, tins and fruit and potatoes bouncing along the street. The tins roll away from her faster than she can pick them up, moving down the incline into the gutter. As the first goes barrelling past, Liv stops it with her shoe.

The woman is crouched to the floor, dusting the dirt from her carrots. Liv hands over the tin, and starts picking up other things too. The ground is damp from the overnight frost and the paper wraps on the tins are bleeding, crumpling away from the metal.

"Thank you," the woman says without looking up, "thank you."

"You're welcome." Liv's accent sounds unmistakably foreign, city-slick and southern, so easily told apart from real islanders. The woman looks up at her, taking in the black of her uniform, the smart set of her tie and hat. It's clear from across the road that the weight of her stare rests on the badges and sigils, all the signs of Liv's allegiance.

The grateful smile slides from her face. She snatches the food from Liv's hand, piling it into a fabric bag. Without another word, she stands, and Liv follows her up.

"All alright? We caught everything?"

Instead of replying, the other woman's throat works soundlessly. Oh no, Solveig thinks, reading her intention a mere second before the woman draws the edges of her coat together, squares her shoulders, and spits right in Liv's face. Liv makes no move to wipe herself with a gloved hand, to back away. Instead, she advances, shorter than the other woman but still casting her into shadow.

"What's your name?"

"Go to hell."

The street hangs suspended in shock at such open defiance. The mid-afternoon shoppers slow their steps, all waiting to see the reaction.

"Bloody idiot," Aase hisses to Solveig, "is she suicidal?"

The words must carry, for Beate turns towards them, eyes wide in a desperate search for support. Then Liv lunges for the other woman's arm, fingers outstretched. She misses, just, as her prey jumps back out of reach, looking now for help from passers-by. At least they're more sensible than she is, gaze diverted and heads bowed. Liv stands in the street, half off and half on the pavement, wiping the thin spittle from her face with the sleeve of her uniform jacket.

"Tell me your name!"

Beate ignores her, hurrying down the street, arms wrapped awkwardly around her shopping.

"Your name!"

Of course, she doesn't get an answer.

"Someone," Liv shouts, "tell me that bloody mare's name."

She stops an old man, grabbing hold of his shoulder. He cringes visibly beneath her grip, his suit puckering beneath the strength of her fingers, but doesn't pull away.

"Tell me her name."

"I'm sorry - I can't see. My eyes..." He gestures uselessly into the distance. Liv pulls a face, biting down on her lip. She makes the demand again, louder and slower this time.

"Her name."

She's beginning to draw a crowd. As she waits for an answer, they close ranks, a wall of stone-faced disapproval.

"I don't know." His voice cracks with strain, as though he's on the verge of tears. "I didn't see her."

Liv lets go of his shoulder, ending the movement with a push. The old man stumbles backwards, caught by onlookers. Liv straightens her uniform jacket, smoothes out her skirt, and shakes her hair back from her face. Breathing deeply, she turns to leave, the crowd parting for her like grease around a drop of soap.

Solveig draws Aase back into the shelter of the doorway, hoping to any god listening she passes them by. Instead, Liv waves and calls out loudly.

"Hei! Hei, Solveig!"

"Hello Miss Sunde." Solveig swallows, acutely aware of the eyes turned their way. "This is my friend from my schooldays, Aase. Aase, Liv Sunde."

Liv smiles, holds out her hand in greeting. Aase returns neither.

"So, I've heard," she says. There should be something tacked on to the end of that sentence, some surface skimming enquiry after her health, some pleased-to-meet-you pleasantry, but Aase adds nothing else. Instead, she folds her arms, leans back on her heels, dares Liv Sunde to make something of it.

Liv's smile stays as wide and bright as before, even as she turns to indicate the emptying street behind her.

"Did you see the woman in the street?"

Solveig shakes her head.

"I saw a crowd of people, and then you. But, um, that's it."

"A woman spat at me. Can you believe it? Right in my face."

Solveig tries to look shocked, but beside her Aase makes no such effort, her own face impassive and unmoving under its plume of black capercaillie feathers.

"Did you see her? Do you know her?"

Beate, Solveig thinks. Her name is Beate. Her sister was in my year at school.

"No," she says, "sorry. I didn't see her."

Liv sighs, smoothing hair off her forehead.

"Ah well." She shrugs, as though it means nothing. "I asked someone else, an old man. He said his eyes were too bad, but he's lying of course. I'm certain of it." She huffs through her nose, a snort of percussive disbelief. "He'll have known her from the day she was born, something like that. They live next door to each other. She's his daughter, his niece, his God damned child bride for all I know. Whatever the case - he wouldn't tell me who she is."

Solveig shrugs.

"Perhaps he really didn't see her - I didn't, and my eyes are absolutely fine."

Liv looks at her for a long moment.

"Are you sure you didn't? Not even a glimpse?"

"Sorry," Solveig says again, pulling a lopsided smile that creases one eye in assumed sympathy. "Aase and I were catching up on each other's news. She's engaged, you see - I wasn't paying any attention."

Liv smiles, and if it looks strained, forced, Solveig tries to ignore it.

"Anyway, you having a good day in the sun?"

"Not bad," Solveig says, and that's all she intends to say. Then she can't hold the words back, feeling them climbing her throat. "Been out with the sheep. Lambing's started, see."

She cuts herself off: she's making conversation with a traitor, breaking the code of silence. All around them, people are judging her. Throw her over, she can feel them thinking. Just walk away, deny all association. Unless, of course, you're one of them. But something she refuses to name, something completely separate from their circumstances, urges her on, making her smile and step forward, perform to win Liv's approval.

Aase shifts impatiently on the spot, pulling back her sleeve to check the time.

"Solveig, we're going to be late."

"Ja ja, Aase, I know," she says. "I'm sorry, Miss Sunde."

Aase is impatient now, tapping her foot. Every second spent with that woman is another mark against her name.

"Solveig, come on. Far will be waiting for me. I don't want him to have to hang around in this weather."

Liv smiles lopsidedly at Aase, her face pulling into a knowing smirk.

"Yes, Solveig," she says, "you really ought to run along."

"Yes," Solveig repeats, "we ought to."

"Well, enjoy lambing," Liv says, brushing the hair out of her eyes. "Birth many sheep, or however it goes."

"You'll have to come out with me sometime: see the sheep, have a picnic."

The words escape her without thinking, and she can't take them back. Aase elbows her hard in the ribs, abandoning all pretence of subtlety.

"I'd like that." Liv nods, pleased. "All right, it's a deal."

Thirteen

It would be easier to break her word, to just continue to avoid the teacher. But the next dry Saturday, Solveig finds herself arriving at the schoolhouse, bringing the spring with her. The sea and sky overhead are almost too blue to be believed, something from a painting, from a pirate's fireside tale of Caribbean seas, teeming with shoals of exotic fish, and great monsters that wash up on golden sands.

In the distance, the mountains of the mainland are hazy smudges of darkness against the sky, their shapes just distinguishable on the horizon. The sea is as flat as it ever gets, waves gently lapping, barely breaking into white horses against the lighthouse. No chance of seasickness on water like this - Solveig could swim between the lighthouse and the school, float on her back like bathers at a beach.

Liv seems surprised to see her, but the width of Solveig's smile brings out one of her own.

"Solveig. What brings you by?"

"You free?" Solveig asks, grinding the toe of her boot into the dirt. "To go lambing?"

It's a little prosaic, perhaps, not as polished or as eloquent or as suave as she's imagined and practiced. But really, fancy words are Liv's suit, not hers.

"Lambing?" Liv hesitates, hand on the door frame. She's forgotten, Solveig thinks, fighting to keep the disappointment from her face. "Well, I do have lessons to plan…"

"Oh, come on," Solveig says. "Sandvik was always fond of endless sums when I was there. Whole days of them. That takes no planning, right?"

"And I'm going to dinner later with the Løviks."

That'll be more chore than treat, with Else Løvik wittering on about Hitler's charms in German as though no-one at the table speaks plain Norwegian. Her company's better than theirs for sure, but a sheep-focused picnic can't beat the social climbing potential of their dinner party.

Solveig forces a smile.

"All right then. Another time maybe."

She's halfway back to the boat when Liv calls down after her.

"Solveig - wait! Two minutes."

It's not two minutes - and really, Solveig should have expected that - Liv is gone forever, no doubt fiddling about with something unnecessary. Doing her hair and make-up. Fixing the seams of her nylons just so and matching the colour of her coat and shoes. The kind of thing that would never occur to Solveig before a trip out to the outer islands.

The sheep are hardly discerning judges of fashion - they don't care if your hair is unwashed or standing on end; they don't mind practical footwear and last year's couture. They don't care about fancy words and clever sentences either.

By the time Liv does finally return, Solveig has moved from the jetty to the shore, idly kicking stones into the water. At the sound of footsteps, she looks up, hands in her pockets, and squints through the unaccustomed sunshine.

Whatever Liv had been up to, it wasn't unnecessary. This is Liv Sunde the skier, Liv Sunde the Resistance hero, Liv Sunde the very embodiment of the Aryan ideal.

Her hair falls in clever waves to her shoulders, a monochrome contrast to her slim fitting outdoor trousers - the grey twill smart and carefully tailored - and clearly new jumper. Even her socks, above the high ankle of her boots, are precisely folded and startlingly white. Even when dressing down, solidly practical, she seems like a silent movie starlet come to life, a walking black and white vision.

Solveig can picture the scene precisely, can frame the shot, can almost see the air crackle between them with poor quality static - the white school in the background, the contrast of the rocks, the woman coming down to the shore to meet her lover. Solveig can feel herself flushing at the thought, at the implication. But such thoughts mean nothing, she reminds herself.

That's purely the plot of the film, a product of Hollywood's propensity for too much romance, for shoe-horning love into the most unlikely of places, between the most incompatible of characters. Solveig is so caught up in her role as director, watching the way Liv's shadow falls unevenly across the rocks, that it's a surprise when Liv speaks.

"Here I am," she says. "Eventually. And I brought refreshments."

She holds up two bottles, beer visible behind the brown glass, hands them over like a peace offering, like a bribe.

"You sure you want to take that outfit lambing?" Solveig says. "It's not exactly a sanitary business."

"These old things?" Liv laughs airily, again a star in front of her adoring audience. "They'll be fine - whatever we encounter."

The outboard runs smoothly, kicking up cold white eddies, and Solveig guides the boat easily out to sea between the rocky outcrops. The silence in the boat is less tense this time. More companionable than when they were running from the storm, less sickening than Liv's arrival to the islands.

It doesn't take long - ten minutes at most - before the bottom of the boat is scraping up a shallow beach and Solveig is all but pulling Liv onto the shore. They have to splash a few steps through the surf, the salt water leaving dark tide marks on the leather of Liv's boots.

"I ought to check the sheep first," Solveig says, "before we just fritter away the afternoon."

"Really?" Liv lingers by the boat, catches Solveig's arm lightly. "Are you sure I can't persuade you to eat first? It's been an absolute age since breakfast and the sheep have waited for you all morning. Surely they could wait half an hour longer?"

Solveig checks her watch. She's late already - she ought to have been out all morning, rather than sorting Liv's picnic - and her father wouldn't approve of a further delay.

"Oh go on, Solveig."

Solveig can feel herself give in, resolve melting in the glare of Liv's smile, in the heat of her hand, the slow rub of her thumb on the exposed skin of Solveig's wrist.

"If you really insist, Miss Sunde," Solveig says, gesturing inland. "Well, I'm sure I can oblige. In fact - I know just the place."

Liv follows her over the tufting grass, spotted with bursts of columbine flowers, their bright purple partially shrouded under thick drifts of dandelion scatter. Solveig stops on an unflowered patch, the grass sloping down to the edge of a pond. Across the water, the land rises gently on all sides, forming a natural barrier against the breeze.

"Here, I think," she says, shaking out the blanket. Liv sits down carefully beside her, watching the ground with an unimpressed expression. It's obvious why: the whole place is crawling with life. Moth-like caddisflies swarm out of the grass at their feet, buzzing up around their ankles. There are midges too, practising tight formations over the surface of the water. Over on the rise stand a few skeletal trees, their branches not yet budding with fresh growth. There's no shade, and the day feels hot and still.

Solveig leans back on her elbows, head tilted towards the sky, hair brushing the tips of the grass. The material of her shirt pulls tight across her shoulders, across her chest, casting dark shadows against the whiteness. The afternoon sun slants across her face, wreathing her in a halo of light. She's virtually off the blanket, swallowed by the spiked grass beneath. She shifts and fidgets as its barbs prick through the linen of her shirt, but she stays at a respectful distance.

"You can actually sit on the blanket, Solveig."

Solveig smiles, waving away a cloud of flies.

"At least this early in the year they're not biting," she says, shifting infinitesimally closer. She pulls the satchel closer, digs with one hand under the closing flap. After a moment, she brings out the beer and an opener. "*Skål!*"

The beer is warm but drinkable, and the day itself seems made for picnics. Out here, in the sunshine and the quiet of the islands, the catastrophe of war might be an imagined foe.

Liv doesn't reply for long moments and then, speaking down into the bottle, she says: "Do you know, I think that's the first friendly wishes I've received in a long time."

"What about... you know..." Solveig stumbles, hides her awkwardness behind another pull on her beer. "Your NS friends."

"Genuine wishes."

It's said lightly, as though it doesn't hurt. Your own damn fault, Solveig thinks, fighting an urge to class herself as uncharitable. She might have said something, but after the first swig, Liv shifts, tucking her legs crosswise beneath her. In the new position, her knee just touches Solveig's thigh, a soft pressure against her trousers.

Don't be daft, Solveig thinks. Don't over-react. You swore to stop it.

To distract herself, she leans away, returning to the bag, searching for something else. When she emerges, she holds out two parcels of wax paper and makes sure her leg is nowhere near any part of Liv.

"Hey," she says, roughly. "What do you want - cheese or egg?"

"Real eggs?" Liv sounds surprised.

There must be some things even the Germans can't magic up for their friends. Solveig laughs, holding the egg parcel further out.

"I live on a farm - we have eggs." She waggles the sandwich in Liv's face. "Here."

The moan Liv lets out around the bread sends Solveig's face blushing crimson. She knows the sandwiches are good: the bread is fresh and springy, the eggs cooked just right. Her mother's cooking, not her own. She had taken no chances.

"Really, Solveig," Liv mumbles, all her sophisticate urban manners disappeared. "This is so..."

She eats like a woman possessed, cramming her mouth, as hungry as if she's been starved for weeks. Even Lars doesn't fall on his food with such desperation. When she's finished, she looks up, embarrassed.

"Sorry. But that was delicious."

"Look - fulmars!" Solveig interrupts her, sitting upright. She follows the flight of the stubby birds with her finger, tracing their low path across the skyline. She turns, smiles. "Isn't that great?"

"Yes, great." Liv doesn't sound convincing, unenthused by the soaring feathers, the careful positioning and navigation. Solveig turns back to the pond, in the direction her birds had disappeared. Solveig supposes she shouldn't be surprised. It's hardly revolutionary for Liv to be so uninterested in the world around her. That's what city types are like, focused only on how it can serve them.

In the silence, Solveig can feel herself working up to be bitter about it.

Here I am, she thinks, risking reputation and self-respect for a traitor who can't pretend to be interested in the things I have to say. She sighs loudly, fishing for a response. Gamely, Liv takes the bait.

"What kind of gull was that, then?"

"Not a gull at all." She sounds truculent, even to her own ears. "A fulmar - they're related to the albatross."

"Hey," Liv says, poking one hard finger into Solveig's side. "Tell me about the islands."

"What about them?"

"Oh." Liv waves her hand vaguely, "I don't know. Anything. Something I don't know."

Solveig laughs.

"An easy enough homework, Miss Sunde."

She names the grasses, the flowers, the birds overhead. She tells Liv about the rhythm of the years, the cycle of seasons. There's no Latin, no precise biological details - knowledge that hasn't come with a diploma or textbooks, that she's learnt outside of school. It probably doesn't hold a candle to things Liv's friends in Paris and Berlin could tell her, with their book learning, their debating societies and after dinner lectures.

"It's pretty impressive that you know all this," Liv says after a while. Their beers are finished, bottles lying empty on the rug.

Solveig shrugs, spreads the palms of her hands wide.

"I am very clever, of course. I thought you knew that. Hidden genius, really."

"Oh, sure. Smoke?" Liv asks, holding out that silver cigarette case again.

Solveig hesitates, taking in the German branding. A gift, of course, from a Wehrmacht admirer. Turkish made, officer quality - far better than the wood shavings that pass for tobacco in Norwegian shops these days. Liv throws her the packet and strikes a match for her own. The wind blows it out almost instantly, and she has to turn and hunch into the lee of her own body to get the thing to light. Solveig's less successful, burning through the matches.

"Come here, I'll do it."

Liv strikes another match, sheltering it in the cradle of her hands. The flame has barely touched the tobacco before Solveig leans back, putting space between them, not meeting Liv's eyes.

"Here, it didn't take. Go again."

Liv smiles, cocks her head. Solveig leans in closer, their faces just a cigarette length apart. The breeze catches her hair, sends it flying about their faces, perilously close to the flame. Liv holds the match with one hand, using the other to tuck the flyaway strand behind her ear. The fingers trail along Solveig's cheek and she cannot help but smile at that, drawing on the cigarette to make the end catch and glow.

"Takk."

She moves away again, laying back down on her elbow, face turned to the sky. Liv takes a drag on her cigarette, letting the smoke linger in her mouth, before blowing the smoke up, over her shoulder, away from Solveig, and lies down, letting the spring sunshine warm her cheeks.

Fourteen

"Right then," Solveig says, standing up and flicking the cigarette stub into the grass at her feet.

"You came to see the sheep, so I think it's time we went and found one."

When she does, it's a feral-looking thing, all rolling eyes and dirty tatters of wool.

"It's hard to believe," Liv says, "that this is the inspiration for all those pastoral idylls: the shepherdess tending her sheep."

"Yes, but books are never like real life, are they? That's the fun of them."

The sheep bucks and kicks out between her legs, her knees holding it still while she feels its legs, looks in its mouth.

"There, girl," she says, "nearly done. We just need Auntie Liv to stroke you, and then off you go."

"Me?"

"Yes, you. It's what you came for, after all."

Liv reaches out a hand, rather unwillingly. The sheep is calling, loud and strident, not the romanticised baa-ing of children's books. She peers at the wool, which is greasy, spattered with dirt. "I'm sure I can see things moving in there."

Solveig says nothing, hands staying firm in the sheep's wool, stopping it from bucking, fighting its way free. There will be things hunkering down beneath the wool strands - the sheep are crawling with mites, with ticks and lice. It's been months since their last dip, and parasites are a simple fact of livestock farming. That would be hard to explain to someone like Liv, though, used to the cleanliness, the hygiene-obsessiveness, of the city.

Eventually, Liv pats the top of its head lightly, barely making contact.

"There we go," she says. "Done. Thank you."

"Let me guess - this is your first time with sheep?"

"You don't exactly see many wandering round Oslo, being herded up and down the streets of Frogner." Liv smiles, wipes her hand on the thick twill of her trousers. "So yes - first time with real live sheep."

"There are other kinds?"

"Of course. There's children's toys, jumpers, skirts, mutton, mince." She runs out of fingers, so stops counting and points instead. "There's fictional sheep."

Solveig looks up at her, squinting into the sunlight.

"You've got a lot of experience with fictional sheep, have you?"

Too much, she thinks. You need to stop before you say

something even more stupid, lay yourself bare, all soppy-eyed and soft-voiced. She knows what the problem is. At the schoolhouse and outside the butchers, she was nervous, hesitant. They were proper places, populated by other people. But these islands are her domain and out here amongst the breeze and the sea, where the only other creatures are the sheep, she's positively bold.

Liv smiles at her from the side of her mouth.

"I have, as a matter of fact."

"Oh, yes?"

As she looks at one sheep after another, she lets Liv talk, listening patiently to endless travels through literary shepherds. The creations of Virgil and Spenser, Don Quixote's friends. It's all real literature - Liv barely touches on the endless, nameless herders that populate the Eddas and sagas, full of clues and riddles, ever ready to help the hero on his way.

"Then the sheep all swell up, from eating too much or something..."

Solveig stops her checks, sheep clamped between her thighs.

"Bloat, that's called. Doesn't happen so much out here, with the matgrass, but on the mainland..."

"Well, Bathsheba's sheep go bloated and Gabriel is the only one who knows how to," Liv drives the heel of her hand sharply into the other palm, "prick them to save their lives. But just so, or they'll die, anyway."

"Right," Solveig says, distracted again. The ewe in her hands is desperate to get away, carving grooves into the dirt between her feet. "I can do that."

"Of course you can," Liv says, a strange choke to her voice. "Of course you can."

Solveig lets the sheep go, scanning the low scrubland.

"Come on," she says and pulls Liv by the hand over the grass. They appear to be heading straight into the sea, but then she stops. Hidden behind a bush is the ewe pen and, in the corner, sat out of the sun and panting, a ewe in labour.

"We're just in time - can you see the nose?"

Solveig half lies across the ewe, knees in the dirt, her hand disappearing somewhere unmentionable. Liv hovers behind her, a safe distance away.

The first lamb comes quickly, head and legs neatly arranged. Solveig appears to be pulling at the lamb with all her strength, her hand slipping from the legs. Finally, one last combined heave has the lamb sliding from the ewe and collapsing in a steaming heap onto the floor.

"Good lamb, that," Solveig says. She picks it up by the legs, swings it over her body to land by its mother's head.

"Really?" The lamb is yellow, covered in mucus, and barely moving. It lies limp in the grass while Liv and the ewe watch it suspiciously. "We must have different definitions of good. Look at it - it's a thing of nightmares."

The lamb coughs and shudders, surprising both observers.

To Solveig's amusement, Liv takes a startled step back, but its mother reaches out to lick its elongated head. At first, she's tentative, but as her lamb continues to shudder and shake, she grows bolder, cleaning with more confidence. Liv is so wrapped in disgusted fascination that she misses the birth of the second lamb. Solveig drops it next to the other, and the ewe switches her attention to the new arrival.

"Is that it? Just the two?"

Flies have begun to circle lazily over the newborns, buzzing around the women as well. Solveig waves them away with her hat, the movement of air reminding her how unseasonably warm, how still the day is. One seems to bite, a pinprick of pain. There are dark patches of sweat forming with the effort of lambing along the line of Solveig's back, at the bottom of her collar.

"No," she says, wiping at her forehead with the back of her bloody hand. "I think there's another one."

Liv's mouth clenches in a small moue of disgust as Solveig's hand disappears inside the ewe, gently feeling for the lamb. There is another, and it's this third lamb that's the problem.

"It's more difficult than normal, but not impossible," Solveig tells Liv, opting for a broad strokes approach over exact biological detail. She doesn't add: easier if the lamb is dead, of course. Liv seems like she might be too squeamish for that depth of detail: it's not the kind of thing you expect city girls to be good with. "We just have to bring the feet forward, and then all should be fine."

She waits for a break in the contractions, pushes on the lamb, its mother clenching around her hand. The bag is slippery under her fingers, but she can feel it move another fraction of an inch, its head sliding further back into the ewe, exposing its shoulders and the tops of its legs. The ewe bleats insistently at the unnatural movement, tries to twist out of Solveig's grip.

Solveig grins up at Liv, her head resting on the broad curve of the ewe's back.

Slowly, carefully, so as not to damage the inside of the ewe,

Solveig feels for the top of a foreleg, pulling it towards her. She covers the sharp edge of each hoof with her hand, until the lamb's head is resting on its knees, ready to dive into the world.

"Virtually there now, Liv. Just a pull and then…"

The lamb slithers from its mother in a rush of heat and fluid. Solveig breaks the bag with her fingers, pulling it from the lamb's head and down around its neck. She rubs once, twice, clearing the nostrils of mucus.

"Here," she says, guiding Liv's hand to the wet muzzle, "like this."

The lamb coughs, weakly, and then begins to bleat, calling its anxious mother.

"One life saved. You're practically a shepherd."

Liv smiles politely, staring down at the mess on her hand: fingers spread, sticky strings of blood and bag spanning the gaps between them.

"Have you got a handkerchief I can use?"

Solveig, busy marking the lambs, gestures with her head towards the shore.

"Just use the grass or something."

In the end, Liv washes her hands in the sea, scrubbing her nails against her palm. When she comes back up the shoreline, the wind blowing her hair forward into her eyes, she's still fretting at the skin between her fingers.

"Stop being prissy," Solveig says, not standing up from the ewe and lambs.

"Prissy?"

"The salt kills everything. Known facts."

Solveig tries for another charming grin, but this time it cuts no ice.

"Take me home, Solveig."

Her tone rankles, and Solveig is reminded of her instant irritation on the quay at Kristiansund. The way Liv's blasé, self-important attitude put her back up immediately.

"Farming's a full-time job - not like this teaching lark of yours. Start late, finish early. What d'you get, thirteen weeks' holiday or something like that?"

Liv sighs loudly, tapping the ball of her foot against the turf. Solveig pats the ewe, all three lambs already pulling milk from her udder.

Fine.

Fine.

This had been a bad idea from the start, and she should have known it would end like this.

"Look, let me take you home and then I'll come back, finish off."

"Only if it's not too much trouble, of course."

"Just get in the boat, Liv."

The boat journey, this time, is tense. Liv stares resolutely out to sea, eyes fixed on the horizon. Occasionally she sighs, grinds her teeth together. It's an obvious message - one she seems desperate for Solveig to pick up on. She wants an apology. But what does Solveig have to apologise for?

"Are you cross 'cos I called you prissy?"

"I'm not cross, Miss Eik."

Hands on the tiller, Solveig smirks.

"I'm *not*," Liv insists. "And I am not prissy."

"Sure thing. Still, I guess you won't be coming out again."

"No, I don't think so."

The boat bumps against the jetty and Solveig helps Liv out, a rough hand on her elbow she's safe on the planking. Well, she'd tried at least. Extended the hand of friendship when others wouldn't. It's not something she'll repeat.

Liv is still standing on the jetty, one foot turned inward. Her teeth worry at her lip, and her hands fiddle awkwardly with her blanket and bag.

"At least," she pauses, ducking her head to meet Solveig's eyes, "not when there's lambing to be done."

Liv leans down, steadying herself with a hand on Solveig's shoulder. She goes to press a goodbye kiss to Solveig's cheek, but the boat moves in the swell and her lips end up bumping against the corner of Solveig's mouth. Solveig freezes, suddenly unable to move. For a moment Liv looks as though she might step back into the boat, tighten her grip on Solveig's jumper, move ever closer.

Then the boat moves again, Liv's lips peeling away. Liv's hand is still heavy on Solveig's shoulder, her face as stunned as Solveig's own must be. Only her eyes are moving, searching for any reaction. Solveig's never seen her look so afraid.

"Well," Solveig says, unable to disguise the shine in her voice, to prevent her smile from spreading across her entire face. "I'll see you again soon, then."

It was just a mistake, just an accidental miscalculation of space and time. That's all it was, all it could be.

"Yes," Liv says, withdrawing as though burnt. "Yes. Goodbye,

Solveig."

Fifteen

As April moves on, news filters out past otherwise watertight censors that high profile French agitators have been arrested, tried, transported to some nameless prison on the edges of the Reich. In the islands, keen not to make the next set of headlines, the Germans' poster campaigns move up a gear, steely-eyed Aryans staring out over harbours and shopping districts, in the toilets on the ferry to the mainland.

At Kristiansund docks, there's a smell in the air that still feels burnt, charred, despite the sea-salt tang. As they disembark, the ferry passengers are stopped, lined up for an identity check, while soldiers search the hold for stowaways.

The message is quite clear: sedition will not be tolerated.

Behind the checkpoint, the soldiers - no more than boys really, too young or poorly trained or simply lucky to be sent to the front - take longer than usual, squinting between the photograph and Solveig's face, checking her name against a list of wanted or suspected criminals. People behind her shift - either nervous or impatient - and Solveig's hands sweat inside her gloves.

They don't have anything on her.

She knows they don't.

If they knew about Lars, she'd have been arrested by now. The lighthouse would have been searched for evidence of other crimes against the German state. They don't know about the radio, either, still tucked away in the schoolhouse roof.

They can't have anything on her.

After all, what has she done that they could hold against her? Fed a starving man, clothed him in the middle of winter. That's just Christian charity, basic human kindness. She doesn't know he's Resistance, he's never said outright that's who he is, he's always - sensibly - refused to answer.

She could deny all knowledge, say she thought him homeless.

They'd have no proof.

Eventually the soldier nods, his helmet too big and sliding down over his eyebrows.

"*Fortsetzen*," he says, waving her through.

Solveig doesn't pause to stow the identity cards back in her purse, just hurries, head down, towards her aunt's house.

She tries to complain to Karl about it.

"Not here," he says. "Come for a walk."

He pulls on his boots, whistles to his mother's old setter, and sets out from the back gate. Solveig walks along beside him, hands thrust into the pockets of her coat. They follow the paths out into the fields in silence; the dog running between them.

When they're on their own, the houses receding behind a line of trees, he stops, leans one shoulder against a slim birch trunk, and lights a cigarette. He won't meet her eyes.

"I hear," he says, "that you've been out and about with the NS."

Solveig stops on the other side of the tree, tries to affect the same coolly detached expression.

"Oh really? Who told you that?"

He shrugs, squints against the smoke as he takes another drag.

"I have my sources."

He refuses to be drawn on this source's identity, drops heavy handed hints about Resistance networks and secret plants. Solveig suspects its more mundane than that: a gossipy call, a dashed off letter from Bjørghild, full of spite and always looking for an opportunity to cut her sister down.

"And did this mysterious source tell you the reason?"

"The reason?"

Karl turns his head, blinks at her. There, Solveig thinks with a vicious stab of satisfaction. That's wrong-footed him.

"There was a reason?"

"Of course there was a reason," she says. "I'm not stupid, and not a traitor, either."

"No, no. I didn't think you were."

Solveig steals a cigarette from Karl's pack and, as she smokes, tells him about her picnic. Just the bare bones, the outline of the day. Tells him it was about gaining the enemy's trust, sliding unnoticed behind their lines.

She doesn't mention the way Liv's lips had collided with hers, doesn't mention the way their legs had felt, casually touching. She keeps the memory of the storm locked tightly away, doesn't even allow herself to think of it for a second.

"That's good," he says, "pulling her in like that. A good start."

"You think? I didn't mess it up at the end?"

Karl shakes his head. "I don't think so. People argue, especially with someone like that."

"What do you mean by that?" With a push to his shoulder, harder than she intended, Solveig forces him round to face her. "Someone like what? You don't even know her."

Karl looks surprised. To him, Liv Sunde is just a means to an end. A way into the NS, a source of knowledge and gossip otherwise unavailable to him. She's useful, for now, but come the end of the war, she'll just be another traitor to be dealt with, punished. But for Solveig, it's not that simple. Not anymore, if it ever was.

"You know what I mean - the people that join up, they're never exactly laid back and easygoing, are they?" Solveig shrugs and they walk on. "Did she tell you anything interesting?"

"No. Well, nothing of interest to you - just about her, about books."

"We found the same."

"You've spoken to Liv?"

He looks at her strangely.

"Not her, not exactly. It was an initiative that... um..." He hesitates, checking about him for listening ears, and stops under a tree, as though the shade will obscure his words. "Our friends abroad thought to try. Try to get some of our own people to infiltrate them, you know. But the fact is we're not going to get anywhere, socially. These NS types are too careful, too cautious. That's the same all over - in Oslo, in Bergen - but out here it's worse. They know us, have always known us, and they're going to be slow to believe you're one of them."

He leans in his shirtsleeves against the trunk, ash building on his cigarette.

"They've got to be convinced, and that's what we can't work out how to do."

The dog squats down at their feet, emptying her bladder onto the grass.

"I could," Solveig says. "I bet you I could convince them."

Perhaps she's too eager, too keen to join the enemy; Karl shakes his head, grinds his cigarette out beneath his boot.

"I won't hear of it," he says. "Out of the question. Too dangerous, especially for a girl, and not enough reward."

He whistles for the dog, heads back towards the town.

Solveig calls after him: "Karl!", but he doesn't stop or turn and she follows him, kicking twigs and stones out of the mud.

Over coffee her grandfather tells stories, long and rambling and mixed up halfway through, like a dream you can't quite control.

"Did I ever tell you," he says, "the one about the trolls and the glass hill?"

Karl fidgets in his seat, checking his watch and bouncing his knee under the table. He has somewhere to be, that much is clear. Off to his Resistance friends, probably, the ones who couldn't find a way into the NS, couldn't find a Liv Sunde of their own.

"You mean the princess and the glass hill," he says.

"No, no." The old man's voice trembles with confusion. "The one on the glass hill, with the trolls, and the horses, and the apples."

"I haven't heard it, *Bestefar*," Solveig says to placate him, reaching out to touch his hand, feeling it shake around the handle of his cup.

"You can tell me."

Her grandfather's smile is watery but direct.

"You're a good girl, Solveig," he says pointedly, "unlike some people."

Karl rolls his eyes, sawing impatiently through his sausage and potatoes.

"A long time ago," their grandfather starts, "when the mountains were young, there was a poor farmer made poorer by having to feed three sons, and the third was Boots. To make it worse, every year a monster would come down and gobble up their hay meadow." He makes grabbing motions with his fingers, nibbling at Karl and Solveig's arms. "Look, says the eldest son, this can't go on. I'll go and guard the field this year and scare away the monster. But part way through the night, he hears an earthquake and runs crying back to his mother and the hay is eaten."

Solveig watches Karl fidget impatiently in his seat, check over his shoulder for his mother, bite his lip. No wonder he fails at espionage and loses at cards, she thinks.

"Here, Solveig," he whispers, "forget what I said earlier. About the thing. It's too dangerous, and besides, no-one'd believe it of you."

He's wrong, she thinks. People would: trust is easily lost these days, people nervous and withdrawn. It's the strength of the Occupation - they've divided and conquered, sown suspicion in those on all sides, split the most hardened of loyalties.

Just look how easily Karl had believed her a turncoat, a traitor, just on the strength of one springtime picnic with a neighbour. She fiddles with her drink, turning the cup round and round in her hands, feeling the warmth burning through the pottery, picturing her own social fall. Her parents wouldn't cave to rumour, and Gunnar is loyal to a fault. Bjørghild would believe it, programmed since childhood to think the worst. Arne would believe his wife, and he'd be influential: he'd convince the men on the boats, they'd convince their wives, their children, cousins, friends.

Quickly enough, she thinks. The islands would believe it quickly enough.

"I could do it," she hisses. "Just tell me where and when."

"Stay out of it, Solveig. We know what we're about - let us get on with it. Just keep doing what you're doing, and don't interfere."

"Ha!" Their grandfather's sudden shout startles both Karl and Solveig. "His older brothers laughed. You try if you like, Boots, but if we couldn't stop the monster, you certainly won't!"

Sixteen

"He won't let me do anything," Solveig says, kicking straw from a bale across the floor of the barn. Lars watches her silently, carefully tapping the ash from his cigarette onto a plate. For once, she is the one complaining, and he is listening to her. "He treats me like a child, like I'm worse than useless to him."

"Maybe he's right," he says. "These things don't always turn out like you think they will. Before the war, my friends and I were just like you: Norwegian, proud to be so, desperate to protect our country from any threat."

"That's all I am," Solveig says. "I'd do anything, and he doesn't see that-"

Lars looks up at her, smiling lopsidedly around his cigarette.

"Exactly. I was as young as you, as passionate, naïve. And then the war came, and suddenly we were fighting actual battles.

We were firing proper bullets, not training blanks, and they wanted us to kill. I did it for a while, took orders, did what I was told. And I knew, I knew, that I was doing the right thing - risking life and limb to protect Norway, as I'd always said I would."

Lars stops talking, runs his hand through his hair, scratches at his skull. The story must run on in his head without making it past his mouth.

"He was just a boy, younger than me. His uniform was too small, his collar was so tight that his neck was red from the way it pinched."

Lars drops his own hand from his neck, bunches it into a fist around the material of his trousers.

"He was frightened. I could see that. But I had my orders - shoot to kill - and I did. I hit him right here-" He presses his fingers too hard into Solveig's shoulder, pushing her backwards into the hay.

"And what then?"

"And then I went back, reported." He moves back, removing the pressure of his hand against her shoulder, looks away towards the cows at the other end of the barn. "After a week, I said I had to visit my family for my sister's birthday. I left, and I haven't gone back."

Solveig sits up, rests her elbows on the hay and looks at him.

"You just... ran away?"

"You don't understand what it's like when you've killed someone. When you've watched him drop and die in front of you."

Solveig reaches for his knee, tentatively. He needs comfort that she feels ill-equipped to give. Killing pigs or sheep must be nothing like killing a man: there's no guilt to it at all, and the memory is short-lived, forgotten before the meat is even hung to drain and cool.

"You were doing the right thing," she says. "You have to believe that. And besides, you had orders, and a soldier needs to obey them without question, unflinchingly."

Lars tries to smile at that, though the movement is small, just twisting the corners of his mouth.

"That's true enough. My father would agree with you there." The smile slips from his face. "It's what he did say, that weekend of my sister's birthday, when I said I wasn't going back. By then I'd already stayed away too long, and I knew they'd be looking for me, so I came out here. Somewhere I thought no-one would find me."

Solveig can see the logic, she supposes. Who would look for a deserter out amongst provincial sheep herders and fishermen? It's not exactly an obvious place to hide, about as far from help and crowds and anonymity as it is possible to get.

Those are the things Solveig would look for, if she were an escaping fugitive, if she were important enough to be chased. That's just another sign of her inexperience, another reason for Karl to think her useless. A real operative would choose the obscure option, not the obvious. They'd think ahead, play their opponents like a chess game, laying down forks and pins and clever gambits designed to conceal and confuse. Then, when the moment was exactly right, they'd reveal their plan: checkmate.

Surely that is what Lars has done. He might have been backed into a corner by fear and panic and guilt - as any rational person would have been - but he's had time now to plan, to look at the board and think.

"So, what's the next move?"

"I won't be here forever, that's for sure."

Lars shakes his head, stands up and begins to pace. The cows are used to him now, undisturbed by the noise, the motion. One shifts, the splatter of her shit only marginally proceeding the smell.

"I can't. It'd drive me mad. This barn, the smell. Having nothing to do, nothing to think about, no-one to talk to except you and..."

He cuts himself off, nods. He's working himself up to something, to a decision, Solveig can see it.

"They'll have me back, of course. I just need to bring them something useful - that's what I've been doing these weeks. Watching, learning. I see the comings and goings around these islands. I could draw you a timetable of who goes where, when, and how often. That's valuable information." He stops pacing, stares at her. "I know their secrets, if not their names."

"Well," Solveig says. "Names round here are something I can do."

Lars grins at her, runs a hand through his hair. He seems steadier now, swinging back to a more even keel.

"Yes," he says. "I suppose it is."

The barn, for all its size, is suddenly too small for the both of them.

"Well," Solveig says, nodding her head toward the barn door, "there's no time like the present."

The day is cold but bright, light reflecting in dazzling bursts off the water. Lars pauses at the door of the barn, leaning against the frame, arm raised to shield his eyes from the unaccustomed brightness. Solveig sits on the rock, leans out to brush her hand through the water. It's cold, the strong spring sun unable to compete with the deep currents pulling water down from the north, from icebergs and melting fjords. Further south, it's the cold water that draws the cod, gives Gunnar and Arne their living. After a moment, Lars joins her, carefully lowering himself to the rocks.

"Perhaps we've picked the wrong day," he says. "No-one in sight."

"Maybe it's better." Solveig turns to Lars, screws up one eye against the sun. In full daylight, he looks even more drawn, almost ill. She'll have to feed him more, be braver in her acquisition methods. "No-one to catch us, either. You'll just have to tell me who you've seen, and I'll tell you who they are."

"There's quite a lot, actually, coming and going. You, people I think are probably your family. Germans, obviously, running up and down wasting petrol. And what I think is probably the ferry, way out over there."

Solveig leans back on her hands, tilting her closed eyes up to the sun. There's enough of a breeze to ruffle her hair, to whip Lars' musty smell away. Somewhere, on one of the neighbouring islands, a dog is yapping and circling seagulls call overhead.

For a moment, she can pretend that Lars is Gunnar or some other island boy, a friend. Someone she might actually talk to, gossip with.

"That's all very interesting," she says, tricked by the sunshine and the ease of the moment into playful teasing. "But you promised me secrets."

"Sandy hair, flashy boat, hard to miss. Sometimes being shouted at by a big, fat woman."

Solveig nods, lets herself smile. She knows that description.

"That's the Løviks. Magnus and his wife, Else. Local sheep farmer, not far from here. One of them."

"Right," Lars says. "Noted. Løvik - one of them. And over there? Lots of interesting traffic over there."

Solveig lazily cracks one eye open, screwed up against the sun, follows his pointing finger.

"That's the schoolhouse," she says, leaning forward, no longer relaxed. "That's why there's a lot of boats going backwards and forwards."

Lars doesn't seem convinced. He picks at his thumbnail, bites the inside of his lip.

"And school children around here regularly arrive in Navy patrol boats?"

"No." Solveig scratches her cheek. Lars has been watching closely. "The teacher over there, she's..."

"You know her well?"

"No!" Solveig deliberately suppresses the memory of Liv out on the islands, stretched out on the picnic blanket, beer bottle raised to her mouth. "We've met. I know her a little. My sister was the teacher before her. But Liv Sunde's not... she's a real fanatic. Hosts their meetings, dates their officers, that kind of thing."

"One to watch, then," Lars says. "And what about..." He stops. "What about us?"

He seems more intent than he had before, serious and focused. The back of Solveig's mouth floods with sourness, building up behind her teeth. She doesn't have anything to tell him. A hidden radio and a few ripped posters don't seem so heroic with the image of a boy's too tight collar in her head.

"There's me, as you know. And there's, well, there's... I probably oughtn't tell you," she says.

After agonising, silent seconds, Lars sucks in a breath, jerks his head in agreement.

"Ja, ja. Of course. In case they find me, and all that."

He's disappointed, of course. A local chapter would have given him some purpose, some direction to his days. Solveig bites the inside of her lip, her insides tense and twisting with anxiety and irritation. Her pleasant afternoon in the sun is ruined: once again she has to dissemble, cover the gaps in her experience. It's insufferable.

"I'll tell you what," she says. "I'll get you your information instead."

"Solveig," he says. "That's not-"

He sounds too much like Karl. Not necessary, not a good idea. It's meant to dissuade, but it only hardens her. She'll do what Karl and his uniformed buddies can't: she'll infiltrate the NS, learn their secrets, help the war effort for real. It'll be just the start: Solveig Eik, the hero, is just waiting in the wings, and this could be her cue.

"I will," she says. "I'll get it. I know just where to start."

Seventeen

In the dark, the lights of the schoolhouse stand out across the water. It's a clear breach of the blackout, but she doubts Liv will be punished.

There are boats all along the schoolhouse jetty, blocking the mooring points, and Solveig has to tie her own to another, flashier, big petrol-engined thing before climbing across the seats onto solid land.

In the darkness, it would be easy to turn around, go back to the lighthouse and never mention this to anyone. She should

She hovers outside the door, smoothing the unfamiliar weight of her skirt, imagining she can hear Liv's voice: do it. Screw your courage to the sticking-place, it says, and you'll not fail. She takes a few breaths, tenses the muscles of her stomach as though preparing for a blow, and knocks.

"Oh, hullo Solveig." Liv looks back over her shoulder, watching the people move behind her. "Do you mind? It's just that I have people here..."

Solveig holds out her hand, stops just short of blocking the door with her foot.

"Wait!" She pauses, stutters over the next words. For Norway, she thinks, summoning the images of her future glory. For the Resistance. "That's why I came - for the meeting."

"The meeting?"

"Yes. It's just, you see, that I've been thinking about things. About what you said, ages ago. And I think that - it's difficult to say this, out loud, you know - that maybe, well, that maybe you might be right."

"Oh." Liv is blank, unmoving. The buttons on her uniform catch the light, the fastenings on the epaulettes more obvious now than in the daylight. "That's unexpected. I'd taken you for one of the kind ones."

"Not really," Solveig interrupts, the leather of her gloves sticking as she twists her fingers through each other. She's afraid she isn't kind, deep down, where it really counts. She's full of want and desire and secrets, and those are stronger than the urge to be kind, selfless. That's not what Liv needs to hear, not what will help Solveig on tonight's mission. "I don't mean I'm not kind, just that it shouldn't be a surprise, I mean, because you're so persuasive and I..."

Liv holds up a hand, and Solveig comes to a grinding stop.

"Unexpected, but not unwelcome." Liv smiles, as though Solveig were something she'd achieved. "Anyway, where are my manners? If you've come for the meeting, you ought to come in."

The schoolhouse has been rearranged for the occasion: the children's desks have been pushed aside, piled neatly along the walls. The chairs have been left, and their rows are sparsely filled by men and women in the black uniform of the NS. There aren't many of them - fifteen at the most - but at her entrance the conversation in the room swerves awkwardly then dies away, the air poised and tentative; the silent question as loud as if they had all spoken together.

It's not as though Solveig expected anything else. As Liv leads her across the room, Solveig decides it's not her duty to break the ice, spew out distasteful platitudes just to satisfy them.

"Sit here," Liv says, indicating a chair in the second row. The chair is uncomfortably small, designed for growing children, not adults, and the edge presses into Solveig's thigh. She shifts, uncomfortable in her suit.

It used to be Bjørghild's, before she got too big to fit it, and the belted waist shows more of Solveig's figure than she'd like. If the schoolhouse weren't so cold, those loose boards letting the chill spring air in, she would let the jacket sit open.

She hasn't come here to seduce anyone, after all.

"There's not many people here," Solveig whispers up to Liv. "I thought there'd be more."

NS flyers had claimed a hundred members from the main island alone. She shouldn't have believed them - they were just propaganda, like the newspapers, crafted to make good, honest Norwegians think they were in the minority, that the rest of the country, the world, were united against them. Liv shrugs, leans her head to speak directly into Solveig's ear.

"We've a lot of 'passive' members," she says. "Local businessmen, mostly. Who understand the work we're doing, but sometimes..."

She pauses, lowering her voice even further, as though she doesn't want to give the others lined up in her classroom any ideas.

"Sometimes, they lack the courage of their convictions."

"I can understand that."

Liv's attention is drawn away, towards the front of the room. She's being waved over by a man with a thin, sandy moustache that quivers as he rearranges things on the desk in front of him.

Solveig recognises the man, though his name escapes her. He's a grocer, over on the other side of the islands. One of Liv's local businessmen, clearly. He must be high ranking: his uniform is enhanced with various patches on his sleeves and across the top of the breast pockets.

"Good evening," Herr Moustache says and the meeting quiets, people falling silent together. "I'm delighted that you've all turned out tonight, both constant companions and new friends."

Solveig tries to sink into her chair, to make herself as inconspicuous as possible. At least half the room is staring at her, some nudging their husbands, some leaning their heads to gossip into their wives' ears.

"Tonight we're very grateful to Miss Sunde - both for the use of the schoolhouse as always, but also as she has agreed to be our speaker for the evening."

He gestures for Liv to take his space, nods to her benevolently across the schoolroom, and turns to sit in the front row. Liv shuffles for a moment, her face twitching into an uncharacteristically nervous smile.

"Good evening," she says. "I'd like to start with a story that will be... familiar to many of you, I'm sure." Liv tells them of meeting Beate in the street, how even the smallest kindness could meet with suspicion, with derision. "This is disheartening, I know."

Liv pauses for a moment, and Solveig can see her judging her audience.

"But surely none of us expected our struggle to be easy: this path is hard, because we are fighting for something great, and great things are not easily gained. We are fighting for nothing less than a revolution in the spirit of our people. You can't expect everyone to understand what we understand, what we have seen to be coming. People are so used to passivity, to the little men of old Norway, blown here and there by every gust of convenient opinion, gossiping and chattering about the prospects of the next five minutes. They have let the years of peace and prosperity blind them to the threats of the East, erode their loyalty, endurance, their staying power.

"And in the face of the greatest threat that life in Norway has ever faced - the threat of Stalin, of his pogroms, of the creeping, pernicious influence of Communism - this weakness is shameful. It is the opposite of everything we stand for. Constancy, loyalty to cause and comrades, determination and stability of nature. These are the qualities of the true Norseman and the true revolutionary. It doesn't matter if we win tomorrow morning or in ten years, or at the end of a lifetime of labour and of struggle. All that matters is that we win - and we will win, because the very future of our country demands it of us.

"Through good and ill - no matter how many people spit at us in the street - we must march on, till our victory is won. Together in Norway, and with our brothers and sisters across Europe, we have lit a flame that shall not extinguish. It must not be extinguished."

Liv doesn't get the reaction she perhaps expected: she isn't met with shouts and calls, none of the fervour that follows a speech of the Führer's, or England's Oswald Mosely or even Vidkun Quisling.

Instead, there is a smattering of polite applause, an indistinct murmur as people turn to their neighbour and offer their own opinion. It's what happens, Solveig supposes, when you pour out your heart for an audience of pragmatic farmers and shopkeepers rather than university intellectuals.

She makes sure to smile even wider, clap louder than the people in the surrounding chairs, as Liv nods an acknowledgement at the sandy moustache and heads back down through the rows towards her.

"You're a wonderful speaker," Solveig says. "I can imagine you teaching now, holding sway over a class."

Solveig can see it too, as clear as any actual memory of this classroom. At the front there, Miss Sunde would be lit by the beams of afternoon light from the tall windows, bent over the books on her desk like a living statue, haloed by shining dust motes. When you finished your work, you'd raise your hand, and she'd cross to you, ignoring the others and heading straight for you, only for you.

"You thought it was alright?"

"Yes, of course." Solveig looks back up at the moustached grocer, who now appears to be reading some official pronouncement or other. She really ought to be concentrating - writing things down, enthused and zealous as a new convert - but Liv is leaning towards her, the soft press of her thigh flush against Solveig's own. "It really was."

Liv does a better job than Solveig of keeping her concentration on the speaker at the front, eyes front, but the corners of her mouth slide into a pleased smile.

The meeting is wrapping up, and Solveig tries to commit names and dates and off-hand remarks to memory, parsing through the information for that one golden nugget that will earn Lars' respect.

"You're coming in for a drink, then?"

"Oh," Solveig says, checking her watch. She ought to be getting back: if she stays any later, her parents will be watching the water, waiting for her. In the long spring evening, she'll be easy to spot, her point of departure obvious.

"Well..."

"It's not very formal," Liv says, "just a drink, a chat. It wouldn't fly in the bigger branches, in Oslo or Molde, but out here we think it's... neighbourly. Besides, Standarternfuhrer Rastic will be here."

"Who?"

"You don't know? He's the commander of the Germans stationed on the island." Liv pauses, her attention drawn by a passing woman asking something inconsequential about drinks. "You'll like him, Solveig, I'm sure. He's very handsome."

Liv's arm is hooked through Solveig's elbow, virtually pulling her along. Solveig still hesitates, watching the NS members filter into Liv's sitting room, yellow light spilling between their legs onto the wet asphalt of the playground.

She hasn't learnt anything yet, has nothing of value to take back to Lars, to the Resistance. She squares her shoulders - Daniel in the lions' den, Loki in the halls of the ice giants - and lets herself be swept along.

Eighteen

Liv installs her in the corner of the divan and disappears to fetch a drink. She reappears, tumbler in each hand and sinks down beside Solveig, passing a glass without looking. This time, with an audience, she's more conventional, sitting upright, doesn't throw her leg over the arm. Solveig misses the informality, awkward under the gathered weight of attention.

Solveig puts the glass to her lips, sips it, then empties it with a swift jerk of her wrist. Liv's shout of laughter startles the room, another dip in the hum of chatter.

"Stay there," she says. "I'll get you another."

In her absence, Liv's space is filled by a less welcome companion.

"I didn't believe Miss Sunde when she said we'd one day see you here, Solveig Eik." Else Løvik, drink in hand, settles into Liv's space on the divan. "Does your father know?"

"No."

Too abrupt, she thinks, and softens it with an attempt at a shaky smile. Even under her pretend circumstances, a little nervousness is allowed.

"He doesn't."

"I'm not surprised. He was never a very imaginative man."

Solveig grits her teeth. She mustn't take offence, startle back, stand up and throw her drink right in Else's lap. After all, by his own admission, her father isn't imaginative. Steady instead, reliable, not grubbing and cheating and scraping through other people's dirt for an extra kroner per wool bag. And he's respected for it - liked, trusted – while Magnus and Else wind up here, with sharks for friends.

"Magnus Junior would have been here tonight," Else says, "but he's had a terrible cold."

The absence of Magnus Løvik Junior is little loss to Solveig's evening. On first acquaintance, the elder Magnus comes across to most people as a limp sort of man, too cowed by his wife and son, too devoted to his sheep, to have any opinions of his own. But that flaccid appearance disguises a ruthless streak that had local wool merchants and livestock auctioneers tightening their belts and steeling themselves at his arrival.

Magnus Junior has no such camouflage against his real nature. At school, before they were allowed out on the water alone, he'd been the boy to avoid. All too keen to stick the first knife in the fish's gills, to pick fights with younger children, to lead the boys with flaming torches down to the teachers' wooden boats bobbing quietly in the water. It was no surprise to anyone the day he'd first swaggered across the islands in his new, overly tight, black uniform.

"That's a shame," Solveig says. "It's the change in weather. Everybody's sneezing at the moment."

She's lucky, she supposes, that all this thinking goes unnoticed by her new companion, too eager to revel in the fall of her rival's daughter to draw any meaningful conclusions. Instead, Else wriggles herself into the cushions, pulls at the front of her uniform blouse, fanning herself with the fabric, readying herself.

"So, as a new convert, you'll know about Hitler."

Honestly, Solveig thinks, everybody knows about Hitler, even the senile. Surely she must have something specific in mind.

"Know what about him, exactly?"

Else laughs, high and trilling. She leans in, drops her voice to a conspiratorial whisper.

"Oh! How handsome he is, of course. My youngest sister was at school there, and the girls were all just crazy about him. I mean, I'm a married woman, but I understood: those blue eyes, those arms, that voice." She shivers with some kind of suppressed sexual excitement, staring across the room at her husband. "There's just something so alive about him, something so physical. Don't you think?"

"Oh," Solveig says with as straight a face as she can manage, "absolutely."

It's the right answer. Else carries on, in her rapid gossipy voice, with some dull story about the Führer's car passing by her sister's school, how she was so close she could have reached out and touched it. It appears to be the defining moment of her life, and the driving reason behind her membership.

The drinks have been ages. Liv is caught in conversation across the other side of the room. Solveig uncrosses her legs, leaning into the arm of the divan.

"And what about you, dear? How did you become *ein Gläubiger der Führer?*"

The German itself might be lost on Solveig, but the meaning behind it isn't.

I'm not, Solveig wants to say. I'm not like you people, all natural patriotism inverted, twisted into something repulsive. But that will hardly win her information, win her the trust she needs.

"Here," Liv says, interrupting the conversation. "Strong as the first, so you might want to take this one slower if you're to survive the row home later."

Liv lowers herself to the divan as well, settling in between them, forcing Else to shift. After a moment, the Løvik matriarch pretends to hear Magnus calling her, makes her excuses, and sails out into the standing crowd.

"I'm sorry," Liv says when Else has gone, working her way across the room towards her husband. "I didn't mean to leave you with her. Was she wittering on in German again, as though none of us speak plain Norwegian?"

"There was quite a bit of German."

Liv's mouth twitches with amusement, rolls her eyes in camaraderie. She crosses her leg and leans back, her arm pressing gently into Solveig's side.

"So this is us." Liv indicates the rest of the room with her glass. "Everyone's here, I think, although Leo will be coming along soon," she says, as though this should be enlightening.

"Leo?"

Liv's face softens, or tries to, Solveig thinks, in an imitation of love. It's too exaggerated, Solveig feels, with too much facial movement, for it to be real. When she replies, her voice is still the professional Miss Sunde's, not the light laughing of their island picnic.

"Colonel Rastic. The commander of the garrison up on Edøya."

"Ah, I know."

She doesn't. Before Karl put the idea to come here in her mind, she'd deliberately avoided the Germans, shunned as much knowledge as she could. Solveig shifts, attempting to cross her legs in Liv's more modish manner, sending her foot straight down rather than angled awkwardly outwards. It makes sense, she supposes, in a hollow kind of way; the way two lepers, with nothing else in common, might band together against the world's unkindness.

The thought that Liv Sunde could be, should be, more than a simple stooge to the occupiers is hard to shake and disappointment rises in her throat. What a waste, what a shame.

The Colonel is a hard, bright type of man, Solveig thinks, not at all as Liv had described him.

He's blandly good-looking, his hair greying at the temples: the typical soldier's soldier, at home in any army. His eyes seem naturally narrowed, as though constantly appraising a room full of people not quite up to snuff. Although to him, of course, Norwegians will never be completely acceptable society. Savage barbarians, he must think, too stupid to accept their rightful overlords. At least, unlike the Poles or - even worse - the Russians, any of those Slavic dogs, northerners are *Volksdeutsch*, of Aryan descent. Strong-boned, fair-haired and blue eyed. In time, with enough controlled cross-breeding, the Nordic countries would be as racially pure as the Germans themselves.

The thought is sickening and unavoidable. Perhaps that's his interest in Liv - turning the schoolhouse into a high-class, one-man exclusive Lebensborn home.

"What we'd like from you is information," Rastic says. He has that same casual authority that Solveig sees in Liv: an assumption he'll be listened to, obeyed. It works, too: the room falls silent at his quiet words. "You know these people: their opportunities for sabotage, the strength of their convictions. You may not realise how valuable this knowledge is - the smallest detail can give a traitor away."

"There's something suspicious about the Nygårds," Liv says absently, too consciously moon-eyed to give a focused answer. "I went to their house the other day to discuss the boy, Leif. He's doing absolutely terribly. Disrespectful, slovenly. That's not suspicious in itself, but they wouldn't let me inside. Made me speak to the boy in the cold. The house seemed full of people."

Around the room, the other members mutter between themselves, nodding behind their hands.

"The old woman's always been a busybody," Else says. "It

wouldn't surprise me if she'd taken it into her head to interfere."

No-one else volunteers anything. Rastic glares expectantly around the room, disappointed by their silence. For Solveig, it's a relief: she can tell Karl exactly how little the NS knows, how few people are suspected. She allows herself a small thrill of satisfaction, of smug knowledge, and settles down into the divan, digging herself deeper into the corner.

It's short-lived, her movement drawing Rastic's attention, his tooth-filled smile.

"What about you, Miss Eik? Perhaps you hear things that our members don't?"

She shakes her head.

"I don't know anything." Solveig's gorge rises in her throat, while Liv smiles encouragingly. "Everyone I know is law-abiding. Always have been. My father's very keen on fairness."

Magnus Løvik grunts something to himself, folding his arms over his chest. There's a long silence. It feels like a test.

Liv leans forward, touching her leg.

Solveig says nothing, Liv's hand squeezing her thigh. This could be the way into the NS the Resistance was looking for, an opportunity to be trusted by the right people. But she has to play it right, reveal just enough.

She could give up the radio in the school roof, but the Germans will know it didn't hide itself. If she knows its location, she'd know its owner.

There's Lars, hiding in her barn.

Or Karl and his newspaper.

Not a single one of them is an acceptable option. Every one

implicates herself, dooms a friend to torture.

"We understand," Rastic says, "that it is hard to give up friends and neighbours. It is hard even for us Germans. It feels like a betrayal, I know. But I assure you, it is absolutely for the best. If you know anyone to have committed a crime, you must report it."

She could give up Beate, the so far nameless spitter. She's not a close friend. Just an acquaintance, really. Almost a stranger. And what would the punishment be for such a petty crime?

A fine at most.

If it even was an actual crime, rather than just nastily repugnant behaviour.

Just a warning, maybe.

Giving Beate's name wouldn't be much of a betrayal, wouldn't put too heavy a stain on her soul. But, Karl would say, you have to give to receive. Sacrifice the one for the good of the many. It's a motto she has to stick to.

"Olav." Solveig's voice is little more than a whisper. "The butcher."

The Colonel sits forwards, motioning to his man to write this down.

"What about the butcher? What exactly is his crime?"

She's started, she can't finish there.

"He, he hands out meat from the back of the shop. Doesn't ask for ration stubs. Takes fish or wool or whatever as payment. Sometimes asks for nothing."

There are mutters from the black uniformed Norwegians - suspicions realised and confirmed, small exclamations of surprise. Beside her, Liv smiles in benediction, golden as a young Freja on the fields of Fólkvangr.

"Where does this meat come from? Why is it not missed in the weekly accounts?" Rastic seems to be speaking more to himself than to Solveig, but now she has started the confessions won't stop.

"Rumour says it comes from the army's allowance. He prepares it, see. An ounce here, another ounce there. Over time, it adds up."

Rastic smiles at her, leaning back in his chair. He seems calm enough, but Solveig has the terrible feeling that there's frantic movement going on beneath the surface.

"We will confirm your story, of course. And if we find it to be correct... Well," he says with a tilt of his head, "you shan't go uncompensated, I assure you."

And just like that, Solveig is unimportant again.

In the wake of the Germans' departure, the NS members stand in clumps, clinging to family groupings and old pre-war friendships. They talk quietly, but Solveig knows it is about her. Their eyes give them away, constantly slipping in her direction, through lowered lids and lashes, catching her gaze in the mirror above the fire. The Løviks are a wine-drinking barricade; Liv is nowhere to be seen.

Longing to be gone herself but too acutely ashamed to row home, Solveig fumbles in her pocket for a cigarette, leaning awkwardly back into the cushions. In the stillness of the room, the smoke hangs in a screen about her, not thick enough to hide her from purposely raised eyebrows and unsubtle smirks. Beside her, the divan sags.

"Hey," Liv says, low enough that only Solveig can hear. "That was brave."

Solveig shakes her head. It was foolish; it was wrong; it was what she had - implicitly, of course, in careful gaps in otherwise straightforward sentences - been told to do.

"It wasn't."

"It was!"

Liv is too loud for close quarters, one arm propped on the back of the divan, dangling her glass in lazy fingers, the other hand warm on Solveig's thigh. She smiles again, that proud, possessive smile.

"It was brave, if a little..." She doesn't say stupid, but Solveig hears it none the less. "Why did you do it?"

"Well..." This was always the error in the plan. Her reasoning, her motivations, the slow long trek to conversion - she should have thought about them before. "I wanted, I thought..."

"You should go home, Solveig."

Liv swallows a large mouthful of her drink, watching the movements of others over the rim of her glass. She lowers her voice, keeping it soft and quiet, intending it now for one set of ears alone.

"I don't know why you came, and why you said what you did, but I don't think you belong here, with us." She pauses, leaning closer, her arm slipping along the back of the divan around Solveig's shoulders. Her breath tickles Solveig's neck, thick with gin and sweet. "Don't do it to impress me."

The boat, with its scattered carpet of straw and sheep dip cartons and pellets and bits of rope, is too ordinary, too everyday, to row just yet.

Solveig's heart is still hare-fast, darting here and there inside her chest. If she were to row now, with her head buzzing like this, like she's drunk or mad, surely she'd capsize, drown, sinking into the inky night time waves. It's movement she needs, a physical distraction, to calm herself down.

She can't think when she's moving, her brain occupied with simple commands: step here, breathe now. She walks briskly around the school, picking her way between the rocks in the dark.

The light from the windows spills out in long yellow rectangles, shadow puppets moving in its glow, and Solveig skirts them, sticking to the shadows. She wants to stay unobserved, unwatched, by the judgemental eyes inside the walls she circles. At each corner, she stops and shakes herself, urging her blood to flow normally again, to fill the hollow places in her legs and arms, to unknot the tension in her stomach.

It works enough to get her in the boat, to get the oars in their locks, to push off from land. Then, as before, she watches the lit schoolhouse retreat into the night. Only this time, Liv Sunde does not watch her go.

Back in the darkness of her bedroom, Solveig lets herself cry. She gave away information, betrayed a friend to certain punishment, and gained none in return. That's terrible tactics, an awful waste of resources.

Idiot.

Willingly, uncomplainingly throwing herself headlong into a

situation she should abhor because it might score her points with the Resistance. And because, on top of that, it would score her points with Liv Sunde.

And Liv had known.

That was the worst part - it shouldn't be, but it was. It was almost as though Liv understood. She saw Solveig for who she was, who she really was, and instead of raising the alarm, of alerting her precious Leo, she sent her home.

Of Else and the Magnuses, of the other traitors, Solveig can believe the very worst. But surely not Liv, not really. If Solveig can see the cracks in their arguments, then Liv, intelligent, educated Liv, has to see through the carefully choreographed poise of it, the propaganda and lies.

Oh, she wears the uniform, sings their songs, hosts their gatherings, but it seems impossible to match the politics of it all - the intolerance, the supercilious judgement - with the other side of her: concerned teacher, foreign book collector, carefree picnic companion.

No.

She can't believe it, won't believe it.

She fills her mind with pictures of Liv, the hero. The other thoughts, those that crowd her stomach with cramping guilt, she buries under the brightness of her re-imagined world. And if Solveig admires this version of Liv, if she looks up to her, wakes slickly wet with a hand between her legs, there's nothing wrong with that. After all, how could she not?

Nineteen

The next morning she's sulky and withdrawn, too wound up with guilt and worry to manage her breakfast. Even her father comments on the change in her.

"You seem off, Solveig," he says over his morning eggs. "Nothing wrong, is there?"

She shakes her head.

"Are you sure?"

"No," she says, resolute. "Nothing wrong."

She can't say: I've sold out your friend to the Germans, and I can't explain why. Not even to myself.

In the end, her mother intervenes.

"For God's sake Solveig," she says. "Stop moping about. You're not a child anymore. Call Gunnar, go fishing. His mother says he's got a permit to be out during curfew, and we could use the extra catch."

She doesn't want to see Gunnar. There are too many things undiscussed between them, too many things she doesn't want to have to tell him.

"Mor..."

"Besides, you've kept the boy waiting for an answer. The least you can do is see him occasionally."

There is that.

"Fine," Solveig says, standing back from the table. "I'll try to phone him, leave a message down at the docks, and then, if I'm to be out on the water all night, I'm going back up to sleep. Call me down when he's here, will you?"

"Herregud," Gunnar says, fighting the swell. "This is much harder in the blackout."

"I know." Solveig looks up at the lantern room, the top of the lighthouse just another dark shape against the midnight dusk. "Bloody Nazis. Lighthouses are there for a reason, you know."

The prow finally swings out and moves off, wake churning under the jetty. The sea is white under the moonlight, picking out the shape of the islands, the line of the mountains rising up out of the mainland. There are no patrol boats in sight, the Germans clearly unafraid of night-time saboteurs. They're smugger than they have any right to be, Solveig thinks, too comfy in land that's not their own.

"You haven't given me an answer yet," Gunnar says eventually, picking at the nail of his thumb, eyes still fixed on the water's swell. He turns to her then, facing away from the rod and line. As his weight shifts the boat rocks from side to side, rolling against the motion of the waves, and her hands fix around the edge of the seat.

"An answer?" Solveig's stomach clenches and churns, and not only from the pitch and press of the sea under the boat.

"It's all right, you know, if it's a no."

In the near-darkness, his voice is steady, controlled, trying hard to convince himself as much as her.

"It's not a no, not outright like that. It's just... Look, Gunnar, you're a friend. A good friend, one of my best. But I always thought you were supposed to feel more than that, for a husband."

"Yes," he says, "I think you are."

There's a hitch to his voice, a tightness, that's either anger or a barely repressed sob. Maybe both, she thinks, watching the set of his jaw under his beard, the sharp, jerky movements of his head.

She feels awkward, and inside the waterproof boot her foot itches. She grinds the heel of her other boot into the offending toes, valuing the pain as a sign at least that the flesh's still alive.

The roar of engines overhead has the lines jumping excitedly in the water. Solveig leans back, trying to measure the shape of the planes against the stars. Big engines, deep. Bombers, she thinks, headed down past Bergen in the darkness across the North Sea to the busy ports of Scotland. Or maybe not that far, their cargo to be discharged over the Sea itself, hitting British Navy transports or smugglers or innocent fishing boats, out trawling for cod.

"Bastards," Gunnar says. He stands, anonymous enough in the night-time sea, sending the boat rocking so fiercely Solveig lets go of her rod with one hand, clings to the side of the boat. He laughs, shaking his fist in the air. "Fucking bastards!"

"Herregud, Gunnar. Sit down - you're frightening all the fish."

He does as she says, turning back to his rod.

"We'll get them when the war's over. Each damned one of them." He flicks the line and his fingers twitch, fifteen feet away, the spinning lure through the water. "Them, and all their bastard friends."

"Yes." Solveig agrees reflexively, before the words dry up in her throat. Rastic, sure. Magnus Junior and his parents, absolutely. But what about Oberleutant Meyer, the farmer's son? He let her go after all, though he couldn't have believed the spiel about her lunch. Solveig swallows, eyes back on the thin shadow of the line.

What about Liv?

"Have 'em worked over first, I would. Same methods they use themselves, down at Grini, over in Poland." Gunnar is turned to her, eyes fixed on her face, unusually intense. It feels like he means something more by his words, something personal, directed just at her. "Then, when they're good and softened, that's when you haul them in front of a court. Anyone they've ever scammed money off, informed on, locked up, stole a job from, the families. Have them all up there, as a jury. And if guilty, which they are fucking are, then - bang – you will be shot. And sign me up for rifle duty."

"Oh, come off it. You're not a killer."

"Aren't I?" He tips his chin, indicating the crate of dead fish. "Anyway, it's no more than you used to say. Nothing was enough for you, enough for them." He sniffs. "You've had a change of heart though, I think."

"I haven't!"

The float on the end of her line bobs indignantly.

"They're still traitors, criminals. I just..."

Gunnar's line twitches. Just a soft bite at first, a nip at the bait. Then a bigger bite, the hook driving through the soft fish palette, and the line sinks suddenly, reel unwinding fast.

"Hey," he says. "Hey hey - big boy here."

Solveig sits silent while he coaxes the cod to the surface, brows concentrated into a frown, the line snaking back and forth across the waves. Perhaps the fish will distract him enough that he'll drop the topic, let her conflicted loyalties go unexposed a while longer. When the fish is alongside the boat, the red length of it just breaking the surface, she's ready with the net. It's too heavy to lift straight up, straining down back towards the safety of the deep. Leaning back, she uses the side of the boat as a pivot point, levering the thrashing fish out of the water. The pole bends and strains under the weight, the net threatening to break.

"Careful," Gunnar grunts, leaning forward to support the fish with both hands, rod wedged between his knees. "Don't break my net on the first decent catch."

Together, they heave it into the bottom of the boat in a splash of salt water. It lies there tangled in the netting, twitching and jumping, searching for cool water over its gills. Solveig fiddles with the handle of the club, wraps her fingers round the handle, feeling the smooth wood beneath her glove.

"Kill it - don't let it just flap about for God's sake," Gunnar says, and she starts, pulled from transfixed contemplation of the unlidded eye. She lifts the club above her, feels the coil of the muscle in her arm, tense with the weight, and brings it down, cracking into the back of the fish's head, feeling the snap of the thin bones travel through the wood.

"Decent size," she says, already lifting it into the waiting crate. "What d'you think? Twenty, twenty five pounds?"

"Something like that."

Gunnar reaches into the bucket, working his hook free from the cod's mouth. He looks over their catch, tails spilling out over the sides of the crates. Besides Gunnar's big cod, they've got a fair selection of smaller fish - cod and ling and pollock.

"Let's call it there," he continues. "Go and check the traps, see what they've caught."

It doesn't take them long to reach the pots, Gunnar manoeuvring so the buoys bob within an easy arm's length of the boat. To distract herself from Gunnar's silent hurt, Solveig leans out, pulling the wet rope up from the sea. The trap feels heavy, dragging in the water. The force of it pulls the boat off an even keel, bringing the water line closer to spilling over.

"Careful," Gunnar grunts at her again, idling the engine.

"Here," she says, "look at this!" It's a lobster, carapace translucent blue in the thin early morning light, easily as long as the span of both her hands, claws snapping angrily in her direction as it's pulled from the water. The thick gloves make her hands clumsy, struggling with the finicky catch of the cage. Gunnar leans over, hands off the tiller, and beckons for Solveig to pass him the trap.

"Let me do it, if you can't." He turns the lobster over. Its belly is covered in black roe, tiny dots of life. "Krauts would pay a fortune for that," he says. "If I were the kind to cosy up to them, you know, be their under-the-counter friend, I'd pay for that boat you were so keen for me to have in no time."

He shrugs, catching her eye, and throws the lobster back into the sea. It disappears beneath the surface fast, sinking back to its hunting grounds.

"It's closed season on lobsters anyway," Solveig says. "They'd sooner arrest you than pay you for it."

Other than the lobster, the traps have only caught four or five decent sized crabs. The others - those too small to make any kind of meal - Gunnar throws back into the water. Not a bad catch, for summer fishing. Her mother will be pleased: even split between the two of them, it's enough to eat well now and salt some as a precaution against the ever-tightening meat rations.

Solveig yawns and stretches, pulling her shoulder blades together until the folded skin between them complains and the bones of her neck click and pop into place.

"Hometime?" She catches Gunnar's hand, sliding his coat cuffs up beyond the face of his watch. Three in the morning - well past her bedtime. "I've got to be awake later. Mother has the priest coming for dinner, in lieu of a service."

It's meant to elicit a sympathetic groan, a roll of the eyes, but when she looks up Gunnar is staring intently at her hand covering his own.

"Look," he says, "I'm not gonna go on about it, but if you ever decide having a husband who's a friend is enough for you, then..."

"I will."

Solveig lets her hand stroke up Gunnar's arm. She owes him that kindness, at least.

"No, you won't," he says, and it's calmly resigned. "We're different people, me and you. And friends won't ever be enough for you."

He clicks his jaw visibly from side to side, delaying the hurt as long as he can.

"Not while there's Liv Sunde in the world, eh?"

It steals the breath from her, and blood rushes to her face. In the half-light, Solveig knows her face is bright red.

"What?"

He shrugs, not even pausing to acknowledge her question.

"I thought her shine would wear off pretty quickly, you know, and you'd realise she's nothing more than a bloody traitor. You should see what the papers say about women like your new friend."

"She's not my friend," Solveig protests weakly. "I don't really know her."

"Please."

He rolls his eyes, digs in his pocket for something. He pulls out a square of folded paper, the same as Karl had passed her at Christmas. Solveig checks the horizon for patrol boats, listens for the sound of approaching motors.

The morning light is strengthening, but she still has to strain her eyes to read the small, smudged article - it seems to have been written by the same sarcastic author that praised the bombing of Kristiansund, and the passing months have done little to ease his bite.

FRIHETEN

16 April 1943

WILDLIFE REPORT: A new invasive bird species - the tyskertøser - has been spotted recently in the streets and cafes of Kristiansund. Often with bright plumage, smartly turned out, these birds use their song to attract mates. Interestingly, as magpies are attracted to silver, these birds are attracted to the smell of bratwurst and sauerkraut. Oh, yes - the drab males of the lands of their birth hold no interest for them anymore. Instead, they long for the corn yellow hair and blue eyes of the master race and all the cigarettes, silk stockings and treason their new beloveds provide.

This all sounds innocent enough, bird-like and natural. After all, birds are simple creatures without the developed morals of humans: they act according to their lusts. Their couplings are not the product of romance, of sweet deep feelings of love, but of their dirty and obscene natures. It is the opinion of expert ornithologists that these birds represent a threat to the health of our native wildlife populations as, given their association, they are likely to carry all kinds of foreign parasites and diseases.

The ordinary Norwegian citizen is advised for now to avoid them: not to feed, befriend or encourage them in any way lest they begin to settle and multiply. Should you find a *tyskertøser* nesting alongside purer native species pretending cuckoo-like to be your family, there is no shame in ejecting them. After all, these are times of food rationing and belt tightening - we are at war, remember, and have little to spare for traitors.

Once peace arrives, country-wide eradication programmes are expected.

"Dirty and obscene? Eradication programmes? I don't think that's very kind," Solveig says primly, handing the newspaper back.

"It's not supposed to be kind. It's supposed to remind you that women who go with Germans are... are..."

He fumbles for the right words.

"*Untermensch*?" Solveig offers, remembering the German just in time. "Subhuman? Like Herr Hitler says, you mean?"

"Don't give me that," Gunnar says. "You know damn well what I mean. And if you're their friend, then you're tarred with the same brush. Anyway, when the war started, it was fun, dreaming up all those games with you. Thinking that we were blowing up trains and sinking boats and sneaking messages across the border. Talking about how we'd do it, how we'd get away with it. But then it all settled down, became the new everyday, and I got over it. There was still fishing to be done, and I thought you'd get over this obsession with being a hero, being resistance and all that, like I did. A few months, I reckoned, and we'd go back to normal, back to how we were before."

Solveig leans forward, reaching out for him. Gunnar pulls back, leaning on the tiller, and the boat bumps sharply down a wave. Solveig lifts from the seat and lands back on the metal, stomach crunching up, stealing her breath and words.

"But you haven't and I get it now. You want adventure, excitement, right? Just being decent, being ordinary's not enough - you've got to have the glory, have people praising you, falling at your feet. You've never been any different."

"You don't make me sound very nice," Solveig says, "for someone who says he loves me. You make me sound like I've rejected you out of pure selfishness."

"Well, maybe that's how it feels. But I guess that's how it is. You want to be Sigurd – off killing dragons and rescuing damsels - rather than plain old Solveig, and that means friends is never going to be enough for you. You want the grand romance, love against the odds, all that shit. It's all dreams with you, all stories and you're too damn dumb to realise the world doesn't work like that."

The boat swings round under her, bumping back alongside the jetty before she has a chance to answer.

"See you, Solveig." Her throat is tight, painfully knotted just below the line of her jaw. She climbs out of the boat and stands looking down, testing the feel of her boots against the wood. He rolls his eyes, as though she'd intended to ignore him. "I'm going out again soon. We've got a permit for some deep-sea stuff - we'll be gone three weeks, a month, something like that."

"I guess I'll see you when you're back, then."

"Just so," he says. "I suppose you will."

Twenty

Her mother is waiting for the catch, already in her apron, filleting knife ready on the counter.

"That didn't look terribly friendly," she says.

"No, not terribly."

"I suppose you turned him down, then?"

Solveig nods.

The bucket is dripping saltwater onto the kitchen floor, slick and shining in the early light. Solveig lifts it, wriggling round corners into the square sink.

"Oh well," her mother says, already moving on, focused on the fish. "There'll be someone else if he isn't for you."

Solveig considers it. She even opens her mouth, lets her lips form the first syllable. Then her mother hands her a fish and a knife, and Solveig remembers the impossibility of it all. They make bacalao again, a traditional dish brought back from Portugal with the akevitt and other delicacies. The tomatoes came dearly, and the olives even more so - an exotic luxury paid for with money and ration stubs and an exchange of stored up bacon.

It's extravagant, Solveig thinks, for an unemployed pastor and his twittering wife. And then, for her sins, she's made to sit in between the guests and is forced to make polite conversation.

"I remember your confirmation clearly," the pastor says after a few mouthfuls. "Quite separately from all the other years."

"Oh, really?"

"Yes. Same year as Magnus. I remember it distinctly. You laughed the whole time. You and... who was it?" He clears his throat as though that will help him remember. "Gerd Iversen?"

"Gerd, yes." Solveig swallows, washes it down with another sip of her water. "It would have been her, yes."

"I remember the two of you, thick as thieves. Laughing the whole day."

Solveig remembers it too, remembers how Aase stood there sour-faced, left out of their delicious new secret.

"You were a delight, a real bright spot."

He smiles at her through a mouthful of fish and sauce, eyes crinkling to slits beneath the smooth fatness of his cheeks.

"Do you speak to her much anymore, Gerd? Still friends?"

"Not really." Solveig shrugs, as though it were just one of those things. "Not much."

"Hmm, shame. I ministered for her wedding not that long ago."

"Yes," Solveig says, and almost chokes on the single syllable.

She takes a sip of her water, forces herself to smile. "I suppose you would have done."

"You didn't come, I think."

"No. I was working in Molde, couldn't get back in time."

Hadn't tried to. Had sat in her room at Aunt Asbjorn's with a half bottle of wine, and drunk herself into an early bed.

"Right," he says. "That's right; I remember now. How time flies." He smiles at the wall, lost in some memory or other. "So, how are you these days, Solveig?" He's an earnest man, and intends to be kind, even to the patchiest of his flock. "I haven't seen much of you lately, since... well..."

Since he went on strike, he means, since he gave up his calling in protest, in solidarity.

"I see your mother, of course. And Bjørghild is still a regular guest. Your father too. But it's been a while since you and I met."

"I've been busy," she says. "With the animals. We've got more ewes this year, and less and less feed to give them."

"Yes."

He nods as though he understands, but he's not a countryman, not really. Grew up in a town down south - Stavanger or Fredrikstad or something like that - where the fields and forests were just a day trip away, a romantic folk memory to indulge in when you had the time and money to do so.

"It is a hard time for everyone, this war. But I really believe that the Lord will help..."

Solveig tunes him out. He'll be quite happy for a chance to deliver a personalised sermon. He's not the author of those angry articles, of the pieces prophesying fire and brimstone for traitors and their friends. It's a shame - if he had been, he could have been useful. Instead, he's just an ordinary, oppressed man, like everyone else.

"Oh! Solveig!" His wife is talking through half a mouth-full of food, waving her knife so vigorously in Solveig's direction she almost trims Far's beard. "Solveig, I meant to say congratulations!"

There's a pause while Solveig swallows her food. She thinks she knows what's coming next, what the islands' gossip mill has churned up.

"Really?" There has to be some attempt at surprise, or the denial will fall flat. She's been managing the way islanders think they know her, know what's best for her, her whole life. "What for?"

Fru Christensen laughs, a false trilling sound all too reminiscent of Else Løvik. It takes Solveig a moment, but of course that's the Magnus - Løvik Junior - the pastor had meant, his nephew. How could she have forgotten the pastor's wife and the Hitler fancier? A sisterly double act, before the war, lynchpins of housewifely society.

"On your engagement, of course, silly girl."

"Oh. But I'm... I'm not engaged."

"No? Your mother said... Gunnar Josøy, wasn't it?"

The pastor's wife looks to Solveig's mother for support, but she has her head bent determinedly to her plate, mouth stopped with fish.

"No." Solveig lifts her bare hand. "Nothing like that."

"But I thought..."

Her husband clears his throat, tries unsubtly to shake his head at his wife.

"Must have been mistaken. Never mind, Solveig, eh? Won't be long, pretty girl like you, I'm sure."

"Oh, well," Solveig says. "I don't know about that."

"Nonsense! You ought to have chaps queueing out the door for you, at your age. If not the Josøy lad, then there'll be someone else." He looks like he's about to start listing people, others from that golden confirmation year. His own nephew maybe, although given the circumstances, that's unlikely.

Solveig cuts him off.

"Maybe. After the war, I mean. When things are settled again."

"Well, don't wait too long," he says. "They won't wait forever. Best not hang about, end up some old spinster, girl like you." He hums contentedly into his drink, apparently satisfied with his handling of the situation.

Later, as the guests leave, Solveig busies herself with the tidying up, stacking the plates and glasses near the sink, removing the tablecloth, shaking the crumbs and fish bones out of the door for the gulls to find. Her mother hovers behind her, following each movement, but not saying anything.

"Mor, what is it?"

Her mother fidgets.

"As the pastor said, Solveig, if not Gunnar, then perhaps someone else?" She drops a copy of the woman's magazine *Alle Kvinner Blad* - no doubt deliberately filched from one of the pastor's daughters - onto the table, a few adverts conspicuously circled. "I'm sure there's lots of nice boys out there, just waiting for you."

"Mor..." Solveig rinses the glasses in warm water, sets them upside down on the rack. "I meant what I said. If I meet someone, maybe after the war. But not right now."

Her mother sniffs, patience wearing thin.

"You're not getting any younger, Solveig, remember that. After all, I was married at your age, and only two years later, a mother."

"Oh, for God's sake, Mor-"

"Solveig!" Her mother raps the table with her knuckles. "Language!"

Solveig rolls her eyes, scrubs intently at a patch of dried gravy on a plate, starts again.

"Oh, for goodness' sake, Mor! I'm twenty-two, not ninety - I don't need marrying off. And certainly not to some pathetic..." Solveig hesitates, then decides to continue with the profanity, drive the point home, "bloody sod advertising in a magazine."

Her mother huffs, squares the line of her shoulders.

"I was only trying to help, Solveig. There's no need to be rude about it, I'm sure."

She moves off, leaving Solveig leaning on the ceramic bottom of the sink, soapy water swirling about her wrists. Solveig sighs, wipes one hand on the seat of her skirt and picks up the magazine from the side.

16. Country boy from Romsdal wants to correspond with a

straightforward, genuine country girl, 20-30. Cinema, good books, homely touch.

24. Hallo. Write to me and you'll get an answer from a boy of 24 years. Straightforward farmer type.

92. Christian boys and girls. A country boy, 24, wants to write to you.

128. Rural boy, 25. Looking to talk to a kind and straightforward rural girl, 18-22. Send a photo. Response promised!

189. Lonely country boy, aged 30, wants correspondence with a straightforward country girl, 20-25. Send a photo, will reply.

273. Young, bright boy, 22 and a half. Interests: books, music, film. Wants to correspond with a straightforward, firm of character Nordmore girl. Photo.

Her mother seems to have a definite idea of Solveig's type. She's got the interest in books right, at least, but the rest of it - those few repeated words - sound like cardboard cut-out replacements for Gunnar, or her father.

Then a thought hits her.

Oh, God - perhaps that's just her mother's type, and she's superimposed her own desires onto Solveig. The thought of her mother having anything as vaguely romantic as a type fills her with horror.

Well, that aside, and despite a twinge of sympathy for poor number 189, Solveig has no intention of writing to any of them. Firstly, life is quite complicated enough. Secondly, you'd have to be pretty desperate to write such an ad, have exhausted all other possibilities. And thirdly?

Thirdly...

Solveig sits heavily on the bench, idly wipes crumbs from the table into her hand.

Thirdly, there are some things it's better to leave not just unsaid but unthought. Even so, she checks the lists on the unlikely chance that one of the terse missives catches her eye. You never know, after all. But no - the others are the same: all straightforward, country boys and girls looking for a pal to write to, maybe meet, maybe marry. Where's the spark of personality, the first hint of attraction that should compel you to write back? It's all romance crushingly dull.

Solveig finishes her cigarette, stubs it out onto the pastor's dirty plate, the ash congealing into the smears of gravy, and thinks about lighting another. There might be cleverly coded Resistance messages, she supposes, in amongst the limp appeals for attention. A book cipher of a kind: look on this page of that issue and find coordinates disguised as ages, instructions hidden in the interests sections. She looks them over again, a finger tracing each line so as not to miss anything, but if there are messages hidden, they're too well disguised for Solveig to spot.

Twenty-One

The Germans love printing, and the islanders receive endless leaflets and pamphlets and propaganda posters. Someone high up must fancy himself a writer, buoyed by complicated turns of phrase and miles of gothic typeface. For all that, it is just another proclamation - strictly forbidden and pain of death and so on.

This time the leaflets announce a new rule: all 'poor' literature must be turned in. From there, it will be catalogued, denounced, burnt. Solveig's first thought, the leaflet crushed roughly in her palm, is of Liv Sunde. How many of her precious books are now unacceptable?

LIST OF FORBIDDEN LITERATURE

THIS PROHIBITION INCLUDES ALL EDITIONS OF THE BOOKS ON THIS LIST, WHETHER THEY CAME OUT IN NORWAY OR IN OTHER COUNTRIES.

AAKERMAN, ALFRED: ALT AV HAM.
AAMOT, PER: UNDER HAKEKORSTYRANNIET
AASEBØE, CARSTEN OLIVER: IDRETT OG KLASSEKAMP; VAKT I GÆVER
AASVESTAD, LARS: KLAR TIL KAMP
AHLBERG, ALF: MARSJEN MOT ROM; TYSKLANDS ÖDESVÄG
ALVING, ROBERT: VEIEN VI GÅR; FOR DAGEN GRYR; ARBEIDERSANGBOK
ARMSTRONG, H.F: MÜNCHEN – OG DEREFTER

The list goes on and on and on... Liv can keep her Hamsun, of course: he's got his nose far enough up Hitler's arse to make even Quisling uncomfortable.

But for the rest?

All the heroes are banned by the Reich, forced to flee across the Atlantic. Surely Liv's English books are even less desirable, higher up the burning list. For another person, an NS member out of necessity, not conviction, the choice is simple.

You keep the books, hide them under the floorboards, bury them in chests in the ground, slip them between the rafters. Then you say, of course, I don't have poor literature in this house, Herr Colonel. I am a good citizen of the Reich.

That's what Solveig would do. Will do, without hesitation, if any of her mother's books are on the list.

Liv, however, is a different proposition. She believes in the new order. Solveig stuffs the pamphlet down into the pocket of her coat; her father will want to see it. She doubts that his ragged bookshelves will come under scrutiny, but still. Worth knowing.

Information, these days, is often all that keeps people alive. The butcher's shop looks, if possible, more dreary than ever. The window display is virtually empty, and the green paint on the sills is peeling. At least her accusations have brought no harm to Olav or his shop. It's been more than a week, almost two, and the Germans have made no move.

Perhaps they won't.

The queue is as long as always. Solveig waits impatiently, hunched over into her coat, trying not to draw anyone's eye, to start any kind of conversation. News of her presence at Liv's will no doubt have spread, for now just rumours, but still as dangerous as the truth. Rumours – as the pastor's wife has reminded her – take root quickly in the islands' thin and salty soil.

And if they knew, if they really knew...

It doesn't do to dwell, she tells herself. Get herself all worked up, give herself a stomach upset, an early-onset heart attack. No - the best thing is just to forget it, push it down beneath more recent layers of memory, and not to let it surface again. With that hanging around her neck – however insubstantial the rumour, however quietly whispered – she doubts Olav will serve her kindly now, even round the front. But if he will, she'll try her luck round the back, persuade Erik to let her have off-cuts again. He knows her, after all, must suspect that the extra meat is going somewhere.

Even apparently passive attendance at one NS meeting changes things, but she needs him to see through that - though God only knows how he's supposed to do it - to intuit her real motivations for joining. She won't ask for much this time, won't push her luck. Just some blood sausage, maybe, or cubed mutton. Something to supplement the fish and stale bread she's been feeding Lars.

The chance of being discovered grows each time, but she has no other choice. Now that he's in the barn, there's even less chance of him fishing or catching game for himself. And - if he wants to survive the war - he certainly won't be butchering her cows like he had her sheep.

When Gunnar's back from the sea, in a few weeks' time, she'll make him take her fishing. He has a permit, one of only a handful not snatched up by various Adolfs and Wilhelms and Josefs, and a few plump crab claws would make a difference to her food reserves.

Across the other side of the road, a group of soldiers stand, idly watching the crowd. They're more relaxed than they used to be, smoking and chatting among themselves. So comfortable, while all around them the islands' rightful inhabitants cower against the shop fronts, backs turned and shoulders hunched as though to ward off blows. Tall among the soldiers, blond hair still flopping boyishly into his eyes, is the farmer's son - Heinrich.

He catches her eye and smiles. The other men catch the look and erupt into laughter, poking him and making crude gestures.

She can imagine what they're saying, the kind of joke that has them in stitches.

Men are the same, whatever language they operate in.

Solveig looks down, away from the soldiers, focusing her gaze steadfastly on the shop front. She doesn't want their attention, their crude admiration. She's not like the women in Gunnar's newspaper reports, desperate to spread her legs and further the great Aryan race's future. But more than that, she can't afford to be spot-lit, picked out from the crowd, not when she's standing here planning her defiance of them.

Clearly, they're not going to read her thoughts - divine her treachery just by looking at her – but perhaps they could read her guilt on her face, in the protective hunch of her shoulders. You're being ridiculous, she chides herself, but diverts her mind anyway.

Dull, mundane farm tasks and to do lists.

Two boys, children of a woman further up the line, are running in and out of the queue, playing hide and seek between the waiting legs and baskets. The youngest, sliding from his brother's grip, barrels full force into an old woman three spaces down from Solveig. Glad to escape the attention of his comrades, Heinrich moves forwards, setting his gun down on the ground, folding down the legs of its stand.

"Hey, boys." At first, the boys hang back, casting furtive glances at their mother, but she's too busy gossiping with her neighbours to keep track of them. "Here, look."

They're only young - six, seven, maybe eight, she's hardly an expert on children - and the lure of the gun is too much to resist. Slowly, as though approaching a wild animal, the boys move in, crouching down on their haunches. Heinrich keeps talking to them, single words at a time. His voice is too low for Solveig to hear if he's speaking to them in Norwegian or German, but it clearly doesn't matter.

The oldest boy, braver now, reaches out to touch the barrel of the gun, encouraged by the soldier's nods and smiles. The boys' jumpers, red and blue in traditional patterns, are bright, obvious, against the smart dullness of the soldier's uniform. Then their attention is drawn skywards. From out at sea there is the low rumble of engines running together. Soon, overhead, three fighters in low formation fly over the islands.

"Messerschmitt 109s," Lieutenant Meyer yells above the noise. "Friedrichs. Look at the wings."

The boys stare upwards, mouths open, hanging on his every word.

"Hey Oberleutnant, have you been up in one?"

"Yes, Obber... Oberl-l-l..." The younger boy - not old enough yet for foreign language lessons at school, though Liv Sunde's NS government friends will no doubt soon change that - stumbles over the foreign word, gives up. "Yes, have you been up?"

Heinrich smiles, slinging the gun over his shoulder.

"Not me," he says. "Boats for the Wehrmacht. Besides, I'm scared of heights."

The boys look at him, suspicious. Their laughter is clear, mocking, and carries easily to the line of waiting women.

"Boys!" Their mother's voice is sharp, shrill. Heads all along the line turn in her direction. "Come here, now!"

Her sons obey her immediately, abandoning the soldier and

his gun without a backwards glance. Heinrich watches them go, half-said words dying abruptly. He starts folding the gun away, evading the gaze of the assembled Norwegians. Then, unerringly, he looks up, locks eyes with Solveig. He's going to speak to me, she thinks, wants to discuss piglets, here in public. He's going to force me into conversation.

She can feel the weight of expectation from people around her. I should never have spoken to him, never responded that first time on the boat.

It let him in, let him think he knows me. It's another thing to blame Liv Sunde for.

If he speaks to me, she thinks, I'm just going to have to ignore him. But Heinrich barely looks at her. He folds the gun stand away neatly, swinging it over his shoulder, drawing himself off the pavement. With the eyes of the crowd on him, he stands up, neatly, heels together. His arm comes up, straight from the shoulder, hand flat and pointing.

"Heil Hitler!"

It seems he's saluting to make a point, as the others behind him salute as well, their arms and voices a synchronised chorus of ritualism. Then, from behind her, comes the sound of boots marching in time.

She turns, shielding her eyes against the low, spring afternoon sun. A small platoon of soldiers is approaching. Whoever they are, the soldiers already stood by the butcher's, straighten their uniforms, stub their cigarettes out beneath their boots. A few more steps, and the figures resolve themselves into recognisable faces.

At their head is Rastic, decked out in the dove grey of the SS.

The medals and decorations on his uniform glint in the sunlight: the Knight's Cross at his throat, the oak leaves on his collar and gold braids on his shoulders. In the light of day, it's even clearer that this is a professional soldier, not some farm boy conscripted away from his cows.

"You don't see him down here much," someone in the line murmurs. The tone of voice says: and you don't want to either.

If Solveig had felt uncomfortable before, forcing her thoughts down, her discomfort is amplified in front of the Colonel. Her stomach twists like she's falling, like the acid in it is boiling. Her secrets, she feels, are too close to the surface, plain to see.

The approaching soldiers barely slow down as they near the front of the queue. The Colonel waits outside, leaning on one leg, while his men enter the shop. His bearing telegraphs his attitude perfectly: long before racial purity, these islanders would come to heel.

There are raised voices, unintelligible shouts of indignation. Then the soldiers reappear, dragging something between them. They move away from the line of customers, and now Solveig can see Olav hanging roughly from their hands, his lip already split and bleeding.

They drag him right past her.

His eyes catch hers, wide and frightened. There's no trace of accusation there, just fearful resignation, as though he had always known she would turn him in.

No, she wants to tell him, the desperate lie rising up her throat. It wasn't me. Believe me, Olav.

She takes a half step forward, fingers reaching for him. The soldier nearest her turns, hand on the butt of his pistol. Behind her, someone closes their fist into her coat, pulls her backwards. She stumbles slightly, back into the queue, lets her hand drop to her side. The hand belongs to one of her mother's friends.

"I have to..." Solveig knocks the older woman's hand from her coat, brushing her away. "I have to stop..."

Fru Nygård shakes her head, her face all thin lips and narrowed eyes.

"Stay still," she hisses, standing up on her toes to reach Solveig's ear. "Stay here, unless you want to go with him to Grini."

When Solveig looks back, Olav is feet away. The soldiers throw him roughly to the ground, just where Heinrich had crouched with the boys. Olav hits the ground hard - hip, shoulder, head - his hands fastened behind his back.

The queue watches for a moment in shocked silence as the Colonel orders his men in, hands and boots flying. Slowly, the mass of islanders changes shape, compresses, tucks round into a fleshy amphitheatre, a circle of witnesses.

"Hang on," calls someone from the crowd, as mild and polite as any German could hope. "Surely you can't just drag people off - they have to have done something first!"

The Colonel turns sharply toward the voice.

"Who said that? Come forward."

For a moment, no-one moves. The crowd stays as one unbroken block of people, solidly protecting their own. The Colonel takes two steps, shakes Olav roughly by the collar, presses his pistol to his head.

"Come forward!"

Finally, after breathless seconds, the people part, like the Red Sea before Moses, to let the speaker through. He's fair and tall, a well-built man. Solveig knows him. A Josøy, she thinks, some cousin or other of Gunnar's. A local lad, an islander and a good Norwegian.

As he steps forward, he reaches up, holds his hat in his hand. A show of deference, perhaps, or ready for when the punches fly. The Colonel looks him up and down, appraising with one sweeping glance.

"This man," he says, pointing to Olav, held roughly in the hands of his men. His words are apparently directed to Gunnar's cousin but are loud enough to carry to all the assembled crowd. "This man is a traitor - to his country, to the Reich, but most of all to you, his neighbours." A suppressed, unsympathetic murmuring starts up among the crowd. "The law-abiding people of these islands only lose by this kind of behaviour. You lose your rations, you lose the trust of the Wehrmacht. And of course, with loss of trust comes loss of privilege - we have more searches, stricter rules."

He speaks well, at least. His Norwegian is accented, but perfectly correct. Practised. He starts and stops; the right sounds drawn out, others cut precisely short. Liv Sunde must be an excellent teacher.

"It is in the interests of all Norwegians to co-operate."

There are other words, Solveig thinks, that would make better replacements. To collaborate, to collude, to betray their friends and neighbours. Yet the discontented murmurs have lost some of their urgency, their conviction.

They're all out for themselves, Solveig thinks. Each person there is stock-taking: I have this radio hidden, that quilt. My sow had twelve piglets, when I declared ten. My son has not joined the Hird, my daughter secures razor blades behind the paperclip on her lapel. Like Solveig herself, some among them likely have even deeper secrets, more dangerous activities to hide.

Like her too, they'll have heard things - awful, barbaric things - whispered tales of brutality. Of torture, slow and painful, of starvation, sly unkind games of give and take, crucifixions. Behind Rastic's carefully social face, behind the polished manners and the effort to speak their language, the crowd fears a monster. So they say nothing. They do nothing. They stand there, silent, while the Colonel talks on. Without looking at Olav or Gunnar's cousin, he gestures to his men.

"*Nehmen Sie beide.*"

Unlike the rest of the speech, these words are quiet, but they are effective. Held between two soldiers, the Josøy boy - his name is Per, Solveig remembers at last – is dragged away towards the Germans' boats. The Colonel waits, expectantly, almost eagerly, to see if his authority will be challenged again. The crowd outnumbers the soldiers three to one, but no-one moves. Solveig watches as Rastic allows himself a little smile. It's the brightest dogs that learn the fastest, she can imagine him saying, and those with the most determined masters.

"Any person coming to the Wehrmacht with further information on traitorous or suspicious activity will be rewarded. In the meantime, the butcher's shall remain closed."

The soldiers pick Olav up from the street, his body hanging

limply from their hands. At a nod from Rastic, they march off, trailing the butcher between them. The last patch of winter snow where he laid is scuffed up, discoloured: specks of red hard to spot against the dark pavement beneath. The crowd stays silent for long moments - shamed, not catching each other's eyes - until a motor starts up in the distance. As though at some signal, the crowd disperses silently, people turning into the wind and away.

Fru Nygård's hand is at Solveig's elbow again.

"Come now," she says, "come away."

Three days after Olav's arrest, the crew of a local fishing boat hit a body floating in the water at Brattvær. The way Gunnar tells the story, as they're crouched round the radio, he didn't fall in by accident.

"It wasn't, wasn't..." Solveig can't bring herself to name him. "Your cousin."

"No." Gunnar shakes his head around a mouthful of smoke, the smell of his tobacco creeping through the darkness. "Damn Krauts are cleverer than that, leaving bodies lying around."

Solveig turns the volume on the radio down.

"Who was it then?"

"Erik Pettersen."

Solveig's not sure she can bring him to mind. A smudge of a face, maybe, but that's all. She barely dares ask.

"Who?"

"You know. Erik, worked for Olav?"

In the darkness of the schoolhouse attic, Solveig forces herself not to flinch. The butcher's boy. She does remember. He'd handed her the mince that first time.

Get along, idiot, he'd said. You'll get me shot.

"Erik, of course."

The story comes more slowly than the judgement. Pettersen was liked, trusted. Except that recently, without any increase in pay, he'd been wearing a new winter coat and new boots. And of course they were all German made.

"Rumour has it," Arne adds, "that when they pulled the body from the water, it was black and blue from bruises."

"Traitor deserved it," Gunnar says flatly. He switches the radio off, the Norwegian broadcast finished for the night. "And more, probably."

Outside, as they go their separate ways, Solveig looks at Gunnar's knuckles and for now they seem unscathed.

Twenty-Two

The seventeenth of May, Norway's national day - one hundred and twenty-nine years since the country's constitution was first signed - slips by officially unnoticed, outwardly unmarked. There are no parades, nobody wears their bunad, a few brave flags flutter at half-mast.

The soldiers grip their rifles a little tighter, eye passers-by a little more suspiciously, ready to punish any who are dare dissent from the true, Germanic spirit. At the butcher's, the shop front is shuttered and closed, but the rest of the shops are open as usual. The queues of women chat amongst themselves, their children scrambling in and out of the forest of legs. The last of the snow has melted or been swept away, any sign of the scuffle, of Olav's blood, gone with it.

People stop and speak to Solveig as always, their voices

cheerful and their cheeks flushed with the wind and with good health. It's as though the scene the week before - Rastic's voice projected carefully into the crowd, Per Josøy's brief defiance, every person weighing their secrets, their caution, against doing the right thing - never happened, quietly erased by a tide of deliberate forgetfulness.

Solveig picks through the grocer's shrunken carrots, their wilting selection of green vegetables. She's too late to get the best, the queues starting while she was still out with the sheep. There'd be more out the back, if she smiled at the right people, made the right noises. She's been doing it for months now, got cleverer at it since that first bumbling purchase of extra mince. She knows what to offer in trade, how much to take.

Or did, at least.

Since Olav's arrest, there's been no smiling, no making the right noises. Her mother hasn't noticed, yet, the few sausages here and there, the way the milk churn empties faster these days, even if the sow has noticed the drop in her sea beet rations.

Lars has never once thanked her.

Solveig pays for her purchases and is about to step down into the road when she looks up. Everybody else in sight is still, even the children, their backs to their shopping, their eyes fixed on a cart coming down the road. There's nothing particularly special about the horse - it's dark coat turning a dirty grey around the eyes and the mouth, head down, steps steady - or about the flat-bedded cart, which on normal days would be used to transport barrels of fish, of grain. It's a working cart, a farm cart and, today, a hearse.

Solveig steps back onto the doorstep of the grocers, into the path of the woman coming out behind her.

"Sorry," Solveig says over her shoulder, "I was just getting out of the way."

The woman hums noncommittally, rustling her shopping basket as she rearranges her purchases. Solveig doesn't recognise the family at the front of the procession, black coated, hair covered in an array of scarves, fedoras and flat caps. A middle-aged couple leads the way, both broad-jawed, heads downcast. The man's greying moustache droops along the line of his jowls, twitches as he sniffs back tears. The woman carries a young girl on one hip, pulls another older, curly-headed daughter along beside her. Behind them a thin gaggle of family follow the cart, fewer than Solveig would expect.

"Who is it?" Solveig whispers to the woman behind her.

"It'll be Erik Pettersen," she says flatly. Solveig turns back to the procession, the flower-laden coffin now directly in front of her. The cart wheels creak and groan with the weight as they bounce over the uneven cobblestones. She feels dizzy,cold, blood rushing to the ends of her fingers and pooling somewhere in her stomach.

The name isn't uncommon – neither Erik nor Pettersen exactly unusual – and for a second Solveig holds onto the forlorn hope that there might be two dead Erik Pettersens.

"Erik, the butcher's boy?"

"The traitor."

The woman taps Solveig on the shoulder, slides her basket between Solveig and the bay shop window, forcing her way out into the street.

"Excuse me, please."

She steps out of the shop doorway, the only moving person in sight other than the funeral cortege. Erik Pettersen's mother looks at her, turns her head to follow the woman's progress down the road. Maybe she expects sympathy, Solveig thinks, maybe she hopes that the other woman will swell the meagre ranks of mourners. Solveig only hopes the woman won't take after Beate Estrem, will keep her spit to herself.

Solveig waits in the shop doorway until long after the Pettersens have disappeared around the corner, long after the creak and groan of the cart has faded from hearing. Slowly, the other people start to move again, shopkeepers serving their queues, counting ration cards conspicuously.

A pair of soldiers patrol the street, each with one hand firmly on the stock of their guns, the metal gleaming in the spring afternoon light. Solveig's eyes sting in the wind. She blinks resolutely, checks her shopping list. She still needs thread, soap.

Lars would like meat too, no doubt. But there's no chance of that. There's no butcher to run the shop, no boy to hand her offcuts through the back door.

Solveig sniffs again, resolutely squashes the memory of those few moments after she'd spoken, Liv pressed up against her side, the shocked murmurings of the Løviks and their cronies, a slow smile curving across the Colonel's face.

It was necessary, she tells herself. She had to gain the trust of the NS somehow. She learnt things from that meeting, important things - she could warn Fru Nygård, for a start - and you don't get something for nothing. And after all it wasn't her who killed Erik, wasn't her who beat him bloody and left him floating in the sea.

Rastic had wanted to confirm her story - maybe that's where Erik got his coat, his shoes.

All new, Gunnar had said, all German made.

She wipes her eyes fiercely - it's just the unseasonal strength of the wind making them well with tears - squares her shoulders and steps out into the street.

Twenty-Three

In the following days, Solveig avoids Liv or any other encounter with the NS.

She avoids the shops too, not caring to see the butcher's empty and raided, Olav's wife or Erik's mother wailing and beating their breasts in the streets. She can't bear to hear Arne run Erik down, can't stand at his scorned graveside and watch people spit at his mother. She can't spend ten minutes with Gunnar without seeing his cousin in the lines of his face, hear that polite defiance in every word he says.

It's all she can think about, all she can see when she closes her eyes.

Olav's face as they dragged him past her, the thud of his body as he hit the ground. She spends long hours out with the sheep, watching the small lambs grow and fill out. A few need extra help, a little boost here and there. She ekes out her sheep pellets, bought at an exorbitant price from the mainland, a handful here and there, half a bucket for the neediest. Their mothers lose weight and gain wool, getting progressively thinner and shabbier. Shearing will be needed soon, she thinks, pulling the thin fibres from the nearest ewe's coat.

Even the sheep provide little distraction.

Solveig watches the horizon, listens for the sound of Nazi boats approaching, the stamp of jackboots on the jetty. Olav will have been questioned, interrogated. He'll have been asked who he supplied, and when, and why. Each suspicious person and act named, written down, recorded.

The resistance papers say that the screams of prisoners can be heard for miles, that innocent men come back with broken fingers and deep burns, and some men never come back at all. Olav is a good man, of course, principled and honest, but Solveig cannot imagine the butcher holding out for long against such methods. It's only a matter of time before he cracks.

How could she have been so stupid?

Like her ewes, she's losing weight, her appetite deserting her.

"Eat up, Solveig," her mother says. "With no butcher, meat'll be tight round here till the pigs are ready."

The mince sticks in Solveig's throat, the thought of Erik's body, battered and bloated, in the water swimming before her tired eyes. At night she wakes from dreams of the Gestapo and the Statspolitiet, heart thumping, lungs heaving.

When she lays back down, she turns to face the other wall. A different position, a different dream, her mother always says.

Dream of something else, she tells herself, something nice.

A fairytale, perhaps - the one about the bear prince, or the dwarf's banquet, or the old man in the cave. Not the Bishop of Bingen. Most of the time, it works.

Some nights, however, the Gestapo return, or mix swirling with thoughts of the resistance fighter in the barn, no longer a friend but an enemy, strong, relentless, unforgiving. Lars's eyes are hot coals burning in the darkness, waiting.

She's avoided the barn now for days, ashamed of her cowardice, sickened by fear. He must be hungry. He must be concerned, wondering why she's disappeared.

The barn, as always, looks uninhabited, but she's felt him watching her, eyes in the shadows. The thought of Olav's confession makes her wary of food reserves, of taking that stored up against harder times.

All food belongs to someone, and someone will be keeping track of it.

There's blood sausage left, easily available, if she can persuade people that she ate the whole thing herself. Her parents are gone for an entire weekend - visiting her aunt and the boys in Kristiansund - but Bjørghild is still at the lighthouse. Arne's out at sea, and she doesn't want to be alone. She's a month off dropping, too fat to make the crossing comfortably, and the baby takes up too much space to leave her with any kind of useful appetite.

No, Solveig's best bet is the sea.

She sets her lines on the other side of the skerry, using the lighthouse to block the view from the barn. Her lines watch out over the sound to the mainland, mountains rising up in the distance. The waters are quiet. No trawlers or cargo ships in sight, the pleasure boats of childhood summers restricted by order of the Colonel. Even patrol boats are at rest, it seems, and the gulls have the sea to themselves.

Everything about the water speaks of wind: the tall poured-glass arches of the waves frozen motionless at the peak before they crash down into frothing, muddy crests, and then into thin scum that lasts only till the next wave, the next crest. The gulls themselves hang lazily on the thermals, drifting up and down on invisible eddies. Then, with great effort, they fly away from shore, diving into the sea after the shoals of fish that taunt them just under the surface. The sun, for the moment, is shining, although dark clouds hover ominously on the horizon.

As long as I catch something before sun down, Solveig thinks, I'll be happy. Enough to salt and to share would be better.

The lines are quiet for a long while. Solveig sits in the sun and watches them, occasionally twitching the floats, stopping them from drifting too far. Fishing is supposed to be mindless, relaxing, something people do empty their minds and escape their worries. The inactivity, however, is like the moments before sleep; the attempt to empty her brain only leaving worry and fear, all her looming disasters crowding, hustling for space.

Once she's caught a few fish - only seven and too small really, but they'll have to do – she wraps up the lines, retreats to the kitchen to gut and clean her catch. She cooks the fish on the stove, boiling them simply with potatoes. Two fish each for her and Bjørghild, three for Lars.

It's not fancy food, not even a stew, but it's enough to keep him alive.

Inside, the barn is dark.

There are windows, but the glass is dirty, opaque, and all their light is soaked up by the bales of hay and straw. She can see the cows, tethered close to the door, see the switch of their tails as they beat away flies. She can see the carefully stacked dairying equipment, the stools, halters and milk churns, far more than they need for the two cows they currently have. Most of it is old, worn, a remnant from her grandfather's time. It ought to be sold, the profits reinvested in new tups, better feed for the sheep.

She cannot see Lars.

"Hello?"

In the back of the barn, someone is moving. For a second she thinks it's Meyer back again - a displaced farm boy finding refuge from his uniform. Worse, it's a real Nazi, and they've found Lars.

A leak, somewhere higher in the chain, spilling a list of names and addresses, radio operators and saboteurs, all the men and women in hiding.

The bowl of fish and potatoes shakes in her hands. She could throw it at him, follow it up with the cutlery, and hope her aim is good enough to escape, run back to the lighthouse and bolt the door. But if the Reich is here, in the barn, then they already know her name, and what she's done.

She steps further into the barn, balances the bowl and spoon on the top of a churn. The stew slops against the side but does not spill. Behind her, the big barn door is still open - she has an escape route. She can see better now, into the dim corners of the barn.

It's not the Germans skulking in her barn - not unless they've got nowhere else to do their press ups and squats.

"Lars? Is that you?"

He jumps up, brushes his hands on his trousers.

"Sorry," he says. "Old army routines, again. It's the first thing they teach you. You've got to keep moving, always, even as a prisoner. Especially as a prisoner. If you're strong, fit, both in muscles and, you know, up top, it'll be harder for them to break you."

In every single one of Bjørghild's romance novels that Solveig had read, there was always a scene where the heroine stumbles upon her love sword-fighting or wrangling horses or some other manly physical pursuit. The exertion makes his shirtless chest rise and fall, exaggerating the depth of muscle under the tanned expanse of glistening skin.

It's supposed to be attractive.

The reality is just slightly different, Solveig thinks: Lars's current state is decidedly unappealing. He stinks, a rank combination of fresh sweat and lived-in dirt, and his hair is wet and lank with grease.

She takes a step back, out of range of the smell.

"I've brought you dinner," she says. She sits with him while he eats, planted firmly on a hay bale, feet planted and knees wide. Hardly ladylike, a scolding voice in her head says, but then she's not one of those romance heroines, swooning or buckling at the knees. She's a soldier in a hidden war, trying to keep the man alive, not seduce him. Lars seems hungry, cleaning the ceramic pattern with all the enthusiasm of a hungry dog, fish barely touching the sides.

"Good to see someone likes my cooking," she says. "My sister just picked at hers."

"Then she's a fool. This is all right."

He pauses eating for a moment to reach behind him, brings out a newspaper, crumpled and folded, but with today's date blazoned across the top.

"Where did you get this?"

Lars just shrugs, flips through the pages until he finds the one he wants.

"Here," he says. "Read this."

SMØLA DAGBLAD

13 MAI 1943

Today, the authorities announced the execution of Hillel Louis Feinsilber, a Jew, for attempting to cross the border from Norway into Sweden. This is the first case of a Norwegian citizen being executed for violating the order forbidding Norwegians from fleeing to Sweden. Hitherto, only those attempting to escape to England have been executed. However, the government in Oslo and in all provincial centres wishes to reiterate its commitment to the law, and advises all those considering this cowardly and traitorous act to expect to face the full extent of punishment for their crime.

"Still keen to get me to Sweden?"

Solveig shakes her head, folds the paper as small as it will go.

"That wasn't ever really a plan," she says. "Just a... just a thought."

The need to talk about the meeting, to tell someone about Olav, what she'd done and why, is overwhelming. It's bubbling up inside her, threatening at the top of her throat. She needs to spill, to break her silence somehow.

Of all the people she could confess to, Lars is the most likely to understand. The resistance are always acting in tight situations, under cover. They know what's its like in that pressure cooker environment, how easy it is to cave, how sometimes you have to give to receive.

"So," she says. "I did something."

Even as she says it, she knows it's not a tone that reassures. She should sound more confident, prouder. After all, despite the outcome, she'd been brave, well meaning, took a risk for King and Country.

"What?"

He looks at her intently, face still and alert. His whole body is tense - she can see corded muscles standing out in his neck, his fingers white and bloodless against the bowl.

"What did you do?"

"It's nothing - nothing bad."

It is, of course, but now she can't bring herself to discuss it, to tell him about Olav. He won't understand - she doesn't understand - he'll despise her.

"It's just that I've been thinking about what Karl said. About learning what they know. So I went to their meeting, made Li... made them let me in."

Something stops her from naming Liv, even by profession.

The schoolhouse is visible from here. On a clear day, someone with good eyes might pick out individual figures, separate the teacher from pupils by height.

"Did you tell them anything? About me?"

The cow in the corner of the barn lows, and Solveig takes it as a warning.

"Of course not," she says. "I wouldn't. Not about you, or anything."

He still hasn't relaxed, sat forward on the edge of the bale, ready to flee or fight. His eyes are wild, staring, his breath coming in controlled bursts. The threat of danger, always felt but never seen, seems very real. His hands around the empty bowl are huge, and she can almost feel them wrapped round her throat, banging her head into the ground.

"I swear."

He doesn't relax.

"I swear! On my life, on the King's life."

"Right."

He nods, leans back on the hay.

"And?"

"And what?"

"And what did you find out?" He rolls his eyes, speaks each word slowly, as though she's an idiot, a child, reporting the outcome of some silly game. She hardens her voice, turns it into something that she imagines more closely resembles the tone a soldier might take at a debriefing: clipped, steady, confident.

"They talked about the conditions in Germany, how things are on the home front there. Locally, they don't know anything. They suspect an old woman of being a busybody."

Lars snorts.

"The pig-shits know more than that, I bet. They're just waiting till they trust you more, till you're good and snared and sharing in their guilt. You'll learn more next time."

"I'm not going back."

"You're not? They'll expect you."

"No - they don't."

Solveig sighs, can't quite meet his eyes.

She's a coward.

She was at the meeting, and she is now. What would he think of her, if he knew that she'd condemned a decent man to the Gestapo's less than tender treatment and got nothing in return?

"They don't?"

He doesn't sound concerned either way. If only she'd been able to hide so well, disguise and dissemble. To an experienced operative like Lars, like Karl, she must look so naïve, so stupid.

"The teacher, the one who runs the meetings, sent me home. She thinks..."

Solveig doesn't know what Liv Sunde thinks. Not really. Liv had let her in, brought her drinks, and then sent her home. She'd saved her from Else's smug attentions, mocked the other woman even, and encouraged her to betray Olav. Liv's opinions on anything are staggeringly unclear, as unreadable to Solveig as one of the foreign books lining the schoolhouse walls.

"She thinks I don't have the guts for it."

He wipes his mouth on his sleeve, contorts his cheeks to move the last morsels of fish out of his teeth.

"Well, she's right, isn't she? You don't."

There isn't much she can say to that. He nods and looks at her, weighing her judgement, before lowering his head to the bowl to clean the last scraps of flavour from her mother's china.

"Thank you," he says, wiping his chin with the back of his hand. "For the food, and the company."

"It's alright," Solveig says. "You must be a bit lonely out here, all on your own."

"The cows aren't particularly delightful conversationalists." He smiles at her wryly, hands the bowl and spoon back. "And their opinions are terrible."

"Really?"

"Oh, absolutely. It's like being back at university amongst all those bloody Commies and queers. Got out of there as soon as I could, joined the army straight up." He grins up at her, unaware of the building nervousness in the pit of her stomach. "I find you tend to win more arguments with a gun in your hands."

"I'll try to come more often." Solveig has to work to keep her voice steady. She backs away, towards the door. "Bring you another book or something, maybe. Try and stop you going cuckoo, you know?"

"My sister would say you're a brick, Solveig," Lars says with a lopsided smile twisting the corners of his mouth. "I bet she'd say you're a real brick."

"You think so?"

She takes it with a sigh, seeing Olav's reproving stare, Erik's mother's tear-stained face, her puffy eyes and threadbare coat, instead of the familiar barn.

"Well, take it from me, I'm really not."

Twenty-Four

The rain is falling in a thick curtain by the time she returns to the lighthouse, fat, heavy droplets with barely any space between them. Her father would be stoic, unflinching, face unaltered. You don't get any wetter if you walk, he says. If you run, you just catch rain that would otherwise hit the ground.

He might be right, but Solveig always runs. Head down, arm raised over her forehead, water collecting in her eyebrows. She's too busy concentrating on the rain, and getting out of it, to see the figure waiting at the lighthouse door. A face looms out of the darkness at her, lank hair and wild eyes like a hell spirit in human form, come to take her hostage, back down to the depths of the sea. Liv pushes her hair back off her face, her usual careful styling sodden and shapeless.

"Christ, Liv. You startled me."

Solveig looks out across the choppy water, toward the schoolhouse. The waves are tall enough that she'd think twice before setting out, let alone Liv, who says her stomach deserts her on millponds.

"Did you row yourself over here?"

Liv nods, holding a bottle out like a peace offering.

"I heard you were on your own tonight. I thought you could use the company." She offers a half smile, blinking to clear her eyes of rain.

"That was nice of you," Solveig says stupidly, her heart only now slowing from the run and the fright. "But I'm not on my own - Bjørghild's here."

A flash of lightning, somewhere behind the lighthouse, lights up the world, too bright for their night-darkened vision.

One second.

Two seconds.

Three.

Thunder.

"Are you going to let me in?"

Liv has to shout over the crashing. It wakes Solveig to action, pushing the door open and hurrying Liv inside. In the porch they shake and stamp, wringing the water from their hair in rivulets onto the floor. As they shiver their way into the kitchen to stand by the stove, the old dog creaks to his feet, greeting Liv with a friendly sniff and a thump of his tail.

Solveig feeds the burner another few logs, stoking the fire. She leaves the metal door open, letting the heat blast straight out into the room. Liv shuffles close, almost touching her hands to the flame. Their clothes steam gently, sending clouds of vapour up to hang on the ceiling.

Their chatter disturbs Bjørghild, who comes rolling out of the small living room and into the kitchen.

"Who is it?"

Her smiles falters briefly at the sight of Liv Sunde standing in her parents' kitchen. Just a flicker, but noticeable.

"Liv came to keep me company," Solveig holds up the bottle, "and she brought payment."

"You didn't tell me you had guests coming."

Solveig takes a breath, swallows her quick comeback. She can't blow up at Bjørghild, not in front of Liv, and not with the baby due any day. That's the last thing she wants to disturb her evening, now that Liv is here.

So she shrugs, in that particular trouble-at-school movement. Late again, Miss Eik? No homework, late homework, failed tests, fighting again? Shrug, just one shoulder, truculently flinching. Liv - who no doubt charmed her teachers into forgiveness, a few eyelash flutters, a few well-timed tears - comes to her aid.

"In Solveig's defence, she didn't know. And I didn't mean to impose on you. I just saw your parents heading for the ferry this afternoon, you see, and I pictured her - wrongly, as it turns out - all alone out here. I didn't plan on the weather being as bad as this. Just thought I'd pop over, have a drink and, well, a chat, that kind of thing, and then go home."

Very bad planning, Solveig thinks to herself, smirking down at the ridged black top of the burner, considering the forecasts all over the radio and papers.

"I see." Despite herself, Bjørghild makes a renewed effort at a smile. "Well, Miss Sunde, now you're here, you must stay the night, as you say. It's too bad to try to get back to school in this weather, for someone as inexperienced on the water as you. Solveig, you'll sort things out, will you? I'm in no state to be trudging up and down the stairs in search of towels and nightclothes and so on."

Solveig rolls her eyes as she watches her sister heave herself back into the living room. Bjørghild isn't ill, after all - is only suffering as women have always suffered - she's being overdramatic, chafing at needing a chaperone overnight; it wouldn't kill her to offer a towel, a hand with their wet things.

"She seemed pleased to see me," Liv says quietly once the door has shut behind Bjørghild. "Was it something I said?"

Solveig shifts to face Liv, holding the side of her shirt out away from her body. The cotton is cold and clinging and she waves it over the burner, sending warm gusts of air between the fabric and her skin, causing it to pucker and pimple.

"No, don't mind her - she's a grumpy so-and-so when she wants to be. Which, you know, is all the time."

"It's a shame." Liv turns around, warming the backs of her legs. The semicircle of steps brings her closer to Solveig. Her voice is low, intimate, full of promises. "I thought I'd have you all to myself."

Solveig shivers, and she tells herself it's from where Liv's arm is pressing her clothes closer to her body. She doesn't move away, but stays where she is, eyes fixed determinedly on the wall over Liv's shoulder.

"You did?"

They still haven't discussed the night of the other storm. Solveig would say there hasn't been a chance, but there has. They've had months to talk like adults, privately, carefully, and yet it has taken another storm for Liv to find her courage.

"It's not that I don't... that I wouldn't..."

Liv seems uncharacteristically nervous, inarticulate. I make her nervous, Solveig thinks. Or Bjørghild's presence makes her nervous, when she's with me. It might mean nothing, of course, might be wholly unconnected - a product of the storm, of Bjørghild's ever-present disapproval. But anyway, Solveig lets her hand drift upwards, lets her fingertips just touch Liv's forearm, exert the smallest pressure.

"I know," she says.

Liv smiles and her own hand drifts to Solveig's hip, rests there for a moment. Something tentative passes between them, something more honest than anything they've shared before. Another time, Solveig thinks, another place, and it might have been easier between them, been smooth sailing and calm seas. If they hadn't been resistance and collaborator, islander and incoming tide, they could have just been Solveig and Liv.

Solveig moves into the small living room, throws another few logs onto the fire and brings out the glasses. Liv pours yet more of her generous doubles, passes one to Solveig and holds another out to her sister.

"Brandy wine," Liv says, holding her glass high in salute. "Fru Dahl? Bjørghild?"

Bjørghild shakes her head, raises both hands as a refusal.

"No, thank you."

"She doesn't," Solveig says, intercepting the drink, "not ever. Doesn't think it's proper, do you?"

She pours Bjørghild's portion into her own glass, handing back the empty tumbler. They sit on the window seat under a blanket, legs tucked underneath them, feet touching, watching the lightning.

"Listen to that," Liv says, peering through the curtains. "A lion in the wilderness, according to Ibsen."

"He said a lot of things, apparently." Bjørghild sounds less than impressed with the great playwright, hitches her arms up over the bump, settles into a defensive, arms-crossed position. Liv, though, is unfazed.

"He did, and lots of it right. I read a lot of Ibsen at university."

For the first time in the evening, Bjørghild leans forward in her chair, interested in what their guest has to say.

"Really? Were you in Oslo?"

And then they're off. So where did you go? What did you read? Oh, of course, his essays were always beastly. Did you know this girl, what was her name?, or Fru Sorensen's son from over the way?

They laugh in odd places, at things that don't quite make sense. Solveig sits back, determined to ignore them as long as they're talking in ways she can't contribute to. Liv came to see her, after all, not her sister. She's barely thought it before Liv's focus swings round to her again, Solveig's attention drawn by a soft hand on her ankle.

"And you, Solveig?"

"Oh, no. Not me. I left at fifteen, like normal people." She frowns at her sister's barely suppressed snort. "I'm not fanciful, like you educated lot. You and Bjørghild. I'm practical, you know; I do things, rather than thinking about them."

She puts venom in the words, and that shuts Bjørghild up, breaks the flow of conversation. Bjørghild heaves herself to her feet and makes her excuses. The kitchen door slams in the wind as she makes her way outside to the privy.

"Your sister's a surprise," Liv says, lighting another cigarette. "I hadn't realised she was so well read."

Solveig huffs, biting back a retort: I'll leave you two alone then, shall I?

"She is," she says instead. "Kinda seems a shame, doesn't it, seems a waste - all that studying, all that time reading and debating and all that, just to give it up two years later to start popping out babies, when I-"

Solveig sniffs, takes another sip of her drink.

Liv shakes her head, reaches out to place her hand back on Solveig's ankle. Without Bjørghild watching, she runs her thumb back and forward across the soft skin, and the touch sends sparks through Solveig, jittering and dancing along her nerves.

"I don't think it's a waste. No education is ever wasted - you just find other uses for it." Liv pauses, considers the drink in her glass. "So you didn't fancy staying on at school, being a teacher too?"

"Me?" Solveig shrugs. "Oh, well - there's only space for one clever girl in the family, right?" She knows she sounds bitter. She doesn't say it out loud so often – there's nothing to be gained by rehashing old ground – but she is. She still is. "So I left school at fifteen, soon as I could. Got a job as a bookkeeper - I'm not stupid – for the wool merchant, over on the mainland."

"But you came back." Liv's face behind her cigarette is considering, eyes and mouth scrunched with thought. "It didn't work out?"

It's said sympathetically, as though she can guess the reasons. At the fall out with Gerd, with Asbjørn, at the complicated web of family ties and responsibilities that meant the islands, the sheep, owned Solveig as much as she owned them. It's important, somehow, to make the point. She's not Bjørghild, sure, she doesn't have shelves and shelves of books. But she's not just some straightforward country girl.

"Far broke his leg, thigh bone, and couldn't work, couldn't walk for weeks. We let the land on the bigger islands - got rid of the crops, you know - but Mor knows nothing about sheep, except for looking after the odd orphan lamb, and Bjørghild's worse than useless with practical stuff. So, it had to be me."

It was always going to be her, eventually.

"You didn't go back once he was better?"

Solveig's reminded again that Liv's a city girl: there's no point raking over things that can't be fixed, wasting her evening explaining how expectations were portioned out in the absence of a brother and the face of ten unbroken farming generations. Liv just doesn't see the high fences that have surrounded Solveig all her life - the privilege and restrictions of farm life that guarantee her a home, an income, that tie her down, root her so firmly to the thin, salted soil.

"It took ages, till he was back to before and my job had gone. Then the Germans came and... Well, I didn't. Probably won't now."

"Do you miss it?"

Solveig shakes her head.

"It was a job, you know, good money. But you had to sit on this stool all day, in silence, and it was all *Frøken* this and *Fru* that. Told me off for sneezing, once. And Molde was fun, but I lived with my great-aunt who was ancient, and it wasn't exciting. And it wasn't home."

"You were in Molde too?"

"For four years, thirty-five to thirty-nine."

Liv taps the end of her cigarette, knocking ash into the saucer beside her. She takes another drag, watching Solveig's face.

"I wish I'd known you then," she says. "We'd have been friends, I think."

Aren't we friends now?, Solveig wants to say. Didn't you come to see me, in the middle of a storm, with the lighthouse dark, because we're friends? But something in Liv's tone suggests that's not all she meant, and the implication stills Solveig's tongue, forces a self-conscious grin onto her face.

The front door bangs again, and Solveig can hear the sound of Bjørghild's wet boots on the kitchen tiles. Liv leans back, spell broken. She stubs out her cigarette and stands to fill their glasses again. At Bjørghild's return, the conversation turns to lighter things. The weather, the price and quality of bread. The music of Richard Tauber, and wasn't he a dish? Ancient now, of course, but in older photos, well.

A casual outsider listening in would never know they were

Occupied, never know how deep the divisions run. Of course, it can't last for long. Like a compass twisted in hand but pulled back north, eventually they can no longer avoid the one topic Solveig least wants to discuss.

Twenty-Five

"There's a difference, all right," Solveig says, "between things you do to get by, and holding the door for the buggers on their way in."

Liv looks at her over her cigarette, idly picking loose strands of tobacco from her lip.

"That's a bit rich, isn't it," she says, "coming from you."

Without looking, Solveig can feel Bjørghild's frown, can feel the question mounting. She sits up, shifting along the window to the very edge, as far from Liv as she can get. Every muscle in her body is tense, coiled up, ready for action. Any second, any moment now, her secret will be out.

Liv sits back, lounging against the upright of the window, takes a steady sip of her drink.

"Well, anyway, everybody does what they have to. It's not that

I don't love Norway, Solveig, quite the opposite. This - the Germans, the NS - is the best option. The safest option."

She grinds out the butt of her cigarette into her saucer, smoke rising from the crushed paper in a thick curl.

"That's patriotism, Solveig, self-sacrificial. Not this half-baked idea of us versus them. If we don't act, and soon, there won't be a Norway left to love."

She's so self-righteous, so irritatingly smug. Right now, she's like nothing more than the kid that gets knocked over in the playground, the one that has you just itching to punch out. The kind of kid that had Solveig in trouble all through childhood.

It's the same self-satisfied smile that got Solveig in trouble last time, that had her leaning across the gap and crashing her lips to Liv's. Everything in her wants to do the same now, push Liv back against the back of the chair and wipe the look from her face, have her panting and compliant.

Liv's eyes dart across to meet hers, and Solveig knows she's thinking it too, is doing it deliberately.

"No?"

Like Solveig, Bjørghild has just never known when to back down, when to disagree silently. Her presence is like a splash of cold water, and Solveig would love nothing more than to manhandle her out of the room, up the stairs to bed, out of earshot.

"No," Liv repeats. "You'd like to still cling to this idea that Norway will be free and democratic after the war - no matter who wins - that we will somehow slip backwards into the old, familiar ways. You've got to be joking, right? That old world is gone,

Solveig, done and dusted. If we lose, Russia is waiting."

"That's not..." Bjørghild looks to Solveig for support. But Solveig is focused on her own thoughts, lost in a fantasy that's just out of reach. If only Bjørghild hadn't been here, if only Arne hadn't been away. That was Liv's plan. It must have been. Pay a social visit, get trapped by the storm, rinse and repeat.

In the meantime, Liv has started up again.

"It is. Just look at Finland. You think the Germans are bad - they're well organised, well supplied, they're polite." She snorts with theatrical derision. "They're an occupying army to envy."

"Have you heard them, though? Women can't do this, natives can't do that. And, God, Poles and Jews and the rest might as well just give up now, really be *Untermenschen*. Liv, think of the books they've burnt. You, surely, can't be in favour of that."

"Of course not. Not actual books, at least." She shrugs. "But there's so much dross published these days and some of it is so bad it ought to be criminal."

It's clearly a joke, but Solveig and Bjørghild remain silent, left out of the mirth. Something about it, however, rings false. Perhaps it's the manic stretch of her mouth, the unnaturally lengthened laugh. It gives Solveig a burst of confidence. They're in private here, no Rastic or Else Løvik to impress, to convince of ideological loyalty. If she is ever going to persuade Liv to crack her NS facade, to confess her real loyalties, this is the time to do it.

Solveig sets her drinks down, turns to face Liv. Her breath sticks in her throat for a second - the moment is rapidly fading. She swallows, takes another lungful of air.

"But you don't really believe in it. National Socialism, I mean, do you? In the philosophy of it all?" Solveig leans in, as intense and serious as she can be. "A girl - a woman - like you, you see through that claptrap, right?"

"Well, I do. I am."

"You can't be. I don't believe it."

Liv's voice is bitter and thin. The space beneath her eyes gleams in the low light, wet and heavy with suppressed tears. She wipes at the skin there, smearing the wetness across her cheeks, polishing them to an oily sheen.

Bjørghild looks up, hands stilled in her lap.

"Solveig," she says in warning.

"You should listen to your sister," Liv says, standing up and stretching, rolling her neck. "You could probably be shot for talking like that."

She leans against the chimney breast, looks down at the iron stove for a silent moment.

"This is what I'm telling you, Solveig. For someone like me, like you, it's better to be the Devil's right hand than in his path. Do you understand?" It was the closest she had ever come to acknowledging what lay between, what drew them together, and bound them despite their differences. "And besides, at the moment they're the only thing standing between Norway and being crushed under the Red Army from now till Ragnarok."

All the tension between them earlier has gone, replaced with simple awkwardness and the simmering edge of an argument. Solveig hadn't meant to upset her, to push her too far. She just wanted to know the truth, and maybe now she did. Self-preservation on two fronts – personal and philosophical.

Self-preservation has never been something Solveig has paid much attention to. Even so, she thinks it's time to change the subject. She casts about for some safe topic, something to break the argument up.

"How's your brother these days? Have you heard from him recently?"

Once again, the change is too clunky, too obvious to flow.

Liv fixes her with an inscrutable look.

"No," she says, slowly. "I haven't."

Solveig could kick herself: another conversation dead end. She looks around for something to latch onto, something uncontroversial to say.

"Oh, well. D'you fancy warming up the piano, having a song or two?"

Bjørghild shifts, hands splayed wide over her belly, and breaks her diplomatic silence.

"Not for me, you've worn me out, all this philosophising. I'm going to bed." She rocks in the chair, levering herself up on the arms, groaning through stiff knees and swollen ankles. "Night, you two. And try to stay friends until the morning."

Her words are hectoring, given out in her real school-teacher voice, as though she were scolding ten-year-olds for a fistfight. The tone must work, for though Solveig finished school years ago, and Liv herself is a teacher - both grown-up, responsible - when the door shuts, they burst into laughter like children suddenly unchaperoned.

"Look," Solveig says, unable to bear the thought of going to bed at odds with Liv, "I didn't mean to fall out. It was just a..."

"Just a debate, I know. I was at university, remember?" Liv leans back, letting an unlit cigarette dangle loosely from her fingers. "What's more than that, I did philosophy, not science. Besides, these days, I'm used to being disagreed with, though perhaps you aren't."

"No, not so much. As you say, moral high ground and all." Solveig pauses. "Thank you," she says, "for not saying anything about, you know."

"The other night."

They watch each other with flat expressions, the knowledge of Solveig's betrayal dangling.

"Yes, that."

Liv sits back down, tucking her legs up under the blanket again. Her hair is escaping in thin tendrils from its pins, snaking darkly across the seat's lace cover. Her stockinged-covered knees press lightly against Solveig's.

Solveig realises, considers it for a moment, that she could reach out and touch them, run her hand up the plane of her leg, the rough imperfections of her skin catching at the fibres. She smiles lazily, bringing her brandy wine to her mouth. She leans down, glass dangling from her fingers. It hits the floor again with a solid thump, the liquid crashing in waves against the side. Liv reaches down too and wipes spilt drops up with her sleeve, hair falling forwards, catching the light.

"Liv," Solveig says, and stops.

The alcohol burns in the pit of her stomach, warm and hot and encouraging. Liv turns her head and waits, eyebrows raised, for the words to continue.

"Thanks for coming over tonight."

What Solveig says is not at all what she means. The truth is harder than she thought. After all, as Liv surely would tell her, a word is a terrible thing when it suddenly says out loud what the heart has secretly harboured.

Liv smiles as though she understands and reaches out to tuck Solveig's own stray hair behind her ear.

"Solveig," she says, as her nails linger across her cheek, "you're very welcome."

She hadn't split, hadn't confessed to her resistance leanings, and perhaps she never would. Perhaps Solveig had the truth of it now – that fear of the alternative, not love for the Führer, was what lay behind her alliances. That seems somehow more understandable to Solveig, more palatable. Maybe, with an understanding of that truth, they could come to some kind of peaceful middle ground. Be just Solveig and Liv.

She won't bring it up, obviously, won't discuss it head on. That only lead to arguments, to unkindness and anger. But it seems to Solveig that Liv's feelings are always in the silences, in the spaces between words. And so, in a heady rush of bravery, Solveig kisses her.

Liv's mouth is cool, soft. Just the press of their lips, the warmth of her skin under her palms. Liv tastes of akevitt and tobacco, and it makes Solveig feel giddier than all the alcohol in her father's cupboard. God, what have they been doing all this time? All that time they spent out on the islands, just talking.

Gunnar's fumbling, inexperienced kisses will never match up, she thinks. Not even with time, and practice, and a lot more skill.

The width and set of his jaw, his bristles, the tented front of his trousers. They felt wrong - unnatural, to pervert a phrase - and far below the beauty of having Liv so close.

Liv's hands move to rest lightly on her shoulders, sitting up, Solveig following close behind, unwilling to lose contact, breathing hard, their hands still in place, and staring at each other. Solveig finds she does not want to meet her gaze, eyes staying firmly trained on the floor beneath her feet. That's it, Solveig thinks, between us now. We both know, and we both understand.

Liv slips through her grip, and she stands, brushing down the front of her skirt as she does so. The firelight casts an uneven glow across her cheeks, flashing off her necklace. There's a colour to her cheeks Solveig tries to believe is emotion, excitement, the same that runs like acid under her own skin. She stands too, hand half reaching for Liv, willing her to stay, to look in her direction. Instead, the corners of her mouth are briefly forced upwards, her eyes still focused on the fire.

"It's time for bed, I think," Liv says, voice tight and controlled.

Unlike the larger lighthouses nearby, there's not room enough on the skerry for a separate keeper's house. So the bedrooms are all up the inside, a room to each floor. Behind her, the teacher bumps and bangs her overnight bag against the paint, huffing at the climb. Not quite to the top, but close enough.

On summer nights, the top room is light, airy, with views over the strait all the way to Kristiansund. In the summer, visitors fight each other for it, but in the winter you can see your breath, shiver still under three or four blankets, and in a storm Solveig wouldn't wish it on Adolf himself. So really, there isn't a choice. Either Liv has the living room, or she bunks with Solveig, in her sister's old place.

Solveig nods, ready to speak, but Liv is gone, the door to the room shutting firmly behind her. Solveig waits, hearing the teacher's footsteps climb up the staircase into silence. Without her, and as the fire dims and sputters without new logs to consume, the room is growing chilly. Enough to make her sit on her hands, curl her feet under her knees and shiver. Solveig thinks about going up after Liv, chasing her down, forcing a resolution. She hasn't misread the situation, she can't have done.

After all, someone like Liv Sunde would know herself, surely. All those books, all those stories. There must be enough romance between their pages to give away the look of love when she sees it. Then again, perhaps she does know and is better than Solveig at avoiding it, at running away from those dark corners in her mind. Gerd was good at that: driven by the fear of being exposed, found out, cast out, Gerd had become practised at pretending.

In the end, good enough to convince even herself.

Solveig could manage it, couldn't draw a firm enough line between her private and public selves. Within limits, of course. The ones you read about in the paper, the targets of the fiercest whispers - men - seem to more than accept, to embrace it fervently, arms wide open.

Well, that's why they're in the paper, of course.

Perhaps it works in the cities, is necessary, where the press of people lends a false sense of anonymity. There, someone in search of others would have to work that much harder, be that much more obvious, even if such a thing is neither desirable nor safe.

She waits for what seems a lifetime, but can barely be ten minutes. Long enough for the fire to die down in the grate. The lighthouse is quiet, despite the occasional rush of wind outside and the crack of rain falling on the windows. She lets the dog out for one last sniff, although he doesn't go far from the door. At the first crack of lightning, he runs back in, tail between his legs, and heads straight for his bed. Solveig stands, indecisively, in the kitchen.

Their glasses need washing up, and the counter could use a wipe down. All the endless domestic chores her mother would like her to help with. They're still there, waiting, and suddenly rather tempting.

Outside, the storm still rages.

Inside, the lighthouse is deliberately silent.

The dog opens one eye and watches her, reproachfully. With nothing else left to do downstairs, Solveig climbs slowly up to bed. At the staircase window she pauses, watching the waves break against the rock, white foam highlighted by the lightning. Beyond the rocks, out into the sound, there's only darkness.

The light should be on, she thinks.

The room is lit periodically by the flashes, highlighting the shape of Liv under the blankets. Solveig slides in next to her, waits for her to turn, reach out, hand stretching in the darkness, as she had before.

"Liv," she says into the space between them. "Are you awake?"

She reaches out tentatively, her hand on Liv's shoulder.

Liv says nothing, doesn't move, her breath even and steady. Solveig pulls, just a gentle pressure, an encouragement, not a demand.

"Liv," she says again.

Liv rolls to face her, close enough to kiss. She places a hand on Solveig's hip, caresses lightly through the thin material of her nightgown.

Solveig shifts closer, brushes a stray tendril of hair back behind Liv's ear. She traces the outline of her ear with her fingertips, trails down the taut line of her neck.

"This is a terrible idea," Liv says against her mouth. "You know that, don't you?"

Solveig says nothing, waits for her to decide. Liv's hand on her hip is still tracing abstract patterns back and forth, up to her side, down along the length of her thigh. Her hand is getting braver, bolder, slipping to lightly scratch the back of Solveig's leg, the curve of her bottom.

Solveig's breathing is getting ragged, and she can feel Liv's, too, is coming in short bursts, hot against her face. Then Liv's lips are on her, insistent. The hand on her hip pulls her firmly into Liv, crashing their bodies together. She slots her leg between Liv's own, drags the nightgown up to her waist, presses high with her knee. Liv is wet already, sliding skin against skin, and her sharp intake of breath is all that Solveig needs. She pulls Liv's leg further across her own, grinds against her.

Their gasps and moans are covered by the crash of the sea outside, and Solveig feels the bright, sharp peak of her orgasm approaching quickly. Her stomach muscles tighten with each thrust of her hips, each slide of Liv against her. She's lost in the moment now, letting her body take the lead.

There's no fantasy, no imaginings that can compare to the feel of having Liv in her arms, in her bed. The way Liv is moving, craving more pressure, more friction, the urgent press of her mouth, has the tension in Solveig's muscles ratcheting with each movement.

Liv's breath is shuddering, her movements suddenly losing their pattern, and she stiffens, clamping down on Solveig's thigh. Her quiet moan pulls an answer from Solveig's throat too, and the tension in her stomach bursts free, running down the back of her legs. Solveig comes too, muffles herself in Liv's hair, shaking and curling together.

Liv rolls onto her back, one arm still resting against Solveig's face, tender and gentle, the other flung up, the back of her hand pressing against her eyes. She's panting hard.

"I told myself," she says, "that I wouldn't do this."

"But you came to me," Solveig says, still loose limbed and basking, still pulsing from the inside out. "You sought me out. Isn't this what you wanted?"

"I did come to you," Liv repeats, "because I apparently can't help myself."

Solveig grins back at her.

"What you're saying," she says, slowly, reaching out for Liv's hand and fondling it between her own, "is that I'm irresistible."

Liv turns her head to look at her, face suddenly illuminated by the lightning. She rolls her eyes, but she's smiling, and Solveig leans over to kiss her again, slow and soft.

"You're not irresistible," Liv says, but her body gives the lie to her words. She's already moving again, reaching out in the darkness, grinding against the thigh still trapped between her own.

Liv's hands are in her hair, and Solveig opens her mouth to let Liv kiss her.

"Tell me," Solveig says, "what you want."

Liv sits up, pulls her nightgown over her shoulders, flings it somewhere into the corner of the room. In the flashes, Liv's skin shines pale, luminous, and she pulls Solveig towards her. Solveig pushes herself up, holds herself above Liv. Her hair falls around her shoulders like a curtain, making the dark room darker.

Liv's hands are on her shoulders, kneading and pressing.

"Please," she says.

Solveig resists the press of Liv's hands, takes her time. She kisses her way down the sharp line of her jaw, follows the column of her throat, her collarbones. Then she moves lower, down over the soft blonde down on Liv's stomach, pressing kisses to the sharp jut of her hipbones. Liv groans and shifts, opening her legs wider to give Solveig better access. She starts slowly, focusing on the bundle of nerves, too gentle to draw Liv to a peak. Teasing. Her world narrows to the smooth glide of her mouth against Liv, the scratch of Liv's nails against her back.

Liv's hand is fisted in Solveig's hair, twisted against the roots, pulling with every swipe of her tongue, pressing her closer.

"Fuck," Liv breathes - the first profanity Solveig has ever heard from her. "Fuck, Solveig. I'm going to…"

Solveig pushes in, reaching, feeling for the rough patch of nerves, and twists. Liv's second orgasm is stronger but still quiet, barely a gasp escaping her mouth. Solveig stills her fingers but keeps running her tongue in long, slow movements through Liv's wetness, wringing every pulse and tremor she can from her. Eventually, Liv tugs gently upwards on Solveig's hair, detangles her hand from its death grip.

"Come up here," she says.

They lie there together, not speaking, Solveig's head on Liv's shoulder, arm around her waist, leg flung over her hips. The crashing waves against the rocks are loud outside, broken only by the occasional fizz of lightning.

It's exactly as Solveig had dreamed it - the hero of the Resistance and the double agent, worn out from fighting, taking comfort in each other's bodies.

"You're not going to run in the morning, are you?"

Liv's voice is thick with sleep, and her arm tightens briefly around Solveig's shoulders. Solveig shakes her head, content to lie in Liv's arms all night. There's nothing that could make her move from this spot until morning.

Twenty-Six

The room is quiet and dark. Liv still sleeps soundly next to her, but Solveig is awake.

More thunder?

She waits, listening; the lighthouse's creaks, knocks and noises seeming different, unfamiliar in the storm. Liv's breaths have lengthened into light snores. Her arm is thrown up above her head, just resting on her hair. The way her arm falls leaves her neck exposed; clear to see, even in the room's twilight, is a rounded darkening bruise.

The sight makes Solveig swallow and her heart clench. She shifts, feeling the slick movement of her thighs. Stop it, idiot, she tells herself. Don't get greedy. What you had together, what you did, it's only the start of something new. Something as secret and exciting as hiding Lars, and slightly less likely to get you shot. But push her now, and she'll run.

Solveig turns onto her side and throws her own arm over her ear, blocking out the sound. There isn't another crash, nothing more to shatter sleep, and she lets herself drift off again under the warmth of the covers. It's only moments - long, heavy moments of undisturbed sleep – before she's awake again, eyes staring unseeingly into the dark.

"Solveig, Solveig. Wake up."

Liv is shaking her, hands hard and panicked through the layer of blankets. As Solveig adjusts to the darkness, Liv's face blooms towards her, pale and wide eyed, hair for once out of place and wild.

"Just a dream," Solveig says, her mouth thick and dry. "Darling, it's all right, really."

She tries to turn over, press the other cheek into her warmed pillow, but Liv's hands are relentless.

"No - listen."

From outside, the sounds of the storm. Wind, creaks. The same as earlier, the same as always.

"I can't hear..."

She stops. On the wind, a sound like a draug's triumph. It sends shivers along her arms, pulling every hair upright. The scream of twisted metal, shearing bolts. The sound lighthouse keepers fear the most: a boat on the rocks.

All her life, they've prepared for it, watched for it. All her life, the light has burned at the top of the tower, keeping countless sailors from the rocks. And now the light is out.

She's up and out of bed, pulling Liv with her. Sleep is

banished, her legs powered by long years of inherited worry. Up past the cold third bedroom, past windows looking out to sea, over the islands. The light has been out for months, the solid metal door unused. The metal handle is cold to the touch and stiff to turn. Solveig throws her weight behind it, putting every hard-earned muscle into the movement, banging the door with her shoulder. Liv is too close, in the way of Solveig's charge and teetering on the top stair.

"Move back," Solveig says.

She hits the door again and again. The door gives way and Solveig falls through into the empty light room. She gags on the musty smell and her shoulder aches, but there's no time to stop. The space is filled with the bulk of the lantern, unused now for almost three years. A thick film of dust covers the lenses.

"Watch the floor," Solveig says, "don't trip."

Ignoring her, Liv rushes forwards towards the viewing deck. The force of the storm rips the door to the viewing platform from her hand, slamming it into the light room's glass walls.

Liv staggers back into the light room, her hands on the doorframe. Solveig reaches to steady her, but Liv is moving forward again, pulling herself hand over hand along the railing. The metal grating is slippery underfoot, and the wind threatens to push them over and onto the rocks below. It's hard to see anything - the rain is falling sideways, swept into a thick curtain by the wind. The sea too is storm-lashed, the spray sent high above the rocks.

Liv moves round the platform, searching the darkness for the source of the noise. Solveig follows her, stops where she's leaning over the railing. She can't see anything. Then: "There!"

Solveig follows the line of Liv's outstretched arm, squinting into the rain; a dark shape down on the edge of the water. She moves back into the light room for a moment to pull the station's telescope from the wall. Through the lens she can see men, lit by lightning and dim running lights that poke above the water. Some stand apparently on the surface of the water, feet covered by crashing waves, while others climb from a hole in the sea.

"Oh, fucking Christ."

"What?" Liv is pressed against her, trying to fit her own eye to the telescope. "What is it?"

"A U-boat," Solveig says, "scuttled on the rocks."

At that moment, the man climbing from the conning tower looks up, catches the glint of the telescope. To Solveig, it seems he points straight at her, more concerned by the lighthouse than the sea, and shouts something indistinct, words lost in the storm. Others turn too, and the men reverse their frantic escape, piling back into the submarine, disappearing hand over hand into the sea.

"What's going on?" Liv is impatient, too close to Solveig, her hand pressing at the small of Solveig's back. Liv's breaths are warm huffs on her cheeks as she tries to share the single-lensed view. Solveig leans away and Liv takes the telescope, presses it to her own eye. At that moment, the thunder dips, and the sailors' cries rise above the crashing waves.

"Maschinengewehr!"

It means nothing to Solveig, but Liv stumbles back, hand at her throat.

"What?" Solveig's hand is on her arm, urging. "What is it?"

"Machine gun, they said. They think we're the enemy."

We are, Solveig thinks. I am.

"Oh god. They'll all drown, and it'll be my fault."

Liv takes two steps back into the light room, stopped by Solveig's hand on her sleeve.

"What are you doing? You can't go out in that!"

"They're drowning, Solveig!" She gestures wildly, arm outflung. "If it was Gunnar? Or Arne?"

Then Liv is off before Solveig can agree. Over the crash of the storm, Solveig can hear men shouting in fear.

"Liv! Wait!"

Solveig hurtles after Liv down the spiral stairs, steadied by the press of hands on either wall, skipping steps, jumping into the hallway. The noise of the storm and the door has woken Bjørghild, and as they hurtle past her tired, drawn face appears at the door to her parents' bedroom.

"What is it?"

Solveig doesn't stop, can't stop, with Liv pulling away down the stairs.

"Boat," she shouts over her shoulder, "boat, on the rocks."

At the door, Solveig catches Liv's arm, holding the fabric tight enough that the seams start to creak and unravel. Liv wrenches her arm free, pulls on her coat, closing it over the front of her nightshirt. Solveig's father's boots are large enough just to slip her feet into unlaced, and Liv is out of the door before Solveig even gets one shoe on.

Solveig pauses for a moment to light the storm lantern, then follows her out into the night.

The rain is more like sleet, heavy, cold, stinging at any patch of bare skin, worming its way under their coats, into their boots, falling sideways into their path. In the wet the rocks are black against the dark night, drops and gullies and outcroppings all hidden, treacherous even to those on land. The bladderwrack and kelps slide underfoot, the strands catching at their heels.

Even Solveig, who scrambled over the rocks towards the sea every day of long childhood summers, slips on her way down. Liv, in borrowed boots, stumbles ahead, the storm lantern swinging wild shadows at their feet.

As they get closer, Solveig can see the scale of the damage - the hole in the hull is visible now, a gaping darkness edged by sea foam. She peers down, trying to work out what it hit, before reeling back.

There are bodies in the water.

Solveig holds the lantern above her head, throwing light down onto the rocks. There are bodies there too - not moving, at odd angles. As she watches, another man gets swept through the hole in the side of the U-boat. He swims for a moment, his face a pale speck against the rushing water, then disappears.

Liv is shouting in German, voice straining to be heard above the sea. There's only one word Solveig recognises, and she too repeats it, over and over.

"Freunde! We are Freunde!"

Some of the men standing on the deck stop and listen to Liv's shouting. But they issue no orders, and no-one reappears from the hatch.

Liv is pleading with them, talking too rapidly, running words together in her haste to convince them of her sincerity. Liv shrugs off her coat, letting it fall to the rocks. Underneath, her nightshirt is already soaked through.

"What are you doing? Liv, what are you doing?"

But Liv ignores her.

Then she grinds her boot into the rock, working out a safe foothold, and jumps. It's stupid, foolish, and Solveig knows before Liv hits mid-stride that she won't make it. The boat is too far, the wind too strong. She moves forward herself, ready to pull the teacher from the water, carry her with broken bones back up to the house.

The laws of physics, not that Solveig knows them, dictate that Liv Sunde will not - cannot - make it.

And then she does.

She's pulled over the railing by the sailors, clothes plastered to her skin, hair whipping across her face. Solveig can't hear the conversation on deck over the crash on the waves and the stinging whip of the wind. Liv seems to be pleading, pointing, motioning to the darkened lighthouse.

"We are *Freunde*," Solveig calls again, uselessly. Water runs down her face, across her lips, into her eyes. She tries brushing it away, but her fingers are numb and clumsy, and the rain keeps falling.

Out in the sound she watches lightning hit the sea, the world hanging frozen for a moment in the brilliant glare. At that moment, the U-boat heaves and shudders against the rocks. Waves crash high over the stern, which dips and drops.

Solveig can feel as much as hear the scream of tearing metal.

On the deck, Liv and the officers stumble, shaken by the size of the movement of the boat below them. The officer in the peaked cap looks for a moment towards Solveig, towards the darkened lighthouse, and nods. He shouts to the men next to him, and they move to call down the u-boat's hatch.

Men start to re-emerge onto the deck, unbalanced by the force of the waves and wind, stumbling along the deck. They move together, extending a walkway from the boat to the island.

Liv is first over the walkway, forced forward by the officer behind her. A few more scurry across, and they try to hold the walkway steady. But it's designed for calm jetties, ports, not jagged rocks and slips from their grasp. One man curses, clutching his hand to his chest. The man that followed Liv ashore shouts something to the men still on the deck, beckoning them to jump, to reverse Liv's leap into the darkness.

In moments, the rocks around Solveig are covered in German sailors, some unmoving, some crying out in pain, stumbling towards the house and barn.

Twenty-Seven

The old dog is barking solidly, stood stiff legged in the doorway, hackles raised and teeth bared. A crowd of sailors are starting to form a ring around the doorway, held at bay by the dog. As Solveig pushes her way through, some are trying to coax it out, speaking to it in sing-song voices.

Somewhere to the side, an authoritative voice cuts above the others.

"*Nur shießen sie.*"

Solveig ignores them all, elbowing her way through the crowd. For the moment, she doesn't care about offending the soldiers. This is her house, her dog.

It wasn't her idea to shut the light off.

She takes the dog by his collar and shuts him in the small living room. He snarls through the door, protecting his house against these invaders.

"I know, old lad," she says through the wood, as though he might understand. "Don't worry about it. They won't be here long."

In the kitchen, the first men are already inside, warming themselves by the cooling stove. They have colonised the long table, slumped on the benches. Several have blood oozing through their uniform, down their faces, between their fingers. One man, stretched out on the tabletop, moans.

Their coats have been dumped in a wet pool on her mother's counters, dripping onto the flagged floor. Men are still coming in, pushing their way through the door, layering up against the wall. Solveig opens the connecting door to the hallway and through to the large living room.

"In there," she says, pointing. They don't move, bunching together in the kitchen. "In there!"

Pointedly, Solveig pulls the mop from the cupboard and makes a show of attacking the growing puddle on the doorstep. She sighs once, then again, louder. Still, none of the men passing her stop, or even look her way.

She's invisible to them, just another half-human facilitating their rise to glory and power. She's just a woman mopping when they've escaped the grip of the northern seas.

The noise of the sailors' conversation suddenly swells, then dies. From the hallway, Solveig can hear her sister's voice, upbraiding the men blocking her path.

"What do you think you're doing? Get off! Get out!"

Solveig leaves the mop propped against the wall and pushes

her way through the kitchen. Her sister is stood on the bottom step, hand wrapped protectively across her stomach.

"Bjørghild," Solveig says, one hand on the banister. "Go back upstairs. I'll be up to explain soon."

"It better be good, Solveig." She raises her voice above the men's chatter. "And you lot - *Halt die Fresse!*"

A few unmanly titters break out, schoolboys shamed by their teacher. The laughter dies at Bjørghild's withering look. With a sharply directed "I'll be waiting," she climbs the stairs again, each step laboured and slow.

The last of them are still coming in, Liv on the arm of an officer. Another shiver runs down Solveig's sides and arms. Despite the nearness of the men, she cannot help herself. Under her coat, Liv's nightdress is soaked through, virtually transparent. The stiff peaks of her nipples are dark and obvious against the thin fabric. Her hair is only roughly tied back, her face clear of make-up for the night. No wonder Rastic - and every other German on the islands, it seems - likes her.

"*Kapitän,*" Liv says, "this is Miss Eik, our hostess."

He smiles at her and clicks his heels. Solveig waits for the introduction to be reversed, for Liv to explain to her exactly who these people are. It's not forthcoming. Instead, Liv guides her new escort and the other officers to the long kitchen table.

"Solveig," she says as she settles herself on the bench, "why don't you get us a drink?"

Really, it shouldn't sting as much as it does - she's known who Liv Sunde is, right from the first - but then there are things you know, and things you feel. And right now, Solveig can still feel the ghostly press of Liv's lips, of her fingers.

"Up from Bergen to Trondheim," the captain is saying, "and damned lucky not to be further out when we wrecked."

Another Dane, by his accent. Bloody volunteers. Gunnar's right - they all ought to be shot, and give her the first rifle. She hates him more than she'd hate a German, for his obvious politics, for his presence in her house, for the way Liv is staring at him wide eyed.

Solveig smiles thinly at the group of officers.

She leans down behind Liv, her mouth flush with her ear. At this distance she can smell the salt on Liv's skin, the traces of her perfume.

"I need to speak to you now."

"Gentlemen, please excuse us for one moment," Liv says, getting up. Solveig pulls her into the cold room, shutting the door behind them. Their boots stick icily to the floor, each step cracking. Liv stands close to her, trails her hands up Solveig's arms, smoothing the skin under her palms.

Solveig thought she'd be running by now, making sure the captain thought she had only eyes for him, but Liv doesn't say anything, doesn't complain at being roughly removed from his company.

She strokes Solveig's hair behind her ear, presses a soft kiss to the corner of her jaw. It's more tender, more fond, than Solveig could have expected.

"What is it?" Liv asks gently. "What do you need?"

"They can't stay here." Solveig leans into Liv's hand against her cheeks, sighs. "I can't have them here."

"Where are they going to stay, then?" Liv is still gentle, still touching her, but her voice has sharpened. "The submarine at the bottom of the sea? Or perhaps you'll row them to the mainland."

Solveig clenches her jaw, feeling the muscles pull tight under her cheeks, and looks away. She's going for stoic, resigned, but it's cold and she shivers, the hairs on her arms standing on end.

"You're no less Norwegian because you help these men, Solveig."

"Even if I wanted to, there's forty of them. Where are they all going to fit?"

The house is built for six, eight at a push, and the topmost room is still colder than is comfortable. Putting only the officers up would mean filling every bed, and that means...

"They can't sleep in my bed!"

"Your parents', then."

That is even worse.

"My father would never forgive me."

Liv sighs, shakes her head.

"Fine. And, of course, the barn isn't an option either..."

For a few terrifying moments, Solveig is certain she's having a heart attack; at least some form of near-death experience while her heart flutters irregularly, full of long pauses and frantic thumps. Her chest feels hollow, empty of all air.

There isn't any legitimate excuse she can give.

There's a trick to lying, a knack. Things need to be detailed, but not so you lose track of what you've said. They need to be believable, but most of all, you can't defend them too strongly.

She rubs her eyes, doesn't have to pretend to be thinking.

"No, not the barn. It's not insulated, and there's nothing to sleep on."

That, at least, is not a lie.

She sighs, leans back against the pantry shelves.

"Look, how many officers are there? Senior ones. They can..." She wipes her hand across her face. "God, they can have my room and the upper. The others will have to take the downstairs rooms."

"And us?"

"You and I, and the dog, I suppose, will share with Bjørghild. She won't like it, but we've got no choice, have we?"

Of all the smiles in the world at that moment, Liv's is surely the brightest.

"You're a good woman, Solveig Eik. A brick, as they say."

Solveig does not feel like a good woman.

Oh yes, Solveig Eik, people will say. Not quite a collaborator, but there was that business, with the meeting and then the night of the storm. And after that, well. I could never quite trust her the same again. A shame, too: she had all the makings of an underground leader. I was so sure, but I suppose people do what they have to get by.

If only it weren't for damned Lars, she thinks. Then they'd have the barn, and I'd sleep easy. Instead, it's going to be a long night for all.

Despite the adrenaline dredged up with the submarine, Solveig drifts into a fitful sleep, cold saltwater closing around her dreams. She's startled awake by a high keening that seems to set the windows shaking.

"Solveig." In the dark, Liv's voice is high up, as though she is standing right over her. Solveig blinks, eyes fuzzy and blurred with lack of sleep. "Solveig – wake up."

"Hmm?" Her mouth feels dry, cooling saliva stiffening the corner of her mouth. "Not another wreck, is it?"

"No-"

The noise comes again, more distinguishable now as a human noise. It rattles through the floorboards and echoes snaking up the stairs, filling the lighthouse. The wind can make strange noises sometimes, deceptive, like a child's crying or a woman's scream, but this isn't one of them. Which means... it takes a moment for the importance to sink through to Solveig's sleep-addled brain.

Bjørghild.

The baby.

Solveig gets up from her makeshift bed, reaching for the kerosene lamp and Liv.

"Come on," she says, fiddling with the switch. It flares into life and Solveig winces, waits for her eyes to adjust to the sudden light. When she can see again, she makes her way to the bed, patting the mattress as she goes. The bed, the sheets, are soaked.

"You've not wet yourself, have you?"

It's an attempt at a joke – a poor one, Solveig admits – but Bjørghild is calling out in pain, twisting and arching off the mattress.

"Solveig." It's more a moan than any actual words. "Get the doctor. It's coming."

"I'll call him, don't worry. You, you just stay here."

There's an outbreak of half-hysterical sniggers and catcalls – *schöne Nachthemd, heh*? – as she pushes her way through the least wounded German sailors in the kitchen towards the telephone. One officer follows her, standing awkwardly behind her as she presses the handset to her ear.

"*Fräulein?*" he says, just as the doctor answers.

"Doctor Berntsen? Solveig Eik, my sister-"

The windows rattle as the wind gusts, whistling past the lighthouse. The line crackles, breaking up in the storm.

"Who?"

"Solveig Eik, out at the lighthouse."

She waits, this time, for the doctor to hum his acknowledgement.

"My sister Bjørghild needs you - she's gone into labour."

"At the lighthouse, you say?" The line hisses again. "In this weather? My dear girl, quite impossible."

"Please, doctor." She's not above pleading down the phone line. "You have to come - I'll row out and get you. I don't mind the storm."

"Miss Eik, I'm sorry. But if you just stay on the -"

The line goes dead. Solveig hangs up, redials. Still nothing.

"Fräulein," the officer says again. "*Ist alles in Ordnung?*"

"Nein," she snaps, crashing the telephone back into its cradle. "It's not all bloody *in Ordnung*."

He lingers at her shoulder, blocking her way back to the stairs. Bjørghild calls out again, the sound dimming the hubbub of German chatter, and over the officer's shoulder Solveig can see Liv appear at the top of the stairs, her expression drawn and worried.

"Get out of my way," Solveig says, pushing the German to the side, elbowing her way through the crowd of men.

"So?" Liv is hovering at Bjørghild's door.

"He's not coming." Solveig sighs.

"With this storm, can you blame him?" Liv shrugs. "But you're ready for this? Of course you are – that's why she stayed here with you."

It's a fair assumption, but Solveig's not ready for this, not at all. Solveig shakes her head.

"No - I was just a convenient babysitter. Someone to cook and clean up, to shove her up the stairs at the end of the day."

"All that lambing experience," Liv says, "surely you should be fine with this."

"It's not exactly the same, is it? Especially not when it's my sister's..." She waggles her hand disgustedly toward the area between her own legs. "I'm hardly going to put my hand up there, am I?"

Twenty-Eight

Bjørghild, in between contractions, looks up hopefully at Solveig's return.

"Is he coming?"

"I spoke to him. The line was bad, but I got through. Bjørghild, that storm is not slowing down, and we've had one wreck already."

"Is he coming or not?"

Solveig bites her lip, leans back from the bed.

"No. He's not."

The doctor's not coming and, in the circumstances, a shepherd's about as close as they're going to get. What had she seen in films, heard when her mother's friends had discussed these things? Hot water, the midwives were always calling for hot water. And towels too, presumably for the water and the blood.

Time to take charge, Solveig, she tells herself.

"Liv, go downstairs. Grab hot water, towels, anything else you think useful. And, God, grab me a drink."

Solveig turns to her sister, currently curled on top of the mattress, hugging knees to her chest.

"Do you feel very terrible?"

"Not very," Bjørghild says, her teeth clamped together against another wave of contraction. She falls back, breathing in irregular huffs and sharp intakes, twisting her hands into the sheets. "I'm being brave, see."

Being a regular martyr, Solveig thinks, determined to get the most mileage out of the situation. It's unkind, she knows. It's not Bjørghild's fault the baby is coming in the middle of a storm, with their parents gone and no chance of external help. Bjørghild sits up, grabbing for her sister's shoulder.

"Need to move around," she snaps. "Walk me round the room."

They stumble round the room together, Bjørghild in a semi-trance state, her hands clasped round Solveig's upper arms in a mockery of a dance. Occasionally Bjørghild stops, leaning all her weight on Solveig, overcome with the force of the contraction. There was something, Solveig thinks, remembering kitchen-counter conversations she'd tried to block out, about the timing, how close together they came. She probably ought to be measuring the dilation down there, though Solveig would sooner be damned than look.

It's quite one thing to attend to the cows, or to the ewes, even to assist the sow with her twelfth piglet of the day - and quite another to put your hand, your face, down in the shaven, gaping place between your sister's legs.

Bjørghild comes to, shakes her head to clear the fog and lays back down on the bed.

"Herregud, Solveig. What were you doing? Making me walk round like that? I should be lying down - safer that way."

Solveig lets out a breath and runs a hand across her forehead, feeling the sweat cool against her palm. Next to her, Bjørghild moans again, writhing under the sheets.

"Where the hell is Liv with that water?"

If only birthing babies were like birthing lambs. She'd be of some use, then. Or if Bjørghild had gone over to the mainland with their parents, where roads not water separated her from the doctor. Then the responsibility would be their mother's, their aunt's, the hospital's: people experienced in the art of babies. In the old sagas, birthing women would have rooms full of attendant women, instead of just a sister, the sister's almost-maybe - even now, Solveig's mind stumbles over the word, skirts round the actuality of naming Liv her lover - and a house of enemy soldiers.

"Solveig." Liv, leaning round the door, beckons Solveig over. Next to her, out of sight from the room, is one of the u-boatmen. Stood behind him, two steps down, is another man, gold Hippocratic snakes twirling on both their shoulder boards. "This is Stabsarzt Schulde – the submarine's doctor - and his assistant."

"What about the men downstairs, the injured?" Solveig thinks of Gone With the Wind - read in a hurry at Gerd's insistence, preparation for a visit to the pictures - thinks of Melanie moaning for pages and pages, and the doctor who refuses to come, who won't leave his men for a dammed baby.

"What about them?"

Liv squares her jaw, stares hard at the side of the doctor's head.

"He'll make time for your sister."

"*Ich werde deine Schwester helfen,*" says the officer gently, and Solveig understands despite the language.

Solveig looks between them, at the steaming bowl of water clutched in the younger man's hands. They've found soap, too, and her mother's best towels. It's all been worked out, all been arranged.

"She won't like it."

"Who cares what she's going to like? Care what's going to help her, what's going to help the baby."

Outside, a rumble of thunder rattles the windows.

"Solveig?" Bjørghild's voice is weak, mewling, forced out in between breaths. "Where are you? Come back in. Please, come back!"

Her words are followed almost immediately by a full cry as another contraction hits. The doctor, muttering to himself, thrusts his cap at his assistant, pushes past Solveig, and crosses the room to Bjørghild's side. He picks up her wrist, feeling for the pulse.

"Get him away from me!" Bjørghild lashes out, the side of her hand connecting with the doctor's wrist. "I don't want any of them anywhere near me."

"The doctor is here to help," Liv says. "He saw me getting the water and the towels, and wouldn't take no for an answer."

"He says he's the submarine's doctor," Solveig adds.

"And what does that mean?" In a quiet moment between contractions, Bjørghild finds it in her to laugh. "Is he qualified?"

The German says something, taps the thick and thin gold bars on his sleeves, on his shoulders, makes rocking motions with his arms.

"He was a doctor for ten years," Liv translates, "before he joined the Navy. His wife has four children, and he delivered them all."

Bjørghild looks to Solveig, unspeaking, eyes wide and mouth scrunched. Her hand tightens, the squeeze punctuation to her silent question. Solveig knows that look, understands its meaning.

Sister, it says, I trust you. Sister, tell me what to do.

Despite the cold, Bjørghild's face is flushed, red tendrils snaking down across her neck and shoulders. All the pale, white places - the hollow of her throat, the dip behind her collar bones – are filled with deep crimson, the skin under her silver crucifix the last to go. At the end of the bed, poking out from under the cover, her feet are blue tinged.

Solveig resists the urge to look at Liv - just a flicker of the eyes, that's all she'd need – to pass on the responsibility of the decision. But Bjørghild is asking her, trusting her, and so Solveig keeps her eyes resolutely on Bjørghild's face and nods, her edges of her mouth compressed into a grim smile.

"All right," she says, "help her."

The doctor smiles reassuringly, but his assistant seems embarrassed, his eyes focused on the floor, the walls, the side table - anywhere, in fact, other than the bed.

"Es wird gut werden," the doctor says, rolling up his sleeves.

"Du kan es schaffen, ich verspreche."

Liv translates easily; it's the usual platitudes. The doctor washes his hands in soap and water, drying them on the clean towel his assistant holds out. Then he leans forward, hands on Bjørghild's thighs, and Solveig looks away. On the wall at the foot of the bed is her mother's crucifix, nailed at just the right height for wooden Jesus on his cross to have an uninterrupted view where Solveig won't look.

"So," she says lightheartedly to her sister. "You'll be dining off this story for years."

Bjørghild grimaces, another wave of pain causing her to clamp her hand around Solveig's. As the contraction subsides, the doctor says something to Liv, asking her to translate. When he's finished, Liv draws Solveig aside by the elbow, pulling her out into the staircase.

"Schulde says the baby is... I don't know the word. It's coming the wrong way round, buttocks first."

"Breech," Solveig says. "The word is breech."

"He also says that there can be complications, when a baby comes like this. That there is a chance..."

"No." She shakes her head, a stab of her finger emphasising her words. "No. She'll be fine. They'll both be fine."

For the second time that night, Solveig is faced with delivering bad news to her sister.

"Bjørghild," she says, "the baby's coming backwards. Breech. It's fine - lambs come like it all the time."

She doesn't say: and they're often dead, or malformed, or so weak they die within days. That's sheep, after all, not humans.

"I know," Bjørghild says. "I know it's breech; Dr Berntsen told me weeks ago. Said we'd deal with it, said he'd deal with it."

"You'll both be fine, all right? It might take the baby a little while to get going, afterwards, but the doctor..."

Solveig sighs, cocks her head.

"This doctor knows what he's doing. And he says you'll be fine." Bjørghild nods weakly, her head falling back onto the pillows.

"I wish Mor were here."

"I know."

"Or Arne." Bjørghild's teeth are gritted, her voice strained with the effort of pushing. "Even Far."

"I know."

Anyone - a stranger off the street frankly would be better. But they haven't got a stranger. It's Solveig stuck here, and Bjørghild doesn't need to know how thoroughly unprepared Solveig is to see this through.

"You and me though, we'll be fine, won't we? And surprise them all when they get back."

Bjørghild's moaning is hard to listen to: her insistence she was going to die, the baby was going to die, that the storm and the war were to blame for it all. And where was Arne - the cause of all this trouble - and her mother? Why had they left her here with these Kraut bastards and only bloody Solveig for comfort?

She pauses in between contractions, head thrown back onto the pillow, panting, sweat running down into her eyes.

"Who's he?" she asks, nodding her chin toward the door. A sailor, jacket missing, the leg of his trousers torn and crusted with dried blood, stands waiting for the doctor's attention.

When the doctor looks up, he fires off some rapid German, gesturing back down the stairs.

Schulde nods, stands up away from his patient.

"*Ich komme,*" he says. "*Ich komme.*"

Even Bjørghild, in the midst of her labour, can translate that.

"Don't you dare let him go, Solveig!"

Her university accent has slipped, and she sounds like Solveig again, like their parents. Solveig reaches for him, tries to summon any scrap of schoolgirl German that would help, but the doctor steps back out of her reach.

"Doctor, please," Solveig says. "You're needed here."

Schulde is washing his hands, cleaning the evidence of his volunteer duty off his hands before heading back to what he thinks really matters.

"Please," Solveig says again. "Please."

He doesn't pause in his ablutions, using the damp cloth to clean his own forehead. He reaches for his jacket.

"Your assistant," Liv says. "Send him."

It's a good choice – he's not cut out, it seems, for women's medicine, blushing and fluttering at every sight and sound, averting his eyes from his patient. Schulde hesitates, but he lets Solveig push the young man out of the door and close it behind him.

After that, Liv becomes Schulde's right hand, fetching and carrying, translating words of encouragement to both sisters, opening the window when the room becomes too close with sweat. Solveig's hand, clasped in Bjørghild's, feels bruised and swollen from the pressure.

"Here." Liv's beside her, holding out a glass. "Aqua vitae to the midwife," she says. "Drink it, you'll feel better."

With her free hand, Solveig takes it, throws it back and wipes her mouth on her shoulder; it's becoming something of a habit around Liv Sunde.

"Got any more?"

"Sorry - that was the last of the bottle."

"You've had enough anyway," Bjørghild grunts. "You're turning into a terrible drunk these days."

It's just like her, Solveig thinks - puritanical even in the teeth of a long labour.

"I'm not drunk," she says, squeezing Bjørghild's feet in an attempt to get the blood moving in them again. They're freezing, victims to the night air. "I am going to get you some socks though - I'll be right back."

She stands up, wiping her hands on the front of her dressing gown.

"Don't be long." Bjørghild lowers her voice to a whisper, dropping further into a broad rural accent to disguise her words from Liv and Schulde at the end of the bed. "Don't leave me alone with them for long."

Solveig stops at the door, watching as the doctor directs her sister to move onto all fours, her head hanging down between her shoulders. The stairs and the room above are dark, all the kerosene lamps requisitioned by the doctor and his countrymen. Solveig had expected the stairwell to be full of noise - laughing, singing, a tune hammered out on her mother's piano – but the lighthouse is quiet except for the wind outside and the occasional disembodied moan.

There are men in her room – wounded, those not well enough to stay downstairs and too heavy to be dragged further up the twisting staircase. They've been laid on the bed, on the floor, and without a light she treads on one, stumbles across his ankles.

"Herregud," she says. "I'm so sorry."

The man doesn't reply, doesn't make any kind of noise – not a moan, not a whimper. He doesn't move, either, his leg flopping with the blow, the toe of his boot making a dull thump against her rug.

"*Tot*," says a voice in the darkness. She can't tell which man it's from. "*Er ist tot.*"

Four steps up from the door to Bjørghild's room, she stops, resting her back against the cool wall, letting the socks hang by her leg. She stays there with her eyes closed for long moments, gathering the courage to go back into her parents' room.

Bjørghild's moans echo up the stairwell, merging with the crash of the thunder outside and the noise of the men below. Footsteps on the stairs stop directly in front of her, and Solveig doesn't need to open her eyes to know who it is.

"Hey you," Liv says, her hand stroking Solveig's cheek. "Chin up. We're almost there."

Solveig sighs, head leaning against the brickwork behind her. There's a disturbance of air in front of her, twisting eddies of movement, and Solveig is unsurprised to feel Liv's lips warm and soft against her temple. Liv's hand is on her shoulder, curling into the small hairs at the nape of her neck.

She stays there much longer than she should, much longer than propriety or simple comfort calls for.

When Solveig opens her eyes again, Liv is gone, and the stairwell is dark. By the time she gets back to the room, the baby's feet are already out, dangling down between Bjørghild's legs. The doctor isn't pulling, doesn't appear to be doing anything to actually help, just watching the slow progress.

He says something indistinct to Liv, who nods and rubs Bjørghild's back in a practised motion.

"Almost there, he says. Just a few more pushes, and the baby will be here."

Bjørghild nods weakly, leaning back on the heels of her hands. Solveig takes a damp cloth from Liv and wipes the sweat from Bjørghild's hairline, the drool from her mouth.

The rest doesn't take long at all, by comparison.

"A daughter," Solveig says. "It's a girl."

"Just the afterbirth now," Liv translates for the doctor. "He says it shouldn't take long."

"There," Solveig says. "Easy now – you've done the hard bit."

The doctor towels the baby's face carefully, removing the usual fluids and blood. At the touch of the rough flannel, it gives a choking little cry, arms and legs waving angrily above the swaddling.

"Ei ei ei," he croons, his face close to hers. "*Nicht weinen, mein Mädel.*"

Slowly, the baby calms down, its cries fading into snuffling hiccups. The doctor turns to Liv, says something, before handing the baby over to Solveig, taking time to correct her hold, to run a caressing finger across the baby's crumpled face. "Stabsarzt Schulde says, before he goes – what's her name?"

"I don't know." Bjørghild doesn't seem up to explaining, her skin pallid, eyes heavy with exhaustion.

"I don't think they've decided," Solveig says.

She looks down at the baby in her arms, smoothing back the dark crown of hair from her forehead. Babies are ugly and helpless compared to piglets or lambs, born underdeveloped, but the little frowning face is endearing, and Solveig can't help her smile.

"Something Norwegian," Bjørghild manages. "Kristine, Hanna."

"Oh, Bjørghild, no! They're all old lady names."

Solveig moves forward, propping up the baby's head for her sister to get a good look.

"What does she look like? Not a Hanna, that's for sure."

At the foot of the bed, the Stabsarzt is listening carefully to the Norwegian conversation. He's worked out, or Liv has told him, that they're discussing names.

"Jutta." He taps his chest. "*Meine jüngste Tochter, die Jutta heisst.*"

At the doorway, his uniform jacket and cap back in place, the doctor smiles, makes an efficient salute - Heil Hitler! - and ushers Liv and the bloody sheets out of the room before him.

Any other time Bjørghild would have made some cutting remark – who does he think he is? I'm not naming my child for some bloody Kraut – but she just lifts a hand, reaches out for her daughter, runs an awkward hand over the baby's head, fingers stiff, afraid to touch the downy skin too hard.

"Well," Solveig says, "you've got time to decide. There's no rush, is there?"

Solveig stands, strokes the baby's head again. She ought to be tired, but she isn't: she feels vibrantly awake, enlivened by the new life in front of her, fizzing with the lightning storm's electricity.

"Do you need anything? A glass of water, maybe?"

Bjørghild nods.

"Please."

"All right, I'll be back soon."

"Thank you, Solveig, for everything."

Through the closed door, Solveig can hear her sister murmuring to the baby.

"Jutta," she says, experimentally. "Jutta. Hey Jutta, just wait till your daddy meets you."

Twenty-Nine

Liv wakes early, throws open the shutters to the bright morning light, sits brushing and curling her hair in the window. Bjørghild and the baby are already awake, curled up together on Solveig's parents' bed. Bjørghild looks better in the morning light, colour returning to her complexion. She converses in low voices with Liv, inconsequential nothings about the baby, the turn in the weather, their downstairs guests. Solveig watches through gummed eyes from her spot on the floor. She'd like nothing more than to press her face back into the pillow and ignore the movement around her: after that kind of night it's too early to be alive, let alone up and beautifying herself for the enemy's benefit.

Still, there are animals to feed, cows to milk - the necessary rhythms of her life undisturbed by either babies or tempests. She heaves herself up, grabbing yesterday's clothes as she stands.

"Morning Solveig." Liv is far too awake, too put together for Solveig, whose watch says they've only had two hours sleep at most.

"Morning," Solveig grunts. She pulls her clothes on, stripping with her face to the wall, shoulders hunched inwards. "Pigs, cows, then talk."

She stops at the door, steadying herself with the handle. She'd paid even less attention to post-natal care than she had to birthing procedures.

"Do you want anything, Bjørghild? Water? Coffee?"

Her sister shakes her head.

"Go and look after the animals - Liv can sort me out in the meantime."

Bjørghild shifts the baby in her arms, sends a wide, genuine smile towards Liv at the foot of the bed. That's new, Solveig thinks, an abrupt about-face.

"Sure?"

"Go," Bjørghild says, flapping a hand impatiently. "We'll be fine."

Solveig hides a yawn behind her hand, blinks away involuntary tears.

"She never was good in the mornings - once, when I was twelve..." The rest of Bjørghild's story is lost as Solveig turns her way down the stairs to the kitchen. It's tidier than she expected; her mother's furniture seems relatively unharmed by the deluge of men, the piles of coats and clothes moved somewhere out of sight.

The captain is still sitting at the kitchen table, talking earnestly to one of his officers over a cup of coffee: the larder might not be as untouched. They stand at her entrance, holds their arms out in a salute.

"Heil Hitler!"

Solveig has no desire to return the salute, but waves awkwardly, descending the last few stairs without catching their eyes.

"Good morning," she says. "Would you like a cup of coffee?"

The captain motions to the countertop, to the cooling pot of coffee. She can smell it already, the scent of coffee, real not ersatz - her father's hoarded stash, put aside for the baby's Christening and now frittered away on these invaders – winding across the room.

"I am afraid one of my officers took the liberty, but we have only made the smallest amount. My men do not know we have such a luxury."

"Where are they?"

"I have sent the men outside," he says, "to salvage what they can."

That cuts through her tiredness - they'll be in the barn, looking for rope or sacks, filching milk from the cows.

Finding, interrogating Lars.

"Outside?" Her voice is sharper than is sensible, and she has to search for a suitable excuse. "They're not in my barn, I hope, messing with my animals. My father won't be happy if they've scared the cows out of milk."

She's hoping the captain won't know this is an impossibility - that his men could startle a hen out of lay, or a sow into eating her own piglets, but the cows need to give milk every day for as long as they have it - gambling on the fact that German High Command doesn't put Danish farmers in charge of its U-boats. He'll be a professional sailor, career Navy from before the war. And officer class too, educated, urbanised. His grandfather's farm, his great-uncle's herd, will only be a distant childhood memory.

"Of course not," the captain says. "They have orders to search only the shore. I have no wish to overstep our welcome."

It's a bit late for that, Solveig thinks. He should have thought of that before his men stole her father's coffee, should have read his charts more carefully and stayed in deeper waters.

"You'll have to forgive me," she says, "if I check on my animals first."

When she enters, the barn is dimly quiet, the only sounds the soft rustle of the cows in the hay, their slow chewing, the swish of their tails against their backs. She checks over her shoulder, makes sure there's no listening ears.

"Don't come out," she hisses. "It's not safe."

She doesn't get an answer, and she hopes Lars has heard her, that he's not simply asleep. If he's awake, he will no doubt have seen the visitors, heard the harsh German accents filter through the barn doors. God knows what he makes of all this, what it looks like from the outside.

There isn't time to consider his feelings, his perception of events. Not now, not with the sailors still straggling off the island and livestock to feed. As the last squirt of milk fires into the churn, Solveig leans her head against the cow's warm flank and closes her eyes. She ignores the muted voices beyond the barn walls, the creaks of the rent u-boat, the soft splat of shit against the straw.

With Lars in hiding, the barn is a haven.

The cows are unaltered, untouched by the storm, by the sailors, by Solveig's own exhaustion and confusion. They don't know that she kissed Liv, that Bjørghild could have died, that she named her baby for a German, that Liv kissed Solveig back.

It's much simpler for cows, she thinks. You spend all day chewing, being milked and fed, and when the time is right, you're introduced to a bull. There's no courting, no awkward flirting, no next day repercussions. He's in and out, and two hundred and seventy-four days later a calf slips out that's gone a week later and you're back to your chewing and milking.

The cow shifts, irritated by the press of her head, flicking its tail across her cheek. Solveig sits up, moves the stool back against the barn wall: no matter how much she'd like to, she can't hide in the barn forever. The churn is only three-quarters full, one cow coming to the end of her lactation. She'll be dry soon, in the last two months of pregnancy, and the milk yield will drop even further.

Solveig pauses half-way across the barn, gives her tired arms a break from the still heavy weight of the milk churn.

"Lars," she whispers. "I'll be back this afternoon, will explain everything."

As before, there's no response. The barn door opens before her hand can reach the handle. There are three German soldiers stood on the other side, one still with a hand on the door.

"What do you want?"

The soldier looks down at a piece of paper, swallows nervously.

"Do you need any help?"

He says the words very carefully, a parrot with a phrase learnt by rote. Solveig can see the paper more clearly now, the words printed in her sister's best teaching hand.

"Nein," she says. "*Dankeschön*, but no."

She reaches behind her, drags the churn through the door.

One says something, his hands outstretched. He peers round her shoulders into the barn, asks something else. He takes a step forward before she can stop him.

Solveig uses her heel to hook the door, pull it partially closed behind her.

"I don't want people in the barn," she says. "It'll disturb the cows."

The man looks at her blankly, unmoving, blocking her crabwise exit from the barn. Her words clearly don't mean anything to him, don't sound anything like the German, so she resorts to stabbing gestures, sharp shakes of her head.

"You, barn, no!"

It's like talking to a pack of dogs. She has to repeat herself three times, each time getting louder, more forceful, before they nod in understanding and step backwards. She waits until they drift away, back to their shore-line scavenging, before she makes a show of closing the barn door, lifts the milk churn again and carries it down to the jetty.

By the time she's dumped the milk, ready for collection, a terrific squealing screaming starts up. From the window, the cause is obvious: the u-boatmen have conjured a stick from somewhere and are busy teasing the sow, switching her hind quarters, getting her to turn in angry circles, snapping at the perpetually out-of-reach annoyance.

Solveig races back from the jetty, loose rocks and earth dislodged by the storm sliding under the soles of her boots, making her half-scramble up the island to the pigs.

"Stop it!"

The men pay her no attention, caught up in their game, her shouts drowned by their laughter.

"Stop it!"

She's just seconds from beating them, hands thumping their backs out of the way, Liv and the captain following close behind, when they part, turning to face her.

"Get out of there," she demands, pulling her cardigan up onto her shoulders. "Leave my pigs alone."

They don't have to understand her words to understand the tone and step back, clunking the stick over the sty wall. They don't look like soldiers in their knitted sailor's jumpers, their mismatched trousers, as much as some of Liv's naughtier schoolboys facing their teacher's wrath.

"Not him," Solveig says, pointing at the man with the stick. "He's not going anywhere."

Liv barks out an order, her finger skewering the man in place, beckoning the captain further towards the crowd. He stops in front of the ringleader, tapping his foot impatiently while Liv explains.

"Lehmann," he says. It's the man's name, and that's as much as Solveig makes out. It's a display of discipline put on no doubt for Liv's benefit - party member, daring saviour, girlfriend of the local garrison commander - rather than out of any real concern for their host or her pigs.

Solveig leaves them to it, climbs over the wall of the sty, moving out of the way of the sow's initial rush.

"Hey," she says, "hey. It's all right, girl." Solveig half sits on the wall, stretching down to scratch the sow's ear. "They've gone now. They're not after your piglets."

The sow grunts, calming at the familiar touch, and leans against the wall, bathing in the strengthening morning sun. The German tirade stops, and Solveig can hear the click of boots, the movement of their sleeves as the men salute.

"Heil Hitler," one says, and their footsteps return to the lighthouse.

"She's big, isn't she?" Liv is the other side of the wall, nervously leaning on the brickwork, feet well back from the mud and animals. "Is it normal, for her to be so big?"

"Pretty normal, yes."

"The captain says you'll be compensated, of course." Liv waves her hand toward the sty. "For any damage to your livestock, I mean."

"That's not needed."

Solveig doesn't want their money, their over-inflated Reichmarks that would only draw attention and derision if she were to try to spend them. Last night is one thing - that's decent, irreproachable.

No-one can blame her for that, call her a traitor, dredge up that word from Gunnar's newspaper report - tyskertøser - for acting as a lighthouse should and saving men's lives. Profiting from it, taking those thirty pieces of silver - that's unlikely to make her friends in the Resistance, even among her neighbours.

"No permanent damage done - she's calming down already and will have forgotten it by the time her next meal comes round. They've a brief memory, pigs."

Solveig sneaks a glance at Liv, at the outline of her profile in the bright morning.

"Best way to be, I reckon."

"You're probably right."

Liv leans more heavily on the wall, her weight on her forearms, hands clasped together in the air above the trough.

"Solveig..."

She trails off into silence as a group of Germans stagger past the sty, carrying some kind of box or trunk that's been washed ashore and is dripping steadily. Solveig waits until they've passed, turns from the sow to face Liv.

"What were you going to say?"

Liv smiles, steps back from the sty wall. She's got her society face on, and Solveig knows the moment is lost.

"Time for breakfast?"

Inside, the house, in contrast to the outside of the island, is quiet. Only the officers are still inside, smoking happily in the living room. The pot of coffee has, of course, long since emptied. Bjørghild and the baby are placed strategically at the kitchen table, staring balefully at each other, glancing only occasionally at the army occupying their home.

"Morning," Solveig says. She peers into the bundle of blankets in her sister's arms, the baby's reddened wrinkle of a face peering back at her. "She looks about as happy as you do."

"We'll feel better, I'm sure," Bjørghild says, tipping her chin toward the living room, "once they've gone and Dr Bernsten's been. I've called him: I don't trust that Kraut from last night. He said he's a doctor, but we have no actual proof. I want to make sure I'm all right, you know, down there, and that there's nothing wrong with the baby."

"I'm sure you're fine."

Solveig reaches for the kettle and the awful ersatz coffee. It's perfectly drinkable, she supposes, as long as you consciously forget what real coffee tastes like.

"Have you thought of a name for her?"

Bjørghild sniffs as though she hasn't. She drags her eyes up away from the baby, and Solveig knows, is absolutely certain, that her niece will be called Jutta, that Bjørghild is on the threshold of admitting it.

Then the captain, hovering in the door frame, clears his throat.

"Sorry to interrupt," he smiles nervously, uncertain of his reception. "But I just wanted to say we sent a messenger to the garrison and -"

Solveig's head jerks up from her niece.

"In my boat?"

"In mine," Liv says, emerging from behind the captain, her hand on his shoulder. "And he's come back with news: they're sending boats for the sailors soon, from the mainland."

"Pleased to hear it," Bjørghild says. She turns back to the baby, strokes an invisible speck of dirt from its cheek. "They've been here quite long enough already."

The boat arrives soon after, ferrying the u-boatmen away in shifts. Schulze makes sure to stay until Dr Berntsen arrives, has Liv translate his case notes, watches as they carry the dead and injured from the lighthouse down to the jetty.

Solveig stands at the lighthouse door with him, waiting for each motionless, stretcher-borne body to pass her. She can't imagine, refuses to picture, how they carried the lumps she'd stumbled over in the dark the night before down the twisting lighthouse stairs. Her room will need a thorough cleaning, sanding and re-painting, burning the sheets if her mother will let her, just to rid it of the smell of death.

Even then...

She shakes her head, dispels the image. She's never been sentimental, superstitious over death before: the human losses in her life - a grandfather and both grandmothers - happened before she can remember, and she's dispatched too many lambs and fattening pigs and sows that have outlived their efficient reproductive lifespan to worry over the business of body disposal.

Liv is sniffling behind her hand, blotting her tears with her coat sleeve, dabbing carefully to avoid smudging her make-up. They stand, side by side, out on the steps of the lighthouse, the post-storm winds whipping at their hair, their skirts. Liv is shivering, and Solveig holds out her arms, takes her into an embrace. In the circumstances, no-one looks at them twice, thinks anything other than the obvious: two women, bound together by weather and weeping. But Liv, her arms creeping round Solveig too, under the warmth

She waits with Solveig until the last body, the last man, has left the island, leaving with the final boatload, her own boat pulled along behind the Germans.

Solveig watches them go, bumping over the still choppy water.

The island seems quiet, without the sailors' chatter, with the baby finally asleep. Movement in the dark door of the barn draws Solveig's eye, the end of Lars' cigarette burning fiercely.

God knows what he makes of all this, what it looks like from the outside. There isn't time to consider his feelings, his perception of events.

Not now, not with the doctor's arrival and the rest of the Germans still straggling off the island. Later, she knows, they will have to talk.

Thirty

That should be the end of it.

The u-boatmen leave the islands, there's a few thank-yous, and that's that. She's proved herself above suspicion, a loyal friend of the Reich.

She'll be left alone now. Her family, Gunnar, the man in the barn, will all be left alone.

No such luck.

Bjørghild, standing at the kitchen sink, slams a plate onto the side.

"Solveig," she says, "there's people here for you."

For once, she sounds relatively friendly. Perhaps, Solveig thinks, she's finally coming round.

"Who is it?"

"More bloody Germans."

She wipes her hands on her apron, resting them protectively on top of her still distended belly, a pregnancy habit she can't seem to drop.

Down at the water's edge, a delegation is climbing onto the decking. Their uniforms blend with the slate sea, and their movements are easy with practice. Even from the lighthouse front door, Solveig recognises the blond crop of hair.

Heinrich.

Oberleutnant Meyer, she reminds herself.

Clicking their heels officiously, they hand over an official-looking envelope - inside, no doubt, there's more printing to be disposed of. Solveig opens it, feeling her sister's eyes burning on her back. The paper is thick, and the lettering is suitably Bavarian. There's a date and a time, that much translates. The rest, in dense German, means nothing at all. It's signed LV Rastic, in tight script.

"*Ich kann kein Deutsch.*"

It's becoming a bit of a refrain, these days. She makes sure to speak slowly, takes no chances with their understanding. "What does it say?"

The soldiers confer between themselves, their Norwegian little better than her German. It's insufferable, this language barrier. Solveig would have thought by now, after more than two years in the country, the great Aryan race would have at least started to learn to communicate with their new empire.

"An invitation," Heinrich finally manages, "to thank you. For the u-boat."

"Ah," she says. "That."

"You get a medal." "A what?"

"A medal," he repeats, fingering the ribbons on his own uniform. "For your service."

3 JULI 1943

ROVESØYA SCHULHOF - 11.30 am
YOU ARE FORMALLY REQUESTED TO ATTEND A PRESENTATION IN THANKS FOR YOUR ACTIONS IN RESCUING GERMAN SAILORS FROM THE SEA AT HOLM LIGHTHOUSE.

Bjørghild translates more efficiently than Heinrich, before pushing the invitation back towards Solveig.

"Well," she says, crossing her arms, elbows resting on the wooden tabletop between them. "I suppose you'll have to go."

"There's no way out of it?"

Solveig looks towards her parents, hovering awkwardly behind Bjørghild, peering at the foreign lettering over her shoulder. Bjørghild shrugs.

"You could get sick, catch a cold, break a leg. But that would look suspicious." She leans towards Solveig, almost resting her cheek on her shoulder. "And if I know you, little sister, scrutiny is the last thing you need."

"She won't go," their father says. He steps forward, bangs his hat down onto the table, sea spray still clinging to the woollen fibres, to the hairs of his beard. "She can't go. I won't allow it. No daughter of mine is going to stand up in public and have Krauts fawn over her like she's some kind of..." His beard bristles, the salt droplets shining, as he tries to think of a severe enough insult, grinding his teeth together in frustration. "...some kind of Løvik."

"Far," Solveig begs, "please."

"Everybody's saying it, you know. It's common gossip. There's this medal, first off. And then you invited them into this house, let them eat and drink your mother's cupboards dry, scare your mother's hens out of lay. You let their quack..."

Solveig waits for it, waits for her father to run down the doctor who came when their own could not, when he was off the islands, away in the comfort and safety of his sister's house. Bjørghild catches her eye, and Solveig suddenly understands.

At the bottom of her father's anger is that very fact: when the lighthouse was needed, its light was off and its keeper away. When his daughters needed him, he was away and some other man - a man who by all rights should be his enemy - helped them instead.

He looks at the baby, pauses.

"And then there's this friendship with the Sunde woman. You can't tell me you think that's right? Such blatant admiration of the most shameless Nazi-"

Solveig says nothing. What is there to say? It would be stupid to defend Liv – everybody knows who she is. They've always known, right from the start.

"I hired her," Bjørghild says. "Sandvik and I. Do you know how many applications we got before we chose her? And then when she was coming, you sent Solveig to get her, you invited her here for dinner. You knew she was NS, we both did. We all did.

You can't tell me you think that was right, if Solveig's kindness is so wrong?"

From her cot, the baby lets out a little whimper. Solveig's father stands up, reaching in his pocket for his pipe.

"Very well," he says. "This is a lighthouse, designed to save sailors. It's what we do. That's what you did."

He pats Solveig awkwardly on the shoulder, lights his tobacco.

"If you ask me, it was brave, and that's all there is to it."

Thirty-One

"It's just me, Lars," Solveig calls as she enters the barn.

He doesn't respond, probably tucked up in the hayloft somewhere, holding his book right up close to the travel lantern, squinting to read in the semi-darkness. It must be boring, she thinks, to have to spend all your time in the same uncomfortable place. More than boring, with no-one to talk to except cows, nothing to do except old fitness drills and nothing to read except the battered romance novels she'd pilfered from Bjørghild and her mother.

"Milking time again."

She whistles to herself as she sets up, placing the bucket, the stool, warming her hands in her armpits.

"What the fuck was that about?"

"Christ, Lars," she says. He must have been nearby the whole time, standing in a shadow, watching her. He looms out of the dark corner of the barn at her, all sunken eyed and bearded, making her jump. "Warn a girl before you sneak up on her. I almost of died of fright."

He ignores her.

"I said, what the fuck was that about?"

Solveig leans her head on the cow's flank, concentrates on the motion of milking. She knows exactly what he wants her to explain. But she isn't in the mood to rehash the same argument over again.

"Was what about, Lars?"

"The hundreds of Germans everywhere yesterday, of course, all that shit." He steps closer, mindful of the cow's hooves, of the range of her kick, but too tightly wound to stay away completely. "Have you decided to turn for real? Is that it? Decided you do have the guts for the NS, have you?"

"Oh, give over Lars," Solveig says.

She isn't frightened of him.

She isn't, not a jot. He's on her side, for goodness' sake. He knows she's on his.

"I've done this once today. I don't need to do it again."

"You haven't explained to me."

She stops milking, twists on the stool to face him better.

"All right, I'll explain. This is a lighthouse. Around it are rocks. The point of the lighthouse is to keep boats away from the rocks. But the light is off, because the Germans turned it off. So they crashed onto the rocks and I saved them. That's it."

"Just so," Lars says on an intake of breath. He seems to be

calming down, the tapping of his foot less frantic now, less manic. "Just so. But what about this morning? I saw you, all pally pally with that blond officer. An Oberleutnant, by the patches on his shoulders. What was all that about?"

"I'm a hero of the Reich, don't you know: they want to honour me." She rolls her eyes. "A medal, some public ceremony. You know the kind of thing they go in for."

"A medal?"

"Yes," she says. "It's going to be... Oh god, it's going to be awful - I'm going to have do it though, in front of everybody." She runs a hand through her hair, pulling it loose from its set. "You understand, though, don't you? That I have to do it, that I don't have a choice. Not if I don't want to raise suspicions."

Lars is still watching her, eyes scrunched in distrust.

"I'll just get through it and get out of there. That's all."

"That's it? You're sure?"

This is becoming a regular occurrence now, Lars' need for reassurance. He's been trapped within the drafty barn walls for too long, alone with no-one to break the paranoid thoughts as they form. Once the fuss over the u-boat has died down, she thinks, once the Germans' attention has moved away from Solveig, back to shipping movements out in the sound and the hunt for black marketeers, she'll speak to Karl.

It's time for Lars to move on, to get back into the thrust of resistance - he's been hidden on the islands for almost six months now. Long enough.

On this topic, at least, there's nothing else to say. She drops her gaze from him, shifts the stool under her, shrugs as she reaches for the cow's udder.

"That's it."

She tries to talk to him as she finishes the milking, to distract him from the four walls of the barn and things he may or may not have seen through cracks in the cladding, through the open door. It seems to work - he leans against the stall's wooden upright, one leg crossed over the other. He even laughs at one point, lights a cigarette and takes care to flick the ashes away from the straw. Solveig expects the cows to shift and fidget at the smell of smoke, but they don't.

"They're used to me now," he says. "We've been roommates longer than any of the chaps I went through basic training with, at least. Me and these girls are old friends, aren't we, eh?"

Solveig stands up, pushes the stool away with the side of her foot. Her neck and back are stiff with sitting in the same position for too long, and the bones click together as she pores the milk from the bucket into the churn.

"Give us your cup, then," she says to Lars, holding out her hand for the chipped wooden trail cup her mother is still yet to notice is missing. She dips it into the bottom of the bucket, fills it to overflowing with milk. Lars drinks the whole thing without stopping for breath, shudders slightly as he lowers the cup from his face.

"I just can't get used to it being warm," he says, wiping the last remnants from his beard with the back of his hand.

"My father loves it like that," Solveig says. "Sometimes he..." She mimes milking the cow, "straight into his coffee. Says it makes it frothy."

"I know. I've seen him." He shudders again, the movement exaggerated this time. "Won't catch me doing that."

Solveig fixes the lid to the churn, is just about to shuffle to the front of the barn, rolling the churn along the rounded edge towards the cellar for pickup in the morning when Lars catches hold of the rim, keeping her in the barn. Solveig tries to pull it from him, but he won't give it up.

"You better be careful what you say," he says. "About me."

"I'm not going to say anything, Lars. Who would I speak to?"

He doesn't laugh at this.

"To Liv, to your new blond friend, to anyone." He tugs the churn closer, pulling Solveig off-balance. "You bring them down on me, and I'll kill you. Got it?"

She nods.

"Got it."

"Good, good."

Lars drops his edge of the churn, letting it fall to the floor with a metallic thunk. He smooths his eyebrows with his fingertips, one at a time, brushing all the hairs in the same direction. It's an odd, fastidious kind of move, one that hides his eyes, his expression. When he drops his hand again, he's all smiles and friendliness.

"Do you need a hand carrying that?"

"No," Solveig says. "Thank you. I think I'll be fine."

Thirty-Two

The ceremony is anything but plain.

There's a band, for one. Of course there is, Solveig thinks - the Germans do nothing unless there's pomp and ceremony attached. They appear to have press-ganged Liv's students, regardless of musical talent, into performing. The rag-tag band of scraped knees and girlish pig-tails is headed by the younger Magnus Løvik, who scowls down at his child musicians, each stroke of his conductor's baton registering as a blow.

Solveig and Liv are ushered into place, Rastic's hands in the smalls of their backs. Liv is in her uniform, buttons polished and cap set carefully on her hair. She looks the part, Solveig thinks, a uniformed hero. But then there's always something compelling about Liv Sunde, about the way she moves, as though the world were an already choreographed waltz. There's nothing unplanned or incoherent about her - just all poise and grace, each movement falling neatly into place, in carefully measured time.

Solveig is in one of Bjørghild's pre-war, pre-marriage suits. It's a suitably serious brown, too small across the shoulders to button. She can't pick out many familiar faces in the crowd - the other members of the NS are there, stood tightly together in the centre, a person wide gap on either side of them.

She assumes the rest of the crowd has been press-ganged from their shopping, their family visits, their everyday lives to come and stand in the schoolyard and watch. Solveig doubts there would have been volunteers for something pulled so obviously from the newsreels, from the image of such ceremonies back in glorious Germany.

In the bank of assembled faces, she can't see a single smile. They all look coerced, dour. Her parents aren't there, nor are Arne or Gunnar. Her father's foul temper is still in full force, righteously tenuous in his disapproval. Right now, Solveig is glad of it: the fewer people to witness this, the better.

The only people in the crowd she recognises are Bjørghild and her mother's friend, Fru Nygård, the busybody. They're stood side by side, virtually touching, the old woman's hand on the pram, a solid pair. Solveig catches her eye and Fru Nygård, inclines her head, and Solveig decides that it means she understands that Solveig had to save the sailors, to accept the medal, in order to survive herself.

There are a few forced claps, and the band strikes up again, beginning to play the opening bars of something so wobbly Solveig's not sure she can name it. The Horst-Wessel song, probably, or something else with lyrics equally full of banners and bondage and men crying for *die Vaterland*, no doubt.

The sailors and the gathered NS dignitaries stand and salute for long moments, the crowd slowly starting to drift away. Solveig fidgets, bringing her hand up to her mouth, biting at her nails. There's dark crescents of dirt under each one, farm muck that wouldn't quite scrub out.

A sharp tug on her sleeve pulls her arm back down to her side, Liv frowning around the German tune. Without the distraction of her nails, the ceremony seems endless, dragging each second out to four times its natural length. Without apparent warning, Liv stiffens beside her, clicks her heels and salutes. At the same unseen signal, Rastic stands, crossing the open space towards them.

The colonel fumbles the medal at Solveig's chest.

He's over-applied the aftershave, followed by an overwhelmingly masculine smell that makes Solveig want to cough. She watches his stubby fingers, stained yellow with cigarettes, clumsily pinning it to her lapel. She'd expected something grander, more military, hung on a ribbon. This is something else altogether. A bronze circle engraved with a swastika stuck on a hatpin.

It's the kind of thing she'd expect children to win for excellence in sports, not as a reward for saving precious Aryan lives. For Liv, however, he takes his time: smoothing the material out over her breast before, fingers cupping her curves, he pins the ribbon to her uniform.

It's disgusting. Sickening.

Solveig looks up now, searches for Bjørghild's stoic face in the crowd. Liv herself radiates tension, refusing to meet Rastic's gaze. It must be hard for her, Solveig thinks bitterly.

To have us both in touching distance.

Rastic takes a step back, his salute mirrored by the knot of Germans behind him, then retreats, climbing a few steps set out as a speaker's platform. Solveig recognises the lectern from the church, requisitioned and dragged out into the open. Whoever did it wasn't too careful, large scuff marks scarring the wood all the way up the stand. Behind the lectern, hands poised in practised imitation of the Führer, Rastic launches into his speech.

Beside him, her unamplified voice buried beneath his oratory, Else Løvik translates.

Somewhere in the crowd, a child starts crying.

Once he's finished, the band starts up again. This tune is no less patchy than the last, wobbling around the true melody as though drunk. Thankfully, it doesn't seem to have any words, and the crowd disperses efficiently, melting into the buildings on either side, silently slipping their boats' moorings and pulling away out to sea.

"Is that it? All over?" Let me go home, Solveig thinks, away from you, where I can fade into everyday invisibility again.

"There's lunch first," Rastic says, indicating the open door of the schoolhouse.

The NS burst into twitters of delight at the spread laid out before them. It's all translated, each simpering, exaggerated snippet of praise and thankfulness, for the Germans' benefit by a pimpled volunteer soldier stood behind Rastic, murmuring in his ear.

The conversation topics are just as you'd expect: the progress of the war, the price of food, the intolerable nature of most of their neighbours. It's the same kind of things they discussed before the Occupation, surely the same of kind things their ancestors had discussed for generations.

"Wife!" Løvik would shout, slamming his tankard on the table. "Bring me my axe. I'm of a mind to speak to Frditjof across the sound - I lent him gold for a boat to go a-viking across the sea, and after all that raiding and pillaging what's he brought me?"

She'd pass it to him, hair piled up around her furs.

"Be back before dark," she'd say, "I've a new brew to open, despite that malt's so dear these days."

The thought of Magnus Løvik in a horned helmet is so silly that Solveig snorts aloud at her daydream, and the others' heads snap in her direction.

"Sorry," she says, feigning a cough. "Piece of herring went down the wrong way. Sorry."

She bashes her chest a few times for effect, the swastika pin's fitting pressing painfully against her chest. They turn back to the Colonel, urge him to continue holding court. Liv is the last to turn, mouthing "Behave!" before settling her features once again into their lovesick expression. Solveig takes a sip of the water provided and offers a sheepish smile.

"As the colonel was saying," the translator says, as Rastic idly brushes ash from his trouser legs. "Jews and Bolsheviks, homosexuals. All kinds of perverts and traitors. But they're nothing like the gossip, the rumours, that these news sheets would have you believe."

Solveig fidgets uncomfortably in her seat, the edges of the chair suddenly pressing into her thigh. The Colonel watches them all closely, his focus right on Solveig's face.

He knows, she thinks, about Lars, my real loyalties, my links to the Resistance. He's found me out and is playing with me, like a cat with a mouse.

"No?" Liv's question could almost be scripted, it fits his timing so precisely.

Solveig wouldn't put it past them.

The Colonel does not seem like a man who leaves things to chance.

Liv's face, however, is tight, nervous. She won't meet Solveig's eyes, though her eyes flick in her direction. Solveig understands, knows that her heart is beating as fast as Solveig's own, caught on that word, that disgusted tone.

Homosexuals.

Perverts.

Solveig looks away, focuses her gaze somewhere to the right of the translator's ear, forces her face into something she hopes is a vague smile.

"Most definitely not. All lies, from end to end. The colonel was shown Dachau recently, and you wouldn't believe it. It's a marvel of efficiency and discipline. The human wrecks they have there, and yet the orderliness, the cleanliness of the place." As his words are translated, Rastic spreads his hands in an affectation of disbelief. "It's astounding."

There are murmurs and nods of agreement from Rastic's

adoring supporters.

"My nephew," says one, "wrote a letter saying the same thing. He's in the Waffen-SS."

"You see?" The rhetoric, Solveig thinks, loses some of its immediacy in translation. "You see? The enemy is a master of lies, of twisted propaganda. They make us out to be monsters, devils, when they themselves are the degenerates, puppets of their American Jew masters."

The colonel shifts, embarrassed by his outburst, as his translator continues implacably on. The translator pauses, having run out of words, until Rastic is calm again and gesturing expansively to their medals, to the lunch.

"As well as all this, the Reich would like to give you a token of our esteem. Three thousand kroner each, and some food and other goods."

He indicates boxes behind him, and two soldiers move to open the lid. Solveig moves forward to look inside, see what they're offering. Coffee, tobacco, good white flour. There's even, tucked into the corner, real chocolate. Luxuries, for sure, but nothing compared to the money.

Three thousand kroner!

Solveig almost spills her water into her own lap. That's an awful lot of wool, and the Germans are just giving it away. It seems almost sinful to turn it down. Extra feed for the animals next winter, a coat for her mother, supplies for the new baby. Petrol, fuel, food. Everything would be easier with another three thousand kroner in the bank. Still.

"I don't want it," Solveig says, and the room falls into a

shocked silence. "I live in a lighthouse. Saving those in trouble is what we do."

"We understand - your actions were selflessly patriotic, but..."

"Seriously, it isn't needed. My father is paid to be the lighthouse keeper. We expect nothing else: the medal is more than enough."

Liv glares unsubtly across the room and the Germans shift on their feet, gauging each other's reactions. One soldier raises his hand to rest on the shoulder strap of his rifle. The Colonel waves them down, removes his cap. His hair is flat from the pressure of the hatband and he runs his hand through it, sending it straight up like a boy's.

"Now Miss Eik," he says himself, in accented but understandable Norwegian, tone deceptively light, "if you don't accept, some might see that as a..." He pauses, searching for the right Norwegian word, consults his translator. "As a demonstration."

She doesn't take the hint.

"As a demonstration of what?"

Her tone is aggressive, disdain and contempt as plain as day. The humiliation of that ceremony, that speech, still smarts, setting her words stinging.

"Solveig," Liv interrupts, holding up the chocolate, "it's a valuable gift, and very kind of the Navy to thank us so."

It's an attempt at a warning, Solveig knows.

Liv is looking out for her. But Solveig cannot take the money. Gunnar, Bjørghild, her father - they'd never approve, and Karl and Lars would never understand. She might as well start parading up and down the streets in an NS uniform, cut off all her friendships, end up like Erik Pettersen in Brattvær harbour. Solveig says nothing and Liv turns back to pouring over the box of luxuries.

The interruption has given the Colonel time to collect his thoughts, communicate the right words to his translator. Even the boy picks up on his commanding officer's mood, not even attempting to veil the threat in his voice.

"Refusal, Miss Eik, would be seen as a political demonstration. The kind we hope to avoid from free citizens. And, combined with your one time only attendance at the meeting of the *Nasjonal Samling*," he pauses significantly, letting the silence work in his favour, "it would look very suspicious to those in the *Statspolitet* who don't know you as well as we do."

The translator smiles smugly at Solveig, rocks on the balls of his feet. Rastic taps his cigarette into a waiting ashtray.

The entire room seems to be frozen, silent.

"Of course," Solveig finally says. "It is very kind of you."

The notes burn a hole in her pocket, hot and unnaturally heavy. The box of luxuries is more awkward than anything, her arms almost at full-stretch around it. It knocks against her as she walks, forcing her to take short, slow steps down to the jetty.

Around the corner, hidden by the walls of the boathouse, Solveig can hear voices. Out of habit, she stops, waiting. She'd thought resistance work would be noble, exciting: all midnight raids and ski platoons. Instead, she's grubbing around in other people's gossip. That's what the war has made of her - a perpetual eavesdropper.

"I don't mean to interfere," Else Løvik's tone is aiming for confidential, all girls together. "But if I were you, I'd drop Solveig Eik like a stone. That girl's headed for trouble - always has been - and she'll drag you down with her, given the chance."

"Have no worries on that score." Liv's voice sounds hard again, sneering. "After that embarrassing display, I'd sooner socialise with her sheep."

Thirty-Three

"You're going to have to lend me a blouse."

Bjørghild, nestled in the window seat in the small living room, looks up from the baby at her breast.

"What for?"

"To go with my brown suit. My own has got a bloody grease stain right on the..." Solveig gestures to her chest.

"Yes," Bjørghild says, ducking her head back to the baby for an instant, "but why are you wearing your suit?"

She sniffs and the corner of her mouth creeps upwards.

"You haven't won another medal, have you?"

"No."

There's a good five seconds of silence while Bjørghild watches her, face not giving anything away - if she knows, if she suspects - and Solveig has to fight the urge to squirm on the spot, blush, give up on the whole idea. Then the baby pulls away, releasing the nipple with a pop. Bjørghild fixes her shirt with one hand, twists in the seat, looks out across the water to the schoolhouse.

"You'll have to get it from home," she says eventually. "The key's in my bag upstairs."

"Thanks," Solveig says, and turns on her heel to leave the room.

Bjørghild's voice stops her before she's made it three steps.

"And Solveig? Don't go yet." Bjørghild won't look at her now, fixated on her daughter, stroking the tiny fingers between her own. "About six o'clock is the best time - after the children have gone and the marking's done, but before a teacher's standard early bedtime."

Solveig steadies herself with a hand on the doorframe. She stands there for a second longer, but Bjørghild doesn't say anything else.

"Thanks," Solveig says to the back of her head. "Thank you."

For once, despite the evening sun, Liv is obeying the blackout. There are thick curtains drawn across the windows. Not a speck of light escapes.

Perhaps Liv's decided that now she has been held up as a model citizen, honoured recipient of a medal, that she ought to behave like one. As the door opens, Solveig doesn't give Liv a chance to speak.

"I came to see you, to apologise." She lowers her voice, though there's no-one else around to hear. "For, you know, the other week."

Liv looks less welcoming than Solveig had hoped, lips pressed together in distaste. She stands in the doorway, blocks the view of the room beyond. She's hiding something, Solveig decides.

In the room behind Liv, someone sneezes.

Liv stiffens.

"You can't be here," she says. "Someone will see you."

It must be Colonel Rastic - Solveig can see his influence, even in the small sliver of room visible. A new copy of '*Juden und ihren Lügen*' sits openly on the table, carefully bookmarked. There are two half-emptied glasses, one with lipstick smeared round the rim.

Liv hasn't dressed up for this afternoon rendezvous with her admirer - she's rather dressed down. In serge slacks and a dark-blue blouse, she looks styled, effortless; the illusion marred only by a pair of thick, home-made socks.

As Solveig hovers in the doorway, she catches up a brown sweater from where it rests on the back of a chair. It's fine knit - expensive when it was new – but now the wool is thinning at the elbows and the fit has been pulled out of shape. Liv looks solid, real, the very image of the patriotic ideal made flesh.

"Who? Who will see me?" Solveig keeps her voice low. She has no desire to lure Rastic from his hiding place. "Worried I'll put a damper on your afternoon with your boyfriend? Interrupt all the politics and *liebe dichs*?"

"Shut *up*, Solveig," Liv hisses, "you idiot."

Liv checks over her shoulder, holds up a hand to her guest for understanding.

"I'll just be a moment," she says, voice high and bright. "Help yourself to another drink, perhaps some more stew."

Then she steps forward, feet still shoeless, and shuts the door behind her.

"Come on, this way." She grabs Solveig's arm, pulls her towards the schoolhouse. "In here."

Liv spends only a moment unlocking the classroom door before pulling Solveig through.

"Are you stupid?" she says, hands tight around Solveig's arm, nails pressing half moons of pain through the wool of her cardigan.

Liv kicks out behind her, closing the door with a well-placed heel. Solveig notices, distractedly, distantly, that she isn't running, protesting, isn't lashing out, but is backing up against the wall, hiding with the teacher where, just weeks ago, Arne had hidden from the same woman.

"No, I'm not. I just…" She trails off. It occurs to her that a confession of any kind is unlikely to be welcomed. "I thought you'd be alone."

"Well, clearly not." This is not Liv's fake socialite voice: there are no airy manners and disaffected sophistication. "You fucking idiot. Do you have no sense of self preservation?"

Solveig feels the words like a slap - this isn't survival talk, something she says when powerful people are listening. They're alone, and for once Liv is saying exactly what she means.

"Apparently not." Solveig tries to play the hurt off, tries to laugh, but the sounds that emerge from her throat are more animal than human. "Otherwise I'd have just ignored you, like everyone else."

Solveig can see that hit home, a flash of hurt crossing Liv's face before the muscles stiffen again into blankness.

"Was there a reason, other than embarrassing yourself, you came to see me?"

The archness has returned to Liv's voice. She settles herself into a relaxed lean on a nearby desk, but the movements are too orchestrated to be real, too careful. She smiles, tight-lipped, and the muscles in her neck stand out, vibrate with tension.

"I do have a guest, after all." The difference in tone is impossible to ignore. Liv uses her book manners to distract, as a wall - a shallow mask - between the real, raw Liv and everyone else. The realisation leeches the anger from Solveig, leaves her surprisingly calm.

"I just, I wanted to say sorry. I embarrassed you, in front of the Germans the other day..." Solveig grits her teeth, pushes the derision she'd heard in Liv's voice away. "In front of the Løviks."

It sickens her to apologise for staying true, staying decent. She can't help it if she has morals she believes in. A flash of sitting in Liv's sitting room, Olav's secret spilling helplessly from her mouth, is quickly quashed. This is Liv, and she has different opinions.

"No lasting harm done, I'm sure."

"More than that, I wanted to tell you..." Oh come on Solveig, she thinks. Be brave, really brave, for once. "Gunnar has proposed and is pressing me for an answer."

It's not a lie, not exactly. The muscles next to Liv's mouth jump slightly, a brief flicker of emotion.

"Congratulations then."

"Liv..."

"Honestly, Solveig. What do you expect me to say?"

"I wanted you to tell me," Solveig says, slowly, deliberately, caught in an unexpected moment of confidence, "that I had another option."

Solveig reaches up between them and cups Liv's cheek, smoothing the skin with her thumb. She ducks her head to catch Liv's gaze and refuses to look away. Liv's eyes slide from hers, focusing instead on the wall behind Solveig's ear.

"If you persist with it, this," Liv says, gesturing between them, to the hand on her cheek, "if I let you, this is going to get us killed. Or arrested, taken to a camp. Do you understand?"

Her mouth is twisted up, all angry and frightened, her lips pressing into hard lines. She looks wild, her usual rigid control evaporating under the pressure. Even wound tight like this, trapped and dangerous, Solveig wants to kiss her, to curl her fingers into her hair, and press her close against the wall of the schoolhouse where Gunnar kissed her, months ago. And so she does.

Liv is unexpectedly gentle. Despite the urgency, every touch is light, precise, just barely ghosting over Solveig's skin. It's the gentleness that undoes her, sets her legs and arms shaking, narrows her world to that insistent rhythm. Solveig tries for gentleness of her own, but her hands jerk and shake, their movements mere puppets attached to Liv's finger strings.

It's not much, but it seems enough; Liv stretches and tightens beneath her, holding herself rigid for long moments before they sink down together. Heart slowing, the muscles in the back of her legs easing, Solveig lies with open-mouthed contentment. The twill of her suit is rough underneath her, and the classroom floor is not a feather mattress.

Solveig turns and rests her head on Liv's stomach, arm trailing heavily across her hips. The sound of Liv's pulse rumbles under Solveig's ear, less frantic now.

Liv is right there, still close up against Solveig, but not with her. She's just a girl in her arms, getting further away with each passing moment. All emotion has been wiped from her face, her mask is back on, implacable. But as Liv dabs her handkerchief against the corner of her mouth, Solveig thinks there's a chink there, a tiny crack that can be widened, wriggled through.

"We could keep it a secret. I mean, we'd have to but…"

Liv sits up, buttoning her skirt and making sure the seams of her nylons run straight down her legs. There's a ladder near the top, just small for the moment, but deadly in the long run.

Liv looks at Solveig as though to say: see? The first consequence of your actions, and it's not a good one.

"No-one else would know."

Liv moves backwards, sliding the skirt under her through the dirt, leaving a wide trail on the schoolhouse floor.

"Solveig," she says, and it's as close to begging as Solveig has ever heard her. "Please. We can't do this."

"But we are doing this," Solveig reminds her. "We keep doing this. Why not just admit what we want?"

Liv shakes her head.

"It's not about what we want," she says. "About what I want. You know that."

Solveig goes to object, and Liv silences her, a finger against her lips.

"You *know* that. It's about what's safe. And sex is never secret, Solveig. After a while, it's obvious to anyone who looks."

Solveig clambers upright, using a desk as support. The tight set of Liv's hair is dishevelled, drifting loose around her face. She holds out her hand for Solveig to pull her up, stumbling sideways as she rises.

"It won't work, no matter how hard we want it. Not ever." Liv looks away, towards the shuttered window, as though expecting the Colonel at any moment. When she speaks again, her voice is softer, kinder. "Go home. Give Gunnar his answer. Tell him you love him."

"But it would be a lie."

"Not much of one," Liv says. "You'd have married him anyway, eventually, if I hadn't come along."

"I wouldn't. It wasn't like that, has never been like that between us. Not until that night, outside, when I kissed him to..."

The radio is still in the roof above them, there to be found, and Liv - perhaps more now than ever - cannot be trusted to keep things from her friends at the NS.

"When you kissed him," Liv amends, "because you know that is what the world expects."

She steps back and pulls her arm out of the reach of Solveig's restraining fingers. Solveig watches Liv retreat into herself, straightening her blouse and hair, brushing the dust from her skirts, and resists the urge to fall to the floor and beg for a real chance.

"Go home, Solveig."

Liv smiles at her then, as though the goodbye might be forever. They leave the classroom in tight silence, each keeping a decidedly decent distance from the other. Liv does not bother locking the door behind her: she simply leaves, without looking back.

A soft rectangle of light spills from the house before the door closes behind her. Through the window, Liv is clearly visible. She's laughing, head thrown back, drink in hand.

Solveig kicks at the side of the school building, the rubber of her sole leaving a black smudge through the dirt spattered paint. Her eyes well with tears, vision blurring, swimming through the liquid layer. She can't stand there forever, leaning tear-streaked against the wall.

Somehow, she makes it to the boat without running, pushes herself off, stumbling on loose stones and the tiniest tufts of grass, clambers into the boat, her foot splashing the water, sets her oars for home.

After a minute, tears sliding warmly down her cheeks, she stops rowing. She lets herself drift, the boat slowly, aimlessly turning in the rush of oncoming waves. The schoolhouse, like that first day, shimmers on the water, the white reflection bright against the sky and the rust-red of the grass. Solveig wipes at her eyes angrily, scrubbing at her face with the palms of her hands.

"Enough," she says out loud. "That's enough now."

She might make your pulse skip today, flutter at the sight of her, but tomorrow? Or next week, month, in a year's time? Perhaps. But there'll come a time when the fact of who she is will be inescapable - her politics, her disdain for those not versed in

Plato and Socrates, and – perhaps worst of all - her city sensibilities: the theatres, the fancy bars, the bookshops, all the things that Solveig imagines Oslo can provide and Smøla cannot.

That's not to mention what will happen if her side lose, are forced to retreat back into Germany. And then what? Gunnar will have gone, married to someone more sensible, who is capable of feelings the things they ought. Bjørghild, Aase, Gerd. All settled, all sorted. She'll have made her bed, alone, high in the lighthouse - her childhood room - and that would be that.

It's time, Solveig decides, for those childhood imaginings to be put aside. She's not a Resistance hero, not an adventurer or an explorer. It's time for her to grow up, accept the truth of what is, not what she wishes could be.

It's just been spring fever, the weather boiling up in their veins, all the new life spilling over. She'll be over it by high summer - she will be over it, Solveig decides, she will - and Liv will be forgotten by winter.

That's how these things go, Solveig thinks. You meet someone, and they're fun or clever or exciting - sometimes all three combined - and, for a while, you're mad for them. You find a turnip that looks just like old Hans down by the boats, and you think I just have to show Gerd this. She's tender hearted and so you take the smallest piglet and bathe it, screaming, and tie a bow around its neck to make her heart melt. You dream of her - not in that way, of course, although sometimes that too -, you go out of your way to be where she is, bumping into each other outside the shops, or at school or the church. Then one day, for no apparent reason, you wake up and notice how small her teeth are, the way she clicks her tongue between words, that she's constantly biting at her nails and the skin of her fingertips. And just like that, you're no longer mad.

Can Liv Sunde be worth it?

No.

The decision says, her head says, that Liv is not a choice worth making.

All those books have held the answer all along: choose Simon over Erlend, Darcy over Wickham, head over heart. After all, hope is the worst kind of cruelty.

Solveig lets out another brittle laugh and decides, then, there, staring longingly at the reflected school, Liv's lips still tingling against her own, to be joyously in love with Gunnar. If the world wants to be deceived, then she'll let it.

Thirty-Four

Over the next week, Solveig stays away from any possibility of meeting Liv Sunde, brooding, tending to the sows and sheep.

In the evenings, she reads. She could pick something romantic - a book Liv lent her still sits on the shelf in her room - but she chooses an old favourite: Isak Dinesen and the wide, warm plains of Africa. The words and story are familiar, comforting, and the old dog rests his head on her lap as she reads.

Like that, the end of Arne's deep-sea fishing comes quickly. Bjørghild, anxious to have her husband home, sends Solveig off early. The currents are kind, and she lands with time to kill.

She leaves the boat at the quay and wanders inland. The butcher's has reopened, Olav's wife and son behind the counter. The queue is short - just two, three people deep - and silent. People pass by, heads down, eyes averted. The fear in the air almost has a flavour to it. Thin and sickly, like the aftertaste of bile.

Through the open doorway, Solveig waves to Olav's wife, a single hand raised to shoulder height and stationery. The returning stare is blank, a thousand yards long, right through Solveig and out the other side.

She lets her hand drop, shoving it roughly into the pocket of her coat. Down the road, is a gaggle of old ladies. They huddle together, bent against the wind, their headscarves a bright spot in the grey day. Caught up in her own version of the prevailing fearful introversion, Solveig almost walks right past them.

"Solveig!" Aase emerges from the crowd of women, her left hand ungloved. "You heading down to the harbour?"

"Yes. You been showing off again?"

Aase rolls her eyes, wriggles her fingers back into her gloves.

"I'll come with you." She turns back her waiting crowd. "Goodbye ladies."

She kisses the endless, whiskery cheeks of each of them. Fru Nygård is last, reaching up on her toes to meet Aase's face. She kisses Solveig as well, gripping her forearms weakly for balance.

"I suppose you're off to meet Gunnar from the boat."

"Yes, and Arne too."

Fru Nygård starts to speak, but her next words are cut off.

"Miss Eik! Solveig!"

The call is informal, intimate, and freezes Solveig in her tracks. There's only one person who'd call across the quay so breezily, with inflections lifted straight from a book. Across the street, Liv Sunde approaches. A few steps behind her, trailing in her wake, is the Colonel. The other women shuffle and mutter to themselves, fixing their gazes on the floor.

"Miss Eik," he says, inclining his head in greeting. Solveig has to reply - she can stonewall Privates and Sergeants, pretend she hasn't them over the sound of her oars and the gulls, keep rowing until their boat hook stops her, but Rastic is not a man she can ignore.

"Morning, Colonel."

Fru Nygård, it seems, has no such compunctions and gives the teacher and her companion one sweeping, dismissive glance.

"Solveig," she says, laying her hand on Solveig's forearm for emphasis, "how is your sister? Has the baby arrived?"

"Yes - a girl, Jutta."

The old women coo and cluck amongst themselves.

"A good name," says one. "A good Norwegian name."

They all ask other questions, speaking all at once. For simplicity's sake, she focuses on the easiest, from the woman closest to her.

"Is she cute?" Fru Nygård's friend says. "Little Jutta?"

Solveig shrugs.

"She's a baby, got a face, you know, two eyes. Doesn't appear to be deformed."

It's easy to be blasé, now that the baby's actually out, and both it and Bjørghild are alive. The details themselves can be glossed over, forgotten in time. Fru Nygård rolls her eyes, pokes Solveig with one gnarled finger.

"Oh, honestly. You'll feel differently when it's your own child," she says.

But Liv smiles with one side of her mouth.

"Maybe," she says. "Maybe not." Liv's eyes are laughingly knowing, the humour in them unkind. She leans into Rastic, her grip on his arm obvious. "After all, you're not really a family kind of girl, are you?"

Solveig can feel her face flush. Liv's implication is unpleasantly clear; all at once it makes Solveig feel sullied, ugly. The problem is, of course, that it's true. She's said it herself: she's not the family type - but for the first time, her feelings seem wrong and unnatural.

Solveig's throat works soundlessly, the restraining presence of Rastic and the others almost all that stops her from crying, or replying with her fists. No doubt punching an officer's squeeze would be a worse offence than kissing her.

Fru Nygård's face freezes at Liv's words, her smile falling into a grimace.

"Solveig, Aase, get along with you now. You'll be late."

She kisses them both goodbye, and then shoos them away. Aase ignores Liv and Rastic completely, sets out towards the quay with quick, lengthening strides. Solveig nods her goodbyes to the others, barely making eye contact. They hurry along, joining the other women gathering slowly on the quay.

The returning fishing boats are already powering into the mouth of the harbour, trailed by clouds of screaming, swooping gulls that circle the boats, drawn by the smell of fish and the food swirled up in their wake. The thud-thud-thud of the engines is a baseline to the gathered women's chatter. Solveig and Aase stand in silence, and the space between them feels brittle with tension.

The skin is dry and loosening on the pad of Solveig's thumb, shedding in concentric circles inside her gloves, loosened by the cold and the friction. A tag of skin is worrying now in the lining, pulling distractingly with every movement.

The weather is finally easing, the wind less sharp today than a week before, the air above the hard shimmering with heat. Solveig loosens her scarf, leaves it hanging limply around her shoulders, and works her thumb free of her glove.

Absently, she raises her hand in greeting, waves at the knot of gossips, too absorbed by her thoughts and her thumb to notice the gradual drift of people, the emptying of space around her, the sideways whispers and looks. In the old days, when boats were wooden, and the seas were still full of draugs and kraken, women gathered just to see whether the boats would come home. Most of the time they did, but some didn't, victims to the sea's wrath and caprice, leaving broken families scattered across the islands. Sometimes the boat would come back with one less crew - drowned or otherwise dead or jumped. Solveig's own great-grandfather went ashore in Lisbon and never returned.

These days the boats are more stable, and accidents are rarer. But now, for almost the first time, it's not the sea the boats are fighting. The waves are the least of a skipper's worries, with u-boats and floating mines and the risk of air raid.

"People are talking about you." Aase's words are low, hushed. They won't carry far. "About me?"

"About the u-boat, and the medal." She leans forward, covers her mouth with the side of her hand. "You know islanders - we're desperate for gossip."

Solveig rolls her eyes, and the smile doesn't stay on her face for long.

"There isn't any, not really. It scuttled on the rocks in the storm, and Liv insisted we help them."

"Hmm." Aase's mouth stays silent and shut, picking at her teeth with her tongue. "And that's where the gossip is, Solveig. This friendship with a member of the NS."

The denial is quick, insistent.

"I'm not her friend."

"Still, people are talking. They say there's something suspicious about the two of you, and moments like that," she cocks her head back towards Fru Nygård, "don't help any."

"Suspicious how, Aase? I'm not about to start goose-stepping and proclaiming love for the Fatherland."

Aase sighs, says nothing, keeping her thoughts to herself. As children, they knew all there was to know about the other. No secret too big or embarrassing, no grievance too petty to be halved in the sharing. Out on the water, with only the gulls to hear them, they told each other everything. Although later Gerd made their friendship a trio, she wasn't the same. She judged, or they thought she might.

Solveig hadn't realised, though, how easily keeping secrets becomes a habit.

It starts, quite innocently, by forgetting to share a dream, or that your parents argued last night. Then it's intentional, but kind hearted: you don't tell her that your father's dog is expecting, you reveal the puppies as a warm and squirming surprise. Finally, she'd learnt the art of hiding things, even from herself. She'd learnt which parts of herself to protect behind carefully constructed barriers, and which parts to leave out in the open where everybody could see them and nobody noticed. Later still, when their youthful innocence was unravelling, Solveig was glad of those barriers.

Of course, Aase had listened, holding Solveig's head to her shoulder, catching tears in her scarf and hair, but she'd never really understood. Secrets had saved her, then. From censure, from disgrace. From the ridicule and contempt of her friends and neighbours. They had saved her and killed the unreserved trust between the friends. Aase had sensed the distance, the barriers, the secrets, and withdrawn.

"Just be careful, is all. Collaborators get into trouble, Solveig - look at Erik..."

Solveig sighs, rubbing her cold nose roughly.

"I'm not a collaborator. I saved some drowning men. It's a good thing, Aase, not a fucking crime."

"I know, I know. I wasn't talking about you." Aase holds up her hands in surrender, scans the empty sea and horizon for the approaching boat. "But they get into trouble and they can't be trusted, not even..."

"I know, and I swear I'm not her friend." Aase nods. She licks her lips, thrusting her jaw forward to prevent herself from speaking. "All right then."

Before, Aase would have spoken her mind, would have told her exactly what she thought. They stand in relative silence for another fifteen, twenty minutes, occasionally nodding, smiling hello to someone in the gathering mass of people.

"You know best, of course."

Solveig wants to say something, even here amongst the press of people, the listening ears. Words fly round in Solveig's head, searching for the magical phrase, the right combination that will make everything as it was before. I miss you, she's about to say, but her words get lost in sudden, excited chatter as the boat they've been waiting for steams into view round the corner. Their cargo already unloaded in Kristiansund, the crew are eager to disembark.

Gunnar must be more eager than most, for he is the first to barrel down the gangplank, bag thrown over his shoulder, thick coat drawn tight around his shoulders.

He looks familiar, steady and solid. I love him she thinks. The words are a chant, a litany, a statement of hope and belief. She waves to him, up on the tops of her toes. His face is screwed up, perhaps against the cold salt spray, and does not change even as he makes straight towards her.

"Hei Aase," he says, dropping his bag at their feet. "Hei Solveig."

"I want to talk to you," she says, pressing her lips to his cheek, curling her fingers into the thick collar of his coat.

He resists the pull, leans back away from her.

"Don't play with me," he says. "We both know you don't mean it."

Beside them, Aase and Per are caught in their own reunion, her arms twined round his neck, faces pressed tight together. Solveig steps back, hands retreating to her pockets. I love him, she thinks again. I do. She steps back in, pulling him close against her chest, feeling the rasp of short stubble against her cheek. He's unmoving, stiff and awkward in her grip, his arms slow to come up around her back. She drops her voice, purrs into his ear.

"Things have changed," she says into his ear. "Really changed."

Finally, she lets him go, forces a smile onto her face.

"So I'll see you usual time tomorrow?"

Gunnar shakes his head, unclasps her hands from around his neck, lets them drop to her side. He won't meet her eyes, teeth pulling uncharacteristically at his lip, and the movement draws her eye to the length of his beard. Not as trimmed any more, longer, more traditional, more like their fathers'.

The vivid imaginings of their future lives return, settled and steady and dependable. The thought causes a sharp ache in her chest, but she smiles anyway.

"Talk to Arne," he says. "I'll see you in the morning."

"Eleven then?" Gunnar nods.

"Eleven."

He stoops to pick up his bag, hauling it over his shoulder. Before he can move away, her hand on his chest stops him, resting lightly over his lapel. Solveig watches him, his eyes still not fully focused on her face.

I love him, she thinks resolutely.

I am in love with him: he is the love of my life.

The lie chokes her, and she swallows against a sudden surge of bile in her throat.

Arne, at last, has emerged from the boat, and stands on the gangplank, searching for his wife. Aware now of the stares of the other women, Solveig resists the urge to look over her shoulder before pressing her lips to Gunnar's, wet and soft behind the thicket of beard.

"Make sure you come," she says into his ear, allowing a slow smile to spread across her face. "And bring my ring with you."

At first, she can see he doesn't understand. Then he steps back, frowning.

"Solveig," he starts, but she cuts him off.

"I have to get to Arne - take him home to the baby."

He smiles properly then, eyes creasing, teeth white through the length of his sea-beard. He flings his arms around her, squeezing with joy. She leans into it, feeling the strength of his arms around her back. Unwillingly, she thinks of Liv.

Unlike Liv's, the press of his body against her own is...

She stops herself. Don't compare them, she thinks. There is nothing to compare. When he lets her go, she reels back, a few unsteady steps as though dizzied by his nearness.

"See you tomorrow."

He picks his bag up from beside their feet, swinging it over her shoulder. He presses another kiss to the hair at her temple, and heads towards his own boat, smiling hello at the others watching on the quay.

"Hei, Arne!"

Arne is still on the gangplank and doesn't see her until she's almost on him. When he turns, a look of resigned dislike flickers across his face, before he settles into his usual detached pleasantness. Blind as she was to the looks of the other women, Solveig cannot help but notice, and her step falters.

"What brings you by?" Arne enquires, voice loud enough to carry across the whole quay, and then, quieter, more sincerely, "How's Bjørghild? Is she all right?"

"Bjørghild's fine - she's at the lighthouse with your daughter."

For the first time since he saw her, Arne looks genuinely pleased. It takes time to get back to the boat, Arne stopping to speak to each person he passes. There's a lot of laughing and back slaps, but with Aase's words fresh in her ears, Solveig sees how people pull back from her. As they turn from her brother-in-law to her, their laughter seems a little forced, their smiles falling fixed.

A German patrol boat is waiting at the harbour mouth. It stops each leaving boat, checking papers and destinations. Solveig steers the boat alongside, reaching into her pocket for her papers. Boots appear at the railings, and she looks up, squinting into the sun.

"It's all right, Fräulein, I know who you are."

It's Meyer, Heinrich, and he motions to his men to let her through. Across from her, Arne stiffens. His face is set, the dark hollows under his eyes emphasising the frown on his face. As she turns the boat, opens the throttle to pull away, Heinrich calls out after her.

"Have a good day, Miss Eik."

She turns in the seat, raises her hand in goodbye.

"You too, Oberleutnant."

The wave she gives is too much like the German salute, her arm too straight and stiff, her hand too open. She realises a beat too late, caught in the force of Arne's glare, and drops her elbow sharply. Her father's motorboat makes good time along the coastline, but after Arne's first fevered questions - is she well, what's her name? Does she look like me? - they barely speak.

Solveig is still caught up in Liv's smirking cruelty, in Aase's warnings, in Gunnar's distance. She needs things to return to normal, to establish herself again in everyday routines. The sheep, the pigs, the housework. Put Liv and all that well behind her. She did it before, went back to being sensible and ordinary, after Gerd. The first step is the radio.

"I was thinking, tomorrow, I can say I'm going to pick up things for the baby, and meet you at the radio."

Arne is silent for a moment, facing out to sea. When he looks back, his face is set.

"No," he says, "you won't."

"What? Why not?" She shivers in the breeze, not understanding. "No-one will notice we're gone."

"It's not that."

Like Aase, Arne seems uncomfortable, building up to something he knows she will not like.

"People are talking about you, Solveig, they're saying… they're saying you can't be trusted."

"What?"

She sounds like a broken record, scratched, repeating the same word over and over again. It must be a joke, she thinks, just can't be true. Her friends, her neighbours, people she has known all her life: they can't possibly believe that she, of all people, is a traitor.

"Oh Arne, you know that's not true." He's serious, face unflinchingly stern. Her voice breaks with disbelief. "Surely you tell them it's not true."

"Isn't it? You spend all your time with a collaborator, you help German sailors now. You feed them, you house them, and God knows what else." He laughs bitterly. "Poor Gunnar, tied to you, with that rumour floating round the deck."

"But, Arne..."

"And then there's the business with Olav." His words cut her dead, breath hanging in still clouds. "Everyone knows he was supplying you under the counter. Where did the Germans get their information from? Who told them?"

"It could have been anyone." She's indignant now, cross, still barely believing what she hears. That prickle of righteous outrage at being doubted covers her across the lie gives her an air of truthfulness she isn't certain she could muster otherwise. "It certainly wasn't me."

"I'm sure," he says, more gently. "I don't believe you mean badly. Your heart's in the right place. Even so, things are as they are, and I moved the radio." He's not unkind, not vindictive. Just firm, decided. "Before I even went to sea."

She hadn't checked, hadn't risked listening to the broadcasts with Arne and Gunnar away. It hadn't even occurred to her that the radio might not be there anymore.

"So what, that's it? You're done with me now? You'll tell the others, stop talking to me, freeze me out? Because I tried to make a friend? Because I saved men's lives, men like you, men who make their living from the sea?"

The unfairness of it strikes her, the absolute, ridiculous unfairness. When she, likely above all others on the islands, is actually doing something for the Resistance.

What about Lars, she wants to say. I've been hiding a Resistance agent for months, all on my own, while all you do is sit and moan and groan and listen to the actions of others.

"Look," he says, "it's not forever. Stop palling up to the Sunde woman, stay away from the others, be ordinary, quiet. People will soon forget, soon remember who really you are." He reaches out, puts his hand on her knee. "Give it six months, Solveig, and it'll all be forgotten."

For the first time, she allows herself to dislike her brother-in-law. She's never noticed before how narrow his head is. Compared to Gunnar, where the width of his shoulders mirrors the lines of his jaw, Arne looks sallow. Eyes shrunken, low brows, the line of his mouth thin and down-turned. His hair is thinning rapidly, the scalp shining through. He looks, she decides, like a skull in a wig.

"Fine," she says because really, what choice does she have? "Fine."

Thirty-Five

The pig pens are stinking. The sow has another litter of piglets, and her previous litter is getting large now, their backs higher than Solveig's knees. A week or two and they'll be smoked and hung before the end of the month, ready for the table.

The summer heat means more cleaning, more straw, more feed, more work all round. They're Solveig's pigs, and so it is Solveig's job. Bjørghild watches her, bouncing the baby on her hip in silence.

"Looks like you've got an admirer, Solveig." Solveig looks up, wiping sweat from her forehead with the back of her hand. A German motor boat has pulled up at the jetty. It's Heinrich, his blond hair for once dulled against the backdrop of the low afternoon sun.

"No. I don't."

She rakes through the litter carefully, flicking shit into the corner of the sty, looking to save what sawdust she can.

"I don't want anything to do with the Germans."

"I know," Bjørghild says, hoisting the baby higher in her arms.

There's none of her usual rancour, the words flat, without hidden depth. It's hard to take her meaning. She's been different since the baby, since the storm. Solveig has caught Bjørghild watching her in recent days – clearly thinking, using that fancy education to piece things together - and she's been kinder, too, more careful around Solveig than before.

It makes Solveig think of the sow before her first litter. She'd been frighteningly violent then, snapping and biting at anyone who dared enter the sty. It had given her personality, set her apart from her more placid litter mates: it had made her Solveig's favourite. And then, once her piglets were born, she had relaxed - still occasionally snappish, rarely terrifying.

"Want me to get rid of him? Tell him you're taken?"

Solveig nods.

"If you can."

Heinrich is virtually on them now. His uniform jacket is open, dark patches of sweat marring his white shirt. Not quite the untouchable poster boy today.

"You're here for my sister, I suppose," Bjørghild says, laying the island accent on thick. She knows what she's doing, wants Heinrich to stumble over his fledgling Norwegian, stammer out some pidgin answer. She always said: there's nothing men dislike more, nothing guaranteed to send them running away faster than being laughed at by women. "But you know chasing skirts doesn't work when the girl's already been caught by someone else."

Heinrich's answering smile is vague. For a moment, he says nothing. Then he steps forward, rests a hand on the brick wall of the sty.

"I am not," he says, "chasing skirts. This is not a social visit. And it does not involve you."

Bjørghild rolls her eyes in Solveig's direction, shifts Jutta in her arms. The baby's head flops against her mother's chest. She's a good-looking child, Solveig has to admit. Sunny, smiling, hardly ever crying.

"Very well," Bjørghild says. "I shall leave you two alone."

She turns on her heel, as dramatic as ever. Solveig tries not to smile. The baby watches them over her mother's shoulder, bouncing up and down with every step. Solveig waits to speak until the lighthouse door shuts behind them: Bjørghild may have come round, she may even have guessed at part of the picture, but Solveig still has secrets she'd rather keep. Bjørghild will just have to make up her own version of their conversation.

"So, Oberleutnant," she says, "now you've scared off my sister, what do you want?"

"Perhaps you know," he says, "that since the arrest of the butcher-" If he knows of her involvement in Olav's arrest, he gives no sign of it. "-since the arrest of the butcher, my men and I are tasked with finding those who used his services."

"And?"

"And it is a crime, of course."

"Of course," Solveig says. She tries to sound braver, surer, than she feels. "What does that have to do with me?"

The glass of the kitchen window flashes as Bjørghild leans out, flaps a duster in their direction. Heinrich and Solveig watch her, their conversation momentarily broken. She flaps the cloth against the lighthouse wall for far longer than it takes for the dust clouds to disappear. The window closes again. Heinrich turns back to the pigs, idly scratching the sow's back over the wall of the sty.

"Do you remember, back in the winter, that I stopped you? With your lunch?"

"I've been stopped many times. By you, by others." Solveig shrugs. "Germans are everywhere these days. I don't remember them all."

He moves his attention from the pigs, fixes her with an inscrutable look.

"I thought you might not."

"Am I in trouble? Over a lunch?"

"No. Not at the moment. But you have been mentioned as... of interest." He pauses. "These are the pigs I-" He mimes clipping his own teeth. "Yes?"

"Yes. But when was I..."

"They are big now," he says. "Fat. Will be time for the table soon, I think."

"My name? You said it's been mentioned?"

He shrugs.

"You helped to save German sailors. You provided useful information. But you only attended one meeting of the *Nasjonal Samling*, and you almost refused a reward. This is confusing."

There's no simple explanation she can give him, nothing she can say without giving herself away, without betraying Lars. She risks a glance over to the barn, pretending to check the movement of the clouds overhead. They're moving fast, rolling in off the sea towards the mainland. The door to the barn is open. Solveig shifts, moves, leans away from Heinrich. Their conversation is being watched by more than one set of suspicious eyes: in the gap between the frame and the open door, Solveig can just make out the shape of Lars' beard, the paleness of his fingers against the red painted wood.

"But Miss Sunde speaks well of you, and that is important to Colonel Rastic."

Solveig turns back, focuses on Heinrich's implacable expression.

"Liv Sunde was called to speak in my defence?"

This is more serious than just being mentioned in passing, then. This is the first stages of suspicion, the first creaking of the wheels of German justice in motion. Heinrich must be taking a risk, giving her warning, time to protect herself from what is about to arrive.

"You don't have to worry," Heinrich says, mistaking her silence. "This is just talk. If you've done nothing wrong, you have nothing to fear."

It's what they say to children who cower behind their mother's skirts at the sight of the police. These days it's an utter lie, comforting only in its familiarity.

"It's not that," she says.

He's only a boy, she thinks, only a lad her age.

Like Gunnar, like Arne. Nicer than Arne, kinder. She knows him, knows his type. If it was something else - if it was just a falling out with her sister, just a falling out with Gunnar, with Liv - she could ask him, could confide in him. She might even treat him to the truth. But treason is another thing entirely.

"It's just that do you really, I mean if you had the choice, would you actually want things, you know, as they are?"

Heinrich frowns.

"I don't follow you. Don't..." Solveig doesn't blame him. She's barely following herself. "Don't – I don't know the words. Just ask me."

"I mean..." A thought suddenly occurs to her, a memory of pressing herself uncomfortably against the arm of her chair, waiting for Liv to return. "Are you e*in Gläubiger der Führer?*"

Her pronunciation must be awful - in her mouth the words, if they're even the right ones, sound nothing like they did in Else Løvik's - but Heinrich understands anyway.

"I think," he says, "that is not a wise question."

"No. Probably not."

"And not an easy one. Norway was not part of the last war, I think. My father was, and two of his brothers died in France. One to gas, one to bullets. So at the end we are told that the total war - all the gas, all the bullets - was down to Germany, that we must take the..." He trails off, his Norwegian failing him. "All the *kriegsshuld*, you understand? And that now we must do this, we must not do that. That we must pay, over and over, money that we did not have. They blame us for everything, they tell us what to do, and now we must pay them for the honour. You must understand - no-one would like that."

"And yet now you're here, telling us what to do."

"I did not say that the same is not true for you. And then Hitler, he knows it. Like my father, he was there - he knows these rules, these payments, are not fair. So he says no, no more. If you didn't live it, I don't think you will understand."

"Norway was low too," Solveig says. "And I lived that. Every other man without a job, farmers with no money to buy seed, cows thin and starving in the mountains and we… we didn't…"

We didn't become monsters, she wants to say. We kept our heads, didn't set out to conquer the world. But then she remembers Olav, remembers Erik Pettersen, floating in Brattvær harbour. She thinks about Else Løvik, and her quivering admiration for the Führer. The barn door slams. It makes her jump, turn to watch it swing out again, pulled by the wind.

"The wind is getting stronger," Heinrich says, "to open a door like that. I ought to go back soon."

"Yes," Solveig says. "You probably ought to. I'll see you again."

Thirty-Six

The barn seems empty, Lars nowhere in sight.

The cows are undisturbed, chewing their hay. They don't flinch at her entrance, tails switching side to side against the flies.

"Lars?" There's no movement up in the hay loft. Perhaps he's asleep, or simply more cautious since the night of the storm. She keeps her voice down, barely a hiss, and she hopes he can hear her. "Stay in the barn, out of sight - I'm not alone."

"No," he says, stepping out from the shadows. "You've got Germans here again, I see. Saved another boatload, have you?"

First Arne, now Lars. She's not in the mood for their attitudes, no longer patient enough to pacify their patriotic egos.

"It's one German, not a boatload." Solveig shrugs, brushing straw off the wooden boards. She isn't about to confess to her heart-to-heart with a member of the enemy army. "He's a good man. He wants to talk about pigs."

"I don't believe you."

His voice is still friendly, light, but the smile has dropped off his face. He steps closer, reaching out to tuck a strand of hair behind her ear. Close up, she can see how ragged his beard is, how his hair straggles over his ears. Dark smudges under his eyes make his face look sunken, staring. The smell of him brings rising bile to the back of her throat. His voice is gentle, light, but it holds an edge she hasn't heard in months, not since those early meetings in the cave.

"You've told them about me, told them where I am, haven't you?"

"No," she says. "I didn't, I wouldn't. I'm not a traitor. You, of all people, know that." Lars turns, paces, drags his hands through his hair. He's twitchier than he's been in weeks, unkempt and wild.

"You make me sick. Whoring yourself out for petty favours, both of you."

"Both of us? Lars, who-"

He interrupts her, drags his hand through his hair, scratching fiercely at his scalp.

"Her with that officer, you with this boy."

"No. No, Lars. It's not like that. He's just... homesick, that's all."

"And you don't think I am? You don't think I want out of here, out of this barn, cooped up like some bloody animal while you..."

He breaks off.

"Who is this?"

Heinrich's voice is hard with suspicion. The shape of his

trousers, of his jacket-less shoulders, sleeves rolled up past his elbows, are clear in silhouette. His feet are shoulder width apart, hand on the open holster of his pistol.

"Fräulein, who is this man?"

"This is..." Solveig steps towards the door, smiles, waves Heinrich in. "This is Karl, my cousin. He's here to visit the new baby."

"Of course."

The lie seems simple enough, believable. Heinrich returns the smile, but on his face it looks tight, forced. His hand does not leave the gun at his hip.

"Your papers, please."

Lars makes a show of patting his pockets, the breast of his shirt.

"Sorry," he says. He shrugs, casually. "I don't have them on me."

"They must be inside," Solveig says. She rolls her eyes for Heinrich's benefit, the movement exaggerated, theatrical, and moves to stand shoulder to shoulder with her newly minted cousin. "Karl's forever leaving things lying about, aren't you, Karl? Always has, even as a child. Would leave his head behind if he could, some days."

She's aware of her voice rattling on alone, talking too much, the men still and silent. Heinrich doesn't move, doesn't wave away the infraction as she'd hoped. He drops the smile, lifts his chin and pulls his brows together in concentration.

He says something, a question, in quick German that Solveig can't follow. Lars' German must be better than Solveig's - he doesn't blink, just shrugs.

"Nein," he says, hands still hidden in his trouser pockets. "Not me."

Heinrich isn't convinced. "I think I do."

"Happens all the time," Solveig says. "Doesn't it, Karl? People mistake you for someone else."

Lars shuffles his feet, shifting his weight forward.

"All the time." He shrugs. "Must just have one of those faces, I suppose."

"Your papers." Heinrich is determined now, pulling the pistol from its holster. "I want to see your papers."

It happens faster than Solveig can keep up with. Lars steps behind her, his arms coming up to wrap around her shoulders, her throat. He pulls her backwards, into the thin hardness of his body. His breath is rank in her ear, his beard scratching against her cheek.

"*Verpiss dich,* Fritz," he says.

Solveig twists and turns, trying to throw Lars off, but those daily exercises have kept him strong and he just shifts his stance, tightens his elbow around her neck. She tries to scratch her way free, but her nails are short and blunt and do little damage through Lars' jumper. The soldier in the doorway advances, pistol raised.

"I said," Lars repeats, his hands scrunched tightly about the wool of Solveig's jumper, pulling the neck out of shape. "Fuck off, Oberleutnant. Or I'll kill your girl. I'll break her fucking neck."

"Let her go," Heinrich says. "Or I will shoot."

Unlike Lars' threat, Heinrich's words carry little weight,

Solveig thinks. She doubts he's a good enough shot to hit Lars without first hitting her. He's not in some crack sniper unit, after all. Just a called-up farm boy. And Lars is desperate, broken, barely clinging to control.

"No, you won't." Lars sounds confident now, amused. He speaks low, right into her ear, and his arm around her throat relaxes, fingertips stroking along the edge of her collarbone. "Bet he's never fired that gun outside of training. He wouldn't last two minutes in Russia. Not with real soldiers, with real men."

Heinrich adjusts his grip on the gun, trying to disguise the way his hand is shaking. Solveig can see his finger tense on the trigger.

"Let her go," he says.

Lars doesn't let her go. He stays wrapped around her, his hold almost tender.

"Not like us, eh, Solveig," he says. "Not like us, out on the Devil's frozen arse, burning bloody Communists just to keep warm. That's war. Not bobbing about these islands, chatting up girls. This boy would piss his pants if he even saw the border. That's proper soldiering."

"Ich werde schießen."

Heinrich's hands are trembling, shaking, the muzzle of the gun jerking back and forth.

"Go on then," Lars says. "Shoot me then, if you're going to."

Heinrich swallows. His hand closes on the trigger and Solveig closes her eyes, waits for the bang and flash and searing pain. The gun clicks emptily, and Solveig opens her eyes. Heinrich is no longer aiming at Lars, at her. He's focused on his hands, on his frantic fumbling with the workings of the gun. The safety, she supposes, or a jammed trigger.

Lars shifts behind her, releases the pressure of his arms across her throat.

"Idiot," he says and then his hands are on her shoulders, fingers pressing hard into her back. He pushes her and Solveig stumbles, trips, her ankle turning sideways and shoes sliding on the loose straw.

For a second, she thinks Heinrich will catch her.

The buttons on his breast pocket scratch at her cheek, tearing the skin and bringing blood stinging to the surface. She falls heavily, knee then thigh, then shoulder, her out-flung hand skidding away on straw. Her head hits the floor with a crack and bounces, the shock forcing the air from her lungs.

Heinrich's gun clatters between them. It skids along the floor and slides under the straw, just feet from Solveig. Then all at once they're moving, the three of them together. Solveig, out in front, scrambling along the barn floor while the men fight each other as they go, pulling on clothing and hair, kicking out behind them.

It slows them, and it is Solveig's hand that wraps around the gun.

"Zu schießen!" Heinrich is shouting at her, urging her on. Lars is shouting too. *"Schießen!"*

She sits up too fast and the barn spins, the rough ground beneath her as steady as the surface of a wave. The cows are pulling at the ropes that tether them to the wall, metal rings clanking against the wood. She can smell them too, the fresh stink of their shit.

The trigger is harder to pull than she thought, and she uses the fingers of both hands to squeeze it shut. The weapon kicks in her hands, sending the barrel off course.

Thirty-Seven

Solveig opens her eyes, the sharp smell of blood and gunpowder filling her nose. The cows are bellowing, straining at their ropes, twisting and turning their heads to try to escape their restraints.

Lars is only feet away, but he's no longer shouting, no longer surging towards her. The power between them has shifted, and now he cowers from her. She stands slowly, clutching at the stacked hay for support, feeling her way upright.

"Don't shoot," he says, hands spread in front of him. There's no blood on his clothes. He stands easily. Solveig lets out a shaky breath: she missed him. "Don't do it. Please."

Heinrich gasps wetly on the floor beside her, and Lars startles.

I should just shoot him, she thinks. He might be a hero of the resistance, he might not. I should shoot him, put the gun in Heinrich's hand, and blame the one for the other.

It should be easy. Killing at a distance is so much cleaner than clubbing fish to death or slitting the throats of slaughter pigs. She wouldn't have to feel the impact, feel the bones shatter, the squashed flesh splitting under her hand. There'd be no furious rush of blood over her hands, the metallic stink clinging to her clothes.

No wonder the Germans are so fond of firing squads. Just a slight movement, a flicker of intent and - bang - you have been shot. Her palm is sweaty, the gun slipping. She holds it with both hands, the barrel still not steady.

"Please, Solveig," he says. "Don't. I'm sorry. I didn't..."

"Shut up, Lars." The gun in her hands is a Luger, a machine pistol. They're standard issue for the Germans, ubiquitous these days, strapped to every uniformed hip, stolen and traded and detailed in secret publications passed from resisting hand to resisting hand. A Luger has eight bullets in the magazine, one in the chamber.

One bullet fired.

Assuming it was fully loaded, there's still seven bullets left in the magazine and one in the chamber. She's got eight bullets and damp palms and a heartbeat like a frightened rabbit. She has hardly any options.

Lars is edging towards the barn door, shuffling backwards towards the thin sliver of sunlight. She ought to shoot him now, before he gets too far, before they're out in the open, before the noise of the cows, the crack of the gunshot, draws attention.

"You don't want to do this, Solveig," Lars says. He's less cocky than he was facing Heinrich, less certain. He could read the other man, goad him into messing up his shot. Heinrich had been predictable, steady. Solveig doesn't think she's either of those things. Not right now, if ever. "You're not a killer, not really. The German was an accident, self-defence. This wouldn't be. I know you, Solveig: you don't want to do this, you don't want to pull that trigger."

The trouble is, unsteady and unreliable, she does.

He has brought her so much trouble. It's his fault, all of it. If he hadn't been there, if she hadn't found him, helped him, her life would have gone on as normal. Those fantasies of resistance, glory would have stayed just that.

Olav, Arne's blasted rumours.

None of it would have happened. And today, if only he'd just stayed hidden, stayed quiet and out of sight. With eight bullets - despite her failing grip and inconsistent aim - with eight bullets, she's bound to hit him once. It should be easy. She already has one casualty to deal with, another is hardly any more hassle.

The cow bellows again, stamps her feet, disturbed by the noise and the thick smell of blood.

"Solveig, please."

The palms of Lars' hands, held up in surrender, are dirty, filth caked in the lines, underneath his fingernails.

There might have still been rumours. There would still have been Liv, been island picnics and public conversations. There would have still been akevitt the night of the storm, and the u-boat and the medal.

"Get out," she says. "Get off my island."

"How?"

Solveig takes one hand off the gun, wipes her nose, gestures down to the jetty.

"My boat, his boat, I don't care how. Just go."

Lars stops, starts to take a step towards her, back into the barn.

"Go," she repeats, voice firmer now, harder. "Before I change my mind."

Heinrich twitches and gasps on the floor, drawing her attention. She presses trembling fingers to his neck, feeling the unsteady pulse flutter and skip.

"Fräulein," he says. "Fräulein, please."

There's no point calling for help. There's no-one in hearing distance, and anyway the wound is fatal, she doesn't need any medical training to tell that. His eyes are dulled, glassy. Her knees are wet, the hem of her skirt heavy and his starched white shirt saturated.

"Shh, Oberleutnant."

She forces a smile, brushes golden hair back from his head. There's no use pretending the tears in her eyes are just the wind this time.

"It'll be all right. It'll be all right."

She can hear the engine of Heinrich's boat rumble into life.

"Fräulein, bitte."

He coughs once, twice, thick clots landing on his chin. She doesn't know what he wants, what he's asking. It seems important to him - he lifts a hand to her face, trailing along her hairline, tangling in her hair. His arm is too heavy for him to hold and it sags, bringing her head down with it, her ear almost touching his mouth.

He says something about his father - *mein Vater, Fräulein, mein Vater*. Solveig can only pick the easiest words, the simplest verbs. She has no idea what he wants her to know. *Bitte, Fräulein, mein Vater*.

"Yes," she says, "all right." She smiles reassuringly around the lump in her throat, nods her head. "I will." He smiles, weakly.

"Danke schön, Solveig."

Solveig can't move while he gapes at her, mouth opening and closing like a stranded fish. She ought to go and get help, that's what she ought to do.

Run straight to the Germans with tales of a fight in the barn, an accident, her hand no-where near the trigger.

The great Wehrmacht must have medics on hand, surely. And if they were quick enough, then he could be saved. Army doctors must have experience with bullet wounds, even in a backwater like this. But they'd also bring the Wehrmacht's police, the Feldgendarmerie, the chained dogs and their execution squads.

His skin is clammy, cooling under her hand. In the corner of the barn the cows shuffle restlessly, pulling hay from their feeder to the floor, and when Solveig looks back down, Heinrich is dead.

Thirty-Eight

If she leaves him, just lets him lie in the pool of straw and blood, he'd be found by her father, or by another soldier come looking. She could claim ignorance, wide-eyed innocence.

What is there to do?

A dead German is hardly a little thing to hide. Perhaps she could take him out in the boat, tie weights around him, let him sink to the seabed with his country's u-boat. There'd be a few days of frantic activity, inch by inch searches of the islands, and then even the Germans would have to give up, give in, write him down as a mystery deserter, a traitor to the dream of the Reich.

But bodies dumped like that surface all the time.

A year or maybe two before the war there was that woman, sunk beneath the winter ice, who floated up in summer and scared the tourists. Her wedding ring identified her, and the husband's boat still had traces of blood under the seats, in the oarlocks.

And besides, that kind of reputation isn't fair to Heinrich.

She could go to Fru Nygård, her mother's friend, suspect of the NS. Surely she'd offer Solveig food, help.

Even a friendly face would be welcome at this point. She's almost stood up, almost moving towards the door, when she remembers Olav. A memory of the way he looked at her as they dragged him from the shop surfaces, stalling her footsteps.

There's other, even less welcome, pictures at the edge of her thoughts. Not memories, but hauntingly real none-the-less. Her father, mother, Bjørghild, Gunnar. All arrested, imprisoned. Interrogated for information about her, about her harbouring dangerous criminals, about her part in the death of a Wehrmacht officer.

She should turn herself in. Confess. She could say it was an accident, say it was self-defence. That's mostly true, at least. She can make it clear she acted alone.

Solveig remembers all those determined daydreams: wild horses and all the Gestapo's inventiveness wouldn't drag Lars's secret out of her. The anticipation of her bravery is no longer thrilling, noble and stoic. But she can't kid herself anymore. She won't be brave, won't live through those last few moments with honour and dignity. She'll cry, she knows she will, and beg pitifully for her life.

It'll be humiliating, but it'll be the end, and that's enough.

There's another engine out on the water. She can hear the steady thump of its piston getting closer, circling the back of the barn, heading for the jetty.

Please God, Solveig thinks, let it be Gunnar. He'll know what to do - he's sensible and practical. She can rely on him. They'd get away with it.

The problem would be Gunnar, though. He's not an actor: just think of his performance the night Liv caught them with the radio. She could perhaps pull it off. She's lived with lies for long enough, but not Gunnar.

Solveig realises she is almost too calm. She should be panicking, crying, screaming. That's what girls do when they find a dead body. That's what innocent girls do. She lets her breath out erratically. Her hands shake of their own accord, and her stomach churns with sudden adrenaline.

The latch of the barn scrapes, light spilling through the widening crack.

Solveig squints against the brightness, as the silhouette coming through the door resolves into a recognisable figure.

"Oh God, Liv", Solveig says, no longer having to fake the panic in her voice. "Liv, please, you have to believe me…"

Liv doesn't even blink at the scene before her, just steps aside and pulls the door partially closed, blocking the view from outside.

"I know," she says. Solveig wants to shake her, to yell at her. Doubt me, you idiot, disbelieve me. "Lars told me."

Thirty-Nine

"Lars told you?"

"Lars told me." Liv crosses the barn, crouches down next to Heinrich, presses her fingers to his neck. "You told him to leave; he left and came to me for help."

It doesn't make sense.

She'd thought Lars would take the opportunity to snatch Heinrich's jacket along with Heinrich's boat and head for the mainland. With an engine like that beneath him, he could be halfway across the sound by now, the shoreline in sight. He has his reason to return to his colleagues now, another proof of his bravery, of his commitment to the Resistance cause.

Yes, he can tell them, I have been away. But I got information on the enemy's structure, their plans - who on the ground in Smøla is for us, who on the ground in Smøla is against us. And then, when I got too close, when things got too hot...

Well, it'll be in the newspapers soon enough.

So why, of all the people, all the places, Lars could turn to, did he run straight to Liv Sunde?

"I don't understand."

Solveig is still shocked, her thoughts muffled, slow and churning all at once. It doesn't make any sense. She can't put the pieces in the right order, fit the jagged, disparate edges together. Lars has no reason to run to Liv, no reason to turn to a woman he knows is NS, unless: "He knows you, knows you'd help him with anything."

Liv shakes her head at the lack of a pulse, closes Heinrich's eyes with her fingertips.

"He's my brother." She sighs, rocks back on her heels. "Lars is my brother."

Solveig feels numb all over, cold, the hairs on her arms, on her legs, standing up in gooseflesh despite the day's warmth. She stands up away from Heinrich, from Liv. Her legs find a bale of straw and she sits heavily.

"Your brother."

Whose clothes she'd worn, whose picture she'd stared at, trailed her fingers over the glass. Liv's brother, the soldier.

"If he's your brother, and Resistance," Solveig says. "Then the NS, you're not really..."

"No - I really am." Liv stands up, wipes her hand on the dark wool of her skirt, leaving a darker smear along the line of her hip. "He really is."

"What?"

"He was in the army, before. I told you that, Solveig, I think. And I suppose you assumed, what? That when the war came he and his politics had just melted away, ceased to exist?" Liv shrugs. "Perhaps he should have, just disappeared in those first few days, kept his head down, lived quietly."

She straightens her shoulders, shakes her head.

"But that's not what my family do. We do the right thing. You understand, I think."

Liv sits down beside Solveig, lets her head loll back against the straw. She sighs, undoes the cuff buttons on her blouse, rolls the sleeves up towards her elbows.

"So three years ago, while his friends from the academy ran like rats for England, for Sweden, for the forests, Lars stayed and fought. Just in a different uniform than before. First Finland, and then Russia. And then one day – around Christmas - he turned up here, in the middle of my new life, with someone else's ID card, travel papers. Someone else's clothes. Said he couldn't go back, begged me to help him."

"And you did," Solveig says.

Liv nods.

"Yes. As did you."

"Only because…"

Lars had told her he was Resistance.

Surely he had.

That first day, crouching down by his reedy fire, face hidden behind his beard, he'd known her. And then, later on, Karl had –

No.

That was wrong. Solveig cradles her head in her hands. Her skin is cold, clammy, and she can feel her pulse pounding under the thin skin of her temple. Karl had never mentioned it, never asked after the man he'd sent her.

"I mean, all that time I thought I… And then there's Olav, and Erik Petterson. And I told Lars about Karl, about Arne's radio. He told you and then, probably, you told the Colonel…"

"Solveig." Liv's tone is firm, decided. It brooks no argument. "I wouldn't be here now, with you, if my first thought was to tell Leo Rastic everything I heard."

"No," Solveig says. Her head is spinning, the truths of the past year shifting under her feet, as insubstantial as mist. "I suppose not. But you should have done; I'm going to - I'm going to tell them what's happened, confess." She smiles, shrugs. "Just as soon as this dizziness passes."

Liv says nothing immediately.

"Is that a good idea?" she asks, eventually. "There are other options, you know. Other choices we could make."

There's a we, suddenly, an us.

But it's coming too late.

"None that are the right thing, Liv."

Solveig pauses, shifts to face Liv, pulls her face into a wry smile.

"You understand, I think."

"You're decided then."

"I am."

"It just isn't sensible."

"No, I don't suppose it is."

Solveig is not in the mood to argue, her neck still sore from the pressure of Lars' arm, her head swimming from the impact of her fall. She rubs at the skin, tests the depth of the bruises with tentative fingers. Liv breathes out noisily, twisting her mouth into a lopsided smile.

"Here, let me."

Liv peels her hands away from her neck, trailing her fingers across the base of Solveig's throat. She's quiet for a moment, her eyes intent and focused.

"You'll live, I think," she says, hands resting on Solveig's shoulders. She swallows nervously, and her throat works soundlessly, her shoulders bunching against an attack. "When Lars turned up, when he said..."

Solveig understands, hears in the broken sentence the moment of panic, how it had flared through Liv like a flame. How the thought that it was Solveig, not her brother, not some unknown soldier, lying bleeding on the floor of the barn, had gripped her, sent all her high walls and defences tumbling.

"I'm fine, Liv," Solveig says. The Germans are no doubt looking for Heinrich already. They could descend within minutes, within seconds: Liv's still-precious Colonel Rastic might see. It's a lie she's good at telling. "Fine."

Liv withdraws her hand slowly, reluctantly.

"Yes," she says. "Of course you are. It's just that, that I'd also like to think," she says, "that you still... that you would still want..."

A few days ago, dusting school-floor dirt off her clothes, Solveig would have done anything to have Liv talk to her like this, to look at her like this. But things, she thinks, have changed since then. She sniffs, moves out of Liv's reach.

"I thought we'd been over this. It's not normal, certainly not safe. You've made your position very clear, Liv."

"It's not," Liv says, her face suddenly hot with anger. "It's not normal, but I can't believe it's wrong either. It's just that every person I ever trusted, every person I ever..."

Liv shudders.

Solveig doesn't know if it's from the chill air or something else, some memory Liv doesn't want to relive. The day has been warm enough, but Liv is only in a thin cardigan. "Then the war came, and I thought: this is an opportunity, if only I can be brave enough to take it. Lars had already signed up, and my cousins, too. And there was a logic to it, a charisma. The end of poverty, the return of pride, protection from Russia, Communism, all that. I thought I could start afresh, be ordinary. Well, not ordinary, but I could fit in, I could belong."

"You did well with that, then."

"I did, actually." There's a note of pride in Liv's voice, even now, a satisfaction. "Cast in amongst these provincial types, these Else Løviks, how could I not? But there was Lars, and the mess he made of things. It just, just..." A lock of hair falls across her face, and she pauses to push it back behind her ear. "It didn't live up to my imaginings."

"Things hardly ever do," Solveig says.

"But I wanted it, I worked for it, and I couldn't ruin it. You understand. It wasn't because I didn't feel... that I don't... You know that, don't you, Solveig? Just because I haven't said -"

It's hardly the declaration of the century, Solveig thinks. In her daydreams, Liv had been better at this. The reality wouldn't pass muster in one of Bjørghild's paperbacks. The heroes there were always so eloquent, so ready with their feelings. Now, with Liv there in front of her, society defences dropped, with the secrets between them done away, eloquence doesn't seem necessary.

"I know," Solveig says, drawing Liv closer, clenching her hands around the sides of her jacket. "I know."

It's Solveig, this time, who pulls away. She thinks she can hear boat engines circling, the approaching thump of iron-heeled boots. Heinrich is still there on the floor. Liv stands, pulling Solveig after her.

"I'm leaving," she says. "Heading somewhere new, where they don't know anything about us. You can be a whole different person somewhere new." She smiles, huffs out a forced laugh. "Or at least, you can seem to be."

"But after the war, when the Germans have gone, you'll come home and..."

"No." Liv stops her, fingers against her lips. They're warm in the night air, soft and careful. "I won't be coming back, Solveig. Not if the Germans win, not if the English - it doesn't matter who's in charge. I won't be wanted here, either way."

At the jetty, Liv stops, shields her eyes against the afternoon sun. The sea is quiet, for once there are no boats moving back and forth across the flat line of the sea - no patrols, no fishermen checking their nets, no neighbours shuttling ewes between pastures. The waves are whipped up, foaming at the rocks, caught and driven by the wind flowing down off the distant mountains.

"You should come too," Liv says. "Come with me now, while we can."

Solveig shakes her head.

"You ought to go," she says, fiddling with Liv's terrible painter hitch, working the rope free of its knot. "The wind is getting stronger, and you don't want to still be on the water when they arrive."

Liv's hand lands on her shoulder, the grip firm, insistent.

"Solveig," she says. "Are you sure?"

There is a decent swell on the sea under the jetty, shaded in stripes by the planking beneath their feet. Further out, the sun sets the distant islands shimmering, dancing on the horizon. There are gulls overhead.

Either way, Solveig will have to give this up: the lighthouse, her family, her sheep, the sea and the birds and the soft grunting of the sow as she roots for any last speck of food amongst the straw.

It ought to be more dramatic, but there's no Eddic gathering of storm clouds, no omens or portents in the weather. There's no draugs or kraken come to claim her, brand her a monster like them.

It's just another afternoon, the start of an ordinary summer evening. The same that had filled her childhood, and her father's childhood and her grandfather's childhood: the same long, darkless night that pulled fur-clad farmers and fighters from their longhouses, that had followed fishing boats and timber traders up and down the coast, that had lain silent as Kristiansund burned on the horizon.

Solveig smiles at Liv's pale face in the bright evening sun, at her dark halo of hair, at the outline of the distant mountains, and throws the mooring rope down into the boat, holds out her hand for Liv to take.

SMØLA DAGBLAD

12 SEPTEMBER 1943

BIRTHS

On 1 September, to Einar and Kari Sletten, twin sons, Haakon and Per.
On 9 September, to Finn and Agnes Torstensen, a daughter, Jorunn.
On 10 September, to Olaf and Malene Høyvik, a son, Haakon.

ENGAGEMENTS

Miss Berit Virkesdal and Mr Gunnar Josøy, both of Dyrnes.

DEATHS

Petter Moen of Veiholmen, died 8 September 1943. The funeral will be held on Saturday 18 September, Hopen Church.

WOMAN HAS BABY IN OPEN BOAT, BOTH WELL

A baby boy was born in an open boat at Veiholmen, Edøy, yesterday. The mother is Fru Gerd Vejden, wife of an accountant employed by the Møre og Romsdal education board. Matron Nilsson, of the Kristiansund Mother and Baby Home, where mother and child were admitted this morning, said both were in a satisfactory condition.

"Babies can stand up to anything," she said. "The boy was a few weeks premature, but he has been getting along splendidly."

Fru Vejden had been staying at her parents' house in Smøla, the only access to which is via water. Fru Vejden was on her way to have the baby delivered when it was born in the open launch. Her mother helped her deliver her son, who is called Haakon.

WOMEN STILL ON RUN IN SOLDIER DEATH

Lars Sunde, implicated in the death of Oberleutnant Heinrich Meyer on 23rd June, was today executed by firing squad for deserting his post at the Russian front in December last year. Sunde was caught trying to escape by sea to the mainland approximately six hours before the body of

Oberleutnant Meyer was found by fishermen near Tustna. It is believed that Sunde shot and killed the officer after being confronted by Oberleutnant Meyer while hiding on an outlying island, and that currents carried the body towards the mainland.

Liv Sunde, the traitor's sister, school mistress and head of the Smøla Hird Women's Section, and local farmer Solveig Eik both left the islands at the time of the disappearance. Both women are suspected of harbouring Sunde during the months between his desertion and capture. It is believed they are attempting to escape the country, either via Sweden or the North Sea to England. No other accomplices are sought at this time.

Police ask anyone who knows of their whereabouts to contact the authorities. Their capture remains the highest priority for the Statspolitet and German military police across the country and the Reich. A reward of 1,500 kr.- is offered for any information about their whereabouts leading to an arrest.

NEWS FROM ITALY

News reaches us from Italy of the invasion of Rome, Naples and the rest of northern Italy by the victorious Wehrmacht. Inspired by other royal cowards across Europe in recent years, the Italian Prime Minister and King fled in the face of the unstoppable oncoming might of the German Reich. Field-Marshal Kesselring has made a speech, which will be broadcast on NRK, declaring all Italian territory under German military control.

Our glorious Führer Adolf Hitler has ordered that the occupied Italian territory be divided into three zones, with the area around Rome extending south toward the front lines against the Allies, the Alpine mountain region, and the coast along the Adriatic Sea. Herr Hitler also issued strict orders laying out the punishment for any Italian military units that had fought for our enemy: all officers are to be summarily executed, and other ranks to be deported to work camps in Germany.

Let this be a lesson to those segments of our own society still determined to fight the future, fight progress and the New Order.

A NOTE FROM LUCY JACOBS:

I hope you enjoyed ISLANDS OF MICE. This story has been fermenting in my head for years, ever since I went out to the Norwegian islands and heard stories of resistance and collaboration, of great bravery and minor acts of defiance, and wondered which side of the line I would have fallen on.

I'd like to hope I'd make less of a mess of it than Solveig, but I'm not sure.

If you enjoyed ISLANDS OF MICE, consider:
- ✓ Help other people find this book by writing a review - just a few sentences can make the difference, and I always appreciate an honest review!
- ✓ Sign up for my newsletter, so you can be the first to hear any news!
- ✓ Find me on Facebook or Instagram!

Wishing you fair winds and following seas,

Lucy

Printed in Great Britain
by Amazon

48698587R00225